T0049378

Also by Jane Bennett Munro

Murder under the Microscope
Too Much Blood
Grievous Bodily Harm
Death by Autopsy

THE BODY
ON THE LIDO DECK
A TONI DAY MYSTERY

JANE BENNETT MUNRO

THE BODY ON THE LIDO DECK
A TONI DAY MYSTERY

Copyright © 2016 Jane Bennett Munro.

All rights reserved. No part of this book may be used or reproduced by any means, graphic, electronic, or mechanical, including photocopying, recording, taping or by any information storage retrieval system without the written permission of the author except in the case of brief quotations embodied in critical articles and reviews.

This is a work of fiction. All of the characters, names, incidents, organizations, and dialogue in this novel are either the products of the author's imagination or are used fictitiously.

iUniverse books may be ordered through booksellers or by contacting:

iUniverse
1663 Liberty Drive
Bloomington, IN 47403
www.iuniverse.com
1-800-Authors (1-800-288-4677)

Because of the dynamic nature of the Internet, any web addresses or links contained in this book may have changed since publication and may no longer be valid. The views expressed in this work are solely those of the author and do not necessarily reflect the views of the publisher, and the publisher hereby disclaims any responsibility for them.

Any people depicted in stock imagery provided by Thinkstock are models, and such images are being used for illustrative purposes only.
Certain stock imagery © Thinkstock.

ISBN: 978-1-4917-9550-7 (sc)
ISBN: 978-1-4917-9551-4 (e)

Library of Congress Control Number: 2016911920

Print information available on the last page.

iUniverse rev. date: 08/19/2016

In memory of Dr. Semih Mustafa Erhan,
my long-suffering cruise companion

☙

"Would he have been able to get into our cabin if I hadn't answered the door?"

"Absolutely," I said. "I learned today that the captain has keys to every room on this ship, including cabins."

"Jesus Christ," Hal said. "Then nothing in here is safe, including us."

ACKNOWLEDGMENTS

In my so-called golden years, I've done what many people my age do: travel. The easiest way to do that, in my opinion, is to go on cruises. You stay in the same room, you only unpack once, and you get to visit many different places. Plus the food is usually wonderful, you can eat all you want at any time of day, and there's a spa and a swimming pool. There's dancing in the lounge; there's always a great view; there are shops, endless activities, and excursions—I could go on and on.

On my last cruise, I was sitting up on the Lido deck one day, and it started to rain. The roof was open, as usual. They open it early in the morning and close it after dark. They also close it if it rains, as it frequently does in the Caribbean.

So as I watched the massive gears grind and groan to get the roof closed, it occurred to me what a great way that would be to murder somebody and have it look like an accident.

My traveling companion passed away in December 2015. Unfortunately, my BFF, Rhonda, gets seasick just watching a hammock swing in the wind, so she won't be doing any cruises. Therefore my cruising days are probably over unless something changes.

So for now, I'll just write about it.

This is a work of fiction. The characters are figments of my imagination. Any resemblance to any person, living or dead, is coincidental. That being said, I may borrow a trait, a physical feature, or a turn of speech from someone I know, and combine them to make up a whole new person. My ophthalmologist, Robert Welch, MD, encouraged me to use his name. The Constellation cruise line is fictitious as well. The Caribbean islands it visits are real, but the natives are fictitious.

Thanks to Rhonda for reading my drafts and pointing out all my egregious errors, letting me bounce ideas off her ad nauseam, and coming up with ideas of her own that she lets me use.

Thanks also to Susan Scott, wife of Captain John Scott of Holland America cruise line, who wrote a book called *Cruise Qs*, which is chock-full of background information about how a cruise ship works behind the scenes. Thanks also to the officers and crew members of the *ms Noordam*, including Captain Scott himself, who graciously and patiently answered my endless questions.

Not to mention all the folks at iUniverse who helped me get this book into print for my expectant and impatient reading public.

Sunday

BRIDGETOWN, BARBADOS

His hair stood upright like porcupine quills.

—Giovanni Boccaccio, *The Decameron*

I COULDN'T SAY what it was that woke me up.

Whatever it was had jerked me out of peaceful slumber and had me sitting upright in bed, eyes wide and heart pounding, wondering what the hell had just happened.

My husband Hal's gentle snoring had long ago ceased to bother me. We'd both gotten used to the engine noise and the gentle rocking of the *North Star* as she slipped through the darkness of night to the next port. A bad dream perhaps? Usually I remembered those. I didn't remember this one.

Maybe it had been a noise of some kind. Someone walking in the corridor? A cabin door slamming? But why should that cause such heart-pounding wakefulness?

Maybe the person walking in the hall hadn't been alone. Maybe what I'd heard had been a fight. A body hitting the floor. A fist hitting a wall. A scream.

That was it. A scream. Only it was unlike any scream I'd ever heard.

Whatever it was, I couldn't seem to get back to sleep. I lay there for a while, listening, but heard nothing more. So rather than toss and turn and wake Hal, I slipped out of bed, stealthily shed my pajamas and climbed back into the shorts and tank top I'd worn the day before and hung over a chair. I grabbed the turquoise mesh boat bag I'd acquired at our first port of call in the Bahamas eight days earlier, which contained everything I was likely to need, carefully opened the cabin door, and peeked out into the corridor. I saw nobody, so I slipped out of the room, closed the door noiselessly behind me, and ran up the one flight of stairs to the Lido deck.

Up there it was still dark. The only illumination came from the liquor cabinet behind the bar, which was closed, and its reflection in the swimming pool. A faint line of pink along the eastern horizon indicated that dawn was imminent. The Lido restaurant was closed too, but it was still possible to get a cup of coffee, which I did before settling myself at a table where I could best see the sunrise over the ocean. Maybe I could get some nifty sunrise photos with my smartphone, which, unbelievably took better pictures than my digital camera used to.

So I put my feet up on a chair, reached into my boat bag, and retrieved my smartphone and my e-reader, upon which I'd downloaded enough books to keep me occupied for this trip and many more. Luckily, the screen was backlit, so I could read it in total darkness if I wanted to.

I became so absorbed in what I was reading that I completely forgot to watch the sunrise, and I was brought back to reality with a start by the grinding of the gears that opened the roof. That meant it was seven o'clock, because the staff opened the roof every day at the same time.

But they seemed to be having trouble this morning. The grinding of the gears had a high-pitched shrieking quality that definitely wasn't normal. It reminded me of the noise that had awakened me. One side of the roof was opening smoothly while the other seemed to have gotten stuck. No doubt I was hearing the death throes of the motor on that side as it burned out.

I got up and walked around to the other side of the swimming pool where I could see better, and that's when I heard a strangled cry—and running footsteps above me.

And saw something fall. With a squishy thud, it hit the edge of the swimming pool and bounced into the water. Red-tinged ripples spread out from where it went in.

A trick of the light? Or was it blood?

Who was bleeding?

Wait. Was there a *body* up there? Part of which was now in the pool?

I went back to the other side of the pool.

It wasn't a trick of the light. The smear where the thing had hit was bloody, and so was the water that had splashed up onto the deck. The thing that had gone into the pool lay blackly on the bottom in the shadows just below where I stood. It looked like a bowling ball with hair.

A human head?

Surely not.

But what else could it be?

Something dripped on my head. I reached up to touch it, and my hand came away bloody.

I backed up, wiping my hand on my shorts, and grabbed my smartphone. As I did so, a larger object detached itself from the edge of the roof and landed on the deck right in front of me, splattering me with blood. At least I assumed it was blood. If the thing lying splayed out over the tiles was the rest of the body, it would be blood. It was hard to tell. Most of it looked like a cube steak that had been pounded to oblivion, but I was able, in the dim light, to identify an arm and hand, a foot, and part of a leg. The uncrushed limbs were slender, the skin was smooth and deeply tanned, and there was bright-red nail polish on both the fingernails and toenails. Experimentally, I touched the foot. It was warm.

Hmm.

Warm foot. Dripping blood.

Had she been *alive* when she was crushed in the roof?

Wait. The roof was closed every night at seven o'clock and opened every morning at seven o'clock.

If she'd been crushed in the roof at seven o'clock last night, she wouldn't be warm and dripping blood now, twelve hours later.

She couldn't have been dead more than a few minutes. Therefore, someone had had to open the roof, put her in it, and close it on her sometime in the last hour.

Could *that* have been the sound that woke me?

I didn't even want to contemplate the possibility that it might have been *her* screaming that woke me.

I wiped my face with the cleanest part of the front of my tank top, suppressing thoughts of blood-borne pathogens invading my body by way of my mucous membranes, and took pictures of the edge of the opening in the roof, the thing on the side of the pool, and the thing in the pool.

After that, there was only one thing to do.

Aside from getting a better look at the head, I needed to get the blood off me.

I kicked off my Birkenstocks and dived in.

Strongest minds

Are often those of whom the noisy world

Hears least.

—William Wordsworth

It was the head, all right.

I brought it back up to the surface to get a better look at it. The long blonde hair, the red lipstick, and the gaudy, ornate, sparkling earring dangling from one of her pierced ears reinforced my initial impression that the victim had been female. The other earring was missing, apparently torn from her earlobe. The facial features were no help at all; her face was puffy and discolored beyond recognition, with a swollen dark-blue tongue protruding from the mouth. I pried up an eyelid. The iris looked dark brown, but there was not enough light to see the size of the pupil. I turned it over to look at the back and found a jagged laceration about six inches long. I explored it gently and felt the bone underneath give, with crunchy bone fragments grinding together as I pressed on them.

The lady had a depressed skull fracture.

Furthermore, the head hadn't been severed cleanly from the body. The neck ended just below the chin in a diagonal, ragged, red fringe in which it was impossible to differentiate the larynx, esophagus, and great vessels. Even the bones of the cervical spine had been pulverized.

Her neck had been crushed so badly that the head had been avulsed from the body. The evidence of what had done that was right above me, dripping on the floor.

I retrieved my smartphone from where I'd placed it within reach, and took pictures.

Nothing would be gained by further tampering with evidence, so I put the head back where I'd found it, on the bottom of the pool. After rinsing as much blood as I could off myself and out of my hair, I wrapped myself in a towel, grabbed my smartphone, and ascended to the observation deck via the small curved metal stairway hidden behind the bar. Most people didn't even know it was there and used the elevator instead, but I suspected that the crew used it often.

It didn't take a genius to figure out where the problem was. Two Filipino crew members stood looking down at the edge of the opening in the roof, while another lost his breakfast over the rail. By their uniforms, I assumed they were maintenance or possibly engineering. One of them saw me and rushed to intercept me. His badge identified him as Ramon.

"Ma'am, please, you need to leave!" he protested.

I raised both hands to placate him. "It's okay," I said calmly. "I'm a doctor."

He was adamant. "No, ma'am," he said. "I know ship's doctor. You not him."

"I'm a doctor too," I said. "A pathologist. I work with dead bodies all the time." A slight exaggeration, since I did very few autopsies these days. Autopsies are going the way of the dodo bird, thanks to advanced imaging techniques that permit guided needle biopsies from practically anywhere in the body.

His face lit up with comprehension. "Like Quincy!"

This guy was not old enough to remember *Quincy*. I'd watched it during my teens, and it had influenced my choice of career. It was a seventies TV show featuring a crusty medical examiner played by Jack Klugman, which made the whole TV-watching world aware of what a pathologist does: autopsies and testifying before Congress. Since it was a show about a medical examiner, it made no mention of all the other stuff pathologists do. They must show reruns in the Philippines.

I wasn't exactly Quincy, but I figured it would do for now. "Close enough."

Now that he thought I was like Quincy, he was all eager to assist me. "You come this way, ma'am. Come see."

"Thank you, Ramon," I said and followed him back to where his companion waited. The one who'd tossed his cookies had vanished.

There wasn't much to see. All that was left was blood and bits of tissue and cloth on the edges of the two halves of the roof. Some of the flesh had been squeezed out when the roof was closed and now lay in bloody chunks along the edges of the opening. There was no blood in the track itself.

I wondered how the person who'd put her there had secured the body in place while he or she closed the roof on her. She hadn't been secured very well if the head, an arm, and a leg could fall free of the roof edges and avoid being crushed.

"Are you the one who opens the roof?" I asked him.

He shook his head. "The captain opens it. From the bridge."

"Does the captain know about this?"

The other crew member, who had been silent up to now, spoke up. "Yes," he said, brandishing a two-way radio in the general direction of a tall man in uniform approaching in the opposite direction from which I'd come. "Here he comes now."

Captain Colin Sloane stood over six feet tall, and his tanned face and forearms contrasted nicely with his crisp white uniform. He doffed his cap as he approached, revealing a headful of silver hair. All in all, he was a fine figure of a man, as my mother had said when we'd all met him at the beginning of the cruise. I didn't expect him to remember me, though, since there were nearly twelve hundred passengers on board.

Captain Sloane didn't even see me at first; his attention was on the two crewmen. "Fernando, Ramon," he said curtly as he came up to us, "what's all this about a dead body?"

I spoke up. "The body's down there," I said helpfully, "by the pool."

He looked down through the opening in the roof, and his face paled noticeably under his tan. "Oh dear."

"We should be down there," I said, "not up here, don't you think?"

The captain shifted his attention to me. "Madam," he said, "you shouldn't be here. I'll have to ask you to leave."

His British accent made him sound polite instead of boorish. It reminded me of my mother and stepfather, still asleep in their cabin across the hall from ours on the Navigation deck. I repeated what I'd told Ramon. He shook his head. "Nonetheless, you're a passenger, Mrs.—" He peered at my passenger ID which I wore on a lanyard around my neck.

"Doctor," I said. "Toni Day. MD."

"Your ID says Toni Shapiro," he objected.

"Day is my maiden name, which I use professionally," I told him. "And I know I'm not licensed to practice medicine here, but I do know a thing or two about forensics and maybe I can help. Not only that, but my mother and stepfather are on this cruise too, and my stepfather is a retired homicide detective chief superintendent from Scotland Yard."

That got his attention. "Scotland Yard? Homicide? Would that be Nigel Gray?"

"That's the one," I said with surprise. "You know him?"

"I certainly do," he said. "Years ago we had a death on board just as we were about to dock at Southampton. It turned out to be a homicide. Detective Inspector Gray was in charge of the investigation."

"So you've had a murder on board before," I said. "How long ago was that?"

"What makes you think this is a murder?" he asked, ignoring my question.

"What makes you think it's not?" I countered. "You can't rule out murder unless you investigate. Nigel and I can help. In the meantime, hadn't you better close off the Lido deck? Her head's in the pool and the rest of the body's splattered all over the deck down there."

"Blimey!" He went pale again. Turning away from the grisly scene, he unhooked his radio from his belt and gave a series of commands. "It's a good job we're going to be in port today. Maybe we can get this mess cleaned up before anybody notices it."

Good luck with that, I thought. What were the chances nobody would notice that the Lido deck was closed? More than likely the passengers would know about the body before anybody went ashore in

Bridgetown. Those who didn't would know by the time they came back on board.

As if he'd been reading my mind, the captain glanced at his watch. "We'll be docking in about an hour. I've got to contact the police in Bridgetown—and get a cleaning crew in here."

"Not until the police see her," I objected. "They'll need to photograph the scene and retrieve as much as possible of the body. There'll have to be an autopsy to see if there are any injuries that can't be explained by being crushed by the roof, and toxicology to determine if she was drugged or otherwise rendered unconscious before she was put in there."

"Bloody hell," the captain muttered under his breath.

"Nigel would agree with me," I pursued. "Shall I go get him?"

"You keep referring to the body as 'she'," Captain Sloane said. "Do you know her?"

"In my opinion, her own mother wouldn't know her," I said. "But it's been my experience that men don't usually go in for Tickle-the-Toe-Red nail polish."

The captain actually chuckled at that.

"Also," I pursued, "the head in the pool has red lipstick and long blonde hair." I could have showed him the pictures I'd taken, but I decided not to, as he seemed to be a trifle squeamish about such things. "And an earring," I added.

The six-inch gash in the scalp over the depressed skull fracture was another thing entirely. That would be a matter for the police.

At this point the captain seemed to become aware that I was wrapped in a towel and dripping on the deck. "Have you been *in* the pool?"

"Yes," I said. "I saw it fall, and I went in to get a closer look at it."

He scowled and shook his head as if to disperse a cloud of gnats. "What the bloody hell were you even *doing* on the Lido deck at that ungodly hour?"

"I couldn't sleep," I said. "I didn't want to wake my husband, so I came up to the Lido deck to read for a while."

"What did you do with it?"

"With what?"

"The head, of course," he said impatiently.

"I left it where it was," I said.

"In the pool?"

"Yes." I wasn't really lying. I mean, I *had* left the head precisely where I'd found it. Besides, I saw no point in telling the captain that I'd moved it to take pictures. He was obviously in no condition to look at them anyway.

"In God's name, why?" The captain's face had been growing paler and paler as this conversation progressed, and by this point he was taking on a greenish tint. Beads of sweat had popped out on his tanned forehead, and he pulled out a handkerchief to mop his brow.

"Because it's evidence," I said. "If the police want me to go in after it when they get here I'll be happy to do so. I mean, I'm already wet."

He closed his eyes and swallowed hard before speaking. "At least that cuts the job of finding out who's missing in half. If we wait until everyone goes ashore, we can eliminate all those passengers as well."

That made sense, because passengers were required to swipe their IDs through a bar code reader as they disembarked, and then again when they reboarded. This created a record of who was aboard and who wasn't, and it made sure that everybody who went ashore was back on board when the ship sailed. There was only one thing wrong with that.

"You can't let anyone go ashore," I objected. "One of them might be the killer."

"Impossible," the captain argued. "Can't be done. We can't prevent people from going ashore. What would we tell them?"

"I suppose the truth is out of the question?" I asked innocently, although I suspected I knew the answer.

"Absolutely out of the question," he said. "We don't want to start a panic."

"Don't you want to at least wait until the police get here and see what they say?" I asked.

"Now look here, madam," he began.

"Dr. Day," I corrected him.

"Toni!"

I looked up to see Hal coming toward me. I waved. "It's my husband," I told the captain, who did not look thrilled.

My husband, Hal Shapiro, towered over my diminutive five foot three by at least a foot and outweighed me by a hundred pounds. With his blond hair, beard, and mustache, and bright-blue eyes, he resembled a Viking rather than the mild-mannered college professor that he actually was.

"What's going on?" he asked as he got close enough for me to hear him. "They've closed off the Lido deck."

"That's because they don't want people to see the body," I said.

"The *what?*" He stepped closer and looked down through the opening in the roof. "Jesus. Is that ...?"

"A body. Yes." I turned to the captain. "This is my husband, Hal Shapiro. Honey, you remember Captain Sloane."

"Of course." Hal reached out and shook the captain's proffered hand. "How are you, sir?"

"As well as can be expected under the circumstances," the captain said. "Do you have any idea who it might be, Mr. Shapiro?"

"Dr. Shapiro," Hal corrected. "And no, I don't."

"You're *both* doctors?"

"I'm a PhD," Hal said. "I'm a professor at our local college."

"And are you also familiar with forensic science?"

"Everything I know I learned from Toni," Hal said. "You know, who you really need up here is my father-in-law."

"Where are Mum and Nigel anyway?" I asked him. "Eating breakfast?"

"Still in bed, as far as I know," Hal said. "Want me to go get him?"

"Yes, please," I said before Captain Sloane could answer.

Hal gave me that look he always gives me when he thinks I'm speaking out of turn. "I was asking the captain."

"Certainly," Captain Sloane said. "It will be nice to see Detective Inspector Gray again."

Hal looked at me, startled. "Does he know Nigel?"

"Yes," I said. "We can talk about it later. Go, go!"

Hal went.

I didn't. The captain looked as though he wished I had. "Dr. Day, if you don't mind my saying so, you should take this opportunity to get some breakfast before we dock. Nothing's going to happen before then."

I shook my head. "I'm not really hungry, are you? I think I'll just stay up here and admire the view."

"As you wish," he said dismissively. "I have things to attend to before we dock in Bridgetown."

"Like notifying the police," I suggested.

"Precisely. Among other things."

I took the hint. "I'll just be up there watching," I said, indicating an observation point near the bow. "Holler if you need me."

Captain Sloane nodded politely, but I wasn't fooled. I knew that the minute my back was turned he'd do an eye-roll and mutter, "As if."

Or the British equivalent thereof.

As I watched the massive *North Star* slowly make its way into its assigned berth at the port of Bridgetown, I couldn't help thinking that there was something awfully wrong with this picture. Would Captain Sloane have gone ahead and had the crew just clean up the mess and dispose of the body parts along with all the bleach and industrial-strength cleaner, thereby destroying any DNA evidence and probably fingerprints too?

Would he have contacted the Barbados police if I hadn't been there?

Don't be ridiculous, Toni, I admonished myself. If Captain Sloane wasn't a man with scruples, he wouldn't be a captain in the first place. He couldn't possibly have any reason to cover up this murder.

Could he?

Tell that to the marines; the sailors won't believe it.

—Sir Walter Scott

"ANTOINETTE!"

Only one person in the world called me that.

I turned to see my mother approaching. She wore a long-sleeved, mint-green cotton shirt and a wide floppy hat to keep the Caribbean sun off her fair skin. She climbed up to my observation point, using the rail to pull herself up, stood beside me, and heaved a sigh. "Kitten, what *have* you gotten yourself into now? Can't we take a holiday without you finding a *murder* to get involved in?"

My mother, Fiona Gray, formerly Fiona Day, had recently turned sixty-five and retired from the corporate secretarial position she'd had for the past forty years. Celebrating her retirement was the reason we were on this cruise in the first place.

She and I had emigrated from England when I was three years old, at the invitation of my father's parents, who lived in Long Beach, California. That was over forty years ago, but it hadn't had the slightest effect upon her accent, which was as crisply British as ever. She'd always resembled Susan Hayward—still did—and wore her curly red hair in the same style, even though now it was mostly gray. She and I had the same green eyes, but my hair was black and my complexion olive, like my father's had been.

I kissed her cheek. "Good morning, Mum. Have you had breakfast?"

"Not yet, dear. Have you?"

"Just coffee, so far. Did you see the body? Or what's left of it?"

She shuddered. "No, and perhaps I ought not. What d'you mean, 'what's left of it'?"

"Someone closed the roof on her and crushed her beyond recognition."

Mum's complexion, already naturally pale, grew noticeably paler. "Now that's fair turned me up, that has. No breakfast for me, I'm afraid, dear."

I looked around and didn't see anyone else. "Did Nigel come with you?"

"He's down on the Lido deck with the captain," she said.

"Will you be all right up here for a little while?"

She patted my shoulder. "You go ahead, kitten. I'll be fine."

I went back down the stairs and saw Nigel and Hal standing by the body with the captain. I walked over to Nigel, who slung an arm around my shoulders and gave me a mustachioed kiss. "I say, Toni, old dear, couldn't you let me have my holiday without finding me a bloody murder to solve?"

My stepfather resembled the actor Bernard Fox, who played Dr. Bombay on the sixties sitcom *Bewitched*, which I'd watched as a child; but Nigel was grayer and not nearly as pompous, and he clearly adored my mother, who'd been a widow since she was only seventeen and pregnant with me. My young father, an American serviceman, had been killed in a hit-and-run accident on a busy London street. Mum had never shown the slightest interest in remarrying until she met Nigel on the *Queen Mary* five years ago. It had been love at first sight for both of them.

"It wasn't my idea," I told him.

"If there's a murder within a mile of Toni, she's going to find it," my husband said, "more's the pity."

"If you'll excuse me," the captain said, "I need to go down to the bridge and contact the authorities."

He turned to leave, but I stopped him. "You're not going to leave the scene *unguarded*, are you? Someone could tamper with evidence."

Captain Sloane turned back. "Dr. Day, could you possibly allow me to run my ship?"

"She's right, Captain," Nigel said. "You do realize that there's a murderer on board, don't you?"

Captain Sloane sighed. "This area is closed to passengers. In the meantime, I'll notify security. Now, please excuse me."

"Could you please close the roof?" I called after him. "The flies are getting in."

He ignored me. I watched him go, with misgivings. Hal shook his head. "Poor guy. Do you intend to stay here until the police arrive?"

"I think Toni and I should," Nigel said. "Why don't you and Fiona go ashore? There's no reason for all of us to suffer."

Hal agreed with alacrity, gave me a quick kiss, and went back up the stairs to fetch Mum. I imagined they'd go down by way of the elevator, not wanting to pass by the crime scene in deference to Mum's sensibilities.

I became aware that I still held my smartphone in my hand, not wanting to put it in any of my wet pockets. "Now that the captain's gone," I said, "I think I'll take a picture or two."

"Good idea," Nigel said. "Although I imagine the police will do that as well."

I began to take pictures of the remains, while Nigel shooed flies away. I photographed her from her foot with the Tickle-the-Toe-Red toenails to the ragged red fringe that had once been her neck. Whatever clothing she'd been wearing had been crushed into her body, but I could see some residual glittery red-gold material. Perhaps she'd been wearing a red dress with gold threads, or maybe her dress had been gold lamé that was now soaked in her blood. It was hard to tell. If she'd been wearing shoes, they were nowhere in sight. Perhaps they'd fallen off while her murderer had carried her up to the roof.

I also wondered about jewelry. I didn't see any. If she'd worn a necklace, it should have fallen into the pool along with her head, in which case I'd have seen it when I went into the pool to examine the head, but I didn't. There was just the one earring. If all those glittering stones were diamonds, those earrings would have cost a fortune. There were no rings, at least not on the one hand that was still recognizable, her left.

"I wonder how long it will take for the police to get here," Nigel said.

I heard a sound behind us and turned to look. A crewman wearing the tan shirt and trousers worn by the members of the housekeeping staff had brought out a mop and bucket and set it down with a clang. He sloshed the mop up and down in something highly ammoniac-smelling and clearly meant to apply it to the remains.

"No! No! Don't do that!" I exclaimed. "You'll compromise the remains!"

The crewman, a young black man, looked at me in astonishment. He shook his head, smiled a bright-white smile, and spoke reassuringly in a soft island accent. "Scuse me, mum. De captain, he say clean up dis mess."

"Look here, young man," Nigel said in his crispest British. "The police are coming, and this is a crime scene. They won't like it if you disturb it. They could arrest you for tampering with evidence."

The crewman looked from Nigel to me and back again, seemingly at a loss for words.

"He's right, you know," I told him. "He's from Scotland Yard, and he knows about this stuff. You can clean it later, after the police are done with it."

"Yes 'm," the crewman said. He bent over to pick up his bucket and mop, and jumped back, nearly knocking Nigel over. He stared at me, eyes stretched wide, and pointed. "Dat's a foot!"

"Yes, it is," I said. "Did you just now notice that?"

The crewman didn't answer me. He was too busy running for the restroom, his mop and bucket forgotten.

I turned to Nigel, put my hands on my hips, and said, "Well!"

Nigel shook his head. "The captain should know better than that."

"He does!" I insisted. "I told him that myself before you came up here! He completely blew me off."

"Toni, do calm yourself. I rather suspect that someone else told that young man the captain wanted the mess cleaned up, someone who didn't know any better."

"Like Fernando or Ramon," I guessed.

"In any case," Nigel went on, "the police will soon set the captain straight on what should or should not be done with the body." He cast a disparaging glance upon the remains. "Such as it is."

"What would Scotland Yard do with it?" I asked.

Nigel didn't have a chance to answer that. Two officers approached us. One was young, tall, and thin with a full head of dark hair, while the other was shorter and burlier than his companion, with graying hair, and appeared to be in his late forties or early fifties. Two security guards accompanied them.

"Now then, what's all this?" inquired the burly one as he came within speaking distance.

"I'm sorry," said the tall one, looming up behind him. "Sir, madam, I'll have to ask you to leave. This is a crime scene."

Nigel introduced himself, omitting mention of the fact that he was retired. Both officers snapped to attention. "Chief Security Officer Desmond Grant," the burly one said. "I'm responsible for dealing with any adverse incidents or crimes aboard this ship." He indicated his companion. "And this is Chief Safety, Environmental, and Health Officer Roger Dalquist. I didn't know we'd called in Scotland Yard."

"I'm responsible for accident prevention and the safe disposal of waste," Dalquist said. "Although, if you're here, Chief Superintendent, it probably wasn't an accident."

"I don't think it was," I said. "I think the body was put in the roof to cover up what really happened, and to prevent identification."

"And who are you, Madam?" Grant inquired.

I introduced myself.

"What do you think really happened, Doctor?" Grant asked me. "And how do you come to be involved in this? We don't usually consult passengers on these matters."

I decided not to tell him that Nigel was also a passenger. "I was here on the Lido deck, minding my own business, when I saw her head fall into the swimming pool. Then the rest of the body fell onto the deck here. So I went into the pool and looked at the head long enough to see that she had a scalp laceration and a depressed skull fracture, which might have been caused by an accident, but then someone tried to cover it up by putting the body here to be crushed by the roof. I'm surprised the captain hasn't told you all this."

"He did," Dalquist responded. "So someone put this body in the roof, hoping that when the captain closed the roof for the night last night, it'd be crushed beyond recognition?"

"Not last night," I objected. "It had to have been this morning. Her foot was still warm, and her blood hadn't clotted."

Dalquist and Grant exchanged glances.

"You're saying that someone opened the roof, put the body in it, and closed it on her this morning?" Grant asked incredulously.

"Yes, sometime between six and seven."

"How can you be so sure?"

"Something woke me up, and I couldn't get back to sleep, so I came up to the Lido deck so I wouldn't wake my husband. When they opened the roof at seven, the head fell into the pool. Blood was dripping. She couldn't have been dead any longer than that."

"You think the head wound occurred between six and seven this morning also?" Grant asked.

"I don't know," I said. "That could have occurred anytime during the night. She could have lived for hours after that. I suppose she could still have been alive when her body was crushed in the roof. But even if she hadn't been crushed in the roof, the brain hemorrhage would have eventually killed her."

"We've been told that the captain opens and closes the roof from the bridge," Nigel said. "Can anyone else do that?"

"Anybody on the bridge could do it, if directed by the captain to do so," Dalquist said. "That would include the first officer, the second or navigation officer, the third officer, helmsman, and the quartermaster."

"What if repairs or maintenance have to be done?" Nigel asked. "Surely the captain and bridge officers aren't involved in that, with everything else they have to do."

"Routine maintenance and repairs get done between cruises, or when the ship is in dry dock," Dalquist said. "I'm not aware of any repairs having to be done to the roof during a cruise as long as I've been in the cruise ship business. This is a first for me."

"It is for me too," Grant said.

At that moment we heard sirens. "That must be the police," I said and ran back upstairs to see. Officer Dalquist and the two security guards came barreling up the stairs after me, as if they thought I was the perpetrator and might be attempting to escape. We all gathered at the rail. The Barbados police vehicles were white with blue and yellow squares along the side, the word *POLICE* underneath, and flashing red and blue lights on top. The words *Royal Barbados Police Force* could be seen at the bottom of a white wreath inside the blue square on the door, along with the words "To serve, protect, and reassure."

They'd brought a van as well as a police car. Actually, it was a police wagon. I wondered if the van was a mobile lab, like the Twin Falls police had. Two uniformed officers got out of each vehicle and moved toward the gangway.

At that moment I heard the captain's announcement over the PA system that passengers could now go ashore, with the usual admonitions about lining up in an orderly manner and telling us which side of which deck the gangway was on, because it wasn't always in the same place. It varied from port to port, depending upon the facilities available.

No sooner had the captain stopped speaking than a steel drum band began playing on the dock. Nigel came up next to me and leaned on the rail. "You don't suppose the police will make everybody stay on board so they can interview all the passengers, do you?" I asked him.

"I doubt it," Nigel said. "Surely they would have told the captain to keep everybody on board when he called them; but apparently they didn't, because he's made his usual announcement about going ashore—and look, the first passengers are coming down the gangway now."

I looked. They were. A steady stream of passengers came down the gangway. At the bottom, crew members dressed as pirates greeted them and urged them to have their pictures taken. Most people did so, smiling. Those pictures would later be posted so that passengers could order copies of them for ridiculously inflated prices. I wondered what they all thought about the police being there in such abundance. It would definitely cause some speculation among the passengers, who might possibly come up with scenarios even more bizarre than the one we actually had.

"I hope he doesn't regret this later," I commented.

"He won't," Officer Dalquist said. "For security purposes, it's better to get as many people out of the way as possible."

"Even if one of the passengers is the killer?"

"That would be very unlikely," Dalquist said. "A passenger wouldn't be able to operate the roof. Besides, all the passengers will be back on board tonight."

"I suppose that if one doesn't come back on board, it would be a clue," I said. "Would the ship really leave without everybody back on board?"

"Definitely," Dalquist said. "We have to keep to a strict schedule. It's not like we're the only cruise ship out here."

I looked around. "Where did Officer Grant go?"

Dalquist looked around too. "I don't know. I thought he was right behind us."

At that point I heard voices from below, and apparently Officer Dalquist and the security guards did too, because they turned from the rail and headed toward the stairs. Nigel and I followed them down to see the captain standing near the body, accompanied by two men and a woman in suits, and a man in surgical scrubs. I also noticed that someone had erected a barricade around the pool and the remains, and that the water level in the pool was lower. Evidently it was being drained. I was surprised that we'd spent enough time topside to allow all that to get done before we got back downstairs.

The Barbadians flashed their badges and introduced themselves: Detective Chief Superintendent Malcolm Braithwaite, a tall, handsome black man with a cap of thick white hair who spoke with a crisp British accent; Detective Inspector Gordon Jones, shorter and more burly than his companion and having a soft island accent; and the coroner, Marietta Gresham-St. John, a squat, middle-aged black woman with frizzy orange hair and surprisingly pale green eyes. She sounded American.

Captain Sloane introduced the man in scrubs as the ship's doctor, Robert Welch, whom I diagnosed immediately by his speech as a Brit. He was tall and gangly with red hair and freckles and didn't look old enough to have completed college, let alone medical school and a residency. In fact he looked like Richie Cunningham from *Happy Days*. He cast a horrified look upon the remains and recoiled. "Oh, I say!"

Officer Dalquist introduced himself. It was getting to be quite a crowd. Again, I wondered where Officer Grant had disappeared to.

My stepfather also introduced himself, again failing to mention that he was retired. I certainly wasn't going to mention it, and I hoped the captain wouldn't either. As a mere passenger, I had less than no credibility with the Royal Barbados Police, doctor or not, so I looked upon Nigel as a free pass to the inner sanctum of police procedure.

I introduced myself anyway. "Toni Day," I said, "MD. I'm a pathologist."

Chief Superintendent Braithwaite looked down upon me from a height well over six feet with liquid brown eyes. "Really? In what capacity?"

I opened my mouth to answer, but Captain Sloane beat me to it. "She's a passenger," he said curtly. "She has no business being here."

I was afraid that the next words out of his mouth would blow Nigel's cover, so I spoke right up in my defense. "I did, however, prevent the guy with the mop and bucket from sloshing ammonia all over the remains."

"Did you now," said Dr. Welch. "Jolly good show, eh what?"

He sounded just like Nigel.

The Barbadians looked singularly unimpressed, even the coroner, which surprised me. As a fellow pathologist, I'd have expected her to be more receptive, but she wore the same impassive expression as her two male companions.

But then I had second thoughts. Maybe she wasn't a pathologist after all. Back home in Twin Falls, the coroner is an elected official, usually a mortician or a cop. Even if she was a doctor, she wouldn't necessarily be a pathologist.

Only one way to find out. "Dr. Gresham-St. John, are you a pathologist too?" I asked brightly, looking her straight in the eye.

"Yes, I am," she replied, still not smiling. "I trained at Johns Hopkins."

"University of California, Irvine," I said. "Did you do a fellowship in forensic pathology? Are you board-certified?"

"I did, and I am," she said smugly. "So I do know a thing or two about what to do in a case like this."

She sounded defensive. I wondered why. Was it possible that she felt threatened by me? That certainly hadn't been my intention. I was just trying to make conversation. "I'm sure you know a lot more about it than I do," I said. "Everything I know about forensics I learned in the field."

She seemed to relax a bit at that. "Then suppose you and I look over these remains and you tell me what you think."

Accordingly, we walked over to where the remains lay. The smell of blood and feces had become stronger, and the flies had increased in number. Either the captain hadn't heard me, or he'd decided to ignore me when I'd asked him to close the roof. Soon the sun would be high enough in the sky to hit the remains where they lay, drying them out and making the smell even more potent. Dr. Gresham-St. John grimaced. I noticed that the policemen kept their distance, as did the captain and Officer Dalquist and the security guards. But Nigel was right behind us, unwilling to be left out of any of the doings.

"Do you have any idea who it is?" she asked me.

"She," I said. "The remains are female. Check the nail polish."

She peered closely at the feet. "Yes, I see. She's also got the beginnings of a hammertoe. She must wear high heels a lot. Did you find her shoes?"

"No. Not here, anyway. Can you tell how old she is by her feet?"

"I'd guess late twenties, early thirties max. Where's her head?"

"In the swimming pool," I said. "Want me to go get it for you?"

She shook her head. "No, no, I want to see it where it is first."

"That's what I thought. That's why I left it there."

She nodded approvingly. "Let's take a look at it."

We ducked under the caution tape and stood at the pool's edge, looking down. The water level had gone down at least a foot.

The head was gone.

Blind and naked ignorance

Delivers brawling judgments, unashamed,

On all things all day long.

—Alfred, Lord Tennyson

"Oh shit," I said.

"Bloody hell," Dalquist said. "Doctor, are you quite sure it was here?"

"What did you do with it?" Dr. Gresham-St. John asked me.

"Nothing!" I said defensively. "I left it right there on the bottom where I found it. Why do you think I did anything with it? Why would I tell you it was here if I'd done anything with it?"

She shrugged. "You tell me."

"Oh, now, look here," Nigel said reproachfully. "You can't possibly suspect Toni of tampering with the head. She stopped a crewman who tried to clean up the remains with ammonia."

She frowned. "Who told him to do that?"

"He said the captain did," I said.

She folded her arms across her ample bosom. "Oh, surely not. You must be mistaken."

"The captain wouldn't do that," Officer Dalquist said. "He wants to clear this up as much as you do."

I turned to look at the captain, who returned an impassive gaze. I shrugged. "I'm only telling you what the man said."

"Does this crewman have a name?" Dalquist asked.

"I'm sure he does," I said, "but I don't know what it is. All I can tell you is that he's young, tall, black, and wears a tan uniform."

"Terrific," the coroner said sourly. "Well, no matter. Maybe we won't need the head. We can fingerprint her left hand and identify her that way."

I shook my head. "You do need the head," I told her. "She had a head injury. A six-inch gash on the back of her skull and a depressed skull fracture."

"Couldn't that have been an accident? Could she have fallen and hit her head on something?" she asked.

"Or maybe she was pushed," I suggested. "Or beaned with a baseball bat. But whatever happened, someone saw fit to cover it up by crushing the body in the roof. Why would anybody do that if it was just an accident?"

Dr. Gresham-St. John slanted me a skeptical look. "Okay, Doctor, what do *you* think happened?"

"I don't know what caused the head injury," I said. "But the appearance of the face suggests strangulation. You'd agree if you could see what I saw. Her face was all puffy, and her tongue was blue and protruding from her mouth."

"Couldn't that have happened when she was crushed in the roof?"

"Only if she was still alive when she was crushed," I said. "If she was dead when she was crushed, she had to have been strangled beforehand, otherwise she wouldn't have looked like that."

Dr. Gresham-St. John assumed a challenging stance, hands on hips. "You do realize, Doctor, that we've only *your* word for that."

What's up with the adversarial stuff, I thought, doesn't she know we're on the same side? "You know," I said quietly, "several other people besides me saw the head in the pool. Of course, none of them got a good look at it like I did, and now someone's removed it so that they never will. What does that tell you?"

Dr. Gresham-St. John wasn't backing down. "What does it tell *you*?"

"It tells me that somebody's got something to hide. And that tells me that this was no accident."

Nigel too had clearly had enough of the coroner's antagonism.

"Surely you don't think the deceased just happened to fall into the crack while the roof was being closed," he said. "I mean, really, someone would have had to hold the body in place while simultaneously closing the roof."

"How?" asked Dr. Gresham-St. John.

"It would require at least two people," Officer Grant said, startling me. I hadn't seen him come back. "One to secure the body, and one to close the roof on her."

"And from what I've been told so far, the roof can only be opened and closed from the bridge," I said.

Captain Sloane spoke for the first time. "Doctor, are you seriously accusing me or one of my bridge officers of complicity in this heinous crime?"

"Not if there's anyone else who can open and close the roof," I pointed out. "You all know better than I do who that might be."

"Who closed the roof last night?" asked Dr. Gresham-St. John.

"First Officer Lynch," the captain said, "at seven o'clock, as usual."

"We'll need to speak with him," said Chief Superintendent Braithwaite, startling me. He'd been so quiet I'd forgotten he was there. "He won't like finding out that he closed the roof on someone and killed her."

"She'd've had to be killed before seven o'clock last night," the captain countered, "because that's when the roof was closed for the night. But there are still people wandering around up there that early. The Crow's Nest Lounge is open until two a.m. Surely someone would have noticed."

"In which case, it would have been reported last night," I said.

Dr. Gresham-St. John looked at me narrowly. "I'm getting the impression you don't think she's been up here since last night."

"I don't," I said. "When the body fell on the deck, I was already up here. Her foot was warm. If she'd been up there in the roof since seven o'clock last night, it would have been cold."

"How warm?" she demanded.

"Warmer than ambient temperature," I said. "That's the best I can do. Also, her blood was still dripping. And yes, I know, you've got to take my word for that too."

"Are you suggesting that someone opened the roof after it had been closed for the night to put this body here, and then closed the roof on it?" Braithwaite asked.

"I don't see how it could have been any other way," I said.

"And the roof has to be opened and closed from the bridge?" the coroner asked.

"One of the crew told me that the captain does it from the bridge," I said. "But if Officer Lynch did it last night, I guess any one of the bridge officers could have done it as well."

"Are only officers allowed on the bridge?"

"Only a select few," Grant said. "The captain, the first officer, the second or navigation officer, the third and fourth officers, the helmsman, and the quartermaster, to be precise. Others by invitation only."

"We need to get a core temperature," the coroner said. "That should settle the question of when she actually died."

"Have at it," I said.

She removed a liver probe from her bag and plunged it into the remains in the approximate location of where the liver should have been.

"I wonder if the security guards saw anything," Officer Grant said. "I may as well talk to them while she's doing that."

When he left the pool area by way of the door, Nigel and I followed him. The security guards outside looked startled. They clearly hadn't been expecting anyone to exit. "Excuse me, madam," the older of them said to me. "What were you doing in there? How did you get in?"

"It's quite all right, Hodges," Grant said. "They're with me."

"Did either of you see anyone come out carrying a head?" I asked them.

They looked at each other. "A what?" the younger one asked in confusion. I could see why. On boats, the "head" means the bathroom.

"A human head," I amplified.

"Certainly not!" retorted Hodges, clearly offended.

"Gorblimey!" exclaimed the younger one in horror. "Are you 'aving us on?"

Nigel hastened to appease them. "See here," he said. "Did either of you see anybody come out of these doors since you've been stationed here?"

"Just maintenance," Hodges said. "They came to drain the pool."

"And 'ousekeeping," the other chimed in. "Just now."

"Were either of them carrying anything?" Nigel asked.

"Well, the bloke from 'ousekeeping 'ad a mop and bucket," the younger security guard said.

"You're quite sure that was all?" Nigel persisted. "Nothing else?"

They shook their heads emphatically.

We went back inside the pool area.

"The guy from housekeeping couldn't have taken it," Nigel said. "We were already here when he came in."

"Someone could have wrapped it in a towel and thrown it in one of the laundry bins in the spa," I suggested. The spa was located on the Lido deck as well, just forward of the swimming pool. "Or thrown it in the trash. Then he wouldn't have had to carry it out of here at all."

"Maybe," Officer Grant said, "but we can't take the chance. Whatever's in the trash now will get off-loaded here in port, and then it's out of our hands."

"We'd better search both places," I suggested.

"Both of what?" the captain asked.

"Both the trash and the laundry," I said.

The captain seemed to be at the end of his patience. "What the bloody hell are you talking about?"

Nigel hastened to explain the situation.

Captain Sloane sighed. "Officer Dalquist, you'll be in charge. You know what you have to do."

"Yes, Captain," Dalquist said resignedly, and left.

"I suppose it's a mercy," the captain said, "that we can get it done now before everyone comes back on board. The housekeeping staff is all islanders. Superstitious lot. This is going to 'freak them out,' as you Yanks say."

"Shall I go with him?" Detective Inspector Gordon Jones inquired of the captain. "I'm an islander too. Maybe I can talk to the crew and make them understand how important this is."

"I'll go too," offered young Dr. Welch. "They all know me. I did their physicals."

After they had gone, Nigel turned to Officer Grant. "What about the laundry?"

"Laundry is done right here on board ship," Grant said, "so it's not quite so time sensitive."

"Why don't we go search the laundry bins in the spa?" I asked. "Maybe we'll get lucky."

"You three go ahead," the coroner said. "I need to get an evidence tech up here to help me retrieve as much of the body as we can before the ship sails."

"Before the ship sails?" I asked. "You mean you're going to let us sail off at six o'clock tonight as if nothing happened?"

"We can't detain cruise ships," Chief Superintendent Braithwaite said. "We have no authority to do so. If there were a body, we'd remove it, and I'd request an autopsy if I thought it necessary; but in this case all we can do is collect as much evidence as we can before the ship sails."

"In that case," Nigel said, "you'll need us to find the head before the ship sails as well. We'd better get busy straightaway. Is the spa staff all islanders too?"

"Australians," I said, "and New Zealanders." I knew this because I'd availed myself of several spa services during the cruise. So had my mother.

"In that case," Braithwaite said, "would you accompany me, Detective Superintendent Gray?"

"Delighted," Nigel said.

That left me with Officer Grant and the coroner, who'd been on her cell phone during this conversation. She pocketed it as Braithwaite and Nigel disappeared through the spa doors. "There'll be an evidence tech here in just a few minutes," she told me. "Shall we see what we can retrieve?"

"Certainly," I said, accepting the metaphorical olive branch, and we walked back to the body. The area had become quite hot with the sun directly overhead. My clothes were now dry, so I removed the towel and looked around for a place to put it. That's when I saw the laundry bin standing right next to the towel caddy, big as life. I peered into it. It was empty. That figured. Nobody besides me had used any towels yet today.

I put my towel into it and went back to the body, which had dried up quite a bit since seven o'clock this morning. It was getting on toward noon, which meant five hours had passed, and some of the remains had assumed the appearance of beef jerky. It seemed likely that every bone in her body, aside from her left arm and leg, had been broken in multiple places.

"Do you think these fingers will give you usable fingerprints?" I asked her, pointing to the one hand that I could see.

"I don't know," she said. "They look pretty dried out."

"You can cut off a finger and soak it in fabric softener," I suggested.

"Does that work?" she inquired skeptically. "Have you ever tried it yourself?"

"I don't know," I admitted. "I saw it on TV. But what can it hurt?"

She shrugged.

"You could try it and see," I pursued.

Again she shrugged. This woman was a hard nut to crack and no mistake. So much for olive branches. The flies were persistent, and I got tired of trying to keep them off the body, so I quit trying. There wasn't anything I wanted to touch with my bare hands anyway. I didn't have any gloves, and apparently neither did she.

So I got up and moved over to the starboard windows, just in time to see another police car drive onto the pier and park next to the police van. A tall, slender girl dressed in navy-blue coveralls got out, carrying a large case.

"Hey," I called to the coroner, who had also moved away from the body and was now sitting in a deck chair in the shade, "I think your evidence tech is here."

"Good," she said, fanning herself. "It's about time."

A few minutes later, the girl entered the pool area and walked toward us. As she got closer, I saw that she was beautiful. Her features were finely sculptured, her dark eyes large and liquid, and her complexion a flawless café au lait. She wore her hair in a knot on top of her head. She greeted the coroner with a smile. "Whatcha got, Mama?"

"My daughter, Eva Mae St. John," Dr. Gresham-St. John said to me. "She's our evidence tech."

I was having a hard time believing that the short, dumpy coroner and this gorgeous sylphlike creature could be related. I hoped it didn't show. "How handy for you," I commented and then introduced myself.

"Have you touched any of the remains?" she asked sharply.

Like mother, like daughter. "Not without gloves," I replied. "Got an extra pair?"

"Not for you," she returned and turned her back on me to kneel by the remains and open her case.

"I say," Officer Grant commented, "that was a bit rude, what?"

Eva Mae gave him an impassive look and then started unloading containers of various sizes and ignoring us completely. She had quite a few of them, but there was no way she was going to get that entire mangled body into them. She was going to need a body bag or some really big buckets—like those big orange ones from Home Depot.

And a shovel. But I wasn't about to tell her that. I was through trying to help. She and her mama were on their own.

"I don't know about you," I said to Officer Grant, "but I'm done here."

He assented, and we started to leave. The pool was almost completely empty, and something shiny caught my eye. I started down into the empty pool to get a closer look, and Officer Grant said, "What are you doing, Doctor?"

"There's something caught in the pool drain," I said.

The thing that had caught my eye was an earring that had been caught in the drain along with a tangle of blonde hairs. I recognized it right away. Officer Grant whistled when I held it up for him to see.

"Dr. Gresham-St. John!" I called.

The coroner looked up. "What is it now, Dr. Day?"

"You need to see this."

She didn't have a chance to ask what, though, because just at that moment my stepfather and Chief Superintendent Braithwaite emerged from the spa. "What does she need to see?" Braithwaite asked me.

I showed him. "Here's proof that the head was here before someone removed it."

"What is it, Malcolm?" the coroner asked.

"An earring and some blonde hairs in the pool drain," he answered.

She laughed. "All that proves is that somebody with blonde hair swam in the pool and lost an earring."

"It's her earring," I said.

"And how do you know that?" she challenged me.

"I saw it when I examined the head earlier."

"And you think that she's the only one who might have earrings like that," she said skeptically.

I was rapidly losing patience with Dr. Gresham-St John. I opened my mouth, but Braithwaite forestalled me. "It's pretty distinctive, Marietta." He held it up to the light, and I snapped a picture of it.

The coroner didn't answer.

"That woman doesn't want to believe anything I say," I complained sotto voce. "What's her problem?"

"She clearly finds you intimidating," Grant said.

"Really," I said skeptically. "What gives you that idea?"

"Because I find you intimidating as well."

I could think of no possible answer to that, so I just shook my head.

"Don't worry, Dr. Day," Braithwaite reassured me. "If the victim's in the system, we'll find her." He pulled an evidence bag out of his pocket and put the earring in it. Then he pulled out another and said, "Just put the hair in here."

I did so. "I assume you didn't find the head?"

"We looked in every trash receptacle and laundry basket," Nigel said. "Not to mention all the cabinets and drawers. No joy."

"We left behind a thoroughly upset and confused spa staff," Braithwaite said. "It's a good job there were no customers today."

That made me wonder if the murder victim had ever patronized the spa. "You could go back in there and show them that earring," I suggested. "Maybe someone will recognize it."

Braithwaite nodded. "There's a thought," he said, and disappeared.

I heard footfalls on the metal staircase and turned to see Hal emerging from behind the bar. "I thought I might find you down here," he said. He slung an arm around me and gave me a kiss. "Have you figured out who she is yet?"

"No, not yet," I said. "Plus, the head has disappeared."

"What?"

"When we heard the police sirens, we all went topside to see the police arrive. Then when the police arrived here on the Lido deck, we all went back downstairs. During the time we were gone, maintenance came and started draining the pool, and the head disappeared. So Nigel and Chief Superintendent Braithwaite have been searching the spa, and the captain, Inspector Jones, the ship's doctor, and the officer in charge of waste disposal are searching the trash and the laundry, and this is Officer Grant, who's in charge of security."

Hal appeared thunderstruck. "All the trash? On this whole ship?"

"Well, they're a bit pressed for time," Nigel explained, "because they have to collect all their evidence before the ship sails at six o'clock."

"Before the ship sails? You mean the police are going to let the ship just sail on out of here as if nothing happened?"

Braithwaite emerged from the spa in time to hear Hal's question. "That's correct, sir. And you are?"

"My husband," I told him. "Hal Shapiro. Did anybody recognize the earring?"

"Nobody on the staff," Braithwaite said. "But there was a lady there making an appointment, who said it looked familiar. Unfortunately, she couldn't be more specific."

"Well, maybe they'll have better luck with the trash," I said. "Should we go help? What time is it?"

Hal looked at his watch. "Almost two."

"Did Fiona come back with you?" Nigel asked Hal.

"Yes. She said she was going to take a little nap so we could all go to the show tonight."

"We've no time to waste," I urged. "If we're going, let's go!"

"Chief Superintendent?" Nigel said. "Can you use a few extra pairs of eyes?"

"I suppose so," Braithwaite said. "But we've a bit of a problem."

"What's that?" Hal asked.

Braithwaite motioned to the starboard windows. "They're off-loading the trash as we speak. If they haven't found the head yet, it'll be going into that big lorry on the dock."

I looked, and saw rows of trash bags moving along a conveyor belt leading to a huge truck parked on the dock.

"Then where does it go?" I asked. "To a landfill?"

"To be incinerated or recycled," Braithwaite said. "We're an island. We've no space for a landfill."

"What about toxic fumes?"

Braithwaite smiled. "We do have an Environmental Protection Department to deal with hazardous chemicals, just as you Yanks have an EPA."

"So we're basically SOL," Hal said.

"SOL?"

"Out of luck," I translated.

Braithwaite hesitated and then with a faint smile said, "Oh. I see. Yes, I suppose we are."

"So what now?" I asked him.

"Let's see how Marietta and Eva Mae are doing," he replied, and we looked back toward the body.

The coroner and her daughter were gone.

Nae man can tether time or tide.

—Robert Burns

NOT ONLY WERE they gone, but so were all their containers and the remains. Eva Mae must have had a body bag folded up somewhere in her case. The surrounding area had been cordoned off with police tape. Two uniformed Royal Barbados Police officers stood inside the tape, feet apart, arms folded, surveying the mess the coroner had left behind.

Braithwaite lifted the tape, and Nigel, Hal, and I ducked under it. One of the officers turned and saw Hal. "I'm sorry, sir. I can't allow you to be here. You'll have to stay outside the tape."

Braithwaite came up beside me. "It's all right, Officer, he's with me. They're all with me."

"We need to get busy and clean this up," Grant said. "Do the police have everything they need?"

"I'd guess so," Braithwaite said. "My coroner is done with it, in any case."

"We still need to find the head," I pointed out.

"When did it go missing, exactly?" asked Grant. "Does anyone know?"

I looked past him to see a tall, young man with a mop and bucket approaching. It was the same one who had been here earlier and freaked over the foot. I saw relief flicker across his face as he got closer and saw that the body was gone, foot and all. The bucket was actually a large can of industrial strength pool cleaner. "I don't know," I said, "but here comes someone who might."

They all turned to look. The crewman saw Braithwaite, and fear leaped into his eyes. Braithwaite walked toward him, holding up both hands in appeasement. "Relax, Jamal. I'm not after you. We just need to ask you a couple of questions."

"You know him?" I asked.

"Oh yes." Braithwaite chuckled. "Jamal and I are old friends. We saw quite a bit of him down the station during his misspent youth. I trust all that is past now, Jamal?"

"Yes, Chief."

"Excellent." Braithwaite clapped the young man on the shoulder.

"Jamal," I said, "were you here when maintenance came to drain the pool this morning?"

"Yes'm."

"Did you remove the head from the pool, or did they?"

If it were possible for a black man to turn white, Jamal did so. His eyes stretched wide, and he backed away from me, shaking his head. "No, mum, no way. Dere was no head in de pool, I swear."

"Jamal," Braithwaite said, "settle down. Who got here first, you or maintenance?"

"I did, Chief."

"So if he's telling the truth," Nigel said, "the head was removed before either he or maintenance got here."

"I'm tellin' de truth!" Jamal protested.

"Thank you, Jamal. Carry on," Braithwaite said. "We can talk over here," he said to us, indicating the starboard windows, and we moved over to them, out of earshot of Jamal. The giant lorry had ceased loading waste and appeared to be preparing to leave.

Braithwaite sighed. "So much for the trash," he said. "I wonder if they found anything."

"So that means," I said, "that someone else removed the head before maintenance came to drain the pool."

"That could be any crew member," Hal said. "Or even a passenger."

"Not a passenger," I said. "The captain ordered this part of the Lido deck blocked off right after I told him the head was in the pool. Those security guards wouldn't have let any passengers in."

"Then how did that lady get into the spa?" Hal asked.

"What lady?" Braithwaite asked.

"The one who said the earring looked familiar. How'd she get in?"

Braithwaite frowned. "Is there another way into the spa other than from the Lido deck?"

"There's a freight elevator just forward of the spa," Grant said.

"You know what this means," I said. "One of the spa employees could have removed the head and disposed of it before maintenance came up here."

"Disposed of it where?" Braithwaite asked. "We looked everywhere and didn't find it."

"Would there happen to be a laundry chute forward of the spa also?" I asked.

"There is," Grant said. "It goes straight to C deck where the laundry is."

"How did we miss that?" Braithwaite wondered.

Nigel shrugged. "We didn't ask the right questions."

"If that lady was a passenger," I said, "what was she doing using a freight elevator to get to the spa?"

"Could she have been a crew member?" Hal wondered.

"What nationality was she?" I asked Braithwaite.

"She spoke with a British accent," Braithwaite said.

"That doesn't help much," Hal said. "There are lots of Brits and Canadians among the passengers. She could be anybody."

"She might have been part of the entertainment staff," Grant said. "Sometimes they avail themselves of spa services before a show."

"Now we're back to a spa employee," I said. "What could be easier? One of them goes into the pool after the head, wraps it in a towel, tosses it into the laundry chute, and then goes and gets cleaned up in one of the locker rooms. A shower, a hair dryer, a spare uniform in a locker, and Bob's your uncle."

"But why?" Hal asked. "It makes no sense."

"It would," I said, "if one of them was in cahoots with the murderer."

"Sweetie," Hal said in mock disbelief, "did you really just say 'in cahoots'?"

"For that matter," Braithwaite said, "someone from maintenance could be in cahoots, as you say, with the murderer."

"One of them could also *be* the murderer," Hal said. "It would have to be a crew member who could open and close the roof."

"Surely you're not suggesting that the *captain* is the murderer," Grant said, a shocked expression on his face.

"No, but it would have to be someone on the bridge," I said.

The door opened, and Captain Sloane, Inspector Jones, Officer Dalquist, and young Dr. Welch came toward us. They all looked hot and tired. Even the captain's starched white uniform looked a little limp.

"Any luck?" inquired Braithwaite.

The captain shook his head. "How about you?"

Braithwaite shook his head too. "No joy."

I opened my mouth to tell the captain my theory about the spa employee and the laundry chute, but Braithwaite shook his head at me. "The coroner's taken the remains," he told the captain. "So we'll be going back to the station. We'll be in touch if there's anything more that we need." He handed the captain a card. "Keep us posted."

They shook hands all around, and Braithwaite and Jones headed for the elevator.

"I've got office hours at five o'clock," said Dr. Welch. "I must go clean up. It won't do to see patients whilst smelling like a garbage dump." With a smile, he departed, getting onto the elevator with Braithwaite and Jones.

"If you'll excuse me," said Captain Sloane, "I have to get a cleaning crew up here to deal with that mess. It's going to take a lot more than young Jamal and his mop, if you ask me. The passengers are starting to come back aboard, and I can't have them looking in the door and seeing it. Officer Grant, you'll need to assign some of your staff to keep them away until we can get it cleared up." He fixed me with a stern look. "I don't need to tell you, do I, Dr. Day, not to talk about this to anyone? The consequences would be quite dire."

He nodded to Nigel and walked away, issuing staccato commands over his radio as he went. Officers Grant and Dalquist also excused themselves and followed the captain to the elevator.

"Dear me," I said. "Did that sound like a threat to anybody else, or is it just my overactive imagination?"

"It's your overactive imagination," my husband said.

"I don't know," Nigel said, "but he's right about the consequences being dire. We'll all have to be extremely careful what we say from here on out. I'm not sure I should even tell Fiona about it."

"You know everybody's going to be talking about it," Hal said. "Fiona will hear about it soon enough."

"If she hasn't already," I said.

"It's not just that," Nigel said. "Don't forget, the murderer could be anyone. If he or she thinks we know anything, we could be in considerable danger."

I wasn't worried about Mum talking about it. She was very good at keeping secrets. She'd even kept *Nigel* a secret from us right up until she decided to marry him. The problem was, when Mum had a secret, everybody *knew* she had one. She'd get this coy little smile on her face, and a mischievous look in her green eyes. That was what worried me. The murderer might see that and kill her just on the off chance that her secret had anything to do with the murder, whether it did or not.

The only way to prevent that was for none of us to tell her anything.

What were the chances of that?

Slim to none.

The only thing Mum did better than keeping secrets was worming them out of other people.

Particularly me.

I've never been able to get anything past my mother. She could always see right through me.

This time it could get her killed.

Hal and I headed straight for the Ocean Lounge on the Promenade deck. Nigel went to his cabin to check on Mum, after saying that they would join us as soon as she was up from her nap.

Without thinking, I ordered a martini, as usual. Hal vetoed that, reminding me that I hadn't eaten anything yet that day and was no doubt dehydrated—whereas he and Mum had eaten lunch ashore—and dinner was still three hours away. So I changed my order to a Virgin Mary, which would be accompanied by olives, celery, and a dill pickle. I also asked for a large glass of ice water. I could have the martini later, after I'd filled my stomach with vegetables and my third space with water.

The last thing I needed was to blurt out details about the murder while under the influence.

Nigel and Mum joined us about half an hour later. I didn't need to ask what they'd been talking about, because Mum already had that secret look on her face. So much for not talking about the murder to anyone.

But I'd misjudged Nigel. Mum reached into her capacious purse, pulled out a gift box, and handed it to me.

She and Hal had bought me a pair of earrings. They were blue topaz set in white gold, not nearly as ornate as the murder victim's. "Mum, these are gorgeous," I exclaimed as I put them on. "What's the occasion? Did I have a birthday and not notice?"

"Thank your husband, dear," she said. "He said you were having a rough day and might need a pick-me-up."

I hugged Hal and gave him a big kiss. "Thank you both. I love them. And that reminds me: I need to show you something, Mum." I reached into my boat bag, which I'd rescued from the Lido deck, and pulled out my smartphone.

Mum made a face. "No, no, kitten, please, I don't want to see any of those dreadful *gory* pictures."

"I know. That's not what I want you to look at." I went quickly through the pictures in my phone gallery until I came to the one I wanted. "There. Have you ever seen that earring before?"

"Yes, I think I have," she said immediately. "The singer last night at the show was wearing earrings just like this. Don't you think so, Nigel?" She held the phone out to him.

He shook his head. "Now, Fiona, you know I never notice things like that. She could have been wearing barrel hoops and a burlap sack for all I know."

"Oh, you're impossible!" She pouted prettily at him and handed the phone back to me.

"Mum, are you sure?"

"Yes, dear. You would be too if you'd been there. Fairly *blinded* me, they did."

"What did this singer look like?" I asked.

"She was a tiny little thing," Mum said. "Very thin, like one of those supermodels, you know, with long blonde hair and a very dark tan. Quite *leathery*-looking, if you know what I mean. I really don't think these very dark tans are good for the skin, you know, dear, they get skin cancer and spots and wrinkles and end up looking just like little brown monkeys."

"How old do you think she was?"

"Late twenties, early thirties, I'd guess, dear," Mum said. "She was one of those torch singers, you know, all whisky-voiced and sultry. She was rather good at it too. We quite enjoyed her, didn't we, love?"

Nigel nodded.

"Why are you asking all these questions, kitten?"

I looked at Nigel, hoping for guidance, but he was no help. "It's no good trying to keep it from her, you know."

Mum gasped and put her fingers to her mouth. "Hell's bells and buckets, you can't mean … do you mean to tell me that it was *her* body up there?"

Hastily I looked around to see if anyone was listening. Nobody was. I lowered my voice. "If that's her earring, it is," I said. "What else was she wearing?"

"A rather skimpy dress," she said. "Red, with gold threads all through it, and gold shoes. Sandals, you know, all straps, and *very* high heels. I *really* don't think those stiletto heels are good for the feet, you know, dear, they cause bunions and—"

Nigel interrupted the tirade. "Fiona love, do you remember her name?"

"No, dear, but I still have the program here somewhere." She rummaged through her bag and fished out a rather crumpled document.

She flattened it out on the table and ran her finger down the list of performers. "Here it is. Leonie Montague. There's a picture too."

I'd never have recognized her from what her face looked like in the swimming pool, but I didn't think Mum needed to know that, so I said nothing. I noticed that in the program photo she was wearing the same dress that Mum had described, as well as the same earrings and a heavy necklace of woven gold.

"Mum, was she wearing that necklace last night too?"

"Why, yes, dear. Didn't you find it on the body?"

"No. All we found was that one earring. The other had been ripped—"

Hal interrupted before I could finish the sentence. "Toni, stop." But it was too late. Mum put her fingers to her mouth and groaned softly. "Dear God."

"When are you going to start engaging your brain before putting your mouth in gear?" my husband chided me.

Probably never, but Hal didn't need to hear that now. Mum always got squeamish at the mention of gory details, but she usually got over it pretty fast. "I wonder where that necklace is now," I said.

Hal shrugged. "Maybe the killer took it as a trophy."

Nigel stood up. "I think the captain needs to know this straightaway."

I stood up too. "I'll go with you."

Hal objected. "Toni, you don't need to do that."

"Yes, I do," I said. "Really, I do."

"Go ahead, kitten," Mum said. "Hal and I will be just fine here."

In the elevator, I said to Nigel, "I need to talk to you before you talk to the captain."

"About what?"

"When we were talking to the captain up there on the Lido deck, I started to tell him that we thought maybe it was a spa employee that removed the head from the pool, and Braithwaite gave me this look and shook his head, like he didn't want me to talk."

"And so?"

"I think maybe he suspects the captain."

"Oh, surely you're mistaken."

"Well, perhaps he doesn't actually think that the captain is the murderer, but maybe he's not above suspicion."

"You were right," Nigel said. "This isn't something you should say to anyone but me."

"That's what I thought."

The elevator door opened on the navigation deck where our cabins were just aft of the bridge. Of course, passengers were not allowed on the bridge except by invitation, but Nigel was right that the captain needed to know as soon as possible who the victim was so he could contact the Royal Barbados Police and let them know. They'd probably still want to run her fingerprints anyway, but it would just confirm her identity. Then we could all get to the down-and-dirty business of figuring out who would have wanted to kill her and why.

Nigel rang the bell next to the double doors separating the bridge from the rest of the Nav deck, and someone opened it a crack. Nigel said, "I need to talk to the captain straightaway."

"I'm sorry, sir, but I can't let you come onto the bridge without permission from the captain, and he's not here right now."

"Where is he?" Nigel asked. "You see, I'm from Scotland Yard, and this is official police business."

The officer opened the door wider. "You must be Chief Superintendent Gray. Captain Sloane mentioned you. He's in his cabin. I'll show you."

"Thank you," Nigel said. "And you are?"

"First Officer David Lynch, sir. This way, please."

First Officer Lynch was of average height and slightly built. He was handsome in a conventional way that would have made his face totally forgettable if it were not for his exceptionally large ears. I wondered if he'd been called Jughead as a child.

"Did anyone from the Royal Barbados Police talk to you?" I asked him as we walked down the corridor.

He looked askance. "No. Should they have?"

"About the lady who was crushed in the roof," I reminded him.

He went pale. "Dear God. Do you mean to say that I—"

"No, no," I hastened to reassure him. "She was killed early this morning."

He sagged with relief. "Thank heaven. It would be a bit of a facer to realize that you'd accidentally killed someone. Here we are."

The captain's cabin was actually right next to the bridge, but the entrance to it was hidden up a little hallway off the main corridor. First Officer Lynch knocked and announced himself.

The captain opened the door. "What is it, Lynch?"

"Some people to see you, sir. Chief Superintendent Gray and ..." He looked at me questioningly.

"Dr. Day," I said.

"Of course," the captain said graciously. "Please, come in."

"Thank you, Captain," Nigel said.

"Excuse me, Captain, I'll be returning to the bridge now." First Officer Lynch withdrew, closing the door behind him.

The captain's cabin was larger than ours, with a bigger sitting area, more chairs, and larger sliding glass doors leading out to his veranda, which was also larger than ours. His office was in another room, furnished with a large desk, a conference table, and charts all over the walls. The furnishings were otherwise the same as our cabin. I noticed that the coffee table was chipped and stained darker on one corner, and wondered if something had happened to it or if it was a natural defect in the wood.

"Please, sit down," the captain continued. "Can I get you a drink?"

"Thank you, but no," Nigel said. "This won't take long."

"Has something happened?"

"We've identified the murder victim," Nigel said and handed the program to the captain. "The singer, Leonie Montague. There's a picture."

The captain took the program, looked at it, and blew out a breath. He reached behind him, as if to make sure the chair was really there, and sat down slowly, still staring at the program.

"Captain? Are you all right?" I asked. "Do you need some water or ..."

"No, no, I'm quite all right," he said. "How did you—"

"My mother recognized the earring," I said. "She was at the show last night."

"Do you know the lady, Captain?" Nigel asked. "If you'll pardon me saying so, you look a bit shaken."

"Not well," the captain said. "I do know who she is, because this isn't the first time she's been with us. I rather fear that the long afternoon down in the bowels of the ship took it out of me. I'll be quite all right after a shower and a change. And speaking of that, would you and your party consider dining with me tonight at the captain's table?"

"We'd love to," I said. "Wouldn't we, Nigel?"

"Oh, quite," said my stepfather. "Fiona will be delighted."

I never did get my martini.

We all had to go clean up and change for dinner. On board ship, one couldn't wear shorts and tank tops into the dining room. Men were required to wear a jacket and tie, and women had to wear a skirt or long pants, at the very least. Dining at the captain's table, however, required more formal dress, and so I wore a long dress instead of my usual black pants with a tunic top. It was sleeveless and teal green and accentuated my olive complexion and green eyes. With it I wore an opal necklace and earrings. Hal whistled. "That'll make the captain be nice to you, I'll bet."

"Oh, he'll be polite," I said. "He has to. There'll be other people there. You know what, I bet he invited us to sit at his table to keep an eye on us so that we won't talk about the murder."

"Oh, I don't know about that," Hal said. "You and Nigel aren't going to talk about it in any case."

"We won't, but I bet the other people will. They're going to be asking the captain all sorts of questions."

"I'm sure he's an old hand at not answering anything he doesn't want to."

"I think he knew that lady a lot better than he let on. He said he didn't, but it really shook him up."

"Not necessarily," Hal objected. "Didn't you tell me that he said it was because of the heat down on the lower decks?"

"Yes, he said that, but you can't tell me that the captain was down there sorting trash all that time. He was probably down there long enough to issue orders and put a lesser officer in charge of the job while he went around dealing with other things."

"What other things?" Hal argued.

"Like disposing of the head before anybody saw it, maybe."

"I thought you suspected someone from the spa of doing that."

"Only because it would be so easy to do that without being seen. One could just pop out, jump in the pool, grab the head, wrap it in a towel, toss it down the laundry chute, and get cleaned up in a locker room. Nobody'd ever have to know. Since we were in port today, they didn't have any customers this morning."

"Very neat," Hal said. "Now let's go down before you destroy my appetite completely."

"Okay," I said. "But might I suggest that we don't put anything out to go to the laundry tonight, just in case?"

The captain's table was in the choicest location in the dining room. It had the best view of the ocean, which was worthless at the late seating because it was already dark outside. It also had the best view of the dining room, and everyone could see who had the honor of dining with the captain.

I needn't have worried about people asking the captain questions about the murder after all. It was a table for eight, and the four of us were dining with First Officer David Lynch, Chief Engineer Joseph Gerard, and Dr. Robert Welch as well as Captain Sloane.

The surf 'n' turf was prepared perfectly and accompanied by a delightful red wine chosen by the captain. Chief Engineer Gerard explained to us that he was responsible for the ship's engines, propulsion systems, and plumbing, as well as anything else that was mechanical, electrical, or electronic. First Officer Lynch told us that he was the captain's right hand and that all staff managers reported to him. Mum and Hal talked about what they had done and seen in Bridgetown, and the captain talked about our next port, which was Philipsburg, St. Maarten. By common consent, the murder was not mentioned.

Not until the Filipino maître d' rushed up to the captain and whispered in his ear.

I leave this rule for others when I'm dead,

Be always sure you're right ... then go ahead.

—Davy Crockett

THE CAPTAIN STOOD up. "I'm sorry, but you'll have to excuse me. Something requires my attention in the laundry." Then, as an afterthought, he motioned to Dr. Welch. "You'd better come as well. And I suppose you, Chief Superintendent, and you, Dr. Day."

Nigel and I stared at each other. I was sure the same thought was going through his head as was going through mine.

They'd found the head.

"I don't understand," my mother said. "Why do they need a doctor in the laundry? Has someone been injured, do you think?"

"You could say that, my love," Nigel told her. "If we aren't back in time, you two go ahead and see the show. We'll catch up when we can."

The laundry on C deck was accessible only by the freight elevator, which could only be accessed through the kitchen directly forward of the dining room. Passengers rarely got to see this part of the ship.

There was none of the luxurious décor we'd become accustomed to. No carpets, no wallpaper, no pictures on the walls. Just utilitarian tan paint and metal floors. The only things on the walls were warning signs and crew duty rosters. When the elevator doors opened, I was sure we had descended to the bowels of hell. It was at least twenty degrees hotter down here than it was in the dining room.

The temperature inside the laundry must have been well in excess of a hundred degrees. The air was so humid that I felt as if I'd been slapped with a wet towel. Someone had considerately decreed that the walls in here be painted blue, as if to make the crew think it was cooler than it actually was. It didn't fool me.

It didn't take a rocket scientist to figure out where the problem was. All the Filipino crew members were clustered around one of the giant industrial-sized washers, chattering loudly in what I assumed was Tagalog—all except one young man, who was stretched out on the floor being tended to by another crew member, who applied a wet compress to his forehead. The smell told me that he, or someone, had been sick, although the evidence of that had already been cleared away.

The washer had been stopped, and through the glass door I saw pink sudsy water and pink towels.

Captain Sloane removed his cap and scratched his head. "What department uses pink towels?"

I cleared my throat. "I believe those towels are supposed to be white."

The captain put a hand over his mouth and turned away. "Oh dear God!"

Nigel nodded. "You'll need to drain that water before we open the door."

One of the Filipinos objected.

"Do what he says," Dr. Welch directed. "Drain it. Don't use the spin-dry cycle."

The Filipino pressed buttons and turned a dial, and the water began to drain. Slowly the drum inside began to turn, and as the towels inside started tumbling, I caught a glimpse of red. A mouth, with teeth. An eyeball. Blonde hair.

Dr. Welch peered over my shoulder with interest. "Is that her?"

"That's her," I said. "At least I hope it's her. I hope we don't have *two* headless bodies on this ship."

The water stopped draining, and a click announced the beginning of the spin-dry cycle.

"Turn it off," Dr. Welch said.

The Filipino complied. Dr.Welch stepped forward and opened the door. I was pretty sure he wished he hadn't. The miasma of blood and decaying tissue was strong enough to send many of the crew members scurrying for the far corners of the room, or another room altogether. Only a hardy few remained. The captain had disappeared.

Nigel directed the remaining crew to lay a sheet on the floor in front of the washer. They pulled out towels one by one, shook them out onto the sheet, and then threw them into a hamper to be rewashed or possibly discarded altogether.

I stood back while all this was going on, feeling thankful that my dress was washable, but unsure that blood spatters could be completely removed. Nigel, apparently unconcerned about soiling his white dinner jacket, squatted down and closely supervised the proceedings. "Toni, my girl, come take a look at this," he urged. "Grab a pair of gloves. Grab some for me whilst you're at it."

I looked around. One of the Filipinos proffered a box of nitrile gloves. It was only then that I noticed that they all wore gloves to handle the laundry. I grabbed a couple of pairs, tucked up my long skirt, and knelt next to Nigel.

Because of decomposition hastened by the heat and humidity of the laundry and the agitation in very hot soapy water, the head was no longer in one piece. Considerable skin slippage was present, and one eyeball dangled onto the cheek. The color of the iris was now obscured by the postmortem cloudiness of the conjunctiva, but I knew that her eyes had been dark brown. Chunks of skin and soft tissue had sloughed from the skull and cheekbones. The swollen, blue-gray tongue had been caught between teeth exposed by avulsion of the lips, forming an evil rictus of death. The bright-red lipstick was gone.

I looked around at my companions. Dr. Welch stood behind Nigel, staring at the remains of the head with interest. Captain Sloane had returned, but at the sight of the head, he went pale. He turned and made a hasty exit.

With my gloved hands, I arranged the pieces in the closest approximation of their original position that I could manage. I'd seen a mark on the left cheek when the head was still in the pool, and I wanted to get a better look at it. After having gone through the wash cycle in hot water, it stood out much darker than it had in the pool, plus the light was much better here than it had been up on the Lido deck at dawn. I pointed it out to Nigel. "See this?"

He looked closer. "Looks like a handprint. Somebody smacked her a good one. You know, one could almost make out ridge detail."

"Let me get a picture of that," I said. "Maybe someone can enhance it enough to identify who killed her."

"At least who hit her," Nigel said. "It isn't necessarily the same person who killed her."

"True." I stripped my gloves off, took my smartphone out of my purse, and snapped pictures from multiple angles as close up as I could get.

Dr. Welch watched in fascination. "What should we do next, Doctor?"

I looked up at him. "Do you have surgical instruments in your clinic?"

"Of course. What—"

"How about a Stryker saw?"

"Certainly. I do have to remove the odd cast from time to time."

"How about a big jar and a gallon of alcohol?"

"I'm not sure I've got a gallon, but I've got several liters. What do you want to do?"

"An autopsy. Want to help?"

Dr. Welch's eyes lit up. "Right-o!"

We put the pieces into a plastic bag and wrapped the bag in a clean towel for transport to the medical clinic, just in case we ran into anyone on the way.

"So how'd it go with the trash?" Nigel asked Rob in the elevator.

"It was quite an experience," Rob said. "You wouldn't believe how careful they are. There's this big sorting room down there where they separate out metals, aluminium cans, glass bottles—by color, mind you—paper and cardboard, food waste, et cetera. Then they shred the glass, and crush the cans, and bale everything up for disposal. Then a big lorry comes and takes it all away."

"Wow," I said. "I had no idea."

"Well, I knew there was an elaborate procedure, but I didn't know the details until today."

"So there'd be no way a human head could get past them."

"Right."

"What do they do with sewage?" I asked.

"They filter it, treat it with bacteria that digest fecal matter, and then treat it chemically and expose it to UV light. Then the solids are compacted and incinerated on board. Then they can dump the water into the ocean, as long as it's twelve miles or more from shore."

"What about stuff like this?" I asked, indicating the bundle he was carrying.

"That gets disposed of on shore by specialists in biohazard waste."

The infirmary was on A deck, two decks above C deck, and much cooler. Dr. Welch led the way into his clinic and closed and locked the door behind him. "It's after office hours, and we'll just have to hope no emergencies arise."

"Too bad you don't have a morgue," I commented.

"Actually, we do," he said, "but it's little more than a cooler. We have to have someplace to keep a body until we reach the next port. Right this way." He opened a door into a long corridor. "It's all the way back. You can't do an autopsy in it, for example, but there might be somewhere to work on this. We can put it in the cooler when we're done with it." He opened another door and turned on the light. "Just put the doings there in that sink," he directed. He gestured at my dress, miraculously unstained so far. "Want some scrubs?"

"Sure. Thanks."

The scrubs he gave me were much too large, but once I secured the waistband of the scrub pants with a pair of hemostats and rolled up the legs, they were much more comfortable. Dr. Welch changed into scrubs as well, but Nigel just doffed his dinner jacket and rolled up his shirtsleeves. "I believe I'll just watch. Carry on."

After donning surgical gloves, Dr. Welch and I laid out the skull and the tissue fragments on a surgical towel on the counter next to the sink. "When I saw her head in the pool this morning, I saw a six-inch laceration on the back of her head, and underneath it I felt a depressed skull fracture. Right here."

I indicated the spot, and Dr. Welch palpated it. "Blimey. This has got to be the cause of death."

"I'm sure it is. All we have to do is document it," I told him. "I need you to hold the head upright so I can get a picture of the laceration."

He did so, and I snapped several pictures from various angles. "Now," I said, "I need to see if there's anything stuck to the edges of the wound to give us a clue to what she was hit with, and then I need to excise the skin around it and put it in alcohol to preserve it."

Dr. Welch handed me a pair of forceps, and I probed the edges of the wound. "Aha!" I said as I extracted a sliver of wood. "This looks like oak. What's made out of oak?"

"Other than the furniture in the cabins, I don't know," he said.

"You think somebody hit her over the head with a table leg?" I asked. "Or a chair?"

He picked up the head and held it at eye level. "I think it might be difficult to cause a wound in this location by hitting one over the head," he said. "This wound looks more like she fell onto something with sharp corners."

"Like a coffee table," I said, remembering the chip I'd seen on the captain's coffee table. "Or maybe a dresser. Maybe this is an accident and not murder at all."

"Unless she fell because someone pushed her," Nigel said. "And don't forget that even if it was an accident, someone tried to cover it up by putting the body in the roof and crushing it. That's a crime in itself. Obstruction of justice by tampering with evidence."

"I want to take a picture of this sliver," I said. "Can you grab me a paper towel, Dr. Welch?"

He did so. "You know, you may as well call me Rob. We've become quite close over the last few hours."

"Then you can call me Toni," I said. "Have you got a ruler? I need something to show the dimensions of the sliver."

Nigel dug into his pocket and held up a dime. "Will this work?"

"Yes. Just put it on the towel next to the sliver." I snapped the picture at several magnifications. "Have you got a small jar I could save this in?"

"Will a urine cup do?" he asked. He opened one of the lower cabinets and extracted one. "As you can see, we keep supplies in here too."

"Perfect," I said and put the splinter into it, paper towel, dime, and all. "Oh, you know what, I think I'd better save some of her hair for exemplars, just in case. Can you grab me another urine cup?"

Rob did so. I yanked a handful of blonde hairs with their dark roots out of the scalp and sealed them into it.

"Now I think I'd better take the vitreous humor, just in case she was drugged or poisoned," I said. "For that I need a syringe and a needle. And do you have a small tube with a cap?"

Rob shook his head. "I don't think we have anything like that," he said.

"Okay, then, I guess I can use a urine cup," I said, "but it's not optimal. Too much head space. It could dry out."

"Why not just leave it in the syringe and cap the needle?"

"Oh, good idea."

He fetched me two five-cc glass syringes with needles. "One for each eye," he said.

"Cool." I aspirated vitreous from each eyeball and capped the needles. "Do you have anything we could use to label these specimens?"

He reached into a drawer and pulled out a Sharpie. "How about this?"

I wrote "Montague, L." and the date and time on each specimen container.

"We can keep those in the cooler too," Rob said.

"Perfect. Now I need a scalpel," I said.

Rob fetched me one. "What are you going to do now?"

"I need to remove the skull cap. So first I need to peel the skin and subcutaneous tissue off the skull, and then I'll need the Stryker saw."

While Rob held the head steady, I made an incision across the top of the head from ear to ear. With another surgical towel and a little help from the scalpel, I peeled the skin forward over the face, and backward over the back of the head. Then with the Stryker saw I removed the skull cap.

The depressed skull fracture was clearly visible from the exterior aspect, and I photographed it from several angles, including the corresponding hemorrhage in the overlying scalp. It was even more impressive from the inside of the skull cap, with splintery edges that had pierced the brain. Both Rob and Nigel whistled when I lifted it away to expose the extent of the subdural hematoma underneath. I took more pictures.

Next, I removed the brain from the skull cavity, using the scalpel to sever the dura mater and the various cranial nerves that held it in place. "This is what I need a big jar for," I said.

Rob shook his head. "I don't have anything that big, sorry."

"Would a big bucket with a lid do?" Nigel inquired. "Like the buckets that laundry detergent comes in? Or p'r'aps the kitchen might have some big jars—for mayonnaise or mustard, for example?"

Rob stripped off his gloves. "I'll go see."

"Bring me a big knife from the kitchen!" I called after him.

"A big knife? How big?"

"Like a chef's knife."

"You've got it." And he was gone.

"What now?" Nigel inquired.

I stripped off my gloves and pushed my chair back so I could stretch out my legs. "Now," I said, "we wait."

"What do you intend to do with a chef's knife?" Nigel asked. "Fillet the brain?"

"Yes, that's exactly what I intend to do," I said. "It'll show the extent of the hemorrhage."

"And you'll take pictures."

"Right."

"Can you tell," Nigel inquired, "whether or not she was still alive when she was crushed in the roof?"

"Either that, or she was strangled beforehand. If she'd been dead, her face wouldn't have been all swollen up like it was, and the tongue wouldn't have been all blue and sticking out of her mouth. That wouldn't happen unless the blood was still circulating."

"I guess we'll never know," Nigel said. "Any ligature marks would have been obscured when the neck was crushed and the head fell off the body."

"I think she was still alive," I said. "When I saw the head fall into the pool, I got up to look over the edge and blood dripped on my head. If she'd been dead, all the blood would have been clotted."

Nigel shuddered. "I sincerely hope she wasn't conscious."

I gestured at the brain, which sat on the drain board next to the sink with the subdural hematoma covering ninety percent of its surface. "I don't think there was any way she could have been conscious," I said, "with all that bleeding."

"Great Scott," Nigel said. "That means that someone had to open up the roof, put the body in the opening, and close it again, less than an hour before you saw the head fall. That makes a lot of noise. Wouldn't you think someone would hear that?"

"I think I did hear it," I said. "Something woke me up, and I couldn't go back to sleep. The roof made the most awful screeching noise when they opened it this morning. If it made that same sound when they closed it on her, no wonder it woke me up. That's why I was on the Lido deck in the first place, because I couldn't get back to sleep."

"Do you know what time that was?"

"Not exactly. It was still dark, though. I read until I heard the roof opening at seven o'clock. That's what attracted my attention, and that's why I saw the head fall."

"Too bad you didn't look at your watch when you first heard the noise," Nigel said.

"I'd've had to turn on a light. I didn't want to wake Hal. I looked at it when I got up there, though, and it was six thirty."

I heard a key in the lock, and turned, expecting to see Rob coming down the corridor.

But it wasn't Rob. It was the captain. "Where's Dr. Welch?" he asked.

"I don't know," I said.

"He should be back any minute," Nigel said.

Captain Sloane closed the door and leaned on it, folding his arms. "Then I'll just wait." Then he saw the brain. "What's that?"

"Miss Leonie Montague's brain," I said, "showing the massive cerebral hemorrhage that killed her."

"Then that other thing must be ..."

"What's left of her face," Nigel said.

That did it. The captain went pale again. Abruptly he turned and opened the door to leave just as Rob came back. "Captain? What can I do for you?"

"Get out of my way," Captain Sloane snapped and left abruptly.

Rob stared after him for a moment, shrugged, and turned back to me, brandishing the chef's knife. "This do you?"

"Admirably," I said. "What about the buckets?"

"Hang on," he said. "They're right out here." I held the door open while he retrieved an empty laundry detergent bucket and two large glass jars. "How's this?"

"Brilliant," Nigel said. "Just the ticket."

"What did the captain want?" Rob asked.

"No idea," Nigel said. "He got sick before he had a chance to ask anything."

"I didn't realize that the captain had a key to the infirmary," I said.

"The captain," said Rob, "has a key to everything."

"Even cabins?" I asked.

"Well, he doesn't actually carry them around with him, but he keeps master keys to every room on the ship on the bridge. In case of emergency, you know. The security officers do too, for the same reason."

Far from feeling safer, I found this information alarming. "Does that mean that all the officers have access to every room on the ship?"

Rob scratched his head. "I never really thought about it, but I suppose they do."

I gave myself a mental shake. "Well. Let's get this done."

"Right," said Rob. "What do you need me to do?"

"Just arrange these brain slices in a row so I can take pictures of them."

I sliced the brain with the chef's knife, and Rob laid the slices out in a row as I directed. It wasn't easy. The brain is extremely gelatinous when fresh, and even more fragile when decomposed. That's why we let brains fix in formalin for two weeks before cutting them. But this wasn't the usual hospital setting, and we didn't have any formalin. Nor did we have two weeks.

The brain slices demonstrated what I already suspected. The subdural hematoma was large enough to have pushed the brainstem down into the foramen magnum, compressing the respiratory center. I deduced from this that she had been dead or close to it when she was crushed, and couldn't possibly have been conscious, which made me feel better. At least I didn't have to torture myself by imagining what it had been like to be crushed alive.

After photographing the brain slices, I put them into one of the mayonnaise jars, with paper towels between them to keep them from sticking to each other. Rob poured rubbing alcohol over them, and I screwed the lid on. We were getting to be quite a team.

"We'll just put these in the cooler for safekeeping," Rob said, and unlocked the heavy steel door. He had to struggle a bit to get it open though. I guessed it hadn't been used in a while, although one would think someone would lubricate it between cruises. Maybe it didn't get used enough to merit regular maintenance. Oddly enough, however, the interior of the cooler was spotless. It had obviously been recently cleaned. So recently that I could still smell the disinfectant.

"Have you had someone in here recently?" I asked.

"No," he said. "Why do you ask?"

His voice sounded a little strained. I turned to look at him and saw that his neck muscles were tensed. He didn't meet my eyes.

It didn't take a psychiatrist to know that he was lying. I wondered why. What would be the point? That's what the cooler was for, after all, to store a body until it could be taken off at the next port.

Unless, of course, the body had been Leonie's.

"Because it's so clean," I said.

"Of course it is," he returned. "This ship gets cleaned from stem to stern between cruises, and there hasn't been a body in it on this cruise, like I said."

I glanced at Nigel. He shook his head almost imperceptibly, and I took the hint not to pursue it further at that time.

I put the rest of the head into the bucket. "Have you got more alcohol?"

Rob looked in one of the lower cabinets and came up with three more bottles. "Sorry, this is all I can spare," he said. "We can't get any more until we get to San Juan. I need to keep some on hand in case I actually have to stitch somebody up or sterilize something."

"I guess it'll have to do." I uncapped and poured the three bottles into the bucket. It didn't quite cover the head, so I filled one of the bottles with water and added it to the bucket. It just barely covered the head, and Nigel said, "Is that going to be enough to preserve it, with water in it?"

"It should be," I said. "Seventy percent alcohol is strong enough to preserve it without drying it out too much, and this is actually seventy-five percent."

"Right-o," said Rob and picked up the bucket. "I'll just stow this away, and then we can all get some shut-eye, eh what?"

That sounded like a lovely idea, since it was now close to midnight.

Hal was already in bed when I got back to our cabin. I tried to sneak in without waking him, but as luck would have it, I stubbed my toe on the leg of the bed in the dark and lost my balance. I landed on the bed, and Hal woke up.

"Toni?" He rolled over, turned on the bedside light, and squinted at me. "Why are you wearing scrubs?"

I told him about the night's adventures.

"So where are all the specimens now?" he asked.

"Rob put them away in the cooler for safekeeping."

"Rob?"

"Rob Welch. The ship's doctor."

"There's a cooler in the infirmary?"

"Yes. In case someone dies."

"Good. They should be safe there, right?"

"I hope so," I said, "providing he's not involved."

"I see you packed your paranoia, sweetie."

"You may scoff," I said, "but at this point the only people I'm absolutely sure *aren't* involved are you, me, Mum, and Nigel."

"Thank heavens for that." He moved over and patted the bed next to him. I climbed in, scrubs and all, and he put his arm around me. "So what are you going to do with them?"

"I don't know. I took a whole bunch of pictures to document her injuries, so we might not need the actual head and brain. It's just that I don't want to lose anything that could be potential evidence. You just never know. If this goes to court and the defense refuses to accept the pictures because they're digital and can be manipulated, we may need them."

"How do you plan to get them to Chief Superintendent Braithwaite?"

"That's a fine question. You can't just slap a label on them and drop them off at the post office in St. Maarten. They'd require special packaging that won't leak. We might run into local laws that prohibit sending human remains through the mail."

"Well, we sure as hell can't take them home with us," Hal said practically. "We can't carry them on the plane."

"There's always the possibility that Chief Superintendent Braithwaite won't want them," I said. "Maybe we should send them to the coroner instead."

"From what you've told me about her, I bet she won't want them either," Hal pointed out.

"Then maybe we should be sending them to Scotland Yard," I mused.

"We can ask Nigel about that in the morning." Hal yawned. "Hell, it already *is* morning. Let's get some sleep."

I slid out of bed and stood up. "You go ahead. I need to back up these pictures before someone sneaks in here and steals my phone to prevent them from ever seeing the light of day."

Hal slid down in the bed and put his arm over his eyes. "Oy vey."

"Do you want me to do this someplace else so I won't keep you awake?"

Hal shook his head. "No, it's okay, I can sleep with the light on. Besides you're safer here than anywhere else on the ship."

He had a point. Somebody could sneak up behind me and take me unawares while I was engrossed in computer manipulations in the library or any other public area. Luckily, I could get Wi-Fi in our cabin. Not everybody could, I knew. I'd heard people complaining about it.

"I'll just sit over here at the desk and use this light," I told him." You can turn that one off."

"Okay. Good night, hon."

I turned on the desk lamp and pulled out my laptop. For starters, I decided, I'd e-mail them to myself from my phone and forward them to my son-in-law Pete, who was a detective lieutenant with the Twin Falls Police, just in case someone decided to steal my laptop too, and delete my e-mails.

I wished I'd thought to ask Chief Superintendent Braithwaite for his e-mail address. Perhaps it was on the card he'd given Captain Sloane. I could ask him in the morning, assuming that I saw him in the morning. Of course, it was always possible that if he had it, he might not want to give it to me, which would make me suspicious; but he could simply say he didn't have it to give, and I'd never know the difference.

So I Googled the Royal Barbados Police and found their website. Contact us, it said, and gave a phone number and the e-mail address of the public relations officer, Inspector LaShondra Blackwell. I also learned that it was possible to call Barbados from the US by using area code 246, which I might be able to do with my smartphone. I programmed the contact number into it for future use. Then I e-mailed the pictures to Inspector Blackwell, with an explanatory note asking her to forward them to Chief Superintendent Braithwaite. I hoped I wouldn't get one of those messages that said the e-mail address had failed permanently the next time I checked my e-mails.

It was nearly two in the morning by the time I'd finished e-mailing those pictures. They had to be sent separately, because e-mail could only handle ten megabytes at a time. But before I could get out of my scrubs and into bed, there was a tap at the door, which woke Hal. "Who the hell could that be at this hour in the morning?" he grumbled, getting out of bed to answer the door.

First Officer David Lynch stood in the doorway. "I'm so sorry to disturb you, Dr. Shapiro, but the captain just wanted me to check and make sure Dr. Day was all right."

"I'm fine, thanks," I said. "How is he?"

Lynch looked mildly perplexed. "Fine, as far as I know." He

apparently wasn't aware that the captain had spent most of the evening running for the nearest loo.

"Can I ask you something? Is there any other way to open and close the roof except from the bridge?"

"If there is, I'm not aware of it. Why d'you want to know?"

"Just curious," I said innocently.

"Very well." He touched his cap. "I'll bid you good night, then."

Hal closed the door behind him. "I don't think he was expecting us to still be up."

"I think you're right," I said. "Do you suppose the captain sent him to steal my cell phone?"

"Hard to say," Hal said. "Do you suppose he also went across the hall and checked to see if Nigel was all right?"

"Wouldn't we have heard him if he had?"

"I suppose so," Hal said. "Would he have been able to get into our cabin if I hadn't answered the door?"

"Absolutely," I said. "I learned today that the captain has keys to every room on this ship, including cabins."

"Jesus Christ," Hal said. "Then nothing in here is safe, including us."

Monday | PHILIPSBURG, SINT MAARTEN

Man's love is of man's life a thing apart;

'Tis woman's whole existence.

—Lord Byron, *Don Juan*

THAT WASN'T A very comforting thought to go to sleep on, and neither of us slept well, even though I propped the bathroom door open in such a way that anyone entering our cabin would crash right into it. I'd failed to take into account that the motion of the ship in the open sea would cause it to swing back and forth and bang, and I had to get up and secure it. A bungee cord would have come in handy, but who packs bungee cords to go on a cruise? Maybe I could find a hardware store in Philipsburg and get some in the morning, but for now we were at the mercy of anyone with a key.

Finally I settled for sleeping with my smartphone under my pillow, but by that time it was three thirty in the morning, and I was still too keyed up to sleep. So was Hal, apparently. After several hours of tossing and turning, we gave up and got up much earlier than usual, long before we normally met Mum and Nigel for breakfast in the Lido restaurant.

Perhaps that was just as well, because it gave us time to scope out the situation on the decks above us.

To our amazement, the Lido pool area was open and the pool refilled. The roof was closed. We got cups of coffee from the Lido restaurant and went up to the observation deck to look at it from the top, but we saw no evidence of the blood and gore of the previous day. Rather than a miasma of decay, I smelled fresh paint.

As we stood there watching the sun come up, we heard a noise and turned to see the roof opening slowly and smoothly, with less noise than ever before. Perhaps the cleaning required to remove all traces of Leonie Montague had solved other problems as well.

"Wow," I said to Hal, "I never would have expected this to be done so quickly. The maintenance and housekeeping crews must have worked all night."

"It's a minor miracle," Hal agreed.

"I've been doin' this for nearly twenty years, but this is the first time I've had to deal wi' human remains," said someone behind us. We turned to see Chief Engineer Gerard approaching. "I sincerely hope it's the last."

Gerard was a tall, rawboned man with red hair, a red face, startlingly blue eyes, and more than a trace of Scots in his speech. He held a cup of coffee in one hand and a boxlike object in the other. He leaned on the rail next to us.

"What's that thing?" I asked him.

"This? It's a remote control. It's what I used just now to open the roof."

"Really?" I said, surprised. "I thought that had to be done from the bridge."

"It usually is," he said. "But when repairs have to be made, we have to be able to open and close it while we're working on it. We can't be running back and forth to the bridge every five minutes, d'y'see?"

"So does that mean that anybody can open and close the roof?" Hal asked. "We were told that only the captain can do that."

"A bit o' polite fiction for passenger consumption," Gerard said. "As long as it's running properly, the captain is the one who opens it and closes it daily when we're at sea. When maintenance or repairs are needed, we in engineering and maintenance have to be able to access it."

"Can anyone besides the folks on the bridge and maintenance and engineering open and close the roof?" I pursued.

Gerard's expression turned wary. "Why d'you want to know that?"

"Because a woman's body was crushed in the roof sometime between six and seven yesterday morning. Somebody opened the roof, put the body in, and then closed it. If the captain didn't do it, and maintenance and engineering didn't do it, who did?"

Gerard frowned. "How d'you know it was between six and seven in the morning?"

"Simple. Her blood hadn't clotted and her feet were still warm."

"And how d'you know *that*?" Gerard's company manners seemed to be slipping. His Scots was getting thicker too.

"I was there," I explained. "I was on the Lido deck when the head fell in the pool and the body fell on the deck. Naturally I had to investigate—and that's another thing. Who removed the head from the pool?"

"And how would I be knowin' that?"

"Because it disappeared during the time when maintenance was draining the pool and all of us were topside watching the police arrive."

Gerard hunched his shoulders and placed his hands on his hips before closing the space between us. "Madam, I don't appreciate the implication that my department is in the habit of tamperin' with evidence, and I'll thank ye to keep yer nose out of it."

I took a step back. Hal didn't. He and Gerard were practically nose to nose when Hal said, "And I'll thank you not to talk to my wife like that. Is this how you think passengers should be treated?"

Gerard was unimpressed. "What d'you think about your wife going around interferin' in things that are none of her affair?"

"I say more power to her," Hal said. "I took a vow to love and honor, not to be a control freak."

"Y' mean tae say it disna bother you?" Gerard asked in disbelief.

"Sure it does," Hal said, looping an arm around my shoulders. "But I figured out a long time ago that worrying about Toni once in a while is better than not having Toni at all."

Gerard looked as if he'd have liked to come back with a snappy retort, but the radio on his belt crackled, and he had to answer it. "Yes, sir. Right away." He put it back on his belt and heaved a sigh. "I'm sorry, you'll have tae excuse me. It seems one of the washing machines in the laundry requires my attention."

"Probably the one they found the head in last night," I remarked.

Gerard's company manners vanished completely. "Bluidy hell," he snarled and walked away in the direction of the elevator.

"That's spoiled his day," Hal remarked. "I hope he hasn't had breakfast yet."

"Couldn't happen to a nicer guy," I said. "Can you say 'male chauvinist pig'?"

Hal chuckled. "I thought I saw smoke coming out of your ears, but maybe it was a trick of the light."

"Nope," I said, shaking my head for emphasis, "it was definitely smoke."

"What's all this about smoke?" Nigel inquired, startling me. I turned to see him and Mum behind us. I hadn't heard them coming.

"What are you guys doing up so early?" I asked.

"We didn't sleep well," Mum said.

"How come?"

"After we left the dinner table last night, Fiona got into a bit of a dust-up with the Chief Engineer," Nigel said.

"A thoroughly unpleasant man," Mum interjected with a sniff.

"I couldn't agree more," I said. Gerard took the concept of the dour Scot to a whole new level, in my opinion. "We had a bit of a dust-up with him too, just now."

"She rather took exception to his thoughts about what you and I were doing getting involved with a dead body," Nigel continued. "He was of the opinion that we were wasting our time because nothing was going to be done about it no matter what we did."

"You're kidding, right?"

"Not a bit of it," Mum said. "He said that the cruise line would have nothing to do with it because we were in a port, and the port would do nothing because it occurred on a cruise ship."

"Oh, for God's sake," I said in disgust. "So the murderer's just going to get away with it because these assholes can't be bothered to do the right thing?"

"Language, dear," my mother reminded me tartly. "Although that was rather the way I felt about it too."

"There is also the matter of jurisdiction," Nigel said. "Barbados is a

British commonwealth, and the cruise ship sails under the British flag, but one has no jurisdiction in the other and vice versa."

"What about Scotland Yard?" I asked.

"Scotland Yard would have jurisdiction in both," Nigel said, "assuming we were called in by one or the other. That's the rub, you know."

"You know the captain," I suggested. "You could talk him into calling them in. Couldn't you?"

"Toni," said my long-suffering husband, "quit nagging."

"I'm sorry," I said, endeavoring to sound contrite, "I don't mean to be a pest. It's just that Dr. Welch and I collected all this evidence last night and I don't want it to all be for naught."

"I know," Nigel reminded me. "I was there."

"I also took pictures of everything. Last night I backed them up by e-mailing them from my smartphone to my laptop, and I forwarded them to Pete—"

"Why send them to Pete, kitten?" Mum inquired. "He can't do anything with them."

"For backup in case someone steals my laptop. I also forwarded them to Inspector Blackwell, the public relations officer with the Royal Barbados Police, and asked her to forward them to Chief Superintendent Braithwaite."

"That must have taken all night," Nigel said.

"It did, pretty much," Hal agreed. "Then, after all that, First Officer Lynch knocked on our door and said the captain had sent him to make sure Toni was all right."

"We did notice a bit of a disturbance from the room across the hall," Nigel said dryly. "Apparently Captain Sloane wasn't concerned as to whether *I* was all right or not."

"That's because I'm the one with all the pictures," I said.

"Toni thinks the captain sent Officer Lynch to steal her smartphone," Hal said.

"Oh, I can't believe that nice young man would do such a thing, kitten," Mum said. "Besides, your door was locked, surely."

"It wouldn't matter," I said. "The captain has a key to every room on this ship, including cabins."

"Antoinette!" Mum looked shocked. "You can't seriously be suggesting that the *captain* would send someone to break into your cabin and rob you, now, can you?"

I shrugged. "I don't know, but I slept with my smartphone under my pillow, just in case."

Hal chuckled. "Paranoia is alive and well in the Shapiro camp."

I ignored him. "Here's the thing," I persisted. "Is it really true that when a murder occurs on a cruise ship, nobody wants jurisdiction and nothing gets done? Because Captain Sloane told me he knew you from a case where a murder occurred on a ship just before it docked at Southampton, and you were the Scotland Yard detective in charge of the case."

"That's true," Nigel said. "Colin Sloane was first officer on that ship."

"So if Scotland Yard got called in for a murder aboard a ship about to dock in England, why wouldn't it get called in for a murder aboard a ship about to dock in Barbados?"

Nigel pulled thoughtfully at his moustache. "Toni, old girl, you just may have something there. Look here, I'll talk to the captain and feel him out about that old case. He just might see it your way, and if he does, we can send all that evidence to Scotland Yard and let them do the detecting while we do what we came on this cruise to do in the first place."

"Have fun," I said.

"Precisely."

The four of us went down to the Lido restaurant for breakfast, which we carried out to the pool area to eat. "I trust," my mother said sternly, "that there will be no talk of corpses and blood whilst we're eating."

We knew better. My mother had very firm ideas on what was and what was not table talk. Often, during my medical school and residency days, when I started talking shop, she would draw herself up and say in her iciest British, "Antoinette, really, *must* we have bowels at dinner?"

So we limited our breakfast conversation to what we would do while in port at Philipsburg. Mum and Nigel had signed up for a bus tour around the island, and Hal and I had signed up to participate in the St. Maarten Americas Cup 12-metre Challenge regatta. Three of the yachts that had participated in the Americas Cup in years past were permanent residents of Philipsburg Harbor, and cruise ship passengers signed up in droves to participate in a race between the three yachts.

Mum and Nigel would have an interesting tour also, because St. Maarten and the port of Philipsburg were Dutch, while the other side of the island, St. Martin, was French.

In every port, we would look for gifts for Pete, Bambi, and our granddaughters, Toni Amanda, eighteen months old, and Shawna Renee, due in three months. We figured she wouldn't want to be left out just because she hadn't been born yet. I also looked for gifts for Mum and Nigel, which I would stash away in our cabin to be smuggled home in our luggage and given as Christmas gifts, months from now.

After we'd eaten, Mum went back to the cabin to get ready for the shore excursion, while Hal and Nigel and I went back topside to watch our approach and docking in Philipsburg. I prevailed upon Nigel to tell me about that long-ago shipboard murder.

"It was twenty-five years ago, and I was just a lowly detective-inspector," he said. "Colin Sloane was first officer, as I said. The victim was the cruise director, a lovely young woman. She was found at the bottom of a staircase on the Lido deck, not unlike the staircase you were running up and down all day yesterday."

"Was that what killed her?" I asked.

Nigel shook his head. "It was my opinion that someone had punched her in the face. The autopsy showed that her nasal bones had been shoved right up into her brain—something easily done by a blow to the underside of the nose with the heel of the hand. It caused a subdural hematoma that was the actual cause of death. All the other bruising on the body was perimortem."

"Do you mean she was thrown down the stairs after she was already dead?" asked Hal.

"The Home Office pathologist said that the bruising didn't match a fall down any staircase he'd ever heard of. He thought it was more likely that the young woman had been beaten with a blunt object to simulate injuries from a fall down a staircase and was then just dumped there to be found the next day."

"So that one wasn't crushed by the roof," Hal said.

"They hadn't opened the roof," Nigel said. "It was a transatlantic cruise, and the North Atlantic is cold."

"What day was she actually found?" I asked. "Was it the same day that the ship docked, or the day before?"

"The same day," Nigel said. "That was when the ship-to-shore call to Scotland Yard was made."

"Who called you?" Hal asked.

"The captain."

"So who did it?"

Nigel shook his head again. "We never solved it. By the time the body arrived at the Yard and the autopsy was done, the ship had sailed—and any evidence with it."

"You couldn't detain a cruise ship," I diagnosed.

"Right. And then I had to inform the next of kin. A hateful job."

"Her parents?"

"Yes, and then they had to break it to their four-year-old granddaughter," Nigel said.

"She had a child?" I asked in surprise.

"Yes."

"Oh dear. How sad."

We were interrupted at that point by the captain's announcement that the gangway was ready and that we could now go ashore.

Two tall, gorgeous young ladies got on the elevator with us, both dragging overnight cases with them. "Are you leaving us?" I inquired.

"Yes, we were just here for the show last night," one said. She sounded British.

"You don't stay on board for the entire cruise?"

"No, not usually," she said. "We came on yesterday at Bridgetown, and today we'll be meeting another ship."

"Is that usual? I mean, is that what show people usually do, just stay on for one night and then leave?"

"Yes," she said. "That's what we do."

"So what would happen if a performer was to not show up at the next port?"

The girls looked at each other and shrugged. "I suppose they'd try to get somebody else to fill in," the other one said. She sounded American.

"Has that ever happened before?" I asked as the elevator door opened onto A deck.

They looked at each other again. "Not that we know of," the American girl said. "Have a nice day in port!"

By the time we'd made our way decorously down the gangway amid a horde of slow-moving elderly folks, the girls and their overnight cases were already out of sight.

"I didn't realize that," Mum said. "I suppose I thought the same people did the show every night."

"I believe they do, love," Nigel said. "It's just the headliners that change every day. Can't have the same thing going on every night or people would get bored, don't you know."

"I suppose that's true," Mum said. "You and Antoinette missed a really good one last night. Those two young ladies are dancers, and they put on a production number with a young man who sang. I've got the program here somewhere." She dug in her purse. "Now where did that get to?"

"It's okay, Mum," I said. "We can look at it later. You need to get to your bus. That must be it over there, where those people are holding up signs."

"She's right," Nigel said. "Let's go, old girl!"

"Whom do you think you're calling old?" demanded my mother in mock outrage. "Antoinette!"

"Yes, Mum?"

"You two be careful. If anything happens to you, I'll never forgive you."

"Fiona, hush," Nigel said. "They'll be fine."

We waved as they hurried to their bus, and no sooner had they climbed aboard than it started to rain. Sudden rainstorms happen with some regularity in the Caribbean, and Hal and I were already in waterproof anoraks for our yacht race, so we put our hoods up and watched our shipmates dash for cover.

"So I suppose," Hal said, "that means that Leonie Montague came aboard the day before yesterday in Grenada."

"And also that she was supposed to leave us to meet another ship in Bridgetown," I said. "I wonder which one."

"Did you happen to notice another ship in port while we were there?"

We'd been the only ship in port at the time our passengers went ashore, Hal and Fiona among them. But what with everything that was going on with the body and the captain and the guy with the mop and the coroner and the missing head, we could have been surrounded by cruise ships and I wouldn't have noticed. "What about you?" I asked him. "Didn't you and Mum notice what other ships were there when you came back?"

Hal shrugged. "I don't remember which ones. Maybe Fiona does. Anyway, what difference does it make where she was supposed to go? Where she came from might be more important. Is there somebody who schedules all these things?"

A lightbulb went on in my brain. "I bet the cruise director knows," I said. "She's probably around here somewhere, making sure everybody gets to their tour groups." I stood on tiptoe, peering around, trying to spot Jessica, our cruise director, a tall blonde who usually stood out in a crowd, but I couldn't see her.

"Never mind that," Hal said. "We don't have time to talk to her now anyway. We've got to get over to that pier before they sail without us!"

We dashed and made it just as they were choosing up teams for the three different yachts. Hal was assigned to be a grinder, one of those who cranks the sails around when a change of direction is needed. My job was to pass out drinks from the cooler. Everyone was cautioned not to stand up and get hit by the boom, and we were off.

Neither Hal nor I had ever been sailing before, let alone racing a sailing yacht. I was not prepared for the speed with which those yachts moved, or the speed with which they could change direction. I was also surprised at how small they were. They measured twelve meters in length, or roughly thirty-six feet; hence the name of the race. They had looked a lot bigger on TV. The grinders worked their butts off as the captain called out the direction changes, and the boom swished over my head repeatedly with a noise that was probably the reason it was called a boom in the first place: the sound of sails filling with wind. Salt water sloshed over the gunwales during the turns, so whoever sat along the sides got soaked. I was in the center of the boat with the cooler, so I stayed relatively dry, the downside being that my view was blocked by everybody around me. Still, I couldn't help noticing how close we came to the two other yachts during the turns, and I thought it was a bloody miracle that we didn't crash into each other.

Being in the center of the boat had another advantage, though. I could hear all the conversation going on around me without having it swept away on the wind. It's not particularly windy in the center of the boat, so I couldn't help hearing someone say, "I heard there was a murder on one of these cruise ships. Is that true?"

"Really?" said another voice. "Which ship was it?"

I kept quiet. I didn't want to become the one trying to answer all these questions, I wanted to learn something. I sincerely hoped Hal would keep quiet too.

I needn't have worried. Hal and his fellow grinders were much too busy keeping up with the captain's commands as we kept changing direction, and the boom whooshed over my head time and time again.

"It was our ship," I heard a lady say, "the *North Star*." She sounded American, specifically Brooklynese, and loud, and when I glanced her way, I recognized her as someone who had sat with us at dinner a few nights before.

All eyes turned in her direction. I turned my head away, hoping she wouldn't recognize me and try to draw me into the conversation. She knew I was a pathologist from our dinner conversation, and she had all the earmarks of an inveterate rumormonger. At dinner she'd kept pointing people out and telling us who they were and what they did, as well as what she suspected them of doing: A plastic surgeon who analyzed the facial features of everyone seated at their table and told them what he could do to make them look better. "If he has to do that to get patients," she'd said huffily, "he can't be a very good doctor." A lawyer who talked incessantly about all the personal damage cases he'd won. "An ambulance chaser," she'd sneered. A man whose wife suffered from chronic seasickness who took the opportunity to flirt with every single lady on the cruise, as well as several married ones. "Oh, I could tell you about all the cabins *he's* been seen sneaking into in the middle of the night," she'd said in a tone that suggested she knew more than she was saying—and loudly enough for the whole dining room to hear.

Heaven only knew what she'd told other people about me.

"I heard," Mrs. Rumormonger went on, "that it was one of those *ladies of the evening*, if you know what I mean."

"Well, what happened to her?" another voice asked impatiently.

"She fell through the roof of the Lido deck and landed in the pool," Mrs. Rumormonger said.

"That sounds more like an accident to me," said a third voice.

"I think it was supposed to look like one," Mrs. Rumormonger said importantly, clearly relishing her role of raconteur. "But they say that someone strangled her first and then threw her body in the pool."

I wondered who "they" were.

"I 'eard," said a man sitting right behind me, "as she fell onto the deck, not in the pool, and cracked her 'ead open."

"Oh my God," said a young lady with a more upper-crust British accent. "How simply ghastly."

"Do they 'ave any idea 'oo done it?" asked the man behind me.

"Well," Mrs. Rumormonger said, "what *I* hear is that the captain had her in his cabin right up until his wife came on board at Bridgetown. Then he had to get rid of her so his wife wouldn't find out."

A collective gasp ensued.

"I say," a male voice said right in my ear, startling me and causing me to look up. "How about a bit of refreshment, what?"

I passed him a couple of Cokes, and it was at this point that Mrs. Rumormonger recognized me. "I'll bet she knows," she trumpeted, pointing at me. "She's a doctor. She does *autopsies*."

Predictably, someone said, "Eeeuw." I looked around for the offender and saw that everyone was looking at me.

"Don't look at me," I said, shaking my head. "I'm just a passenger. I don't know any more than anybody else."

"You must know something," Mrs. Rumormonger insisted. "Isn't that Scotland Yard man your father?"

"They've called in Scotland Yard?" Coke man asked.

To avoid having to answer questions, I decided to go on the offensive.

"Who told you that she was strangled and thrown through the roof?" I demanded, looking Mrs. Rumormonger straight in the eye. "And who told you that the captain did it?"

A mousy little lady sitting next to Mrs. Rumormonger spoke up. "I told you, Myra, you should be more careful what you say."

Mrs. Rumormonger sighed. "Ruthie, I know what I'm talking about."

"So who told you the captain did it?" I repeated.

She dropped her gaze and looked uncomfortable. "I don't know exactly, but everybody's saying it," she said.

"Do you have any idea how much damage this story will do to the captain?" I asked. "Particularly if it's not true?"

"Then 'e'd better watch 'is p's and q's," said the man behind me, "if 'e knows wot's good for 'im."

"He is rather a bit of a flirt," said Miss Upper-Crust. "I should know."

"And you know this how?" Coke man asked.

She tossed her head. "How do you think? He was all over me the other night when Mummy and I dined at his table."

"He was probably just being polite," I said.

"Polite, my arse," Miss Upper-Crust said rudely. "I'll have you know that he invited me to his cabin for a nightcap. And I'm not the only one."

"Did he invite your mother too?" I asked.

She sniffed. "Don't be silly."

"Did you go?" I persisted.

She tossed her head again. "I'm not that kind of girl."

"Here's the thing," I said. "If the captain had the victim with him in his cabin for the whole cruise up until Barbados, what's he doing inviting another lady there for a nightcap?"

Miss Upper-Crust flushed and dropped her gaze.

"That strikes me as an exceedingly stupid thing to do," I went on, "and the captain's not stupid. He wouldn't be a captain if he was. So if he was in the habit of inviting young female passengers to his cabin, he couldn't have had the victim staying there with him, could he?"

"Wotcher gettin' at, Doc?" asked the man behind me.

"I'm just saying," I said, "that if this lady's story is true, then this girl is lying. And vice versa. You can't have it both ways."

At this point everybody started talking at once, and I shut up. My work here was done. I'd gotten people talking without telling them a thing. I just hoped the race would end before they started peppering me with questions again.

Hal was exhausted. "Remind me not to volunteer to be a grinder next time we do this," he commented as we walked back to the shops in our dripping clothes. It was a lot warmer than it had been earlier, and the sun was out, so we took off our jackets. By the time we'd been through the shops and bought our souvenirs and gifts (and bungee cords), we were dry.

The *North Star* had docked at the very end of the pier, and now a line of cruise ships flanked the pier on both sides, creating a dark sunless tunnel through which we had to walk. Jessica, the cruise director, was waiting at the gangway when we arrived back at the ship. She was busy greeting all the other passengers as they reboarded, so I asked her if I could talk to her later, and we made a date to meet for a drink in the Ocean Lounge, which wouldn't be busy until after dinner when the dance band got started. Until then, everybody would be around the pools on the Lido and Nav decks.

We both took showers to wash off the saltwater residue, and Hal took some ibuprofen and a nap while I went to meet Jessica in the lounge.

She was waiting for me at the bar with something tall and pink in front of her. She greeted me, and the bartender came right over to take my order. I ordered a martini. When it came, I suggested that we sit somewhere else, and we sat at a table at the opposite end of the room from the bar. "Why all the secrecy?" she wanted to know.

I got right to the point. "Do you know who makes the arrangements for the performers in the show?"

"We have an entertainment staff," she said, "and I'm in charge of it. We have special performers that come aboard along the way, and the arrangements for that are made in advance by someone from the shipping line."

"What happens if a performer fails to show up?"

"We have a contingency plan for that," she said. "We have some skits and production numbers that we can substitute for our headline performers, but we've never had to use them as long as I've been here. Why d'you ask?"

"Do you hear about it if someone who performs on this ship fails to show up at the next ship?"

"Usually," she said. "These things get around. Why are you asking all these questions, Mrs. Shapiro?"

"Toni, please. Had you heard that someone got killed on board this ship yesterday?"

She laughed shortly. "How could I help it? Everybody is talking about it. I've heard everything from being pushed overboard to being bashed on the head and thrown in the swimming pool. If you're trying to get the real story, you've come to the wrong place. I don't know any more than anybody else."

"Have you heard who it was?"

She shook her head. "Nobody seems to know. If they do, they're not talking. Except that Mrs. Levine. She thinks she knows everything."

"Who's Mrs. Levine?" I asked, although I had a feeling I knew.

"She's that elderly lady that's traveling with her sister," Jessica said. "They're from Miami. She's the one who does all the talking. Her sister never says a word."

That fit. I recalled that Mrs. Rumormonger, or Mrs. Levine, had been accompanied at our table by another rather mousy elderly lady who talked very little. She was the same one who had reproved her sister on the yacht for talking too much.

I leaned forward. "The captain warned me that the circumstances would be 'quite dire,' to use his words, if I were to talk about it; but I need to know if the reason she was killed had anything to do with her being a performer who goes from ship to ship."

Jessica was not stupid. I could practically hear her brain clicking as she did the math. Her blue eyes grew wide, and she put both hands to her mouth. "Not Leonie. Please tell me it wasn't Leonie."

"You knew her," I said.

Jessica's eyes filled with tears. "I've known Leonie all my life. She was my best friend."

"I'm so sorry," I said.

"How did you know? Did someone tell you?"

"I saw her," I said, omitting the gory details. "I took a picture of the earring she was wearing, and my mother identified it. She saw the show and still had the program."

"She didn't suffer, did she?" Jessica begged tearfully. "Please tell me she didn't suffer."

"She didn't," I said, hoping I was right and that she'd at least been unconscious when she was crushed. "I'm sure she never knew a thing."

Jessica wiped her eyes and blew her nose. "Who are you really?" she asked. "You're not just Mrs. Toni Shapiro from Idaho. How do you know all this?"

"How did you know I was from Idaho?" I countered.

"You and your husband are the only ones from Idaho on board," she said. "Also the only Shapiros. As cruise director, I have to practically memorize the passenger list. People like it when you know their names."

"You memorized twelve hundred names? I'm impressed."

"You didn't answer my question," she reminded me.

I grinned. "You're right. I'm not just a nice lady from Idaho. I'm a *pathologist* from Idaho. Toni Day, MD, is my professional name. I just happened to be up on the Lido deck when they opened the roof and discovered her body. I was there when the police arrived. I was there all day. I never got to go ashore at all." I didn't mention Leonie's head falling into the pool, or her body going splat on the deck. I didn't think Jessica needed to know that little detail.

Jessica gasped. "Her body was in the *roof*? You mean when they closed the roof they …" She put her hands over her mouth and couldn't go on.

I nodded wordlessly.

She swallowed hard. "Was it an accident, or was she …"

"Yes," I said as gently as I could. "In my opinion, she was murdered. She had a depressed skull fracture. She bled into her brain. That's what killed her. Not the roof."

She exhaled. "Thank God for that. So that's how you know she didn't suffer?"

"That's right."

Her eyes filled with tears again. "But who would kill Leonie? And why?"

"That's what I'm trying to find out," I said. "That's why I'm talking to you."

She frowned. "But why would I kill my best friend?"

"I'm not accusing you," I said. "But you knew Leonie. You can tell me about her. Maybe you know something that will give us a clue to her murder."

"You know what's weird? Leonie's mum was a cruise director too."

"Is that why you became one?"

"Not really. Mostly it was because of what Leonie was doing. She works ... worked for this show company that provides entertainment for cruise ships. They really liked the way she sang. She had a beautiful voice."

"So in a way, you two were working together."

"Right, at least we did when we were both entertainers."

"Oh, you were an entertainer too?" I asked in surprise.

"Certainly. Most cruise directors are former entertainers, or former waiters, or former something elses."

"So were you a singer too?"

"Yes, but nothing like Leonie. I was just one of the 'doo-wop girls,' as you Yanks say."

"Did you see each other often after you became a cruise director?"

"At least once a cruise. We always had some time to talk and catch up on things."

"That must have been nice," I said. "Tell me, did either of you ever get involved with any of the crew on these cruises?"

"Oh, no, we weren't supposed to. The cruise line has a policy that crew can't fraternize with passengers or entertainers."

"What happens if someone violates that policy?"

"They get fired."

"Do you know of anyone who ever did that?"

She looked away from me. "Only one."

She stopped. I waited. Finally she spoke. "Leonie's mum had an affair with an officer once."

"When was that?"

"Twenty-five years ago."

"Did she get fired?"

"No. She got killed."

The devil damn thee black, thou cream-faced loon! Where got'st thou that goose look?

—Shakespeare, *Macbeth*

"THE SHIP WAS about to dock in Southampton when they found her," Jessica went on. "They called in Scotland Yard but never found out what really happened."

Oh my God. "Jessica," I said firmly. "You have *got* to talk to my stepfather. Have you got time now?"

She glanced at her watch. "Yes, but why?"

"You'll see. Come on, let's go."

I took her up to the Nav deck and tapped at their cabin door. Nigel answered it, saw us, and stepped out into the hallway, closing the door behind him. "Fiona's still asleep," he whispered. Then he saw Jessica. "And who's this lovely young lady? Aren't you our cruise director?"

"Yes, this is Jessica, and she needs to talk to you," I whispered. "We need to find somewhere we can't be overheard."

"We may as well go back to the Ocean Lounge," Jessica whispered. "There's nobody there this early."

So we did, and there still wasn't anybody else there. The bartender came over and took our drink orders. I ordered another martini. I'd barely touched the first one, and the bartender had taken it away when we left.

"Okay," I said to Jessica when he'd left us alone, "tell Nigel what you told me about Leonie and her mom."

Nigel glanced sharply at me, but I merely tipped my head toward Jessica. "Leonie Montague was her best friend."

Jessica's eyes filled with tears again, and Nigel patted her hand. "I'm so sorry for your loss," he said gently. "Toni and I are trying to find out who killed her, since it's unlikely that either the cruise line or the Barbados police will even try. Nobody wants jurisdiction over a shipboard murder. Even Scotland Yard won't interfere unless asked."

So Jessica wiped her eyes and told Nigel the whole story.

"What was Leonie's mother's name?" Nigel asked.

"Evelyn Hodges," Jessica said. "Evie for short."

"So Leonie's name really isn't Montague?" I asked.

"It isn't even Leonie," Jessica said. "It's Margaret. When we were kids in school, she was Maggie Hodges."

"I'm surprised that Evie would work as a cruise director when she had a four-year-old child at home," I said.

"She didn't," Jessica said, "until Maggie was old enough for preschool. After that she figured her parents could manage while she was gone."

"What about Maggie's father?" Nigel asked. "Where was he?"

"I don't know," Jessica said. "Evie wouldn't talk about it. Everybody just assumed he left her when he found out she was pregnant, like so many men do."

"So how long after that did she get killed?"

"On that very first cruise after she went back to work," Jessica said and started crying again.

"Oh no," I said. Poor Maggie. I felt like crying myself. "So did her parents manage all right after that?"

"They did, thanks to my mum," Jessica said. "Mags spent a lot of time at our house while we were growing up."

"No wonder you two were close," I said.

"Again, I'm sorry for your loss," Nigel said. "As it happens, I was the Scotland Yard detective inspector in charge of that case. The captain asked for our assistance. We were able to determine that Miss Hodges was murdered, and it was made to look like she died from falling down a flight of stairs. But the autopsy showed the real cause of death."

"Who killed her?" Jessica asked.

Nigel shook his head. "We never found out. We couldn't detain the ship, any more than the Barbados police could detain this one. It sailed away, and all the evidence went with it."

"So if it weren't for you two," Jessica said, "we might never know who killed Leonie either."

"We still might not," Nigel said, "but not for want of trying."

"Do you know which officer Evie had an affair with?" I asked.

Jessica shook her head.

"It might interest you to know," Nigel said, "that the first officer on that ship was none other than Colin Sloane, our captain."

Jessica gasped.

"Does that ring any bells?" I asked.

Jessica stared at me, eyes wide, as if in a trance. That deer in the headlights look.

"Jessica?"

She shook her head and came out of it. "No. No, it doesn't. Not at all."

I didn't believe her.

Neither, from the look he gave me, did Nigel.

Love is strong as death; jealousy is as cruel as the grave.

—Song of Solomon 8:6

"Is it possible that Leonie's mother got involved with Colin Sloane when he was a first officer on that other ship?" I asked.

We'd reunited after our respective naps and showers for cocktails in the Ocean Lounge, which was still empty, the better to discuss things best not overheard. The bar staff would soon be wondering what was going on if we continued to meet like this. If that happened, we'd have to find another place for our clandestine meetings.

"I've known Colin Sloane for twenty-five years now," Nigel said. "He knew perfectly well that if he got caught fraternizing with a crew member it could mean the end of his maritime career. He'd climbed the ladder all the way to first officer and was waiting to get a ship of his own. Some wait all their lives and never get one. Why would he jeopardize that by having a fling with the cruise director?"

"Maybe she put the moves on him," I suggested. "Maybe he never had a chance. Maybe she made him an offer he couldn't refuse."

"But kitten, that would have jeopardized her career as well," Mum objected.

"Not as much as it would jeopardize his," Hal said. "Perhaps she meant to get him to marry her. Then she wouldn't have to work."

"That might have worked twenty-five years ago," I said. "It sure wouldn't work today. Most families need two salaries just to get by these days."

"Especially if they have children," Hal said.

"Was Colin Sloane married twenty-five years ago?" I asked.

"I don't know," Nigel said.

"You never asked him? You didn't know him very well, did you?"

"Honey," Hal said. "Guys don't ask those kinds of questions of each other."

"Well, they should," I said. "If he was married, he stood to lose that too. Wouldn't a divorce have an effect on whether he got to be a captain or not?"

"Things like that do tend to come out in a divorce," Nigel said. "That would be the last thing he'd want to have happen."

"He wasn't married at the time," Mum said suddenly, "but he is now. He's been married for twenty-four years. He has one son and no grandchildren. He said so at dinner last night."

"See?" I said. "Women can ask questions like that and nobody thinks anything of it."

"Actually, I didn't have to," Mum said. "I was talking about Little Toni and then he started talking about his son, who also works on cruise ships, and it just went from there, just as natural as can be."

"Does the captain's wife ever sail with him?" Hal asked.

"She does sometimes," Mum said. "She's here now. She joined the cruise at Bridgetown."

That jibed with what Mrs. Levine had said. "Then why wasn't she at dinner with us last night?" I asked.

"I did ask him that. He said she was tired. She'd been at the races all day."

I knew from reading Dick Francis mysteries that horse racing was just as popular in Barbados as it was in England. "Does she own horses, or does she just like to gamble on them?" I inquired.

"She owns racehorses," Mum said. "She comes from a very wealthy family. I believe they even own this cruise line. She spends quite a lot of time in Barbados, especially in the winter when she's not cruising."

"So if they weren't married yet, she probably wasn't with him on that other cruise," Nigel said.

"What ship was that anyway?" I asked. "Was it this cruise line?"

"It was this cruise line," Nigel said. "As I recall, it was the *Southern Cross*."

"Jessica didn't actually come right out and say it was Colin Sloane that Leonie's mother was having an affair with, did she?" Mum asked.

"No, love," Nigel said. "She just gasped and stared into space."

"Like a basilisk," I commented.

"What's a basilisk?" Hal asked.

"A snake," I said.

"A mythical snake," Mum said, "that can kill you if it looks at you."

"That's pretty circumstantial," Hal commented. "She could have had other reasons for reacting that way."

"Like what?" I asked. "Like maybe she's having a fling with the captain right now and is realizing that if Evie had an affair with him back then and got murdered, then maybe she's in danger now?"

"Holy shit," Hal said with disbelief. "You just came up with that right off the top of your head, just like that?"

"Well," I said defensively, "it's another reason for her reaction. Maybe everything we know about the captain is circumstantial too. He could be as pure as the driven snow for all we know."

"What a turnabout," Nigel said. "This morning you were talking about the captain trying to cover up the murder. You were wondering if he would even have called the police if you hadn't been there. Now you're defending him."

"No, I'm not. I'm being a devil's advocate."

"Okay then," Hal challenged me. "Do you have any other suspects in mind?"

"How about Rob?"

"The doctor? I thought he was your new best buddy."

"I told you last night that the only people I knew for sure weren't involved were the four of us. If the evidence suddenly disappears, we'll know it's him."

"Not necessarily. What if the captain orders him to get rid of it?"

"Can he do that?" I turned to Nigel. "Can the captain order the doctor to destroy evidence? That's a crime in itself."

"Only if he gets caught," Nigel said.

"Lovey," my mother said to him, "have you talked to the captain about calling in Scotland Yard yet?"

"Not yet," Nigel said.

"You need to," I urged him. "The sooner, the better."

"What's all this?" Nigel looked at each of us in turn. "Ganging up on me?"

"Here's the thing," I said. "Don't you see? If the captain agrees to call in Scotland Yard, and we go to Rob to get the evidence to send to them, and it's gone, then what?"

"Toni," said my long-suffering husband, "quit nagging."

"She's got a point," Nigel said. "Time may be of the essence here. I'll go see if I can talk to him now. We may be able to send it off from San Juan tomorrow if we're lucky." He drained his drink and got up.

"Want me to go with you?" I asked.

"Toni, old thing, I love you dearly, but the captain doesn't."

"That would be a 'no'," Hal said.

"Okay. I get it. You don't have to hit me over the head with a brick."

"Sometimes we do," Hal said slyly.

"Hal, dear, enough," said Mum. "She's right, you know. We've only three more days. Once we reach Fort Lauderdale, it's out of our control."

The long blast of the ship's whistle made further conversation impossible and told us that our departure from Philipsburg was imminent. It always gave me such a cozy, safe feeling to know that my loved ones and I were safely aboard. I didn't know if anyone ever actually missed the ship, but if anyone did, it wouldn't be me. The panic I'd felt in St. Thomas when I'd bought a ring at Diamonds International and had to wait for it to be sized had been bad enough. I'd heard the ship's whistle while still waiting in the store. Luckily, the ship's jewelry expert had been there too, and they certainly were not leaving without him, I reasoned. But it had been very unsettling all the same, and I determined never to repeat the experience.

People began to drift into the Ocean Lounge, making it unsafe to continue our conversation about possible suspects, so we went up to the Lido deck where we could watch the ship leave Philipsburg while enjoying our drinks. I ordered a second martini with extra olives, as the late seating for dinner was still two hours away, and I was getting hungry. The waiter, a smiling Filipino named Arturo who knew all of us by name, gave me an entire glass full of olives. I thanked him profusely and put a generous tip on the receipt.

I spotted Rob Welch, still in scrubs, at the bar and waved at him. He came over. "Just finished with office hours," he said. "Mind if I join you? Where's your stepfather?"

"Not at all," I said. "Nigel's off talking to the captain. This is my mother, Fiona, and you remember my husband, Hal. This is Dr. Robert Welch, the ship's doctor."

"I'm delighted to meet you, Doctor," Mum said with a smile. "I appreciate your helping Antoinette with this case."

Rob looked sidelong at me. "Antoinette?"

"Nobody calls me that except my mother," I informed him, "and the only reason she does is because I can't stop her."

Rob smiled back at my mother. "Please call me Rob. Everybody does. So," he said to me, "what's Nigel talking to the captain about?"

I thought perhaps I shouldn't mention calling in Scotland Yard just yet. It might give Rob incentive to destroy the evidence sooner rather than later if he was the killer. "They know each other," I said. "Nigel was involved in a murder on a ship where our captain was first officer."

"Really," said Rob with interest. "When was that?"

"Twenty-five years ago," I said. "Nigel was only a detective inspector then."

"Does the captain remember him?"

"Definitely," I said. "He was the one who mentioned it to me."

"Who was murdered?"

"The cruise director, a woman named Evelyn Hodges."

"How did you know that?" Hal asked.

"From Jessica, our cruise director," I said. "Apparently she knew the family."

Rob looked pensive. "Hodges. That's interesting. I went to university with a girl named Maggie Hodges. Probably no relation, though."

I had to physically restrain myself from reacting. Could it just be a coincidence? "That *is* interesting," I said. "Our cruise director, Jessica, also went to school with a Maggie Hodges. This particular Maggie Hodges became a professional singer and changed her name."

"Anyone I might know?"

"She changed it to Leonie Montague," I said.

There was no hiding Rob's reaction. He went white and seemed to have some difficulty catching his breath. "You mean the girl who got crushed in the roof?"

"The very same," I said. "Are you all right? You look like you're about to pass out."

He wiped his brow with a cocktail napkin. "I'm quite all right. It's just a bit of a facer to realize you've assisted at an autopsy of someone you knew in school."

"Are you quite sure," said my mother, "that it's the same Maggie Hodges? That's not such an unusual name."

Rob took a gulp of his drink. "It's her. I've kept track. I went to medical school, and she went to London to become an actress."

"You kept track," I repeated. "Just how well did you know her?"

"Toni," Hal said. "Don't pry."

Rob didn't answer right away. Instead he put his elbows on the table and his face in his hands.

I touched his arm gently. "Rob?"

He looked up. His face looked haggard, his eyes full of pain. "We were engaged. She broke it off just before we graduated."

"Why?"

"Blimey, you don't give up, do you? It just so happens that I don't know why. She wouldn't tell me. I tried and tried to get her to talk to me, but she wouldn't. Finally I had to give up and move on with my life. That do you? Or do you want to *pry* some more?" He drained his drink, shoved his chair back so hard it fell over, and stomped out.

I sat staring after him in consternation. It certainly hadn't been my intention to piss him off, but I knew that running after him to apologize wouldn't do either of us any good. He needed time to cool off.

People at the tables around us were staring. "Now look what you've done," Hal said. "You've pissed off an officer. The captain's gonna throw us all off the ship if you don't watch out."

"You need to apologize, kitten," Mum said. "Although perhaps not right this very minute."

Nigel reappeared. He picked up Rob's chair and sat down. "I say, Toni, old dear, whatever have you done to the medical johnnie? He looked like he was about to kill somebody."

"And naturally you just assumed it was something I did."

"It usually is, isn't it?"

I couldn't really argue with that, so I told him.

"Interesting," was his response. "Do you suppose we've another possible suspect?"

"Maybe," I said. "How did you do with the captain?"

Nigel told me that the captain had grudgingly agreed to call in Scotland Yard, and that he, Nigel, would act as intermediary, thereby obviating the need to fly an agent to Fort Lauderdale from London.

"They do want the evidence we've collected, but we're going to have to figure out how to package it to send," he said. "Any ideas?"

"Well," I said, "we need a couple of boxes about so big." I illustrated by holding my arms about a foot apart. "And a smaller box for the wood chip and the vitreous. Then we need a lot of plastic bags, preferably the kind that can be sealed. They're also going to have to have proper labeling for biohazardous material. Does Scotland Yard have labels or containers that they use for that purpose?"

"I'll have to ask them," Nigel said, "but they can't get them to us in time even if they do."

"Maybe if they can describe what they need, we can imitate it. Maybe the labels can be e-mailed and printed here. If you can find out before we go to dinner, maybe after dinner we can go down to the infirmary and retrieve the evidence. And then maybe the purser can help with finding mailing materials, and then we can mail them in San Juan tomorrow." I was talking so fast that I stumbled over my words.

"Toni, old dear, do slow down," my stepfather begged me. "These old ears can't hear as fast as you're talking. First, I have to see about making a ship-to-shore call. Then—"

"Why do you need to call? Can't you e-mail them?"

"I don't know the e-mail address," Nigel protested. "And I've never sent an e-mail in my life."

"Nigel, old thing, really," I said. "You've simply *got* to drag yourself into the twenty-first century. Wait. Let me go get my laptop. We'll Google them."

"I'll go with you."

We took the stairs down to the Nav deck and our cabin.

My laptop was gone.

Great blunders are often made, like large ropes, of a multitude of fibers.

—Victor Hugo

We looked everywhere, even under the beds, but no joy.

"Do you think you left it up on the Lido deck?" Nigel asked.

"I don't think so, but we can look."

We went back up to the Lido deck. I started looking under tables and on chair seats and windowsills.

"Antoinette," said Mum, "whatever are you doing?"

"Looking for my laptop," I said.

"Isn't it in the room?" Hal asked.

Would I be looking up here if it was in the room? Really? "No, sweetie, it's not," I said.

"Where did you see it last?" Mum asked.

I thought for a minute. "On the desk in our room. I downloaded my pictures on it and then e-mailed them to Pete and to the Barbados police. But it's not there anymore."

"Or anywhere else in that room," Nigel said. "We fairly turned it upside down."

"Did they take the charger too?" Hal asked.

I had to think about that. I always left my laptop plugged in when I wasn't using it, because it only took a couple of hours to use up the battery. I'd noticed right away that the laptop was missing, but the charger? I always packed an extension cord and a surge protector with multiple outlets so I could charge up my laptop, my e-book, and my smartphone. The surge protector sat on the desk with all the chargers plugged into it. Had there been three cords plugged in, or just two?

"No," I said finally. "That's dumb. Whoever took it must not be the brightest bulb on the tree. Unless …"

"If someone took it to prevent anyone from using those pictures, they wouldn't care if it was charged or not," Nigel said.

"Well, it was all for nothing, because those pictures are still on my phone," I said.

"Well, you'd better hang on to it," Hal said. "Now, hadn't we better go get ready for dinner?"

"I'll go make my call and meet you there," Nigel said, "and report the theft of your laptop too."

When we got back to our cabin, I took Hal's advice. I transferred my smartphone from my boat bag to my evening purse, as my dressy dinner clothes didn't have pockets. Then I thought better of that and stuck it in my bra, trying not to think of the rumors I'd heard that young women were getting breast cancer from doing just that. Just this once, I thought, can't hurt.

From the doorway to the dining room, we had a clear view of the captain's table. His wife was with him, along with First Officer David Lynch, Safety Officer Dalquist, Chief Engineer Gerard, and Rob. Next to Rob was an empty chair. I wondered who it was for.

Nigel joined us while we were still standing in line to get into the dining room. He was smiling. "Did you get through?" I asked.

"I did. They want the stuff. The purser will have the containers ready for us shortly. All we have to do is get your young medical friend to let us into the infirmary, and Bob's your uncle."

"Easier said than done," I told him. "Rob's mad at me."

"No worries. I'll talk to him."

After we'd been escorted to our table and given our orders to the waiter, Nigel excused himself and went over to the captain's table, where he sat down next to Rob.

"What's going on?" Mum asked. "What are you two hatching now?"

"Scotland Yard wants the evidence we collected, so we have to pack it up and get it ready to mail from San Juan tomorrow."

"Then what, kitten? Will that be the end of it?"

I shrugged. "I don't know. I hope so."

"Me too," Hal said, "because I haven't seen much of you lately."

"Sorry, sweetie," I said. "I miss you too." I gave him a kiss.

Nigel came back. "The doctor will meet us in the infirmary after dinner," he said. "He also wished me to convey his apologies for his earlier outburst."

I'd have liked it better if Rob had delivered his apologies in person, but one can't have everything. "He's forgiven," I said. "I should apologize to him for prying into his painful past." I turned to look and see if I could catch Rob's eye, but his back was to me, and he didn't turn around. "I'll do that later. Although I'm not really sorry I did. We needed that information."

"I do hope you aren't going to tell him that," Mum said.

"Not bloody likely," I said. "Not unless he turns out to be the murderer."

Two Canadian couples joined us at that point, so the talk turned to more pleasant topics, such as what everyone had done ashore that day. There was no more talk about murder until Nigel looked over at the captain's table and noticed that Rob was gone.

"Now where the bloody hell's he gone? He was there just a minute ago."

"Two possibilities," I said. "Either he had to go to the little boys' room, or he's gone to dispose of the evidence."

"What evidence?" asked one of the Canadian men.

"You really don't want to know," my mother assured them.

"Police business," Hal added. "He's Scotland Yard."

"What's Scotland Yard doing here?" the other Canadian man asked.

"I really can't talk about it, you know," Nigel said reprovingly.

"So," I put in, "we can either wait for him to get back, or we can go down to the infirmary and catch him in the act."

"Or," Hal said, "you can wait here while Nigel checks the men's room."

"Jolly good," Nigel said, rising. "Back in a flash."

"Look here," one of the Canadian ladies said, "just what is going on? Has someone been killed on this cruise? Is there a *murderer* loose on the ship?"

"Hush," said her companion. "Keep your voice down. Do you want to start a panic?"

I looked around. People at some of the other tables were looking at us.

Hal saw them too. "I think that ship has sailed," he said.

"The body of one of the entertainers was found day before yesterday," I said. "Nigel and I are trying to figure out what happened."

"Maybe it was an accident," said the other Canadian lady hopefully.

"Maybe," Mum said, "but my husband and my daughter don't think so."

Nigel came back. "No joy," he said. "The captain says he went down to the infirmary. Shall we?"

"Right behind you," I said.

But the infirmary, when we got there, was locked, and Rob was nowhere in sight.

"Now what?" I asked in frustration.

"Now," said my stepfather, "we go back upstairs and ask the captain for the key."

"You do realize," I pointed out, "that we're about to ask one suspect to help us get another suspect to help us get evidence that might convict either one of them of murder."

"Either or both," Nigel said. "They could be in cahoots, as you Yanks say."

So we rode the forward elevator back up to the Promenade deck where the main dining room was located. Luckily for us, the captain and his wife were still at their table, enjoying after-dinner liqueurs in tiny glasses. The rest of the officers had left.

"Chief Superintendent Gray," Captain Sloane greeted us with a smile, "and Dr. Day. Did you find Dr. Welch?"

"No," Nigel said. "He wasn't there, and the infirmary is locked. We came to see if we could get the key from you and find the evidence ourselves."

"I can't exactly give you the key, you know," the captain said, "but I can go down with you and help you find what you need. Or I can page the nurse and have her do it."

"Oh, don't you think the fewer people we involve in this, the better?" I appealed to both men.

"She has a point," Captain Sloane agreed. "I'll go down with you after we finish our cordials. Would you care to join us? Allow me to introduce my wife."

"Sarah," said the slim, white-haired woman sitting next to him. She reached out to shake my hand. "Please join us. And perhaps your mother and husband would care to join us also?"

I looked over at our table. The Canadians had already left, and Mum and Hal were just pushing their chairs back to get up and leave. I waved at them, and they came over. I made introductions all around. A waiter materialized, and the captain ordered cordials for everybody.

Apparently we were going to have to wait. The captain and his wife weren't going to budge until they were good and ready, and the urgency I felt was of no consequence. I was sure they thought I was overreacting, much like my loving but long-suffering husband.

So I sipped my cordial and otherwise kept my mouth shut. At least I did until Sarah Sloane turned to me and asked me what kind of a doctor I was and what this was all about. Obviously, her husband had told her nothing.

I hesitated, and she noticed. "It's quite all right," she added. "I want to hear all the details. Leave nothing out."

The captain and Nigel were deep in conversation. So I began to tell her all about the body crushed in the roof and the head in the swimming pool, when my mother intervened.

"Antoinette, darling, *really*. Must we have corpses with our cordials?"

"Antoinette?" Sarah inquired with amusement. "Your name is really Antoinette?"

"Yes, more's the pity," I replied with a withering glance at Mum. "Nobody gets to call me that except Mum. Everybody else calls me Toni."

"I see. And do you have a middle name?"

"Yes, it's Ivy."

"After my grandmother," Mum said. "She never uses it, though."

"You know why as well as I do, Mum. If I use all my names, my initials spell AIDS."

"Oh dear," Sarah remarked. "That would never do. So, about this body. What happened next?"

Cleaning up the narrative for my mother's sake, I told Sarah about the coroner, losing the head, finding the head, the autopsy of same, and the gathering of evidence. "That," I told her, "is what Scotland Yard wants us to send them. Dr. Welch put it away for safekeeping in the infirmary, and now we can't find him, so your husband is going to let us in with his key so we can find it. We have to mail it from San Juan tomorrow."

"It appears," Sarah said, "that our young doctor is behaving somewhat suspiciously. Do you suppose he knows more than he's saying about this dreadful affair?"

"He's said plenty," I told her. "Apparently he knew the victim from his college days. They were engaged to be married, and she broke it off just before graduation. She wouldn't tell him why."

"I'm surprised that he would tell you that," Sarah said. "Men, in my experience, don't like to talk about affairs of the heart, especially if they end badly."

"He didn't do it willingly," Hal put in. "Toni bullied it out of him."

"I didn't bully anybody," I objected. "He got upset when I asked him why. Apparently he kept track of where she was and what she was doing and made several attempts to contact her after they graduated and he went to medical school. She refused to talk to him."

"Antoinette," said Mum, "doesn't this story remind you of Robbie?"

"Oh jeez. You would have to bring *him* up."

"Who's Robbie?" asked Sarah.

"An old boyfriend," Hal said, "who wouldn't take no for an answer."

"A most *unsavory* young man," Mum said severely, "who beat her up and then raped her, and then he almost killed Hal."

"My goodness gracious," Sarah said, shocked. "When did this happen?"

"We dated in high school," I said, "and then he went away to college. We got together whenever he was home, though, and he wanted to marry me, but Mum didn't want me to."

"I certainly didn't," Mum said firmly. "She was all ready to marry that boy right after graduation and work to put him through law school so he could just drop her like a hot potato and marry a trophy wife. Not if I could help it, she wasn't!"

"He kept calling me after we broke up."

"After he raped you, you mean," Mum interrupted. "He also kept calling me, and I wouldn't tell him where she was."

"Neither would I," I said, "and after Hal and I moved to Idaho, we kind of forgot about him."

"Until he found her," Hal said. "He came up to Idaho to visit a lawyer friend, and while he was there, he threatened to kill me so he could have Toni."

"Then he kidnapped Hal and tied him up in a crawl space where he nearly froze to death," I began.

"And I got hantavirus pneumonia and almost died," Hal said.

"My God," Sarah exclaimed. "Where is he now?"

"In prison," I said.

"Thank heavens," Sarah said. "What a horrible story!"

"It was that old 'if I can't have her nobody else can either' scenario," Hal said. "Do you suppose that's what happened between our murder victim and our doctor?"

I shivered. "We can't rule it out," I said.

"That settles it," Hal declared. "You and Nigel aren't going down to that infirmary by yourselves."

"We won't be by ourselves," I objected. "The captain will be there too."

Silence ensued. I looked at Mum, then at Hal, and they stared back implacably. Nobody wanted to mention that the captain was a suspect too, not in front of his wife.

"We'll all go," Sarah said. "He can't kill all of us, now, can he?"

Not unless he has a gun, I thought, recalling last year when a serial killer was trying to drown me in a canal, and Hal, Nigel, my son-in-law Pete, and the sheriff had ridden to the rescue, all armed with guns.

"Now then," said the captain, startling me, "shall we?"

We all got up and followed Captain Sloane to the elevator. As we stood there waiting, he looked around at all of us. "You're not all going, you know. Just Chief Superintendent Gray and Dr. Day."

"Not on your life," Hal said. "The man is dangerous. We're not letting you go without us. Don't you have a gun?"

The elevator doors opened, and we all got in. Captain Sloane looked at his wife as he pressed the button for A Deck. "Sarah? Are you responsible for this?"

"Yes, dear. We've been having quite the conversation, and I think Dr. Shapiro is absolutely right."

"You can't very well stop them, you know," Nigel said to the captain.

"You do realize, don't you, that on this ship, I am the law?"

"Sometimes," Nigel said, "the law needs a little help. Speaking for Scotland Yard, I say you shouldn't turn it down."

The captain sighed. "Very well, then, since you're all here. Stay behind me, and do exactly what I say. Is that clear?"

We all assented.

When we arrived at the clinic, the doors were still locked. Captain Sloane knocked. There was no answer. He knocked again. When there was still no response, he inserted his key in the lock and opened the door. Hal, Nigel, and I flattened ourselves on the walls to either side of it as we'd seen so many cops do on TV so as not to get shot through it, but nothing happened. The captain turned on the lights. "Lead the way, Dr. Day," he said to me.

"It's in the morgue," I said, opening the door into the corridor. When we reached it, I found the door to be locked. I turned to the captain. "Now what?"

"No worries," he said, pulling out his keys.

After the captain unlocked the door, I turned on the light. "Here's the cooler," I said. "We put the stuff in here. I may need a little help with this. It sticks."

It took all three men to wrench the door open. When they did, everybody gasped.

The evidence was gone, but the cooler wasn't empty. It had acquired a new occupant. A stout lady in a long floral dress and a cardigan.

"Who the devil's that?" Nigel demanded.

"She's a passenger," Captain Sloane said, "but I don't know her name. I'll have to check the passenger list. Do you know her, Dr. Day?"

"She sat with us at dinner one night," I said, "Jessica said her name was Levine."

"I know who she is," Mum said. "She's that awful woman who gossiped about everybody she'd had dinner with and had nothing good to say about anyone. You remember, Antoinette. She badgered you with questions about autopsies and accused you of taking money to cover things up."

"Blimey," Nigel commented, "who could forget that?"

I took a closer look at Mrs. Levine's face. It was puffy, and her lips were blue. I lifted an eyelid. There were tiny red spots on her conjunctiva. "Nigel," I said, "could you hold her eyelids apart for me?"

Nigel complied. I pulled my smartphone out of my bra and snapped a picture. Next I pulled down on her lower lip and saw more little red spots. The tip of her tongue protruded between her teeth and was also blue. I took more pictures.

"I assume there's no truth to that, Dr. Day," Captain Sloane said. "What are you doing?"

"Examining the body." Mrs. Levine's neck was short and thick, but I pulled the folds apart and saw a ligature mark. I called upon Nigel again and took a picture of it. "Look at these marks," I said to him. "This was a wide ligature, and it looks woven."

"I see that," Nigel commented. "She's still warm too. She can't have been here long."

"She can't have been dead long either," I said, manipulating an arm. "There's no rigor."

"There was that CEO, remember?" Mum said. "You did an autopsy on him, and there was this doctor who kept threatening you if you put something in the autopsy report. I forget what."

I remembered that case only too well. "He'd had a heart attack," I said, "and the intern in CCU started a central line in the subclavian vein and neglected to get a chest X-ray afterward. As it turned out, he'd punctured a lung, and the resulting pneumothorax contributed to the patient's death. It didn't help that the intern's father was on the medical staff."

"Ah," Nigel said. "He was trying to protect his son. What did you do?"

"What anyone would have done," I said. "There were other people in the room with me when I found that. No point in trying to cover it up. Not that I would have done so in any case."

"What happened?" asked Captain Sloane, interested in spite of himself.

"The family sued the hospital. It was a big mess."

"What about the intern?" asked Sarah Sloane.

"Nothing," I said. "It was a hard lesson to learn, but we all have them. Usually they're not this harsh. He was raked over the coals by the Morbidity and Mortality Committee, the Credentials Committee, and the California State Board of Medicine, but he was allowed to complete his internship and go on to a surgical residency."

"What happened to his father?" asked the captain.

"Nothing," I said.

"Didn't you complain?" Mum asked. "I seem to remember—"

"I was a resident at the time, and I reported his threats to the Chairman of Medical Education. Nothing happened."

"That doesn't seem fair," Sarah Sloane commented.

"It wasn't," I said, "but it was another lesson learned."

"Not to cut the story short," Nigel said, "but where's the evidence?"

"Rob did tell me," I said, "that he'd have to move it if he needed the cooler for a body, so it could be anywhere. Maybe it's in those cabinets."

"What exactly are we looking for?" asked Captain Sloane.

"A big glass jar," I replied, describing the approximate dimension with my hands, "a bucket, a urine cup with a splinter in it, another urine cup with hair in it, and two glass syringes, and I know where those are. I'll go get them. Oh, and by the way, this lady was murdered."

I left the others staring after me in shock while I went in search of the refrigerator. I found one in the very last room I came to. The two glass syringes were still there.

"Aha!" I exclaimed in triumph, as I grabbed them and started back toward the morgue.

I never got there.

Something hit me very hard on the back of the head, and everything went black.

Tuesday

SAN JUAN, PUERTO RICO

One eyewitness is of more weight than ten hearsays.

—Plautus

I WASN'T OUT for very long.

I woke up, still on the floor by the refrigerator, surrounded by my five companions. Hal knelt next to me, patting my cheek. When I opened my eyes, he said, "Oh, good, you're awake. Can you sit up, sweetie?"

I was too smart for that. The last time I'd had a concussion, I'd puked all night. No way was I about to sit up or even move my head. "You remember what happened the last time I did that," I murmured.

"Did you see who hit you?" Nigel asked.

"No," I said, still not moving my head. "Did he take the syringes?"

"He must have," Nigel said. "I don't see them anywhere."

"Damn," I said. "What about the rest of the stuff?"

"No joy," Nigel said. "We looked everywhere."

"Dr. Day," Captain Sloane said, "you should see a doctor."

I almost laughed. "Are you serious?"

"Antoinette," said my mother reprovingly, "the captain is only trying to help."

"I'm not staying here," I declared. "For all I know, the doctor is the one who conked me on the head. Maybe he murdered the lady in the cooler. Take me back to our room. Hal can wake me up every fifteen minutes to make sure I'm not bleeding into my brain."

"Oh, thanks a lot," Hal grumbled. "Just what I wanted to be doing all night."

"She's right, you know," Nigel said. "She's safer there than she would be here. Besides, the doctor's missing, so it would be rather pointless to stay here, don't you know."

"Darling, can you walk back to your cabin?" Mum asked worriedly.

"Not unless you want me to throw up," I said. "Surely there's a gurney around here somewhere, isn't there?"

"There's a wheelchair," Captain Sloane offered.

"No, I need to stay flat," I said.

In the end, they found me a gurney—no doubt the same one that had transported Mrs. Levine—and took me back to our cabin where I lay flat on my bed, still fully dressed. Hal offered to help me undress, but I wasn't having any truck with that, as it would have involved movement and probable vomiting. My head hurt, but I wasn't bleeding, thank God, since that would have involved sutures and would have required the doctor.

Mum offered to spell Hal so he wouldn't have to stay up all night. Captain Sloane said he'd check on me in the morning and organize a searching party to locate Rob. Sarah patted my hand and told me if I needed anything to just ask. Then they left, and Mum and Nigel went back across the hall to their own cabin.

Mum and Hal changed places at around three in the morning. At that point I decided that I needed to go to the bathroom, and Mum helped me out of bed and into the bathroom without incident. There was no nausea, so I consented to let Mum help me undress and get into my pajamas, and then I went back to sleep.

When morning came, I felt almost normal except for a slight headache and a very tender goose egg on the back of my head. Mum was gone. So was Hal. Mum had hung my clothes on the back of a chair, but I wondered if they might contain evidence of my attacker, so I put them into the laundry bag and dressed in more casual attire to go meet my family for breakfast.

As I left our cabin, Hal came out of Mum and Nigel's cabin. "Oh, you're up," he said by way of greeting. "How do you feel? Are you okay?"

Then he saw the laundry bag I was carrying along with my boat bag. "What's that?"

I explained. Nigel came out into the corridor in time to hear me explaining. "Oh, jolly good," he said. "Here, let's put that in our room, and then we can examine them after a bit of breakfast, eh what?"

"Are you sure they're safe there?" I asked.

"Safer than they would be in our room," Hal said.

Nigel went back into his cabin, and Mum came out. "Good morning, kitten. How do you feel? Do you feel well enough to eat something?"

Suddenly I became aware that I was starving. "I certainly do."

"Do you remember anything that happened before you were struck?" Nigel asked me as we climbed the stairs to the Lido deck.

I thought a minute. "I remember finding the glass syringes in the refrigerator. I also remember the lady in the cooler."

"Nothing after that?"

"Not until I woke up."

"Did you hear anything behind you before you were attacked?"

"Not that I can remember."

We didn't talk about the case while going through the cafeteria line in the Lido restaurant so as not to gross out the other passengers at breakfast. But a thought had occurred to me, and I ran it by Nigel as soon as we'd carried our plates into the pool area and sat down at a table. "Whoever put Mrs. Levine in the cooler had to move the evidence to make room for her. We didn't have a chance to look for it, because I got conked on the head. We need to go back and look for it."

"Toni, old thing," Nigel said. "Think. If the lady was murdered, chances are that the murderer put her there. Why would he not just get rid of the evidence?"

"Well, then, why leave the syringes in the refrigerator?"

"Perhaps that person didn't know about the syringes," Hal suggested. "Not until you went back there to get them."

"You mean someone waited back there just on the off chance that someone else would come in—and then go after them?" I asked. "Sounds pretty chancy to me."

"Unless that someone knew we were coming," Nigel said.

"Who knew you were going to the infirmary?" Mum asked. "Other than the captain and his wife, that is."

"They didn't know until Nigel asked about it at dinner last night," Hal said.

"But when Nigel went over to the captain's table to talk to Rob about it, the table was full," I said. "Officers Grant and Dalquist were there, and the Chief Engineer, and First Officer Lynch. They probably all heard Nigel asking Rob about the evidence. By the time we joined the captain and his wife, they'd left the table. Any one of them could have gone to the infirmary, disposed of the evidence, and laid in wait for us."

"But kitten, what would be the point of lying in wait?" Mum asked. "Why wouldn't they just get rid of the evidence and be done with it? Why complicate things by attacking someone?"

"Perhaps," Nigel said, "we caught someone in the act of trying to get rid of the evidence. Perhaps that person heard us come into the infirmary and hid, hoping we'd not find the evidence and would go away so he could finish the job. And then when Toni went back to the room with the refrigerator, he coshed her to prevent her from discovering him."

"And to create a diversion," Hal said. "We were too concerned about Toni to go looking for her attacker at that point."

"As I recall," my mother said, "we were also anxious to get out of there, lest we be attacked as well."

"How did your attacker get in?" Hal asked. "The doctor and the captain are the only ones who have keys."

"You're assuming the doctor didn't do this, then," said Mum.

"Not necessarily," Hal said. "But the doctor knew where the evidence was and could have gotten rid of it at any time. It had to be someone who'd found out about the evidence but didn't know exactly where it was and had to wait for us to show him. Only Toni got too close for comfort."

"We're assuming that the person who murdered the lady also murdered Leonie," I said. "It could be completely unrelated. In which case, the person who put the body in the cooler didn't know what all that stuff was and just moved it, and if that's the case, the evidence is still somewhere in the infirmary."

"Two murders in one cruise?" Hal asked skeptically. "What are the chances that they're unrelated?"

"Okay, suppose they're related," I argued. "Why put the body in the cooler? Wouldn't you think he'd want to get rid of it?"

"Chances are she's traveling with someone," Mum said.

"She is. Jessica told me that she's traveling with her sister," I said.

"Well, there you are, then," Mum said. "That mousy little person she was with at our table must be her sister. She'd be missed. Her body would have to be accounted for."

"Then someone would notice that she was strangled," Hal said. "That might start a panic among the passengers."

"Not necessarily," Nigel said. "The petechiae in her eyes and mouth and the ligature mark are hard to find and difficult to see. You and the doctor are the only ones who would know to look for them. Chances are nobody else would even notice them."

"What's going to happen to the body now?" Mum asked.

"She'll probably be taken ashore in Fort Lauderdale," Nigel said, "and out of our jurisdiction. Good thing you took those pictures."

"Let's hope they're good enough to convince the police that she was murdered," Hal said. "The lighting in there wasn't very good."

"They're not bad," I said, reaching into my boat bag. "I'll show you. If I could find my damn cell phone. Where could that have got to?" I continued rummaging in my boat bag, but I couldn't seem to locate my smartphone. Finally I dumped the contents of my bag out on the table. The phone wasn't there.

I felt tears of frustration building up behind my eyes. First the head gets stolen. Then my laptop disappears. Then the evidence disappears. Now my cell phone. When was I going to catch a break here?

"What are you doing?" Hal asked.

"Looking for my phone," I said. "I don't see it, do you?"

"Could you have left it in the infirmary last night?" Mum asked.

"No, I remember putting it back in my bra."

"It wasn't there when I undressed you," Mum said.

"Did it fall out when we put you on that gurney?" Hal asked.

"Surely one of us would have noticed," Nigel said. "It's far more likely that your attacker took it."

"You mean he took it out of my *bra*?" I asked in disbelief. "God, I feel so violated."

"It's of a piece with everything that's happened so far," Nigel said. "And a fine kettle of fish, to boot. If Scotland Yard needs those pictures, we'll be dead in the water."

"Nigel, dear," said Mum, "could you possibly put that another way?"

"We're not dead in the water," I said. "I e-mailed those pictures to the Royal Barbados Police, and also to Pete. Remember?"

"So all we have to do is tell Pete to forward them to Scotland Yard," Nigel said.

"I'll text him from my phone," Hal said, "and tell him to forward them. Tell me the e-mail address."

"Fine," Nigel said, and did so. "Now then, what I want to know is, if the doctor didn't attack you, why did he disappear right after I talked to him. That's suspicious behavior, eh what?"

"That's true," I said, "but Officers Lynch, Dalquist, and the Chief Engineer all left too, while we stayed to have cordials with the captain and his wife."

"What about Officer Grant?"

"He wasn't there at all," I said, remembering. "That's odd. Maybe he was on duty."

"That's another thing," Hal said. "We were all impatient to go down to the infirmary, and the captain wasn't budging. Do you suppose he did that on purpose to allow someone time to get rid of the evidence?"

"That would suggest that the captain was in cahoots with my attacker," I said. "What I was thinking is how anyone would dispose of the evidence. Rob told me that all the solid waste gets sorted prior to disposal. How would anyone get the brain and the rest of the head past that?"

"How about the kitchen?" Nigel suggested. "It could have been handled as food waste. Chopped up and mixed in with meat scraps. What do they do with that?"

"Officer Dalquist would know," I said, "but who would do the chopping up? And how does one dispose of an entire skull?"

At this point, Mum, who had been uncharacteristically tolerant as we were eating during this discussion, lost patience. "Antoinette, really, must we have body bits at breakfast? This is fairly turning me up."

"P'r'aps we'd better change the subject," Nigel said, and the discussion turned to the upcoming excursion in San Juan.

"I think I should go down and talk to the purser," Nigel said after breakfast. "It seems we won't be needing to mail anything in San Juan after all, more's the pity. I should do him the courtesy of letting him know that his efforts aren't unappreciated."

"Are you planning to call Scotland Yard again by any chance?" I asked.

"I do need to let them know that the evidence has gone missing," Nigel said. "Or do you have something else in mind?"

"Well, so far we know that our captain was on the *Southern Cross* twenty-five years ago, but maybe there were others," I said. "I can't get that information, but maybe Scotland Yard can."

Nigel chuckled. "Two suspects aren't enough for you?"

"They might both be innocent," I said. "Don't you think it's worth checking out?"

"Why don't I just ask our captain?"

"If he's guilty," I said, "he might lie to you."

"Toni, old dear, you can't have it both ways."

"You may as well make that call," Hal advised him. "She's not going to give up on this. You know that as well as I do."

"I always said Antoinette would be a good lawyer," Mum said. "She'd fairly argue me to death even as a small child."

"And you love me anyway," I said.

"That I do, kitten. Nigel, love, do go make that call."

"Very well. Where will you be?"

"Right here, dear. Perhaps I can get Antoinette to join me in another cup of coffee."

I'd felt well enough to put away a substantial breakfast, but my headache worsened enough that I opted not to go ashore in San Juan but instead to spend the day lounging by the pool. Or maybe I'd avail myself of some spa services. That would give me an opportunity to question some of the spa employees about what had happened to Leonie's head.

Accordingly, I went to the spa as soon as Hal and Mum and Nigel left for their shore excursion and booked myself a massage and facial. Then I went back to our cabin, set the alarm on the clock radio, and went back to bed. But I couldn't sleep.

A thought wormed its way into my subconscious and niggled at me until I threw off the covers and sat up, thoroughly awake and pissed off.

Why could the murderer not simply have thrown Leonie's body overboard?

It would disappear forever in the vast depths of the ocean and never be recovered. Even if it washed up on a beach somewhere, the crabs and lobsters would have nibbled away whatever was left of the flesh so that nobody would recognize her.

Not that anyone would have recognized her in any case. Even by the time I got a look at her when her head was in the pool, her face was so puffy and discolored that I wouldn't have known her. The next time anyone saw her face, it was falling off the bone. If she hadn't been wearing those earrings, perhaps we still wouldn't know who she was. By the time anyone realized she hadn't turned up in Bridgetown in time to board the next cruise ship, we had already sailed.

But that begged the question of why it was necessary to retain the body at all.

Why was it necessary to make that awful mess by crushing it in the roof?

I could think of only one reason.

Well, maybe two.

It was possible that the murderer might have been seen carrying the body up to the observation deck.

But why carry it up there in the first place? There were probably outside decks all around the ship on multiple levels. If the captain had killed her in his cabin, he'd only need to dump her off the back end of the Nav deck. To do that, he'd have to walk the length of the ship from front to back. The problem with that was the aft pool and bar. If anyone had been up and hanging around the swimming pool, he'd be seen.

Maybe he could just dump her off his own veranda.

Would that work? Could his veranda be seen from the bridge? Someone would be on watch, but what were the chances? Was there more than one officer on watch at a time?

For that matter, would the body clear all the other decks and hit the water if he did that?

Would it clear the other decks and hit the water no matter where it was thrown from?

Clearly this called for some reconnaissance. And what better time than now, while everybody was ashore?

I swung my legs out of bed, stuck my feet into my Birkies, and gingerly ran a comb through my hair. I picked up the booklet containing the floor plans of all the decks, which all passengers had received upon boarding. There was no way I could check out the captain's veranda without being invited, so I went out onto our own veranda and looked down. Three decks below me hung the lifeboats in their davits. A body thrown from any of these verandas would land in one—or on one, since they were enclosed.

They were also motorized. We'd actually had occasion to ride in them, because they doubled as shuttles to transport passengers to the dock in those ports where cruise ships were obliged to anchor offshore.

Clearly that eliminated the possibility of dumping a body from any point on the side of the ship above the Promenade deck. But how about below it, below the lifeboats?

I took the stairs down to the Promenade deck and went outside. Now the lifeboats hung above my head. I recognized the area where we'd had our lifeboat drill the day we'd boarded the ship. When I looked down, I saw nothing to interfere with throwing a body off; it would definitely land in the water and be screened from anyone looking down by the lifeboats.

I perused the pamphlet. The only outside walkway was on the lower Promenade deck, and it went all the way around the ship, front and back—or fore and aft. There were no outside walkways on any of the other decks, and there was no other access to the bow of the ship;

although it was obvious that anything thrown off the ship there wouldn't land in the water anyway, so it didn't matter. Access to the stern could be had from the Lido Terrace, the aft pool area on the Nav deck, or the lower Promenade deck.

But what about the captain's veranda? The only way to check that out would be from the dock, so I went down to A deck where the gangway was and went out onto the dock. Unfortunately, the captain's cabin was on the port side of the ship, and the dock was on the starboard side, but the deck plans showed verandas on both sides. So I stood on the dock, looking up past the lifeboats, so lost in thought that when a voice spoke behind me, I was so startled that I nearly fell off the dock.

"Dr. Day."

Captain Sloane stood behind me at parade rest, his visor shading his eyes so that they looked hooded and secretive.

"Captain! What are you doing out here?"

"I am occasionally allowed to leave the ship, you know," he said dryly. "There's always an officer on the bridge, even when we're in port."

I knew that was a stupid question before it was even out of my mouth. "I just wasn't expecting to see you here," I said lamely.

"I'm everywhere, Dr. Day. Didn't you know that?"

A frisson went down my spine, and the hair on the back of my neck rose. Was that a threat or just a product of my overheated imagination? Standing where he was, he could easily push me off the dock. But that would be ridiculous, I told myself.

Nevertheless, I stepped away from the edge of the dock before I spoke. "I was just wondering if anything dropped from that veranda would hit the lifeboat."

"That would depend on if the ship was underway or not."

"Underway," I said.

Captain Sloane scratched his upper lip. "At our usual cruising speed of twenty-three knots, it might. Of course, one has to take weather conditions into account. Why?"

"I was just thinking about the murder," I said.

"Of course you were. But Miss Montague wasn't thrown overboard, as you know."

"Why not?"

There! It was out.

"Dr. Day, however would I know that?"

"Suppose you were the killer," I pursued. "Why would you choose to mutilate the body rather than just throwing it overboard?"

"Since I'm not the killer, I haven't the slightest idea. Unless one didn't want to be seen by security cameras. We have them everywhere, you know."

Security cameras. Of course. I hadn't thought of that. Some sleuth you are, Toni. "Can I ask you another question?"

"Can I stop you?" He almost sounded amused.

"No. Are there any crew members besides yourself who were on the *Southern Cross* twenty-five years ago when Evelyn Hodges was killed?"

"Ah. Chief Superintendent Gray told you about that."

"Yes, he did."

"Did he happen to tell you how she died?"

"He did."

"And am I supposed to have killed her as well?" His shadowed eyes seemed to bore into mine.

He was trying to intimidate me, I knew, and I refused to be cowed by it. "Not necessarily. I'm just looking for connections between that murder and this one."

"Besides me?"

"Yes."

"Have you found any?"

"Yes, I have."

He took a step closer to me. "And who would those be?"

I stood my ground. "I can't tell you that."

"Why not, pray?"

I looked straight into his eyes. "Because if you're the killer, those people could be in danger."

"If I were the killer, Dr. Day, you'd be dead by now."

Well, now. That threat was unmistakable. If he were the killer, that is.

I changed the subject. "You didn't answer my question."

"Oh, yes. The crew of the *Southern Cross* twenty-five years ago. Of course, I haven't exactly memorized the crew manifests, but to my knowledge, nobody else from that crew is in this one. Are you satisfied?"

"No. I have one more question."

"Only one? You surprise me, Dr. Day."

"I was told that Evelyn Hodges had an affair with one of the officers on that trip. Do you know anything about that?"

He looked away from me. "How would I know anything like that?"

"So it wasn't you?"

"I'm sorry, Dr. Day. I've told you all I can. This conversation is over." He turned and walked rapidly toward the gangway. I stood, hands on hips, and watched him go. *Way to go, Toni,* I thought. *You just pissed off another officer.*

And the big kahuna, at that. He could make the rest of this cruise a living hell if he were so inclined. Maybe he'd already started to by stealing my laptop and my smartphone, which reminded me that I'd better report that to the purser.

But in answer to my question, he could have just said no. Instead he'd walked off in a huff. Did that mean he was guilty as charged, or just offended on principle?

Obviously, I'd touched a nerve.

I glanced at my watch. It was time for my facial and massage. I ran toward the gangway and reboarded. Captain Sloane was already out of sight. I heaved a sigh of relief and took the elevator up to the Lido deck.

Later, while lying stretched out on the masseuse's table under a warmed blanket, luxuriating under the pressure of her fingers as they rubbed and kneaded and worked various aromatic and soothing creams and oils into my skin, I mentioned the late Leonie Montague and inquired as to whether she'd ever utilized any spa services.

"Oh, yes, she came in for a facial and massage before every show," my masseuse, Christine, said. She was a tall, Scandinavian-looking New Zealander with long blonde braids. "I didn't do her, though. Mavis did."

"Is Mavis here?"

"She'll be doing your facial."

"Did Leonie come in the day before she was killed?"

"If she did, I didn't see her. You'd best ask Mavis."

After Christine was done with me, she warned me about the extreme, almost pathological dryness of my skin, which was news to me and no doubt greatly exaggerated to convince me to purchase an exorbitantly expensive assortment of products guaranteed to prevent my skin from cracking and falling off me entirely, or something equally dire. I did consent to a large jar of coconut-scented body lotion, which would be added to my spa bill. Then she escorted me to Mavis's cubicle for my facial.

Mavis was a New Zealander too, but otherwise she was just the opposite of Christine—a short, wiry, talkative brunette. All Christine had to do was mention my interest in Leonie, and she was off. I could hardly get a word in edgewise.

"I've been doing Leonie's facials and massages for about two years now, so I feel like I know her pretty well. Like sisters, we were. I'm going to miss her. Had some real good chin-wags, we have."

"Did she ever talk about her mother?"

"Oh, yes, all the time. She told me her mum died when she was four and that her grandparents raised her. She never knew her father. She asked her grandparents about it when she got older, but they didn't know any more than she did. They told her that her mum had an affair with an officer on one of the ships she worked on and got pregnant, and that she had to quit that job to take care of her child until she was four, and that she went back to work and died on *that* ship."

At this point I had an epiphany. Or perhaps it was an apostrophe. At any rate, I realized that it was not important whom Evie might have had an affair with on the *Southern Cross*. It was whoever had gotten her pregnant on a previous cruise five years *before* that, since Maggie was already four years old when Evie went to work on the *Southern Cross*.

Colin Sloane might not even have been on that cruise.

Nigel and I had been barking up the wrong tree. We needed to ... With difficulty, I wrenched my mind off that subject, because Mavis was still talking, and I didn't want to miss anything. "I'm sorry, what did you say? I seem to have been woolgathering."

Mavis wasn't offended. "I said, she's been looking for that officer on every ship she performed on. She thought it was possible that on her mum's last cruise she might have told the guy that he had a child and that she was going to sue him for child support, so he killed her."

"Did she ever find him?" I asked.

"She told me she had an idea who it was, but she wouldn't tell me. She said she needed to find out for sure before she told anybody."

Damn. Why did people do that? It was a surefire way of getting killed. Just read any mystery novel. "Do you have any idea who that officer was?"

"No, not a clue. Do you think it's got anything to do with Leonie getting killed? Like maybe she found out who her father was and that he killed her mother, and then he killed her to prevent her from telling anyone?"

"Maybe. It's a plausible theory. I should have thought of that myself. Did she ever talk about her boyfriend, the doctor?"

"How did you know about that?"

"Jessica told me. You know, the cruise director?"

"How did she know?"

"She and Leonie grew up together. I'm surprised she didn't tell you."

"So am I," Mavis said. "I had no idea. You don't suppose he has anything to do with this, do you?"

I wondered how much I should tell Mavis. She was clearly a gossip, and anything I told her would no doubt get around. She might tell the wrong person, and that person would come after me. Nigel would tell me not to say anything to anyone for my own safety and to leave it to the police. That would be good advice except for one thing.

Nigel and I had only two more days to flush out the murderer.

How better to flush out a killer than to spread rumors around? If he came after me, we'd know who he was. And who would be better to spread things around than a gossipy spa employee? It would be like confiding in your hairdresser. Maybe I ought to get my hair done while I was at it.

"He might," I told her. "He's on this ship."

Mavis's eyes grew round. "He is?"

"He is. He's Dr. Welch. And the reason I know that is because he told me himself."

"Oo-er! But Leonie said he stalked her for *years*. That doesn't sound like Dr. Welch to me. He's so nice. Stitched up Horacio's finger, he did, when Horacio cut it on his razor that time. Ever so nice, Horacio said he was."

"I know. I think he's nice too. He told me that they'd gone to college together and had been engaged and that she broke it off when they graduated and wouldn't tell him why."

A look of comprehension washed over Mavis's face. "Oh, I heard about that one. Her name was Maggie. It wasn't Leonie."

"Leonie *is* Maggie," I explained. "Jessica told me that. She changed her name when she started singing professionally."

"Oh dear," Mavis said. "Does he know that?"

"He does now," I told her. "And there's something else. The first officer on the ship where Leonie's mother was killed was none other than Colin Sloane, our captain."

"Crikey!" Mavis's eyes grew round again. "How did you know that?"

"My stepfather told me. He was the Scotland Yard inspector assigned to the case."

"Scotland *Yard*?" Mavis exclaimed in disbelief. "Mrs. Shapiro, are you sure you're not having me on?"

"Quite sure," I assured her. "He's here too. We're on this cruise to celebrate my mother's retirement. So we're both poking around to see what we can find out about Leonie and who might have killed her and why, and whether there's any connection to Leonie's mother's death. Her name was Evie, by the way."

"Blimey!" Mavis's agile fingers, which had been patting a moisturizing mask onto my face, stilled. "Do you think our captain killed both of them?"

My initial reaction was not to let that little idea get bruited about in the crew mess. The captain was already mad at me. But on the other hand, why not? Especially since Mrs. Levine had been spreading the rumor that the captain and Leonie had been having an affair and that he'd had to get rid of her because his wife was coming aboard in Bridgetown. "As far as I know," I mused, "there's no evidence at all of any connection between the captain and Leonie and her mother other than that he knew both of them. He probably has no idea that they were mother and daughter."

"But don't they always say that it's the last person you'd suspect?"

"They do say that," I said, "and the captain certainly fits *that* description." Even more so, I thought, since he probably wasn't the one who got her pregnant. Nigel and I needed to find out about who'd been on that first ship. So far, we didn't even know what ship that was. Talk about going back to square one! This was square zero. How were we going to find out the name of that ship? Did it even belong to this cruise line? That would have been, what, thirty years ago, which would have been 1983.

Maybe Nigel could simply ask Captain Sloane what ship he'd been on in 1983. He certainly wouldn't tell me, since I'd already pissed him off.

But that wouldn't help if Captain Sloane wasn't Leonie's father.

I felt as if we'd just been cast adrift without a paddle.

Bother!

Mavis did her best to sell me multiple obscenely expensive products to hydrate and plump my face and remove wrinkles (which I didn't have), shrink large pores (which I did have), and even out my complexion by removing dark spots and redness (not a problem, so far). I told her I could use the body lotion I'd already bought from Christine, and she nearly had a heart attack at the very notion of using the same skin cream for facial skin as I did for the rest of my body. In the end, I consented to a small tube of eye cream, because now that I was pushing fifty, there were a few crow's feet. Whereupon, she made a miraculous recovery. I tipped her generously for the gossip she would no doubt be spreading on my behalf, and her eyes grew wide when she looked at the receipt.

After a massage and facial, one is supposed to rest and drink plenty of water, but all I wanted to do was wash my hair. All those oils and unguents had gotten worked into my hair as Christine extended the massage to my scalp, and now my hair was sticking up in greasy spikes. The problem was that I was loath to shower and wash all those emollients off the rest of me, because they felt and smelled so good. I turned back. "Mavis," I called.

She stuck her head around a partition behind the reception desk. "Mrs. Shapiro? Is everything all right?"

"Oh, yes," I reassured her. "I was just wondering if I might get a shampoo and haircut."

"You mean right now?"

I gestured at my hair.

"Right," she said and ran a finger down a page of the ledger on the desk. "You're in luck. Horacio has an opening in ten minutes."

"Excellent," I said. "I'll take it."

"Just have a seat in the waiting area. Horacio will come get you when he's ready."

As I cooled my heels in the cool, green, potted-plant-infested waiting area, I tried to figure out where to go next. It was only two in the afternoon. Hal, Mum, and Nigel wouldn't be back on board until at least four. Maybe I could put the time to good use by talking to Officer Dalquist. Only I hadn't the faintest idea where to find him. Maybe Horacio or Christine or Mavis or somebody on the spa staff could direct me.

"Mrs. Shapiro? I'm ready for you."

I was so far into my reverie that I jumped.

"Sorry to startle you," Horacio said. He was a willowy young man with dark skin and liquid dark eyes that suggested Indian origins, although his speech was pure Aussie. His wavy black hair hung to his shoulders, and his ears were pierced with small gold hoops.

As we walked back to his station, I asked, "How does an Indian guy get called Horacio?"

He turned with a smile. "Easy. My mum is Filipino. It was her father's name."

His walk and hand gestures suggested that he was gay, which didn't bother me. Gay guys, in my experience, were much more likely to gossip than their straight counterparts.

Horacio didn't disappoint me. "Mavis tells me you were the one who found Leonie's body. Was it awful?"

"Actually, Leonie's body found me," I said. "I was just sitting here on the Lido deck, minding my own business, when her head fell into the pool, and the rest of her practically fell on me."

Horacio shuddered delicately. "How too gruesome, darling. I heard that she was crushed in the roof. Was that true?"

"That's not the worst of it," I said. "Someone took the head out of the pool, and it ended up in the laundry in the washer with a load of towels."

Horacio made a face. "Ugh. How'd that happen?"

"I don't know, exactly," I said. "Someone could have wrapped it up in a bunch of towels, put it down the laundry chute here in the spa, and then cleaned up in the locker room."

Horacio whipped out a towel and a cape and fastened them both around my neck. "Blimey, I hope you're not accusing one of us," he remarked as he tipped the chair back.

I suppose that my timing could have been better, since my head was now tipped back and hanging in the sink, a rather vulnerable position to be in had anyone been inclined to strangle me. Moreover, I'd read articles in medical journals cautioning that older women could easily stroke out with their heads and necks in that position; not that I was particularly old. One shove of the heel of a hand up under my chin could break my neck and sever my spinal cord. Horacio could kill me three different ways without even breaking a sweat.

No, four. He could also drown me in the sink. But I needn't have worried. Horacio briskly massaged the shampoo into my scalp and showed no inclination to kill me.

"Not necessarily," I said. "Maybe it was someone else hiding in the spa waiting for an opportunity."

"Whyever would anyone want to hide the head?"

"To keep us from identifying her," I said. "Whoever killed her expected her head to be crushed in the roof, and it wasn't."

"Right. I hear you're all cozy with Scotland Yard. Do they know who did it?"

"No, not yet."

Horacio rinsed my hair, wrung it out, wrapped a towel around my head, and brought me upright, all in one fluid motion. "Rumor has it that the captain might have had something to do with it."

"I've heard that," I said. "Did you know Leonie well?"

"I did her hair from time to time," he said while dexterously manipulating comb and scissors. "I suppose I knew her as well as one's hairdresser knows anybody. We're like bartenders, you know. People talk to us."

"So Leonie talked to you," I said. "About what?"

"Oh," he waved a hand gracefully, "the odd boyfriend, other people's love affairs, who said what to whom—you know, the usual."

"Did she happen to mention that her mother was cruise director on another ship of the line twenty-five years ago?"

Horacio stopped snipping. "She said she was looking for her father. She thought it might be the captain. She said he was on that same ship."

"Why the captain?" I asked. "Did her mother tell her that? Or tell her grandparents that? I heard that she never told anybody who it was."

Horacio resumed snipping. "Who told you that?"

Bits of black hair flew everywhere, including into my face. I blew them off as best I could. "Jessica," I said. "The cruise director. They grew up together, you know."

"I know," he said. "So if it wasn't the captain, who was it?"

"I have no idea. I asked the captain if there were any other officers on this crew that were also on that crew, and he said that as far as he knew, there weren't."

Horacio put the scissors down and picked up a hair dryer. "I thought it was the captain, because Leonie spent quite a lot of time talking to him on this cruise. Sometimes she went to his cabin at night after dinner."

"Wait," I said. "I thought she came aboard in Grenada. Has she been on this ship all along?"

"Who told you that? She came aboard in Fort Lauderdale. I did her hair before the show that night."

"Was she having an affair with him?"

Horacio turned the hair dryer on and blew the little bits of hair off my face before turning his attention to my hair. "Crikey, you don't have to do much with this lot, do you? It's curling up all by itself."

"I know. What about the captain?"

He shook his head. "She said they just talked. She was only a tyke when her mother died, and I suppose he could tell her what her mum was like."

"Do you suppose he was helping her find her father?"

"Could be." He put the dryer down and removed the cape and towel from around my neck. "There you go. Like it?"

"Love it." I started to get up out of the chair, but Horacio stopped me. "You know, your hair is a bit dry …"

Here we go again. I held up a hand to stop him. "I do use a conditioner, you know."

He picked up a tube. "Let me put a bit of this on your hair, just to see if you like it." He squeezed a small amount into the palm of his hand and used the fingers of his other hand to apply it sparingly to the tips of my curls. "It makes it shiny, see?"

I saw. I liked it. I consented to buy some. I also tipped him generously for spreading the rumor that someone had stolen the head around the crew mess, as I knew he would do.

It wasn't until I got out to the reception desk that I remembered to ask if they knew how I could get in touch with Officer Dalquist. The receptionist suggested that I go down to the main desk and leave a message. So I did.

After that, I felt at loose ends. Hal and Mum and Nigel wouldn't be back on board for an hour and a half yet. I was curious to know what Nigel had found out when he called Scotland Yard. I was anxious to talk to Officer Dalquist about how one might dispose of body parts. I needed to talk to someone about how easy or difficult it might be to throw anything, or anybody, overboard. Perhaps I should talk to Officer Grant about that. So I went back to the desk and left a message for Officer Grant, and also for Hal and Nigel to meet me in the Ocean Lounge. Then I reported the theft of my smartphone to the purser.

I still felt antsy. I couldn't wait to tell Nigel we had to find out about a cruise that took place five years before the *Southern Cross*, during which Evie Hodges had actually gotten pregnant. He'd probably have to call Scotland Yard again.

Perhaps Jessica might know the name of the ship. If Evie had mentioned if to Maggie ... but Maggie had been only four years old when Evie died. Perhaps her grandparents knew. Maybe they'd mentioned it to Maggie when she was older, and maybe she'd mentioned it to Jessica. It was a long shot, but sometimes long shots hit the target. One could hope.

So I went up to the Ocean Lounge and ordered a drink. The bartender was Arturo, who usually worked the Lido bar. "Martini?" he inquired.

I nodded. He prepared it and gave me my glassful of olives without my having to ask for them. I carried my drink over to a table by a window where I could see what was happening on the dock. I grew hypnotized watching crates and crates of supplies being loaded via conveyor belt.

It seemed incredible, the amount of food and consumables required to keep twelve hundred passengers plus crew fed and comfortable.

"Toni."

I turned to see Rob standing by my table.

"Might I join you?" he inquired.

"Of course," I said, wondering what to expect. Last time I'd talked to Rob, he'd gone stomping off in a rage.

He sat down. Arturo came over, and Rob ordered Scotch on the rocks.

"Are you still mad at me?" I asked.

"Toni, I am so sorry about that. Can you possibly forgive me?"

"If you can forgive me for prying."

"Oh, well. You have to ask these questions, I suppose, when investigating a murder."

I offered him an olive. He declined. "I don't think it would go very well with Scotch, do you?"

As far as I'm concerned, olives go with everything—except maybe ice cream. "What happened to you last night? Weren't you going to meet us in the infirmary and give us the evidence so we could mail it from San Juan today?"

"I got an emergency call," he said. "I was told that someone in maintenance had a rather serious injury. When I got there, nobody knew anything about it. I went around the various compartments, asking if anyone was hurt, but nobody knew what I was talking about, and by the time I got back to the infirmary, nobody was there."

"So it wasn't you who hit me over the head and knocked me out?"

Rob nearly choked on his Scotch. "God, no! What the bloody hell are you talking about?"

"And it wasn't you who put the lady in the cooler and moved the evidence?"

Rob looked narrowly at me. "Are you having me on?"

"The lady was murdered, by the way."

"What!"

"She had petechiae on her conjunctivae and oral mucosa, and a ligature mark on her neck," I told him.

"Does the captain know about this?"

"He was there," I said, "when we found her. I told him she was murdered before I went to find the syringes in the refrigerator and someone knocked me out."

"Blimey! Who else knows about this?"

"Mum and Nigel," I said, "and Hal, and the captain and his wife."

"Dear God," Rob moaned, "this will never do. I've got to see this for myself."

"I'll go with you," I said.

He didn't object. We finished off our drinks and headed for the forward elevator. It was like déjà vu all over again as Rob inserted the key in the infirmary door and let us in. We made our way down the corridor to the morgue, Rob unlocked the door, and he and I horsed open the cooler door.

The body was gone.

Eat, drink, and be merry, for tomorrow ye diet.

—William Gilmore Beymer

"What the hell?" I exclaimed.

Mrs. Levine had joined the evidence, my laptop, and my smartphone in the land of the lost. I wondered if the Bermuda Triangle extended this far south.

"There's got to be a reasonable explanation for this," Rob said. "I'll check with the captain."

"Too bad whoever removed the body couldn't have put the evidence back," I grumbled.

"Even if we find it, it's too late to mail it from San Juan," Rob said. "We sail in half an hour."

I hadn't realized it was so late. "I suppose we could mail it from Fort Lauderdale," I said.

"It's a moot point unless we find it," Rob pointed out.

"Let's start looking," I suggested. "It shouldn't take long with both of us looking."

"We haven't got much time," Rob said. "I've office hours at five."

"Then hadn't we better get busy?"

We began opening cabinet doors. "Who was she?" Rob asked.

"Her name's Levine," I said. "Myra Levine. She sat at our table at dinner a couple of nights ago, and she was on the yacht yesterday in Philipsburg."

"Oh, you did the yacht race. How was it?"

"Thrilling. Everybody wanted to talk about the murder. Mrs. Levine was spreading the rumor that the captain was the killer because he'd been having an affair with Leonie and had to get rid of her before his wife came on board in Barbados."

"No wonder somebody killed her," he said facetiously. "Are we now supposed to think the captain did that as well?"

"There's a thought," I said. "Do you suppose that somebody's trying to frame the captain?"

"Who'd want to do that?"

"Oh, I don't know," I said, "but maybe there's someone who wants to discredit him. Somebody who wants his job, for instance."

"Well, that would be Dave Lynch," Rob said, "but it wouldn't do him any good, because that's not the way it works. If Captain Sloane loses his job, it would go to the next first officer in line for a promotion. Dave is much too young to be that high on the list."

"You sound like you know him pretty well," I commented.

"We grew up together," Rob said. "I lost touch with him when he went off to maritime college, but since then we've been on several of the same cruises—and that reminds me."

"What?"

"Someone told me awhile back that Dave was in a relationship with Leonie. That's how she managed to get a job as an entertainer for this cruise line. I heard Dave pulled some strings to make that happen so they could be together."

"Then it must have pissed him off big-time if he thought she threw him over for the captain after he went to all that trouble to get her a job."

"So maybe Mrs. Levine knew what she was talking about."

"And got strangled to shut her up."

By this time we'd made our way through every possible hiding place in the infirmary. The evidence was nowhere to be found. Admitting defeat, Rob and I went our separate ways—I to the Ocean Lounge, and Rob remaining in the infirmary to prepare for evening office hours.

My husband and my parents were waiting for me in the Ocean Lounge, drinks in front of them.

"So how was it?" I asked.

"Hot," said Hal succinctly.

"What did you see?" I pursued.

"What *didn't* we see," Mum said. "We started out at the visitor center right off the pier and got these maps and pamphlets, and I think we've seen everything on them and then some."

"We've been all around Robin Hood's barn," Nigel said. "We've left no corner of Old San Juan unturned."

"We started out with El Castillo San Cristóbal, and then we went to Castillo San Felipe del Morro," Mum said, mangling the Spanish horribly, "and then we went to the Santa Maria Magdalena cemetery where all the high muckety-mucks are buried, and then ..."

"Darling Mum, do you know that your Spanish sucks?" I said.

Mum was unperturbed. "Yes, dear. Then we walked for absolutely miles down this street that runs along the outside of the wall around the city until we got to the city gate."

"Paseo del Morro," Hal said. His Spanish was much better. "And then, once we got inside the old city, we saw the governor's mansion, which was once a fort too, and Ponce de Leon's house—"

"Ponce de Leon, seriously?" I asked. "The 'fountain of youth' guy?"

"He was also the first governor of Puerto Rico," Hal said. "His house was built in 1521 and is one of the oldest buildings in Puerto Rico. And he's buried in the Cathedral of San Juan Bautista, which was built in 1540."

"We saw that too," Mum said.

"Then we walked up and down streets and bought souvenirs and such," Nigel said, casting a disparaging look upon Mum's packages. "Fiona had to go into every single shop and browse, and there must be *hundreds* of them."

"You exaggerate, dear," Mum said.

"Some of those shops are so small that there's only room for one customer at a time, and Hal and I had to wait out in the street," Nigel went on.

"But the streets are so pretty," Mum said. "All those colorful houses and blue cobblestones."

Nigel grunted. "Hard on the feet."

"I told you we should have used the trolley, love," Mum said tartly. "It's free. But you two great boobies had to be macho and walk everywhere."

I sensed that the conversation was degenerating into a spat and it was time to change the subject, but Hal beat me to it. "In my opinion," he said, "it's time to stop talking and do some serious drinking. Where's that bartender?"

"And by the way, did you get a chance to call Scotland Yard?" I asked Nigel.

"I did," he said. "Before we went ashore. I talked to an old colleague of mine who's near retirement himself. He remembered the case. He said he'd get the information and call me back tonight."

"Tonight?" Mum asked. "What's the time difference? Won't that be awfully late for him to be calling?"

"Four hours," Nigel said, "but tomorrow we'll be at sea. It's easier to call ship to shore, and vice versa, while we're still in port. And speaking of which, what time do we sail?"

"Five thirty," Hal said, "and it's four thirty now. You haven't got much time."

Arturo came over to the table carrying a tray with our drinks. "Sorry it took so long. I was on the phone. The purser says the Chief Superintendent has a phone call."

"Jolly good," Nigel said. "Thank you, Arturo. Fiona, will you wait until I get back, or should I meet you in our cabin?"

"I think I'll take these things to our cabin," Mum said, "and maybe take a shower."

"We'll be here," Hal said.

"Very well," Nigel said, and he left.

"How's that for timing?" Hal commented and took a sip of his beer.

"Impeccable," I said. "And speaking of timing, I found out what happened to Rob last night. Maintenance called him and said they had a badly injured crewman, and when he went there, nobody knew what he was talking about."

"Of course," Mum said. "The oft-used bogus phone call, famed in song and story, meant to get someone out of the way for nefarious purposes."

"Which means," Hal said, "that it wasn't necessarily maintenance who called him. I mean, anyone could call and *say* they were maintenance."

"That's true," I said. "I hadn't considered that. But it didn't keep us out of the infirmary. The captain let us in with his keys. So what was the point?"

"Somebody had to get into the infirmary before that to steal the evidence," Hal said, "and to lie in wait for you. That person had to have keys too."

"So who else has keys to everything?" I asked. "Besides the captain. Would maintenance have keys to every room on the ship as well?"

"I should think so," Mum said. "So would housekeeping."

"They probably have master keys that open all the cabins," Hal said.

"Well, hell," I said with disgust. "We've just narrowed it down to maybe five hundred crew members. Now what?"

"Did the doctor know anything about the body in the cooler?" Mum asked.

"No, he didn't," I said, "and when I told him she'd been murdered, he insisted on going down to the infirmary to see for himself—and she was gone!"

"Gone!" echoed Hal. "How could that happen?"

"I don't know," I said. "Either she's been thrown overboard or taken off in San Juan. Rob said he was going to check with the captain."

"Let's hope she's not going to be the next victim of the Lido roof," Hal said.

Mum shoved her chair back. "That's quite enough, Hal dear," she said with asperity. "I need to get all these packages up to the cabin."

"We'll help you," I offered. "We probably should start getting ready for dinner anyway."

On the way upstairs to the Nav deck, we met Nigel coming down. I pounced. "What did Scotland Yard say?"

"Let's go back to your cabin," Nigel suggested.

When we got there, Nigel closed the door behind us. "My old colleague was able to inquire as to the crew of the *Southern Cross* at the time of that murder. He faxed me the list. There are quite a lot of them, as you might guess."

"Where is it?" Hal asked.

"Right here," Nigel said.

"Let's see," I urged. He handed it to me. I perused it while the ship's whistle sounded, and the gentle motion of the ship told me that we were leaving San Juan. Ordinarily I loved to watch while the massive *North Star* moved away from its mooring and headed out to sea, but I was anxious to find a familiar name on that list.

I found it on the fifth page under Technical Department. I handed it back to Nigel. "Check out the third engineer."

Nigel took it and frowned. "Well, I'll be buggered."

"What?" asked Hal.

Mum peered over Nigel's shoulder at the document. "Joseph Gerard," she said. "Can it possibly be the same one?"

"We could ask him," Nigel said. "Or we could ask the captain."

"Then we could ask him why he lied to me," I said.

The phone rang. Hal answered it and held the receiver out to me. "It's for you."

It was Officer Grant. "I got a message that you wanted to talk to me," he said.

"I do," I said. "I was wondering about security cameras. You have them, don't you?"

"Of course we do. Why do you ask?"

"I need to know how easy it would be to throw somebody overboard without being seen."

"Dear God, why?"

"Well, it seems stupid to crush a body in the roof if it could just as easily be thrown overboard."

Grant sighed. "Oh, I see. That girl."

"I figured out all the places where one could throw anyone or anything overboard," I told him, and I enumerated them. "Do you have security cameras in all those places?"

"We have them everywhere, Dr. Day."

"Do you record what they see?"

"Of course."

"How long do you keep the recordings?"

"Till after the cruise ends. Then we delete them."

"Does someone watch them twenty-four seven?"

"We have an officer on duty for that at all times, sometimes two. But you have to understand that they have to check them periodically, because it's not possible to see them all at once."

"So some things could get missed."

"That's correct."

"Only there'd be no way to know when nobody was watching a particular camera, would there?"

"Only the officer on duty would know that," Grant said. "And he's not allowed to leave his post."

"Would it be possible for us to see some of those recordings?"

"On whose authority?" Grant had clearly had enough of this conversation. I passed the phone to Nigel.

"Chief Superintendent Gray here," he said brusquely. "Scotland Yard."

Apparently that was all Officer Grant needed, and he offered to let us see any recordings we wanted. Nigel arranged for us to do that after dinner, and hung up.

"Well, that answers one question," Mum said. "I've been wondering all along why the murderer didn't just simply throw the body overboard instead of making that awful mess with the roof."

"Because he was afraid he'd be seen," Hal said.

"You mean he wouldn't be seen carrying her body up to the observation deck?" I argued. "And what did he do with her clothes? She would have had one of those overnight cases, like those girls had when we talked to them on the elevator. What about that?"

"Maybe he threw those overboard," Mum said.

"Why would he do that and not the body?" I asked.

"Perhaps because it was important that her death be a matter of record," Nigel said. "That's hard to do without a body."

"Why was it important?" I asked. "Was there an inheritance involved?"

"That's the usual reason," Nigel said. "If she had to die to allow someone else to inherit, for example. Or if someone stood to inherit from her, which would be another scenario."

"Then why disfigure her so that nobody would recognize her?" Mum asked. "That would defeat the purpose, wouldn't you think?"

Suddenly a thought came to my mind, one so illuminating that all came clear. "Unless," I said, "the person who killed her is not the person who crushed her in the roof."

"You mean," Hal said, "maybe there's more than one person involved in this. Maybe the person who killed her asked someone else to dispose of the body."

"That still doesn't explain why the body was disfigured," Mum argued.

"It might," I said, "if the person who disposed of the body had a grudge against the person who killed her and did it for revenge."

"Oh brother," Hal said. "Can we possibly make this any more complicated?"

"That is quite a lot to digest all at once," Nigel said. "I suggest we go and digest our dinners and talk about something else."

Our after-dinner movie date with Officer Grant didn't happen as scheduled.

From our table across the dining room, I saw the Filipino maître d' make his way over to the captain's table and whisper in his ear.

"Uh-oh," I said.

Hal looked. "Déjà vu all over again."

Sure enough, the captain rose, and so did Rob, who came over to our table. "The captain requests your presence in the waste disposal department," Rob said.

"Oh, not again," Mum said. "Can't they at least finish their dinners?"

"Maybe," Hal said, "it would be best if they don't."

Mum made a face. "Oh dear."

Nigel and I shrugged and followed the captain and Rob into the kitchen, where we took the elevator down to B deck where waste was sorted for disposal. Rob had described to me what went on down there, but all the same, I was not prepared for the size of the machines that ground up food waste, crushed cans, and shredded glass. Most of them were taller than I was, and some were even taller than the captain. Considering the type of work done, everything was amazingly clean and shiny, including the floor—except for the food grinder that had been opened up and dismantled on a drop cloth.

Officer Dalquist stood over it, hands on hips, while a sullen-looking young man with a nasty-looking scratch on his cheek struggled to free an object from the cutting mechanism where it had gotten wedged. The smell of ozone in the air told me that the motor had burned out or shorted out, and it almost—but not quite—masked the all-too-familiar odor of decomposing flesh.

I turned to Rob. "Is that what I think it is?"

He nodded. "More than likely. When Keith figures that out, he's going to need medical attention."

"Keith? You know him?"

"He's the captain's son. Starting from the bottom up, and not too happy about it."

I watched as the captain greeted his son, and the look on the boy's face was one of pure hatred. Too bad, I thought. Keith resembled his mother, except that his hair was dark, and with a smile on his face, he would have been handsome. The way he looked now, I was glad he had something besides me to be grumpy about. This was one very angry young man. Chances were that his wealthy mother had spoiled him rotten as a child.

I noticed scratches on his arms too and wondered who he'd been fighting with.

Officer Dalquist came over to us. "I do hope whatever that is wasn't part of anything we've eaten. It's definitely gone off."

"I'm pretty sure it isn't food," I said.

He thought about that for a few seconds, and when he realized what I meant, he went pale. "Blimey!"

At that moment, Keith managed to extricate the offending object from the cutting blades. He held it up. "Got it!"

Crew members clustered around, straining to see. I recognized it, and so did Rob. We stayed where we were, and presently Officer Dalquist and the captain made their way to us through the crowd. "Any ideas?" the captain asked.

"It's her skull cap," I told him. "And if that screwed up the grinder, the rest of the head is bound to do even more damage."

"Assuming," Rob added, "that it hasn't already gone through."

"Oh, I can't believe it has," I said. "It's got even more bone than this."

Both the captain and Dalquist had gone pale and sweaty, and the captain looked positively green. I expected him to hightail it for the nearest loo, and he didn't disappoint me. Dalquist took out a handkerchief and mopped his brow. "Are you telling me that we need to go through everything that's in this grinder to find the rest of the head?"

"It might not be in this grinder," I said. "Aren't there others?"

"You'd best check them all," Nigel said.

Dalquist gave us an eye roll. "I do believe this is a job for the captain's son," he said. "I certainly hope he's got a stronger stomach than his father."

"You don't need us anymore, do you?" Rob asked.

Dalquist shook his head. "We've got it in hand," he said.

As he made his way back to the center of the crowd and gave Keith Sloane the bad news, Rob and I beat a strategic retreat. "From the look on that kid's face," Rob said, "Dalquist may be our next corpse."

As we got off the elevator on the main deck, we heard the three chimes that heralded an announcement. "This is Second Officer Ian Bellingham speaking from the bridge. The captain has instructed me to inform you that there is a storm between here and Fort Lauderdale. We may experience rough weather tonight and tomorrow. Be sure to secure your belongings. I repeat—we may experience rough weather tonight and tomorrow. Secure your belongings. Thank you."

Better take a seasick pill tonight before bed, just in case, I thought.

Our table was being served dessert when we got back. Nigel and I were just in time to have some. "Did you hear the announcement?" I asked Mum and Hal.

Hal shook his head. "I heard the chimes, but it was too noisy in here to hear what was said. What was it about?"

"We're sailing into a storm," I said. "We need to 'secure our belongings.'"

"I'd better take a pill tonight, then," Mum said, "to secure my stomach. You too, kitten."

"Yes, Mum."

"So what was that all about?" Hal asked.

"Tell you later," I said. "Let's just say that we don't need to watch as many of Officer Grant's movies as we thought." We didn't need to quiz Officer Dalquist about disposal of the stolen physical evidence either, but I decided not to mention that at the table.

While eating our desserts, I saw the captain and Officer Dalquist return to their table. The captain refused dessert and leaned over to speak to Officer Gerard, who then rose and left the dining room.

"He's gone to give young Keith a hand with the grinder," Nigel muttered sotto voce, but Hal heard him.

"Who's young Keith?" he asked.

"Nepotism is alive and well aboard the *North Star*," Nigel said. "Keith Sloane is the captain's son, and he's working down there in the bowels of the ship. Officer Dalquist told us that the boy is not happy about having to start at the bottom."

"That's throwing roses at it," I said. "You should have seen the way he looked at his father. That's a very angry young man. He could be dangerous."

"How old is he?" Mum asked.

"Oh, I don't know—eighteen, maybe twenty," I said. "Just out of school, I'm thinking, and probably spoiled rotten."

"If the captain hasn't tried to steer him straight until now, it's too late," Mum said. "That sort of thing should start in the cradle."

"He wants watching," Nigel said. "He could be the murderer, for all we know."

There can no great smoke arise, but there must be some fire.

—John Lyly

After Nigel and I left the table, we met Officer Grant on the main deck near the purser's office, as arranged.

"We don't have to look for anybody throwing our evidence overboard," I told him. "It turned up in the food-waste grinder tonight."

"Blimey!" Officer Grant exclaimed. "You don't mean …"

"Someone put it in the garbage," Nigel said. "It wasn't thrown overboard. So what we need now is the footage from the observation deck the night of the murder."

Officer Grant let us into the security room by typing a code into a pad by the door. A younger man, possibly late thirties, with bright-red hair, sat before a myriad of screens on the wall, which showed what was going on in—I counted—thirty-six locations on the ship. As I watched, the scenes changed to thirty-six more locations. How on earth, I wondered, did one person keep track of that many cameras, let alone that many cameras that changed every minute or two?

"This is Security Guard Joe Gerard," Grant said. "You just tell him what you need, and he'll bring it up on the computer."

"Joe Gerard?" I echoed. "That's the same name as the chief engineer."

The man grinned. "He's my dad," he said. "I'm Joe Junior. We don't often get to work the same cruise." His Scots wasn't nearly as broad as his father's, and he appeared to have a much better disposition.

"I'm Dr. Toni Day," I said, "and this is my stepfather, Chief Superintendent Nigel Gray of Scotland Yard."

Joe Gerard shook Nigel's hand. "Pleasure to meet you, sir," he said. "Now what can I show you?"

"Observation deck," Grant said. "The night of the murder."

Gerard looked askance. "The night of the murder? What night would that be, sir?"

"The night before we arrived in Barbados," I said helpfully.

"That would be Saturday," he said. "What time?"

"She was actually crushed in the roof sometime between six and six thirty in the morning," I said, "so that would be Sunday."

"So you want Sunday morning at or around six. Which camera, do you know?"

Nigel and I looked at each other and shrugged. What did we know? "Whichever cameras show the roof of the Lido deck," I said finally.

"From which direction?"

Nigel and I looked at each other again. Nigel said, "We don't know. Best do all of them."

Joe shrugged. "Okay. Here goes. This might take a while."

"We've got nothing but time," Nigel said.

It was disappointing, to say the least. None of the views of the roof showed anything. The roof was closed, and there was nobody in sight.

"What were you expecting to see?" Joe asked us.

I turned my palms up. "Somebody carrying a body, for one thing," I said finally. "Can you run those backwards?"

"Sure. Do you know how they got the body up there and held it in place?"

That was something we hadn't considered. We'd been too preoccupied with who and why to think about how.

"We were rather hoping to see that on these recordings," Nigel said.

"How far back do you want me to go?" Joe asked.

"Can you run them back slowly so we can see if there's anything happening?"

"Okay."

Joe ran the first recording backward until I stopped him. "The roof's opening!"

"Do you see anybody?" Nigel asked, peering at the computer screen.

"No. Keep going!"

"Who's that?" Nigel asked, pointing.

Joe slowed the recording to a snail's pace. A dark figure ran across the roof, knelt, reached down into the opening and did something we couldn't see, and then ran back. Then the roof began to close.

"I didn't see his face—did you?" Joe asked.

Nigel shook his head.

I leaned forward and pointed. "There! What's that?"

It was so dark that I wasn't sure I'd seen anybody, but I thought I saw something odd about the roof. A shadow had appeared along the roof opening that didn't go all the way across.

"Can you run it in slow motion?"

Joe did so. The shadow slid across the roof along the opening and then dropped off the side and out of sight.

"What just happened here?" I asked. "I didn't see anybody. Did you?"

"What was that thing that just slid off the roof?" Nigel asked. "Could that have been the body?"

"If that was the body," I said, "why didn't it fall onto the Lido deck when the roof opened?"

"It must have been secured somehow," Grant said. "Run it back some more, and then forward in slow motion."

Joe did so. I concentrated so fiercely on what I was seeing that my eyes began to burn. I blinked to relieve them just as Nigel exclaimed, "There!"

I opened my eyes just in time to see something suddenly shoot out of nowhere and then drop out of sight, like a shooting star.

"What the bloody hell was that?" Nigel asked.

"No idea," Joe said. "Let me run it in slow motion." He did so. The object soared into the air and disappeared on the other side of the roof. It seemed to have a string attached.

"It's a weight," Grant said, "attached to a rope. Blimey, the guy's got an arm. Those things are heavy. It'd take a bloody discus thrower to get it all the way to the other side of that roof, especially with a rope attached."

"Damn," said Nigel. "He stood right underneath the camera so he wouldn't show up. This fellow is a sharp cookie as well as an Olympic medalist."

"So that's how they got the body up on the roof," I said. "They tied the rope around her neck and threw the other end over the roof, and then ran around to the other side under cover of darkness and pulled her up. But how did they attach the ropes that held her in place while the roof closed on her?"

"Perhaps they attached those before they hauled her up on the roof," Nigel said.

"Then how did they get them off the body so fast?"

"There are all sorts of quick-release knots he could have used," Joe said.

"That must be what that guy on the roof was doing," I said. "Releasing the ropes. He must have taken them with him, because there were no ropes on the body when we saw it."

"Two ropes," Grant said. "One around the torso and arms, and the other around the legs. Leave just enough slack to allow the body to fall into the opening but no farther, close the roof just enough to hold the body in place, and then release the ropes before closing it the rest of the way."

"Well, now we know how it was done," Nigel said, "but we're no closer to knowing who did it."

"Wait," I said. "How did they get the body up to the observation deck in the first place?"

"Good question," Grant said. "Joe, can you go back farther?"

"Certainly," Joe said. "How much farther?"

Grant shrugged. "Just do it. Maybe we'll see something."

The video began to run backward again. At 5:55 a.m., the body slid toward the edge of the roof and off the side and disappeared from view. Joe switched to another camera, but it was too dark to see anything.

"Try the cameras that show the elevator and the stairs," Grant suggested. "He'd have to bring the body up here one way or the other."

"There's no security camera in the stairs, sir," Joe said. "That is, if you mean the stairs behind the bar, sir."

"Okay, try the elevator."

Joe did so. But the elevator door remained stubbornly closed.

"How about the elevator on the Lido deck?" I asked. "Maybe he brought the body up to the Lido deck and then hoisted her up the stairs."

Joe did so. At a quarter to six, the elevator door opened. After about five minutes, it closed again, and remained closed thereafter. The interior of the elevator was pitch dark. Although we ran that tape back and forth several times, we saw no other movement of any kind.

Grant removed his cap and scratched his head. "It would seem that our perpetrator is an invisible man. Is there a camera that shows the interior of the pool area, including the door, the bar, and the bottom of the stairs?"

Joe switched to another camera. The bar showed up just fine, but the door into the pool area and the bottom of the stairs were in deep shadow. As he ran the video back, we saw the door into the pool area open and close, although as far as we could tell, nobody was there. Then I saw it.

A reflection in the glass door.

"There!" I said excitedly. "Right there!"

"Run it forward, Joe," Grant said. "What do you see, Doctor?"

"A head," I said. "And possibly a face. See the nose?"

"I see it," Joe said, peering at the screen, "but I can't tell who it is."

Grant leaned forward to look closer. "Whoever it is is wearing a black hood over his head. If it weren't for the reflected light from the bar, we'd never be able to see even this much." He shook his head. "But I can't tell who it is either."

"Can you e-mail that recording to Scotland Yard?" Nigel asked. "I think our forensics people could enhance it enough to identify him."

"Of course," Joe said, and Nigel gave him the e-mail address.

"This is a very savvy killer," Grant said. "Someone who knows where the cameras are and how to stay out of sight of them. Also someone with access to ropes. This whole thing was done with ropes."

"Sir," Joe said, "if I'm to e-mail all this to Scotland Yard, I'll need some help up here."

"Right," Grant agreed. "Get Meacham up here to relieve you so you can give it your full attention."

"Yes, sir."

"Where do you suppose those ropes are now?" Nigel asked Grant. "They should have DNA on them."

"Whose?" asked Grant. "The killer's or the victim's?"

"Both," Nigel said. "Or at least that guy, whoever he was. He may not even be the killer. He could be just disposing of the body for somebody else."

"The captain should know about this straightaway," Grant said.

"We'll go with you," Nigel said.

For a moment Grant looked like he might object, but then he shrugged and said, "Let's go, then."

We rode the forward elevator up to the Nav deck, where it opened into the corridor leading to the bridge crew's cabins, including the captain's. In the elevator I expressed the thought that had just occurred to me. "What about the stairs?" I asked. "There could be blood on them. Or on the railing. Couldn't there?"

"Certainly," Grant said. "But would it still be there after all of us ran up and down them a multitude of times? And then if Jamal and his mop have cleaned them in the meantime ..."

"Sounds like the stairs are a nonstarter," Nigel commented.

Grant pushed the bell button to the right of the door leading to the bridge, and First Officer David Lynch opened it. "Officer Grant! What—"

Grant wasted no time on niceties. "We need to see the captain straightaway."

Officer Lynch stepped out into the corridor and closed the door after himself. "He and his wife are in their cabin and probably asleep by now. Are you sure?"

"Quite."

"Right, then. Come this way." He led the way down the corridor that branched to the left off the main corridor, as he had done before. I took the opportunity to ask a few questions of my own. "Officer Lynch, I heard that you had a relationship with the late Leonie Montague. Is that true?"

"I'm sorry, Doctor, but I fail to see what business that is of yours," he said huffily.

"You must have been angry that she started spending so much time with the captain," I pursued.

Lynch shot me a hostile glare but didn't have a chance to answer because the captain opened his door—in pajamas and smoking jacket. "Officer Lynch? What—?"

His wife stepped out from behind him, glamorous in a black silk robe. "Darling, where are your manners? Please, do come in. May I get anyone a nightcap?"

Captain Sloane sighed. "Sarah, this is hardly the time …"

"Nonsense," she said. "It's as good a time as any. Please. Make yourselves comfortable. We were just enjoying this wonderful port wine."

"Sarah, this is not a social occasion."

His wife ignored him and handed around tiny glasses of port. "There's nothing like a nightcap on a stormy night like this," she said, and as if on cue, the ship lurched suddenly, throwing me off balance just as I was about to accept a glass from Sarah. Nigel tried to catch me but failed. I landed on my butt, and my head flew back to crash painfully into the leg of an end table. I saw stars, but it didn't knock me out. I sat up, gingerly palpating the goose egg rising on top of the lump I already had on the back of my head. When I brought my hand away, there was blood on my fingers.

If I didn't stop getting hit on the head like this, I'd end up with post-pugilistic Parkinsonism, like Muhammad Ali.

Sarah knelt on the carpet next to me. "You're bleeding!" she said. "Colin, call the doctor at once. She needs stitches." She got up, fetched a towel from the bathroom, and wrapped it around my head, tucking in the ends.

But Captain Sloane sat staring at me as if he'd seen a ghost.

"Colin!" Sarah grabbed her husband's arm and shook it. "The doctor?"

The captain came out of his trance. "Oh, yes, of course. Officer Lynch, would you …?"

"Yes, sir. Right away," Officer Lynch said and left.

"Is this what happened to Leonie?" I blurted without thinking.

A collective gasp ensued. It was then that I noticed that the coffee table had been replaced. This one didn't have the stain and the chip out of the edge that I'd noticed the last time we were in the captain's cabin. I also noticed that the carpet near one corner looked rough and matted.

I hadn't noticed that on our last visit to the captain's cabin, but perhaps it was just the angle of the light from my vantage point while sitting on the floor. Nigel reached down to help me to my feet, but I waved him off and crawled over to feel the carpet. It felt caked and stiff. I parted the fibers. They were discolored brown at the base. I looked up. Everybody seemed to be holding their breaths.

"This is blood," I said.

"It's coffee," Captain Sloane snapped.

Nigel knelt down next to me and felt of the carpet. "It's blood, all right, and someone's tried to clean it, but they didn't get it all. We're going to need to cut away this piece of carpet and send it to Scotland Yard."

Grant pulled out his radio. "I'm on it," he said.

"Where's the other coffee table?" I asked.

"What are you talking about, Dr. Day?" Captain Sloane asked. "This is the same coffee table that's always been here."

"It had a splinter," Sarah said. "Things kept catching on it. Colin's having the ship's carpenter smooth it out."

"Sarah," the captain said sotto voce, "please be quiet." I wasn't sure, but he seemed to be talking through his teeth. What was he trying to hide, and whom did he think he was fooling?

Certainly not Nigel or me. "It's probably got blood on it too," I said.

"I hope you don't think you're sending an entire coffee table to Scotland Yard," Captain Sloane said irritably.

"No need," Nigel said affably. "Just have your carpenter cut that section out and we'll send it along with the carpet."

"I don't know what you think you're going to match it to," Captain Sloane pointed out. "All your other evidence is gone."

"Not exactly," Nigel said. "The Royal Barbados Police coroner removed what was left of the body. Plenty of DNA there."

"Not to mention that your son has been extricating bits and pieces of her from various food grinders down below decks," I said.

The captain's face went pale. I hoped I wasn't sitting in his path to the bathroom should he desire to bolt in that direction. But I needn't have worried. He didn't move.

There was a knock at the door, and Sarah opened it to admit Rob.

He took one look at me with the towel wrapped around my head and said, "Toni, what have you done now?"

I told him.

"Okay," Rob said. "You're coming with me. Can you walk? I've a wheelchair outside if you need it."

"Just a minute," I objected. "We haven't told the captain what we came here to tell him. About the security tapes."

"No worries," Nigel said. "Officer Grant and I can do that. You go ahead and get yourself taken care of."

"Can't this wait?" asked Captain Sloane. "It's nearly midnight."

Sarah stood up. "Thank you all for coming," she said graciously, "but Colin does need his sleep."

We took the hint. Officer Grant said, "I'll talk to you tomorrow, Captain."

The captain nodded wearily, and we left. Out in the hall, Nigel said, "I'll let Fiona and Hal know what's going on," and he and Officer Grant went out through the double doors into the main corridor leading to our cabins. Rob put me in the wheelchair, and we took the forward elevator down to the infirmary, where Rob stitched me up while I filled him in on what we'd been doing. He was particularly interested in the captain's reaction to my injury.

"I can't believe you just came right out and asked him if that was what happened to Leonie," he said admiringly. "I should think he'd have given you all the boot."

"He might have," I said, "if Sarah hadn't been there. She was treating the whole thing like a cocktail party, and he didn't seem to be able to do anything about it."

"I have a feeling," Rob said, "that she wears the pants in that family."

"Perhaps because she's the one who has the money," I speculated. "He certainly wouldn't want to screw that up by having her find out about Leonie."

"The way you describe his reaction tells me that Leonie fell and hit her head in his cabin," Rob said. "So maybe that lady was right about her being in his cabin all along."

"She could have been," I said. "She came aboard in Fort Lauderdale."

"Do you know that for a fact?" he asked.

"I heard it from a reliable source," I told him.

"The cruise director?"

"No, a hairdresser."

"A hairdresser," Rob said skeptically.

"Yes, a hairdresser. I had a massage and facial today while everybody else went ashore, and Mavis, who did my facial, told me that. She said Leonie got a massage and facial before every show. And not only that, but Horacio, who gave me a shampoo and haircut, told me that Leonie was looking for her father, and that was why she spent so much time talking to the captain."

"Blimey, you do get around, don't you?" Rob said. "So does that mean she thought the captain was her father?"

"Not necessarily. Horacio said she talked to the captain so much because he'd known her mother and might help her find her father."

"How?" Rob demanded. "He hasn't had time."

"Maybe he has," I said. "I'm sure this isn't the first time Leonie's been on this ship. Maybe he told her who it was on a previous cruise, and this time she went to that person, and he killed her."

"That means he has to be on this ship right now. We need to ask the captain about that."

"I already did," I told him. "He said that as far as he knows, nobody who was on *Southern Cross* twenty-five years ago is on this ship right now. But that's not the problem."

"What do you mean, that's not the problem?"

"Whoever got Leonie's mother pregnant didn't do it twenty-five years ago. When she went to work as cruise director on the *Southern Cross,* Leonie, or rather, Maggie, was already four years old."

"So what ship was she on before that?"

"I have no idea. We don't know the ship, we don't know which cruise, and we don't know who we're looking for. It's like trying to grab a handful of fog. Where do we start?"

"If we postulate that the same person who fathered Leonie also killed her mother—and then killed Leonie—that person has to have been on all three ships."

"Postulate? Who are you, Socrates?"

"You know what I mean," Rob said patiently. "If we could find out who on this crew was also on the *Southern Cross*, then we could trace that person's work history back four more years, and voila!"

I sighed. "Well, there you are. There's only one person."

"I thought you said Captain Sloane told you—"

"I did," I interrupted, "but Nigel got a list from Scotland Yard of the crew of the *Southern Cross* for that cruise, and Joseph Gerard was the third engineer."

"Joseph Gerard, who is now the chief engineer?" Rob asked incredulously.

"Presumably. Unless there's more than one Joseph Gerard. And speaking of which, our chief engineer's son, Joe Junior, is one of the security guards on this ship. I met him tonight while we were watching security tapes. But it's not him. Twenty-five years ago he would have been maybe ten years old."

"Security tapes?" Rob inquired. "What were you watching security tapes for?"

"To see if we could catch whoever put Leonie in the roof."

"And did you?"

"We saw her body, and we saw the roof open and her body disappear, and we saw somebody run across the roof and do something to the body, and we saw the roof close," I explained. "And we saw somebody throw a weight with a rope attached from one side of the roof to the other, but we couldn't see who either of those people were. So now Joe Junior is in the process of sending all that video to Scotland Yard by e-mail."

"How's he going to do that and do his job too?" Rob objected. "He can't do both at once, can he?"

"No, of course not," I said. "Officer Grant told him to get somebody called Meacham to come and relieve him."

"Meacham?" Rob repeated. "You mean Bert Meacham is here? On this ship?"

"I wouldn't know," I said. "Who's Bert Meacham?"

"It may not be the same guy," Rob said, "but there's a story I've heard about a guy named Bert Meacham who went to the same maritime college that our captain did. Rumor has it that our captain caught him cheating on an exam and reported him, and he got kicked out."

"Well, that would certainly be someone with a grudge against the captain," I said.

"So," Rob continued, "he's had to work his way up from the bottom, rather like our young friend Keith, and oddly enough he always seems to turn up wherever Colin Sloane is. And now he's done it again."

"You mean this guy is stalking the captain?" I asked in disbelief.

"You can call it stalking," Rob said. "Others call it haunting. It's gotten so that whenever anything goes wrong on a cruise ship, it gets blamed on Bert Meacham."

"Like an evil spirit that haunts any ship captained by Colin Sloane," I suggested.

"Exactly."

"Which would give Captain Sloane a reputation for being a cursed captain," I said. "Nobody's going to want him to captain their ships. That could ruin his reputation."

"Except," Rob said, "that his wife's family owns this shipping line."

"If that's true," I said, "he could very well be haunting this ship. I mean, what could possibly go more wrong than a grisly murder?"

"Maybe," Rob said, "but Meacham is a common enough name. He could be a different guy altogether."

Maybe, I thought, but what were the chances? I changed the subject. "This is crazy," I said. "I'm actually beginning to think of our captain as a victim rather than a suspect. You know, maybe he really didn't remember that Joseph Gerard was on that other ship."

"So now you want to give him the benefit of the doubt?"

"Reasonable doubt," I said. "Juries are supposed to vote 'not guilty' if there's reasonable doubt. You know, I asked the captain straight out if he was the one Evelyn Hodges had an affair with, and he wouldn't answer. He said the conversation was over and walked away. He answered all my other questions, but when I asked that one, he refused to discuss it."

"So what is your conclusion?"

I shrugged. "Either he's the one, and therefore Leonie's father, or he's covering up for whoever is."

"Which doesn't necessarily make him the murderer," Rob pointed out.

"Of course not. Why would a father want to kill his daughter, and especially in such a grisly manner? The only reason I even considered that is because somebody murdered Leonie's mother twenty-five years ago. What are the chances that a mother and daughter would both get murdered on cruise ships twenty-five years apart? I thought maybe Evie confronted her lover and told him he was a father and demanded child support, or threatened to blackmail him, and that was why he killed her."

"So you think this person killed Leonie because he was afraid she'd expose him as her mother's killer?"

"I did think that," I said, "but now I'm not so sure. The captain said there was nobody from that crew on this ship except him, and Jessica said Evie never told anybody who Leonie's father was. The two murders may be completely unrelated."

"Three murders," Rob said. "Don't forget Mrs. Thingummy."

"I'm not likely to," I said with feeling. "This was fairly straightforward until she showed up."

"And now she's gone too, and we've no evidence."

"Except the pictures on my cell phone," I said, "which is also missing. Whoever knocked me out saw to that."

"This murderer," Rob said, "has been one step ahead of us from the get-go."

"I know. This has to stop."

"What are you going to do now?"

I yawned. "Get some sleep. Things might make more sense in the morning."

I hadn't noticed the pitching of the ship much from the level of A deck, but when I got off the elevator on the Nav deck seven decks above it, I found myself bouncing off the walls on my way down the corridor to our cabin. If I could have just laid myself out flat on the bed when I got there, I would have been all right. But I had to wash the blood out of my hair first, and that required me to take a seasick pill before getting in the shower, and then the running water woke up Hal.

"What are you doing?" he demanded fretfully, standing in the bathroom doorway, squinting in the light.

"Washing the blood out of my hair," I told him.

"Oh, right," he said sleepily. "Are you okay?"

"Pretty much," I replied. I turned the shower off and stepped out onto the bathmat, keeping one hand on the rail by the door to steady myself against the motion of the ship. Hal handed me my bathrobe, and I put it on. He pulled me over closer to the light and parted my hair to look at my laceration. "Nice job with the stitches. Nigel told us about the security tapes—and that you came right out and practically accused the captain of killing Leonie."

"Not exactly," I protested. "I simply asked if the same thing happened to Leonie as happened to me."

"And what did he say?"

"Nothing. He just sat there, looking as if he'd seen a ghost."

"Were you knocked unconscious?"

"No. I was bleeding, though, and Sarah told him to call the doctor, and he sent Officer Lynch to do that, and then Rob showed up and took me down to the infirmary ... oh my God."

"What?"

"I bet that's what happened when Leonie fell and fractured her skull. He called the doctor then too. Or maybe Officer Lynch did, or one of the other officers. I bet Rob came and took the body down to the morgue. I bet Leonie was right there in the cooler—that is, until somebody took her out to crush her in the roof."

"I'll bet you're right," Hal said. "Looks like our young medical officer has some explaining to do."

By the time I dried my hair and got into my pajamas and could finally climb into bed it was nearly two in the morning. It was delightful to snuggle up to Hal under the covers, listen to the rain lashing the glass doors that opened onto the veranda, and fall asleep to the rocking of the ship. But it was a very short night.

A commotion in the corridor outside our cabin woke us up while it was still dark outside.

"What the hell?" Hal said, raising himself up on his elbows.

"Only one way to find out," I said sleepily, burrowing farther under the covers.

"Easy for you to say," he grumbled. He swung his feet out of bed, went to the door, and flung it open. "What's going on out here?"

I heard Nigel say, "We've a bit of a problem." With his British tendency toward understatement, that was roughly equivalent to "Oh my God, something awful has happened! What are we going to do?"

So I got up too and stuck my head out the door. Nigel and Officer Grant stood in the corridor, Nigel in his pajamas, Officer Grant still in his uniform. "What's going on?" I asked.

"There's been another murder," Nigel said.

Wednesday | AT SEA

'Tis education forms the common mind:

Just as the twig is bent the tree's inclined.

—Samuel Pope

"Hurry and get dressed," Nigel continued. "There's no time to lose."

"What time is it?" I asked, squinting in the bright light from the overhead lights in the corridor.

"Five a.m.," Officer Grant replied.

"Who's the victim?" Hal asked.

"We don't know yet," Nigel said.

"I got a frantic call from our young physician just now," Officer Grant said, "but he didn't identify the victim."

So we got dressed, and Nigel and I accompanied Officer Grant to security, while Hal and Mum went up to the Lido deck for coffee. We were to join them up there once we'd seen what this was all about.

It didn't take a brain surgeon to see where the trouble was. Rob knelt next to someone crumpled on the floor next to an overturned chair. Was it the mysterious Meacham? I wondered. But the person wasn't dead after all; he was moaning. Dead people don't moan.

They don't bleed either. The victim's head lay in a pool of blood and continued to bleed profusely. When I got closer, I noticed that his hair was red, even where it wasn't bloody. I looked up at Rob quizzically.

"Yes, it's Joe Junior," Rob said. "We need to get him to the infirmary so I can sew him up. Dash it all, I'm going to be running out of sutures if this keeps up."

"I thought you told Officer Grant he was dead," I said.

"No, I never said that," Rob said. "What, you think I don't know whether somebody is dead or not?"

"He told us there'd been another murder."

Rob shrugged. "You must have misunderstood him. Joe's still very much alive. Unless somebody else has been murdered."

"Where's Meacham?" Officer Grant asked. "He was supposed to relieve Joe. Why isn't he here?"

We all looked at each other as if one of us was supposed to know the answer to that, but of course nobody did. "If Meacham isn't here, who called you?" I asked Rob.

"I don't know," he said. "He didn't identify himself. Before I actually got here, I wondered if it was another bogus call."

Someone knocked on the door, and Officer Grant opened it to admit a young lady in scrubs who was pushing a wheelchair. Rob straightened up, hands on hips, and sighed. "Phoebe, for God's sake, I need a gurney, not a wheelchair."

She shrugged. "Sorry, Doctor. You didn't ask for a gurney. You just said you needed to transport a patient."

Joe groaned.

"And bring an emesis basin when you come back," Rob added.

He'd just barely gotten the words out of his mouth when the patient vomited. My stomach clenched in sympathy. I knew exactly how he felt.

Phoebe did an abrupt about-face and left the room. Nigel made a face and said, "Do you need us anymore, Doctor?"

"Do you need me to help you suture?" I asked.

Rob shook his head. "Phoebe can assist me."

"I suppose someone ought to tell his dad," I suggested.

"I'll take care of that," Officer Grant said. "You folks don't need to stay. I've got to find out what happened to Meacham."

"What's Meacham's first name?" I asked suddenly.

Grant frowned. "Why do you want to know that?"

Rob came to my rescue. "I told her the story about Bert Meacham," he said.

Grant's face cleared. "Oh, that. No. This is Will Meacham."

"So," I said, "not the same guy. Rob was right."

"Who's Bert Meacham?" Nigel asked.

"I'll tell you upstairs," I said.

Hal and my mother were enjoying plates of scrambled eggs and bacon when Nigel and I got off the elevator on the Lido deck. It smelled so good that Nigel and I decided to get some too. Transporting our breakfasts from the cafeteria line in the restaurant out to the pool area was another thing entirely, as the pitching of the ship made it nearly impossible to keep our footing while balancing loaded plates and full cups of coffee. Still, we managed, mainly because Arturo came out from behind the bar to grab our plates before we dumped their contents all over the floor, which was awash in water that had sloshed out of the pool during the night.

Someone had cordoned off the pool with orange cones and caution tape and had started draining the pool. The water level had dropped considerably, although it was still high enough to slosh. Nobody would be swimming today, because it wouldn't be safe, and in any case the pool area was nearly deserted.

Hal and Mum had picked a cozy table on a raised platform right in front of the bar. It was illuminated by several tall light standards with shades shaped like dolphins and was surrounded by rattan chairs with fat cushions into which one could snuggle while contemplating the spectacle of the storm-tossed sea, its waves reflecting the dark gray sky. Besides which, it was the only place where the floor was dry. All the lights were on inside the pool area in an attempt to counteract the dinginess of the weather outside while the rain beat against the windows and the ship continued to rock and roll. "Where is everybody?" I asked as I sat down.

"I rather suspect a lot of people are seasick," Nigel said. "Young Dr. Welch will have his hands full passing out Dramamine."

"It's early," Mum said. "Not even seven o'clock yet. I expect most people are still in bed."

"I doubt anybody's going to be opening the roof today," I said.

"So who was murdered?" Hal asked.

"Nobody, as it turned out," Nigel said. "The security guard who was on duty last night was attacked, but he's very much alive."

"Reports of his demise were premature," I quipped.

"Well, that's good, isn't it?" Mum asked. "But who attacked him?"

"We don't know yet," Nigel said.

When we'd all finished eating and were enjoying our coffee, Nigel leaned back in his chair and said, "Now, what about Bert Meacham?"

"Who's Bert Meacham?" Hal asked.

"He's a ghost," I said, "who haunts cruise ships. Everything that goes wrong on a cruise ship always gets blamed on Bert Meacham."

"Including that poor girl's murder?" my mother asked.

"Probably. The thing about Bert Meacham is that he always seems to haunt ships where Colin Sloane is."

"No shit," said Hal with interest. "So he's here."

"Presumably. The story goes that Bert Meacham was in Colin Sloane's class in maritime college, and Colin Sloane caught him cheating on an exam and got him kicked out of school."

"That would tend to make someone hold a grudge," Hal said.

"So Meacham was obliged to work his way up from the bottom instead of graduating from college as a third officer, which put him in a position to mess with things and cause accidents and equipment malfunctions and such, and he always managed to get onto the same ships where Colin Sloane was part of the crew."

"So you're saying that this Bert Meacham is a real person," Hal said, "not a ghost."

"Well, Captain Sloane's been a captain for a long time," I said.

"I think Sarah said twenty-two years," Mum said.

"So by now this Bert Meacham has assumed almost mythical proportions, because he always works the night shift, and nobody ever sees him."

"Where did you hear this story, kitten?" asked Mum.

"Rob told me last night when he was sewing up my head. I was telling him that we'd been looking at security tapes and that Officer Grant had asked Joe Gerard Junior to send all the video to Scotland Yard by e-mail and to get Meacham to relieve him so he could devote all his attention to it."

"A different Meacham, I hope," Mum said.

"Yes," I said. "Officer Grant says his name is Will, not Bert."

"So when we went down to security this morning," Nigel said, "we found young Gerard suffering from a bleeding head wound and a concussion, and Meacham was nowhere to be found."

"Well, now, that's spooky," said Hal.

"It gets spookier," said a voice behind me, and I turned to see Officer Grant. "Mind if I join you?"

We all assented, and Grant sat down next to me. "What's spookier?" I asked him.

"Meacham," he replied. "We've looked everywhere. He's still nowhere to be found. Nobody's seen him. It's a real mystery."

"Surely," my mother said, "there's no shortage of hiding places on a ship this size. You must have overlooked something."

"We checked his cabin," Grant said. "His things are gone too. His roommate hasn't seen him. Of course his roommate was partying in the crew bar all night, so he's not much help. It's as if Meacham never existed."

"Maybe he jumped overboard," I said. "Of course, that would show up on security tapes, wouldn't it?"

"That's not the worst thing," Grant said. "All those tapes—or rather video files—that young Gerard was going to send to Scotland Yard are gone too."

"That means Meacham coshed him to knock him out while he made away with all those tapes," Nigel said.

"Actually, they were video files that were deleted from the computer," Grant said.

"Don't they say that deleted files are never really gone, that they're still somewhere on the hard drive if you just know how to recover them?" I suggested. "Isn't there someone in the IT department who knows how to do that?"

"That's an idea," Grant said, sounding happier. "I'll get someone on it right away."

"You might have to get someone trained in forensic computer technology," Nigel said. "You may have to send that hard drive to Scotland Yard. Of course, you'll have to do that from Fort Lauderdale."

"And by then this ship will have sailed with a whole new crew and passengers, and all the evidence with it," I said. "You can't detain a cruise ship."

"So does that mean we have two ghostly Meachams?" Mum inquired. "We've a Bert and a Will. Could they be brothers or something?"

"Could they be the same person?" Hal asked. "Maybe Meacham has a middle name that he's using on this trip."

"Well, let's see," I said. "What's Bert a nickname for? Bertram? Burton?"

"Albert," Hal suggested. "Egbert. Herbert. Norbert. Filbert."

"What's Will short for?" Mum asked. "Besides William."

"Willard," I said. "Willis. Wilton. Willoughby. Wilbraham. Wilbur."

"How about Wilbert?" Hal suggested.

"Wilbert," Nigel repeated. "Excuse me a minute. I need to check something." He rose from his chair and left.

Grant leaned back in his chair. "Looks like you folks have the Lido deck all to yourselves," he observed. "How are you handling all this rough weather?"

"As long as I take my pill, I'm fine," I said. "I'm rather enjoying it."

"I am too," Mum said. "I really feel quite safe. Is it because the ship is so big?"

"That's part of it," Grant said. "But there's a bit of engineering involved. There are stabilizing fins on the sides to counteract side-to-side rolling, and heeling tanks prevent the wind from blowing the ship over by moving water from one side to the other to keep it upright. Unfortunately, nothing can prevent the up-and-down pitching, which is what makes people seasick."

Nigel returned. "You were right," he told Hal as he sat down in the vacant chair. "This is the crew list from the *Southern Cross* twenty-five years ago when Evie Hodges was murdered. Here it is. Wilbert Meacham, Able Seaman."

Hal looked at the document Nigel held out. "Well, I'll be damned."

"Able seaman," I mused. "That means he knows what to do with ropes, doesn't it?"

"And now he's a security guard," Nigel said. "Which means he knows how to avoid security cameras."

"And nobody ever sees him," I said. "He's the invisible man."

"A perfect candidate for our murderer," Nigel said.

Grant signaled to Arturo. "What motive would Wilbert Meacham have for killing an entertainer?"

Arturo leaned over the bar and said, "Yes, sir?"

"Coffee, please," Grant said.

"Right away, sir."

"Toni's already figured that out," Hal said. "He didn't kill Leonie. He just mutilated the body."

"Dear God, why?"

Hal nodded at me. "Ask her."

Grant shifted his gaze to me. I shrugged and turned up my palms. "I just thought that if the person who killed Leonie had a motive that required a body to be found—like an inheritance, for example—it would defeat the purpose to mutilate the body beyond recognition. So maybe the body was mutilated by someone with a grudge against the killer."

At that moment Arturo brought Officer Grant's coffee. I looked up and happened to catch his eye. He averted his gaze instantly, and I wondered how much he'd heard and whether it mattered. But I didn't have time to worry about it, because after Grant signed his receipt, Arturo went back behind the bar—and hopefully out of earshot.

"Also," I went on, "we know that crushing Leonie in the roof took two people. And we also know that Meacham isn't the only person with a grudge against the captain."

"Who else has a grudge against the captain?" Grant asked.

"His son," I said. "Keith Sloane. He works in maintenance."

"You can't be serious."

"You weren't there when they found Leonie's skullcap in the food grinder," I said. "Keith was the one who found it. When the captain spoke to him I saw the expression on his face. If looks could kill, the captain would have been our next victim."

"Dear me," Mum said. "I wonder why. Maybe I should chat up Sarah about it."

"Fiona, really," Nigel said. "You're getting as bad as Toni."

"Nigel, darling, really," Mum returned, "just whom do you think she gets it from?"

Grant shook his head as if trying to disperse a cloud of gnats. "So if you think that Meacham, with help from Keith Sloane, mutilated that girl's body, then it follows that you think Captain Sloane is the murderer. Seriously?"

"I don't want to believe that," I said, "but if it was Meacham and Keith who mutilated the body, and if they did it because they have a grudge against the captain, he must be."

"But darling kitten," Mum interjected, "you don't really have any proof that this Meacham and the captain's son were the ones who mutilated the body. You only know that it took two people."

I sighed. "You're right. But I do know that Leonie sustained her head injury in the captain's cabin. That does tend to implicate the captain, wouldn't you say?"

"That would depend on who else was in the room," Nigel said. "If anyone was."

"Well, if she was assaulted by someone else in the captain's cabin, the captain would know who it was, wouldn't he?" I asked.

"Then why hasn't he said anything?" Grant demanded.

"Perhaps he's protecting someone," Hal said.

"So who would the captain want to protect?" I said. "I can only think of one person."

"His son," Hal said.

"That's the one."

Grant clutched his head in both hands, nearly dislodging his cap. "I'm going to have to talk to the captain. But what the bloody hell am I supposed to *say* to him?"

"You could simply ask him who else was in his cabin when Leonie had her accident," Nigel suggested.

"He won't give up his son that easily," Grant objected.

"You can't know that until you ask him," Nigel said practically. "Shall I go with you?"

Grant shrugged. "It probably wouldn't hurt."

Nigel turned to me. "Toni, old dear, have you any other bright ideas?"

I shook my head. "No. I do have to go talk to the doctor, though."

Nigel nodded. "Right-o. Fiona?"

"Yes, dear," Mum said. "Please extend an invitation to Sarah to join me for breakfast. That should get her out of the way so the captain can talk more freely. There might be some things he wouldn't want to say in front of her, don't you see."

"But you've already had breakfast, love."

"She doesn't have to know that. Oh, all right, then, if she's had breakfast, ask her to join me in an Irish coffee. That would be nice on a nasty day like this, don't you think?"

"Jolly good, then," Nigel said, and he and Grant departed in the direction of the stairs.

I drained my coffee cup and stood up. "I guess I'd better get busy too."

"Want me to go with you?" Hal asked.

"That might be a good idea. You can keep me from falling down and hitting my head again. Mum, are you going to stay here and wait for Sarah?"

"I may as well, kitten. If I move, nobody will know where to find me."

"True," I said, and Hal and I headed for the elevators.

As I'd predicted, the infirmary was a busy place. Phoebe was passing out seasick remedies to a patiently waiting line of passengers, and even a few crew members. Rob was nowhere in sight. A heavyset woman in a white lab coat manned the desk. She looked at us and sighed. "If you need something for seasickness, you'll have to get in line."

"We don't," I told her. "But I need to talk to Dr. Welch whenever he has a minute."

"I'll give him the message," she said. "Who are you, and where can he find you? He can talk to you when he has his break in about twenty minutes, unless he's in the middle of something."

That sounded chancy to me. I was loath to leave and perhaps not get to see Rob at all today. "Maybe I'll just wait here," I told her.

She shrugged. "Suit yourself."

"What about that security guard?" Hal said. "Is he still here? Maybe we could talk to him."

"Who would that be?" she asked.

"Joe Gerard," I said. "We were with Rob when he found him bleeding all over the floor in security. He knows us."

She glanced at her computer screen. "Yes, he's in room three. Doctor wanted to keep him here for observation, at least until he regains consciousness."

Hal and I glanced at each other, startled. "You mean he's still unconscious?" I demanded.

She nodded. "At least he was the last time we checked on him."

"But he was vomiting when we last saw him," I protested. "I thought he'd regained consciousness then."

"Well, he lost it again," she said, "because he's been unconscious since I've been on duty."

"Can people vomit when they're unconscious?" Hal asked.

"I've seen them do that," I said, "with severe head injuries. It's the cerebral edema that causes it. Rob might need to put him on a Solu-Medrol drip to reverse that."

"Sounds like a good idea," said a voice behind me, and we turned to see Rob coming out of an exam room. "Toni, what are you doing here?"

"We need to talk to you," I said.

"Privately," Hal added.

"What about?"

I glanced at the receptionist, who was following our conversation as if it were a tennis match, her piggy little eyes switching from Rob to me and back again. "The usual subject," I said.

"Also we wanted to talk to Joe Gerard," Hal said, "but apparently he's still unconscious."

"He keeps drifting in and out," Rob said. "It's not a good sign. I think he may have a subdural hematoma."

"That's not good," Hal said. "He needs a neurosurgeon."

"I know. I've notified the captain that we need to medevac him to a hospital on the mainland."

"How long will that take?" I asked.

"Several hours, I should think. I'm just hoping it's not too late for Joe. Maybe a Solu-Medrol drip will help."

"Do you have any mannitol?" I asked.

"Unfortunately, we don't," Rob said. "If we're lucky the medevac people will bring some with them."

"Mannitol?" Hal asked me sotto voce. "What's that?"

"It's an osmotic agent," I told him. "It draws edema fluid out of the brain. I remember we used to use it in the emergency room when I was an intern."

Rob glanced at his watch. "I'll have a break in about fifteen minutes. Want me to meet you somewhere? Lido deck?"

"How about the Ocean Lounge?" I asked. "It's kind of chilly up on the Lido deck today."

"Okay. See you there."

"What now?" Hal asked as we got back into the elevator. "Ocean Lounge?"

"Let's go tell Mum where we are, in case she wants to join us," I suggested.

But when we reached the Lido deck, we found it empty. Arturo informed us that my mother had left with another lady. That sounded promising, so we went back down to the Promenade deck and the Ocean Lounge. We were in luck. Mum and Sarah were already there. Mum waved at us and invited us to join them. "We're having Irish coffees," she said. "Would you like one?"

"Sounds good to me," Hal said, and Sarah signaled the bartender. He held up two fingers inquiringly. Sarah nodded. The bartender gave her a thumbs-up and got busy.

"Have you found out anything new?" Mum inquired.

"Rob thinks Joe Gerard may have a subdural hematoma," I said. "He's trying to get him medevaced to the mainland."

"Oh, yes, Colin got that call just before I left to come down here," Sarah said. "It's all arranged."

"Oh, good," I said. "I hope they get here in time."

"Is it that bad?" Sarah asked. "D'you mean to say he might not live?"

"It's possible," I said. "In any case we won't be able to get any information from him, even if he does make it."

"About that awful Meacham person, you mean," Sarah said.

"Or if he was able to e-mail any of the security footage to Scotland Yard before he was attacked," I said.

At this point the bartender—a craggy-faced Indonesian with spiked hair whose nametag bore the improbable but highly appropriate name of Boozey—brought our Irish coffees. I wondered how much he had overheard. Sarah signed the receipt. By common consent, we didn't resume our conversation until Boozey had returned to the bar.

"Security footage?" Sarah asked. "What security footage?"

"There was a reflection of a face that showed up in the glass door leading into the pool area of the Lido deck," I told her, "and Nigel thought that someone at Scotland Yard might be able to enhance it enough to identify it. But now all that footage has been deleted from the computer. We'll never know if Joe had a chance to send it to Scotland Yard before he was attacked."

"Oh dear," said Sarah. "Isn't there an IT person on board who could find deleted files? I've heard that sometimes that can be done."

"Officer Grant was going to check that out," I said. "Nigel said that if the IT people on board couldn't retrieve the files, we might have to send the entire hard drive to Scotland Yard for their forensic techs to do it."

"You'd better hope that Meacham didn't destroy that hard drive," Hal said darkly. "It could have been thrown overboard by now."

"Hal darling, please don't say that," Mum begged.

"It may be okay," I said, hit by a sudden thought. "Those files may be backed up on a main server, or maybe to the Cloud."

"Cloud? What cloud, kitten?"

"Some programs allow data to be stored in cyberspace, and they call it the Cloud. I've even got some on my own computer at home. I'm sure Officer Grant will check that out, though."

"Here comes the doctor," Mum said.

I looked up to see Rob approaching, his scrubs covered by a white lab coat. He sank into a chair with a gusty sigh and ran his fingers through his red hair until it stood on end, like Boozey's. "The helicopter's on its way, but it's probably too late," he said. "He's already starting to have decorticate posturing."

"Oh no," I said.

"What's that mean?" Hal asked.

"It means his brain swelling has damaged the cerebral cortex," I said. "Did you start the Solu-Medrol drip?"

"Of course I did," Rob said irritably. "What do you think?"

"Don't talk to my wife like that," Hal said.

"It's okay," I said. "He's exhausted. I almost hate to start asking him questions now."

"But you're not going to let a little thing like that stop you, are you?" asked my husband, who knew me so well.

Rob signaled to Boozey, who came right over. "Bloody Mary. Hold the veg."

Boozey gave him a thumbs-up and returned to the bar.

"I hate to interfere," said my mother, "but are you sure you should be drinking whilst on duty?"

Rob rubbed his eyes. "I'm not on duty right now. I'm free until five o'clock, except for checking on Joe."

"Good," I said, "because we really need to talk about Leonie."

Rob squinted at me through reddened eyes. "What about Leonie?"

"I told you what happened last night in the captain's cabin. I fell and hit my head, the captain sent for you, and you came and took me down to the infirmary."

"Yeah, so?"

"Didn't he send for you when Leonie fell and hit her head? Did you take her down to the infirmary? Did you put her in the cooler?"

"Of course. What did you think?"

"Why didn't you tell us?"

Rob threw his hands up in the air. "You didn't ask!"

I threw my hands up too. "Oh, for God's sake!"

Boozey, with Rob's Bloody Mary on a tray, took a step back. "You two gonna fight?"

Rob waved a hand negligently. "No, of course not."

After Rob had signed his receipt and Boozey had returned to the bar, I resumed my questioning. "Tell me what happened. From the beginning."

"She was still alive when I got there," Rob said. "Dave Lynch and I put her on a gurney and took her down to the infirmary."

"What time was it?"

"About quarter past five."

"What did you do?"

"I tried to assess the wound. I cleaned up as much of the blood as I could, and then I felt the depressed skull fracture. I knew this was not just a simple suture job. Then I noticed that she'd stopped bleeding."

"Dead girls don't bleed," I remarked.

"Right. So then I checked her pupils and they were fixed and dilated. No respirations, no pulse. So Dave and I put her in the cooler and left."

"What was the time of death?"

"Five thirty-five."

That couldn't be right, I thought. If she'd been crushed in the roof at five minutes after six, she would have been dead for thirty minutes. That was too long. "So what time was it when the captain called you?"

Rob thought for a few seconds. "About five."

"Then the accident must have happened about, what, ten minutes before that?"

Rob shrugged. "Probably. I don't really know."

"Was there anybody else there?"

"No. Just the captain."

"Was he upset?"

"Well, yes, a girl was bleeding and unconscious in his cabin. What do you suppose?"

I sighed. "I guess that was a stupid question. What I was trying to get at was, supposing Leonie was his daughter. Was he *that* upset?"

Sarah spoke suddenly, startling me. She'd been so quiet that I'd actually forgotten she was there, so fixed had been my attention on Rob. "Colin and I don't have a daughter, you know. Just a son."

Oh my God. I thought Mum would have brought that up by now. But maybe she didn't have any more of an idea than I did about how to broach that subject tactfully. But Sarah spoke again, saving me the trouble. "Colin, like most men, has had affairs, but as far as I know, none of them have resulted in children."

Okay, I thought, *now I know what to say.* "This would have been before you were married," I said. "Our cruise director, Jessica, grew up with Leonie. She told us that Leonie's mom had an affair with an officer on another ship where she worked as an entertainer, that she had a child, and that she went back to work as a cruise director when the child was four—and then was murdered on *that* ship."

"I don't understand," said Sarah. "What's that to do with Colin?"

"Captain Sloane was first officer on that ship," I said.

"Oh, I remember," Sarah said. "The *Southern Cross.* It happened just before it reached Southampton. They called in Scotland Yard, as I recall. We were engaged then," she added as an aside to my mother.

"The Scotland Yard detective inspector they called in was Nigel," I told her.

"Ah," said Sarah. "So that's how Colin knew him."

"And Colin never told you he had a daughter?" Mum asked Sarah.

Sarah frowned. "Never," she replied. "Maybe he didn't know, or maybe he was afraid to tell me since we were already engaged."

"But he wasn't," I protested. "I mean, not unless you were engaged for five years. When Leonie's mom worked on the *Southern Cross*, Leonie was already four years old."

Sarah's face cleared. "That must have been Colin's first ship after he graduated as a third officer: the *Seven Sisters.* I didn't even know him then."

Aha! The *Seven Sisters.* Now we had the name of the ship. I mentally filed that away to tell Nigel.

"Are you angry that he didn't tell you he had a daughter?" Mum asked her.

"I have no right to be," Sarah said.

"Why?" my mother persisted.

"Because I kept it from him that I was already pregnant when we were married."

"But surely—" Mum began.

But Sarah interrupted her. "By another man."

"You mean that Keith …"

"Is my son. Not Colin's."

Man is the only animal that blushes. Or needs to.

—Mark Twain

WELL!

That little bombshell had my head spinning. It reminded me of a joke I'd once heard where a young man chose a girl to marry, and his father said, "You can't marry her. She's your sister." So he went to his mother and she said, "It's okay. He's not your father."

All eyes were pinned on Sarah. She blushed. "I trust that stays just between us. I want to tell Colin in my own time."

"You're going to tell him, then," Mum said.

Sarah sighed. "Yes. I think it's time we got all this out in the open. Particularly now that Keith is working on ships now. I'm afraid that he's inherited his father's temper. It's something Colin will have to deal with, I'm afraid."

"So who is his father?" I asked, earning a glare from my husband and an "Antoinette!" from my mother.

"It's all right," Sarah said. "It's all going to come out anyway, but I need to tell Colin before I can tell anyone else. You do see that, don't you?"

Feeling sheepish, I allowed as how I did.

"Does he know that Keith's his son?" Mum asked.

"No," Sarah said. "If I couldn't tell Colin, I certainly couldn't tell him."

Rob glanced at his watch. "I've got to go check on my patient." He drained his Bloody Mary and departed.

Sarah looked at her watch too. "I'd better go too. Thanks for the Irish coffee. It was just what I needed, a bit of Dutch courage." She stood up.

"Are you going to tell your husband right now?" asked my mother.

Sarah sighed. "I see no reason to postpone it. Colin has a right to know who our son really is."

"And you have a right to know about his daughter," Mum said.

"I certainly do," said Sarah. She turned and walked away resolutely.

Mum stared after her. "I don't envy her, kitten."

"Me either," I said.

"Now what?" asked Hal.

I was about to answer that when I heard a clatter outside. I turned to see a helicopter approaching. "That must be the medevac," I said excitedly. "Let's go up and watch it land."

We took the elevator up to the observation deck. It had stopped raining, but the wind had not diminished. Rob was there, his white lab coat whipping about his legs. An orderly accompanied him. Joe Gerard lay on a gurney between them, covered by a blanket strapped down securely to prevent it from blowing off. He was ominously still, legs out straight, toes pointed.

The helicopter landed, but the blades kept turning. As soon as Joe was secured, it took off again. Rob stood staring after it, shaking his head. The orderly had left.

I climbed up to where he stood. "Still decorticate?"

"Nope," Rob said. "Decerebrate. It'll take a bloody miracle to save him now."

"You did the best you could," I told him.

"Tell that to our chief engineer," he said sourly. "He doesn't share your opinion. He called me a bloody quack."

"Really."

"And that's not all," Rob went on. "You'd better stay out of his way too. He said that if you'd kept your nose out of what doesn't concern you, his son wouldn't have ended up like this."

"Oh, for God's sake," I said. "He can't hold me responsible for that. *I* didn't conk him on the head."

"No, but you're the one who wanted to see the security tapes."

A thought struck me. "You know, it was Nigel who convinced Officer Grant to let us look at them. Maybe I'd better warn him."

Rob snorted. "Maybe someone ought to warn Officer Grant too. Especially if Joe doesn't make it."

My immediate inclination was to say that of course Joe would make it, but who recovers from brain damage so severe that it causes decerebrate posturing? Rob was right. It would take a bloody miracle, without which Chief Engineer Joseph Gerard would be on the warpath. So what I said instead was, "How about we talk about something else?"

We stepped down from the helipad to rejoin Hal and Mum. Rob shot me a sidelong grin. "Something like the murder, for instance?"

"Well, I didn't get a chance to ask if you saw anybody hanging around the infirmary after you put Leonie in the cooler."

"No, why?"

"If Leonie died at five thirty-five, and you put her right into the cooler, and we saw the body being put onto the roof at five fifty-five on the security tapes, that leaves less than twenty minutes between when you and Officer Lynch left the infirmary and somebody else went in and got the body out. Was anybody else in the infirmary with you besides Lynch?"

"At that hour in the morning? No way."

"Also," I continued, "the tapes showed the Lido deck elevator opening at five forty-five. That means whoever took the body had to do it within *ten* minutes after you guys left her there."

"And didn't you say that her feet were still warm when she fell onto the Lido deck?" Mum asked.

"I did," I said. "Maybe she wasn't in the cooler for even ten minutes after you left. Somebody had to be just waiting for you to leave so they could go in and get the body."

"I'm beginning to wonder," Mum began, and then she broke off and covered her eyes with her hand. "No, I can't say it. It's just too awful."

"You're wondering the same thing I am," I said. "You're wondering if Leonie was really dead when Rob put her in the cooler."

"She was," Rob insisted. "She had no pulse, she wasn't breathing, her pupils were fixed and dilated … oh God."

"Sometimes it's hard to tell," I said. "Sometimes you have to wait a long time before you give up on a pulse."

"How would you know? You're a pathologist."

"Last year I nearly did an autopsy on a lady who turned out not to be dead," I told him. "They pronounced her dead in the emergency room and sent her to the morgue. I didn't even *look* for a pulse. Why would I? The only thing that stopped me was that she grabbed hold of my apron strings. I had the scalpel in my *hand*, Rob, all ready to do the usual Y-shaped incision."

He turned and looked at me. "Toni, stop. You made that up."

I shook my head. "No, I didn't. It really happened. What I'm trying to do is tell you that nobody's perfect and you aren't alone."

Rob snorted. "Well, I sure feel alone."

"Right," I said. "You young whippersnappers think you're the only ones who ever make mistakes. Well, you're going to keep on making them, because that's how you learn. Why do you think it's called 'practicing' medicine?"

Rob looked at me in disbelief, but I went on talking before he could say anything. "I'm old enough to be your mother, and I know these things. You should listen to me." *Listen to me*, I thought. *I'm channeling my Jewish mother-in-law.*

Rob shook his head. "You aren't that much older than me. I'm thirty-five."

"Forty-eight," I told him. "But that's not the point. The point is to get over yourself and stop obsessing over this. You didn't hurt anybody. Leonie got crushed in the roof through no fault of yours. And Joe may or may not make it, but not because of anything you did wrong. So can we move on now?"

"Yes, Mother."

"What are you two plotting now?" Nigel inquired from behind us. "And could we possibly do it inside out of this wind?"

"She's giving me a pep talk," Rob said.

"What for?"

"Doctor stuff," I said. I looked around and saw that Mum and Hal had disappeared. "Where'd they go?"

"Back to the Ocean Lounge. Shall we do the same?"

Rob and I assented and the three of us took the elevator back down to the Promenade deck. Mum and Hal were waiting for us in the Ocean Lounge.

"How'd it go with the captain, lovey?" Mum asked Nigel.

"He swore that nobody was in his cabin but Leonie and himself," he said. "He said she'd had too much to drink and lost her balance. She struck her head, knocked herself out, and cut her head open, and then he called you, Rob. He said you came, and you and Officer Lynch put her on a gurney and took her away. Then he called housekeeping to come and clean up the blood on the carpet."

"That's all?" I said.

"He said he'd decided to tell her that he was her father, so he told her all about it, and they were celebrating. He'd ordered a bottle of champagne. That was why she had too much to drink."

"So he already knew she was his daughter," I said.

"Yes. He said that Evie told him about her on the *Southern Cross*. Of course, her name was Maggie then, as you know, not Leonie."

"So how'd he make the connection?"

"Leonie had talked to him before, you remember. I imagine she'd already told him her real name."

"So then what?"

"Then Sarah showed up. I thought you were going to keep her busy, Fiona. What happened?"

"Well, lovey, she confessed to us that their son Keith is her son but not the captain's, and the captain doesn't know."

Nigel's jaw literally dropped. "Are you having me on?"

"No, dear. She said she was already pregnant when she and the captain got married."

"Did she already know about Leonie?"

"No," Mum said, "but she does now, and she decided that it was time her husband knew about Keith, so she left to tell him. There really wasn't anything I could have done to keep her here, you know, short of physically restraining her."

Nigel nodded. "Yes, yes, I quite see that. I don't suppose she happened to mention who Keith's biological father is?"

"No," I said. "She said she had to tell the captain before telling anyone else."

"I suppose," Mum said thoughtfully, "that means Keith doesn't know he has a sister."

"Half sister," Hal corrected her.

"Stepsister," I said. "They aren't any blood relation at all."

"Whatever," said Mum. "What I'm getting at is how he might react when he finds out."

"You think *Keith* might have killed Leonie?" I asked. "Why should he do that?"

"Inheritance, dear. Didn't you tell me that Sarah's family is wealthy?"

"Yes, but wait," I said, confused. "Sarah is Keith's mother. Sarah is the heiress. Where's the problem?"

"Think, kitten. If Sarah outlives our captain, there's no problem. But what if she doesn't?"

"Oh." I was beginning to see. "If the captain outlives her, he inherits her fortune. Then he could have bequeathed it to his daughter, Leonie."

"Or at the very least, Keith and Leonie would have to divide it," Nigel said.

"Then why would Keith want to mutilate the body so it couldn't be identified?" Hal asked. "I thought you said—"

"I did say," I said. "I was operating under the assumption that the captain was the killer and that the body was mutilated by someone with a grudge against the captain. But if *Keith* is the killer ..."

"That goes right out the window," Nigel said.

"Exactly. So now we have to find someone with a grudge against Keith."

"So we're back to square one," Mum said. "Who would have a grudge against the captain's *son*?"

"Lots of people, I should think," Hal said. "From what you've told me, he's pissed off everybody he's worked with."

"So a lot of people in the maintenance department don't like Keith," I said, "but do any of them hate him enough to do *this*?"

"One of them might," Nigel said. "Who has to deal with all those disgruntled crew members?"

"Their boss," I said.

It is a wise father that knows his own child.

—Shakespeare, *Merchant of Venice*

"THE CHIEF ENGINEER?" Hal asked in disbelief.

"That awful man," Mum said. "I wouldn't mind at all if he turns out to be the killer."

"Me either," I said, "but would he be mad enough to mutilate the body when he knows it's his department that has to clean up the mess?"

"That's what he'd expect us to think," Nigel said. "It would detract from any motive he might have."

"Next you're going to accuse him of smashing his own son over the head in order to destroy those videotapes," Hal said.

"Well, maybe not that," I said. "We still have Meacham to deal with. I wonder if Officer Grant ever located him."

"I wonder if our chief engineer was in cahoots with Meacham to mutilate the body," Hal said.

"Oh, I hate this," I said in frustration. "We have all these questions, and we can't get to the people we need to ask them of because they're crew and off-limits to us."

"Toni, take it easy," Rob said. "I'm crew. I'm off duty. I can talk to anybody. Where do you want me to start?"

"Who brought the champagne?"

"What? What champagne?" Rob looked bewildered.

"Who brought the champagne to the captain's cabin the night Leonie was there?"

"What's that got to do with anything?"

"If there was anybody else there besides Leonie, that person might have seen who."

"The captain's room steward," Mum said. "He'd be the one to bring anything to the captain's cabin. That's his job."

"I'm on it," Rob said just as his cell phone rang, startling all of us, especially since none of us knew he carried one. He pulled it out, peered at the screen, frowned, and answered it. The conversation was brief, and the expression on Rob's face was enough to tell the story.

"Joe?" I asked.

"Yup. He didn't make it."

"Oh dear," said Mum.

"I'm so sorry," I said.

Rob started to put his phone away, but I stopped him. "Can I see your phone?"

"Certainly. Why?"

"Because I didn't know you could use cell phones out here in the middle of the ocean. What kind of phone is that?"

"It's just like yours," he said.

"You mean I could have made calls on my phone? Before it went missing, I mean."

"Well, maybe not," Rob said. "You would have to be set up for international calling, and your wireless service has to be one that has a roaming agreement with Wireless Maritime Services."

"So can Nigel use your phone to call Scotland Yard instead of going through the purser?"

"I suppose so. Do you need to do that now, Nigel?"

"I suppose I could," Nigel said. "What time is it there now?"

Rob looked at his watch. "Almost five. You'd better hurry."

Nigel fished in his shirt pocket and pulled out a slip of paper. He handed it to Rob. "You'd best dial it for me. I might push a wrong button or something."

"Okay." Rob dialed. After a few seconds he handed the phone to Nigel. "It's ringing."

Nigel took it and held it up to his ear. After a few moments he said, "Chief Superintendent Alastair Hardwick, please. Homicide. Chief Superintendent Nigel Gray here." He covered the speaker and whispered. "We're in luck. He's still there."

"Nigel, you old bastard, have I got news for you!" The current chief superintendent's voice came through loud enough that we could all hear it. Rob must have put his phone on speaker.

"Do tell," Nigel said.

"We've identified your murder victim."

"So have we," Nigel said.

"You didn't tell me that, old boy. Her fingerprints match a certain Margaret Anne Hodges, a.k.a. Leonie Montague. Does that jibe with what you found?"

"Yes," Nigel said. "Anything interesting under her fingernails?"

"Now that you mention it, yes. We found blood and tissue matching Keith Alexander Sloane."

"The captain's son?" I inquired. "What did you have to match it to?"

"Who's that?"

"My stepdaughter, Dr. Toni Day," Nigel said. "She's a pathologist. So what did you match it to?"

"That young man has been in trouble since his first year at Eton. We've had his DNA profile on record since he beat up a classmate and nearly killed him, about ten years ago."

Scotland Yard's version of Jamal, I thought. Which reminded me of the autopsy Rob and I had done on Leonie's head. "What about the handprint on her cheek?" I asked. "Did that match Keith too?"

"As a matter of fact, it did."

"Bingo!"

"That doesn't mean he's the killer," Hardwick cautioned. "It only means he slapped her and she scratched him."

"Okay," I conceded. "It's suspicious but not diagnostic."

"Spoken like a true pathologist."

"Bloody hell," Nigel said. "Ten years ago he would have been, what, twelve or thirteen?"

"Thirteen," said the chief superintendent. "Big for his age. Liked to pick on the smaller boys."

That would make Keith twenty-three now, I thought.

"A bully," Mum said.

"Who's that?" Hardwick asked.

"My wife," Nigel said. "Fiona."

"Congratulations, by the way."

"Thanks. Did you receive any video from ship's security?"

"We did. But we couldn't see anybody in it. I assume you're talking about the ones where the roof opens and closes?"

Two thumbs up for Joe, I thought. He must have done that right after we left. "Didn't you get the one with the reflection in the glass door?"

"Toni," Hal said sotto voce, "quit interrupting."

"We got it, but we can't match it to anyone."

"One more thing," Nigel said. "Do you have any records on a Wilbert Meacham?"

"Let me check." I heard the rapid clicking of a computer keyboard. Rob's phone had really good fidelity, much better than mine had. "Spell it."

Nigel did.

"No, sorry. Your boy seems to have stayed out of trouble. We've got nothing."

I guessed that cheating on an exam in maritime college didn't require police intervention. Apparently pranks aboard ship didn't either.

"What about the crew of the *Seven Sisters*?" I prompted Nigel.

"The what?"

I realized that I hadn't yet told Nigel the name of Colin Sloane's first ship. I rectified that oversight.

"You still there, Al?"

"Affirmative."

"Can you pull up the crew of the Constellation Line ship *Seven Sisters* in 1984?"

"Wish I could oblige, old boy. Those records wouldn't be digitized. If we've got records at all, they'd be on microfiche. If you're looking for something specific, I could assign someone to look for it. Or you could call the shipping line directly. They'd be more likely to have records of their crews."

"Okay, I'll do that, but in the meantime, look for Colin Sloane, Joseph Gerard, Wilbert Meacham, and Evelyn Hodges."

"Right-o. Any relation to our dead girl?"

"Her mother."

"Got it. I say, you are going to tell me someday what this is all about, aren't you?"

"Someday."

"I'll hold you to it, old boy."

"Many thanks." Nigel disconnected. "He may call back when he gets that info. Mind taking the message?"

Rob held out his hand for the phone. "No worries."

Nigel didn't give it to him. "You wouldn't happen to know how to reach the shipping line office, would you?"

Rob shook his head. "The captain probably does. Or any of the bridge officers."

Nigel gave the phone back to Rob. "Then it appears I need to visit the captain again."

A sudden gust of wind drove rain against the window. Mum shivered. "I wonder how he and Sarah are doing."

"You do realize," Nigel said gently, "that it's really none of our affair."

"On the other hand," Rob said, "I do have to notify the captain of Joe's death."

"You have to tell his father too," I said.

"I'm not looking forward to that one little bit," Rob said. "I think I'll tell the captain first. He might want to accompany me while I tell Gerard, for safety's sake. Our chief engineer might not try to kill me if there are two of us."

After he'd left, Mum laid a hand on my arm. "Was he serious, kitten?"

I was reluctant to cause my mother any more worry, and Nigel noticed, as he always did. "It's no good trying to keep it from her, you know."

"Keep what from me?"

I sighed. "Rob told me that our chief engineer called him a bloody quack."

Mum looked narrowly at me. "What else, kitten?"

It was no use. "He also said that his son wouldn't have ended up like this if I'd kept my nose out of it."

"Oh dear. And now his son is dead."

"Nonsense," Hal said. "He can't hold you responsible for that."

I disagreed. A reasonable man couldn't hold me responsible, but Chief Engineer Joseph Gerard was not necessarily a reasonable man.

"I was the one who wanted to see the security footage," I reminded him.

"Well, then he may as well blame me and Officer Grant," Nigel said. "You couldn't have seen those tapes without us."

"Do you suppose we ought to warn him?"

Nigel shook his head. "I'm sure Officer Grant is well aware of Joseph Gerard's temper. Besides, it's probably all bluster. I doubt that Gerard has ever actually attacked anyone. He wouldn't still have his position if he had."

I wasn't so sure.

From the look she gave me, neither was my mother.

Don't look back. Something might be gaining on you.

—Satchel Paige

I COULDN'T WAIT to see who showed up for dinner.

Would both the captain and his wife be there after confessing their sins to each other? Would the chief engineer blame Rob for his son's death and kill both him and the captain? Or would the chief engineer simply lie in wait somewhere to kill me for setting events in motion that led to his son's death?

But it was just past noon, and breakfast had been six hours ago, so we decided that lunch was in order. We went back up to the Lido deck and the restaurant.

After lunch my belly was full but my head was pounding. I'd had exactly three hours sleep the night before, so I decided to take a little nap; but those three Irish coffees before lunch made sleeping impossible. So I tried to read for a little while, but after reading the same page over and over again for ten minutes I gave up on that too and went back down to the Promenade deck. I didn't know where Hal and Mum and Nigel were or what they were doing, but I knew that there were computers in the library and that I could purchase Internet minutes at an exorbitant rate that would allow me to access my e-mail.

The library was quite large, with bookcases lining the walls and comfortable-looking easy chairs and couches everywhere, tastefully lit by table lamps. Computer stations surrounded the pillars that divided the room and appeared to support the ceiling. Usually the room was filled with passengers lounging around reading books or newspapers, and usually all the computer stations were occupied, but not today.

Although the lights were on, the library was completely empty, and nobody was on duty at the reception desk to assist me with purchasing minutes, so I went over to one of the computers and sat down. Instructions for logging on were attached to the top of the desk. All I needed was my cabin number and my name to access the screen for purchasing minutes—and Bob's your uncle, as my mother would have said.

I had accumulated 208 e-mails since my laptop and phone had gone missing. Many of them were advertisements from various retail catalogs and stores. There were also about two dozen Facebook friend requests from people I'd never heard of, and notifications that other friends had posted or shared something or other on Facebook or Twitter. I spent what I felt were too many of my precious minutes deleting those. Of the ones that were left, only four caught my attention.

The first one was from Pete, dated three days ago.

"Toni, what have you gotten yourself into? Those pictures were pretty gross. You guys are supposed to be on vacation. What's going on?"

Damn. I thought I'd explained myself when I sent the pictures. The next one said, "Toni, why aren't you answering my texts? Are you guys okay?"

I clicked on Reply and typed, "We're fine. Somebody stole my phone."

The next e-mail, dated two days ago, was a total surprise. "Dear Dr. Day, thank you for the excellent crime scene photos that you sent. We have duly forwarded them to Scotland Yard, as we feel that they are better equipped to deal with such a crime than we are. Best of luck in your future crime-solving endeavours. Sincerely, Marietta Gresham-St. John, MD, Coroner, Royal Barbados Police Force."

Well, how about that? The old bat finally gave me some credit for knowing what I was doing. And maybe it wasn't fair to call her an old bat either, since she probably wasn't that much older than I was.

Pete's next e-mail, dated yesterday, said, "Hal just texted me and asked me to forward those pictures to Scotland Yard. Hal never texts me. Was he serious?"

Uh-oh. Did that mean he'd never sent Scotland Yard those pictures? Thank God that Dr. Gresham-St. John had. Rapidly I typed, "Don't worry about sending those pictures if you haven't already sent them. Scotland Yard already has them."

I'd barely finished typing that, when another e-mail popped up. Pete said, "Not to worry, Toni, I sent them. You and Hal don't usually kid around about stuff like that. They should have them by now. How come you aren't answering my e-mails? Is everything all right?"

Excuse me? That didn't make any sense, I thought. Then I noticed the date and time on that e-mail, which was earlier than any of my replies. Pete and I were crossing each other in the mail. I'd probably have to wait for his actual replies to my e-mails, using up more of my precious minutes, so I quit e-mailing Pete and sent a quick reply to Dr. Gresham-St. John. "You're welcome. Did you send them any tissue for DNA matching?"

I figured that she probably wouldn't answer me right away either, so I Googled the Constellation shipping line and found that the office was located in Portsmouth, UK, and the address and phone number were provided. I wrote them down on a scrap of paper and stuffed it in my pocket. Then I went to the screen that said "Choose a ship" and typed in "Seven Sisters" What I got was a list of cruises scheduled for the coming year. I saw no screen that allowed me to bring up information on past cruises. So I went back to the original screen and found a box that said "Meet the crew" and clicked on it. That showed pictures of present crew members and a brief paragraph about each one's experience. There was no way to access past crews.

Obviously that was a dead end, so I Googled "Captain Colin Sloane" and found that he had graduated from the University of Southampton, UK, and served as a deck officer on the *Seven Sisters, Orion, Sirius,* and *Southern Cross.* The website didn't specify which deck office he'd held on each of those ships, but obviously he'd spent his entire career with the Constellation Cruise Line. He had been captain of the *Cassiopeia,* the *Andromeda,* and presently, the *North Star.* He'd married Sarah Katherine Faversham of Portsmouth, UK, in 1989. One son, Keith Alexander, was born in 1990. Informative, but really nothing of importance that I didn't already know.

So I Googled Sarah. To my surprise, she was on Facebook. Not only that, she had her own website as a breeder of racehorses. I found no pertinent information that went back beyond 2008. I sent her a friend request, just for the hell of it.

I Googled Keith Sloane. I found a number of Keith Sloans and Keith Sloanes and persons with the last name of Keith, but there was nothing specific about the particular Keith Sloane I was looking for. Surprising, considering that Scotland Yard had had him on their radar since 2003.

Perhaps his family was influential enough to get all that deleted from the Internet. I'd thought that getting anything off the Internet once it was on there was impossible. Perhaps, if Keith hadn't been in any trouble since he turned eighteen, his juvenile record had been expunged.

But no, Nigel's successor at Scotland Yard had access to Keith's juvenile record. So it hadn't been expunged. Or maybe it had, and Chief Superintendent Hardwick simply remembered Keith from back then.

It's hard to expunge things from someone's memory if they're memorable enough.

I Googled Wilbert Meacham. I found that Meacham was indeed a very common name. Wilbert was not that uncommon either. Nonetheless, I found no Wilbert Meacham, dead or alive, associated with any cruise ship.

Just for the hell of it, I tried Bert Meacham and hit pay dirt. I found him associated with all the ships of the line on which Colin Sloane had been a deck officer, *except* for the North Star. I also found an article entitled *The Legend of Bert Meacham*, which pretty much recapitulated everything Rob had told me. I wondered if he'd gotten his information from reading this article.

So then I Googled Will Meacham and found him only on the *Seven Sisters*, the *Southern Cross*, and the *North Star.*

What was going on here?

This didn't make any sense. The crew list Scotland Yard had provided to Nigel for the crew of the *Southern Cross* had a Wilbert Meacham on it.

Could there actually be *three* Meachams?

Perhaps I'd have better luck with Joseph Gerard, Senior. He'd gotten his maritime engineering degree from the City of Glasgow College Maritime Academy. His maritime record included the *Seven Sisters*,

Southern Cross, and the *North Star*, among others. The time periods coincided with those of Colin Sloane.

To my surprise, I learned that the chief engineer of a ship holds a rank equivalent to, or nearly equivalent to, the captain.

"I'll be damned," I murmured.

"Have ye found everything yer lookin' for?"

Startled, I whirled to find Chief Engineer Joseph Gerard standing right behind me, staring at my computer screen.

Uh-oh.

I cannot tell how the truth may be;

I say the tale as 'twas said to me.

—Sir Walter Scott

I LEAPED TO my feet, my heart in my mouth.

Chief Gerard's blazing blue eyes bored into mine. "Well?"

The computer chose that moment to tell me that I'd run out of minutes, saving me the trouble of logging off. But it was too late. Chief Gerard already knew I'd been Googling him.

"What d'ye think ye're doing, Doctor, looking me up on Google?"

Should I go all ashamed and apologetic and hope for mercy, or tell him the truth? It took me less than a nanosecond to make up my mind.

I stood my ground. "I'm trying to solve a murder," I said, looking him straight in the eyes. "What are *you* doing?"

Gerard took a step closer. "So you think I'm a murderer, do ye?" he said. "D'ye care tae explain why?"

He was so close that I could feel his breath on my face, but I refused to back up and let him think he was intimidating me, even though he was. "I don't know if you're a murderer or not," I told him. "It could be anybody. Who do *you* think it is?"

"I know it isna me," he said, sounding suddenly defensive, "and I'll not thank ye for snoopin' into my private affairs."

"Oh, come on, do you think you're the only one whose affairs I'm snooping into?" I demanded with false bravado. "Get over yourself, why don't you? I'm Googling *everybody*." As I said this, I threw my hands up in the air the way Hal does when he yells "Oy gevalt" to the ceiling. The gesture caused Gerard to step back, which was good because I was getting a crick in my neck from looking up into his face.

Gerard opened his mouth but didn't have a chance to say anything, because Hal chose that moment to come charging into the library, distracting Gerard and giving me a chance to stretch and rub my sore neck.

"So there you are! We were all wondering where you got to. I thought you were going to take a nap. Come on, let's go!"

"We're no' done here," Gerard growled.

"You are now," Hal informed him. He grabbed my hand and began to pull me toward the door.

"Someday he won't be there tae save ye," Gerard said very quietly, almost under his breath. My blood ran cold. Hal, seemingly oblivious, continued to pull me out the door and down the corridor so rapidly that I had to practically run to keep up. It reminded me of John Wayne dragging Maureen O'Hara the whole five miles from the train station back to Innisfree in the movie *The Quiet Man*. Furthermore, the motion of the ship made it very difficult to keep my feet under me. "What's the big rush?" I protested. "Where are we going?"

"What does it matter?" he growled. "Anywhere away from that man. He threatened you. Didn't you hear him?"

"I did, but I didn't think you did."

"Well, I did, and I'm not letting you out of my sight until this cruise is over. Furthermore, I'm going to lodge a complaint."

"With whom?"

"The captain, of course."

By this time we'd reached the Ocean Lounge, but Hal kept going, all the way to the aft elevators. He pushed the Down button.

It seemed an age before the elevator came. Hal kept glancing behind him, as if expecting the chief engineer to come charging down the corridor after us; but he didn't, and eventually the elevator arrived and we got on. Hal pushed the button for the main deck.

"Did you know," I said after the door had closed, "that the captain and the chief engineer have equivalent ranks?"

Hal looked skeptical. "You've got to be kidding."

"No, really. I saw it when I Googled him."

"So does that mean there's no point in complaining to the captain because there's nothing he can do?"

The elevator door opened onto the main deck and we got out. "I don't know," I said. "I suppose we can inquire about it, now that we're here. Maybe we should ask the purser."

"Why the purser?"

"That's who Nigel complained to when my laptop and phone were taken," I said. "He should at least be able to tell us who to talk to."

But the purser's office was closed until eight o'clock. Unless we ran into the captain at some point before that, our complaint would have to wait.

"Now what?" I asked.

Hal shrugged. "I suppose we could go back to our cabin and take a nap. We didn't get much sleep last night."

"I tried that," I told him. "It didn't work."

"Okay then, what do you suggest?"

"Let's go back to the library," I said. "Gerard should be gone by now, and I want to see if Pete answered the e-mail I sent him."

"You sent Pete an e-mail? What about?"

"He e-mailed us," I said. "He was worried because we didn't answer his e-mails and texts."

"He could have texted me," Hal objected. "I've still got a phone. I texted him about sending those pictures to Scotland Yard. Did he send them?"

"He did," I said, "and so did the coroner from Barbados."

"Did she send them any tissue from the body?"

"I don't know. I asked her that, and I'm waiting for an answer from her too."

Hal turned up a palm. "Well, then, what are we waiting for?"

When we got back to the library, Gerard was gone. I purchased some more Internet minutes, only to find that neither Pete nor Dr. Gresham-St. John had replied to my e-mails. So we went back to the Ocean Lounge, where Nigel was waiting, sprawled in a chair, eyes closed. He opened them when he heard us approach.

"Where's Mum?" I asked.

"Gone back to the cabin to take a nap. You should do the same, old girl. None of us got much sleep last night."

"I tried," I told him, "but I couldn't sleep. For that matter, why aren't *you* napping?"

He shrugged. "I couldn't sleep either. Too many things to think about."

"Well, here's something else to think about," Hal said. "That bastard Gerard just threatened Toni."

Nigel sat up straight. "You don't say. How? Where?"

At this precise moment Boozey came over to our table and asked if we wanted anything to drink. Hal ordered coffee. Nigel and I asked for hot tea.

"Now then," said Nigel after Boozey had gone back to the bar. "What about Gerard?"

"I was in the library," I said. "He caught me Googling him."

"You Googled him?" Nigel echoed. "Jolly good show, that. Why didn't I think of that?"

"You come from a different generation," Hal said. "Toni Googles everything."

"That's right." I said. "I was Googling everybody. Gerard just happened to walk in while I was Googling him. I don't blame him for being upset. I'm sure he felt violated."

"Don't you make excuses for him," Hal retorted. "He didn't need to threaten you about it."

I didn't really think Gerard was threatening me about Googling him. He was threatening me because his son had died and he held me responsible. But that wasn't the point.

"What exactly did he say?" Nigel asked.

I told him.

"Blimey," Nigel said. "What had you been talking about before that?"

"The murder. He thought that I thought he was the murderer. I told him that he was just one of many that I was Googling and that he should just get over himself."

Hal put a hand over his eyes. "Jesus, Toni. What are you trying to do, alienate everybody on this ship?"

"Hey!" I objected. "Who's alienating who here?"

"She's right," Nigel said. "Our chief engineer has cornered the market on the alienating business, it seems to me. Besides, didn't our young doctor say that Gerard was angry at Toni because his son would still be alive if she hadn't stuck her nose in?"

"So he's got two reasons to threaten me," I said.

"P'r'aps you should file a complaint," Nigel said. "An officer on a cruise ship shouldn't be allowed to go around threatening passengers."

"We tried," Hal said. "The purser was closed until eight o'clock."

"Speaking of officers," I said, "did you know that the chief engineer and the captain hold equivalent ranks?"

"I didn't," Nigel said, "but what's that to do with the subject at hand?"

"I don't know," I admitted. "Maybe nothing. But aren't you forgetting something? If you and Officer Grant hadn't made it possible for me to stick my nose in, I wouldn't have. What I mean to say is—"

"I say," said a new voice behind me, "do I hear my name being taken in vain?"

I turned to see Officer Grant. "Speak of the devil," I remarked.

"May I join you?" Grant inquired.

"Of course," Nigel said.

"Where's your lovely wife?"

"Napping," Nigel said. "We didn't get much sleep last night, as you know."

Grant nodded. "I think I got less than you did."

Boozey came back with our tea and coffee and made a great production of arranging the milk, lemon, and sugar that came with it. If he was hoping to overhear what we were talking about he was out of luck. Officer Grant ordered coffee too, and Boozey went back to the bar.

"How'd it go telling our chief engineer that his son died?" I asked.

"About how you'd expect," Grant said. "He spewed a lot of rot about you and the chief superintendent and me, saying that if we hadn't meddled, his son would still be alive, and so on. The captain told him he was relieved from duty for the rest of the day and confined to quarters. Whether he actually complied with that is anybody's guess."

"He didn't," I told him. "I was in the library on the computer just now, and he came in and caught me Googling him. He wasn't happy."

"Oh dear," said Grant. "Did he threaten you?"

"Not right then," I said. "He backed off a little when I told him I was Googling everybody, not just him."

"But then he did," Hal put in. "Right after I got there and made her leave with me. He said that I wouldn't always be there to rescue her."

"Dear me," Grant remarked. "Seems to me that you both could do with bodyguards."

"So could you," I said. "And Nigel."

"That could be arranged if necessary," Grant said. "But I can't believe that Gerard would actually harm anyone. He's all bluster. He's never been violent."

"On the other hand," I pointed out, "his son's never died before either. Who knows what his limits are now?"

Boozey came back with Officer Grant's coffee. Grant signed the ticket, and Boozey left.

"Not to change the subject or anything," Nigel said, "but have you located the mysterious Meacham?"

Grant shook his head. "Nobody's seen him since Monday night."

"And that's another thing," I said. "I Googled Wilbert Meacham and nothing came up."

"I thought Meacham was such a common name," Nigel said.

"Oh, it is," I said, "there are lots and lots of Meachams—even Wilbert Meachams—but none of them are associated with any ships."

"That's odd," Hal said.

"I thought so too. So then I Googled Bert Meacham, and I found him on the *Seven Sisters* and the *Southern Cross*, but not on this ship. I even found the story about him online, the same one Rob told me. Then I Googled Will Meacham and found him on all three ships."

Nigel looked perplexed. "But I found Wilbert Meacham on the crew list for the *Southern Cross*. How do you explain that?"

"I can't," I said. "Could there possibly be three Meachams? With two of them on the *Seven Sisters* and *Southern Cross* at the same time?"

Nigel frowned. "I suppose that's possible. On the other hand, you can't believe everything you see on the Internet. I'll be more trusting of whatever crew manifests old Hardwick comes up with."

Grant said, "Hardwick?"

"Old Scotland Yard colleague," Nigel said.

"Actually," I said, "if there are three Meachams, they were all on the *Southern Cross* at the same time."

"Did all these Meachams work in the same department at the same time?" Hal asked.

"I don't know. There wasn't that much detail."

"Oh, well," Nigel said comfortably, "the crew manifests will clear that up. There's my lovely wife. Fiona! Over here!"

"Assuming they get here in time," I muttered.

"Hello, loveys," said my mother, looking radiant and refreshed, "and Officer Grant. How nice to see you again."

"Likewise, Mrs. Gray."

"Fiona, please," Mum said.

Nigel pulled out a chair for her. Boozey came back. She ordered hot tea and handed Nigel a sheaf of papers. "The purser called and said he had a fax for you, so I went down and picked it up."

"But the purser was closed until eight," I said in bewilderment.

"I wouldn't know," my mother said. "He was open for me to come get these papers. He may be closed again now. Why did you need to see him?"

"I was going to lodge a complaint against the chief engineer," Hal told her. "He threatened Toni."

Mum gasped. "Antoinette! What did that awful man say to you?"

I told her.

She bristled. Her curly red hair fairly quivered with indignation. "Officer Grant, that man shouldn't be allowed to go around threatening passengers! What are you going to do about it?"

"The captain has already addressed that, Mrs.—Fiona. He's been relieved of duty and confined to quarters for the rest of the day."

"But he didn't stay there," I protested. "He was in the library not half an hour ago."

"You did say they hold equivalent ranks," Hal pointed out. "Maybe he doesn't have to do what the captain says if he doesn't want to."

"Is that true, kitten?" Mum asked me.

"It is according to what I read online," I said.

Grant drained his coffee and rose. "I think I'll just mention this to the captain. Cheerio!" He left, and Boozey came back with Mum's tea.

Nigel hadn't said a word throughout this discourse. He'd been perusing the papers Mum had brought him, and they were now scattered all over the table. Now he looked up. "This is a copy of the crew manifest from the *Seven Sisters* in 1984. Joseph Gerard was first mechanic. And here is Wilbert Meacham, Able Seaman."

"Who was chief engineer?" I asked.

"Why do you want to know that?"

"Just curious."

Nigel turned over a page. "Ah, here it is. William Egbert Meacham. Well, I'll be buggered."

"Could he be Wilbert Meacham's father?" Mum inquired.

"Can't rule it out. Maybe our captain knows."

"Speaking of that," I said, "who was the captain?"

Nigel turned over another page. "Keith Alexander. Why does that sound familiar?"

"Because it's our captain's son's name," I said. "He obviously named his son after his first captain. He must have had quite an influence on young Colin Sloane."

"Who was captain of the *Southern Cross*?" Hal asked.

Nigel picked up another sheaf of papers and leafed through them. "George Lynch. That sounds familiar too."

"Our first officer is David Lynch," I reminded him.

"Who was it that said nepotism was alive and well aboard the *North Star*?" Nigel mused. "Somebody said that just recently."

"I think it was Rob," I said, "when we were talking about Keith Sloane."

"Sounds to me," Hal said, "like it's alive and well throughout the Constellation Line. I wonder if there are any more connections between the Sloanes, Meachams, and Lynches."

"And Gerards," I added.

"How about Alexanders?" Mum asked. "Are there any more of those?"

Nigel picked up one of the crew manifests and began to peruse it again.

"What are you doing, lovey?" Mum asked. "One would think you'd have those memorized by now."

Hal picked up the other two crew manifests and handed one to me. "Here, we can help you look."

I was the one to find it. The third officer aboard the *North Star* was John Alexander.

"How the hell could we overlook that?" Hal demanded. "It was right under our noses all the time."

"Not really," I said. "Until we knew about Captain Keith Alexander, it wouldn't have meant anything. And how about this? Jessica's last name is Lynch. She could be related to Captain George Lynch and our first officer, David Lynch. How about that?"

"But what does it mean?" Mum asked. "Does it have anything to do with our murder?"

"Murders, you mean," I said. "Don't forget Joe Junior and Mrs. Levine."

"Oh dear," said Mum. "I'd completely forgotten about her. But how could she possibly have anything to do with the other murders? She was a passenger. The others were crew."

"Crew is everywhere," Nigel pointed out. "Any crew member could overhear anything a passenger might say. If a passenger said something to indicate that she'd seen or heard something that might implicate a crew member in some wrongdoing, and that crew member overheard it …"

"He'd want to shut that passenger up," Hal said. "For good."

"The only thing she said that I know of was that the captain was having an affair with Leonie and had to get rid of her before his wife came aboard in Barbados," I said. "She implicated the captain in Leonie's murder, which doesn't make any sense because Leonie was supposed to leave the ship in Bridgetown anyway. Sarah would never have had to know she was there."

"Unless somebody talked," Mum said. "Like Mrs. Levine."

"Well, the only person who would've had any interest in killing her would be the captain," Nigel said. "Unless his son did it and the captain's covering for him."

"Maybe the captain had an interest in killing Mrs. Levine too," Hal said.

"Then why did he wait to do it until the next day when Sarah was already aboard?" Mum asked.

"We need to talk to Jessica again," I said.

"Whatever for, kitten?" Mum asked.

"We need to know if she really is related to David Lynch," I said. "Lynch isn't that uncommon a name. It could just be coincidence."

"There are no coincidences in a murder case," Nigel said.

"What difference would it make?" Hal asked.

"Jessica and Leonie grew up together," I explained. "David Lynch and Rob grew up together. If David is Jessica's brother, that means that Leonie, Jessica, Rob and David all grew up together."

"I still don't see …" Hal began.

"Rob was engaged to Leonie," I said. "I should say, to Maggie. She broke it off and then had a relationship with David Lynch. We were speculating that the reason Leonie got a job as an entertainer aboard ship was because David Lynch pulled strings."

"Well, that makes sense," Mum said.

"Maybe, but it wouldn't have been necessary," I said, "because Jessica was her best friend, and she could have pulled strings. Isn't it part of her job to pick which entertainers she wants? Or does the shipping line decide that?"

"Ah," Nigel said, "but who got *Jessica* her job?"

Light dawned. "Her brother, of course."

"I still don't see," Hal pursued, "what any of this has to do with Leonie's murder."

"I don't either," I confessed, "but it puts four childhood friends together on the same ship for the same cruise."

Hal, sounding like a broken record, said, "I still don't see …"

"It would be quite a coincidence for that to occur without somebody prearranging it," I said, "and Nigel says there are no coincidences in a murder case."

"Kitten," my mother intervened, "are you suggesting that three childhood friends conspired to murder the fourth? To what purpose?"

"Well," I began, "Rob had a grudge against Leonie because she broke off their engagement, and a grudge against David Lynch because she took up with him next."

"Except that nobody murdered David Lynch," Nigel said.

"Where does Jessica come in?" Hal asked.

I clutched my head with both hands, wincing as my fingers encountered my various tender lumps and sutures. "I don't know. It's like trying to grasp a handful of fog. It's making my head hurt."

"You need to eat something, kitten," Mum said. "Speaking of which, isn't it getting on to dinnertime?"

I looked at my watch. "You're right. We'd better go."

The captain's table was empty, and it stayed that way all through dinner. Something was clearly going on, and none of us had any doubt that it had to do with Chief Engineer Joseph Gerard's threat.

Nonetheless, it was a bit of a shock when the Filipino maître d' ran over to our table and whispered in Nigel's ear.

Who shall decide when doctors disagree,

And soundest casuists doubt, like you and me?

—Samuel Pope

"All of us?" Nigel inquired.

"Yes, sir. In the captain's cabin. Right away!"

This created somewhat of a stir in the dining room. Everyone was staring at us as we got up from our table and filed out of the room. Luckily, the other people assigned to our table that night hadn't shown up, so we didn't have to answer any questions.

Officer Grant met us outside of the dining room. "I'm to escort you," he said with a faint smile, "even though I'm sure you know how to get there on your own."

The officer who opened the double doors at the fore end of the Nav deck wasn't familiar to me, but his name was. "Third Officer John Alexander," he said in answer to my inquiry.

I wasted no time. "Are you related to Captain Keith Alexander?"

"He was my grandfather. Why do you ask?"

"Because our captain named his son after him. He must have been quite a guy."

Alexander smiled. "Oh, he was. It was mutual, by the way. Grandad was really impressed with Captain Sloane. Couldn't say enough good things about him. He was really excited when I got this assignment right out of maritime college."

"Is he still living?"

Alexander shook his head. "No, sorry to say. He passed away a few months ago. Lung cancer."

"I'm so sorry for your loss," I said.

"Thank you." He tapped at the captain's door. The captain opened it and invited us in. He was still in his uniform, and Sarah was fully dressed also in a tropical print dress and sandals. A light cardigan was draped casually over her shoulders. How did she do that? Whenever I tried to toss a sweater casually over my shoulders it was always crooked and kept falling off.

Alexander excused himself and returned to the bridge.

The genteel cocktail party atmosphere that had been present at our last visit was gone. This was more like a business meeting in a lawyer's office. We sat around the conference table in the captain's office. Instead of the port wine and tiny glasses, a bottle of single malt Scotch sat on the table in front of the captain. I peered at the label. Laphroaig. I'd heard of it but never tasted it.

An elderly Indonesian, undoubtedly the captain's room steward, busied himself filling whisky glasses with ice and passing them around. At a gesture from the captain, he picked up the Laphroaig and began filling the glasses with two fingers' worth. I tasted it and made a face. I like Scotch, but this was way smokier than anything I'd ever tasted.

Sarah noticed. "Don't you like it, Toni?"

"It's okay," I said. "It'll just take some getting used to."

Mum put a hand over her glass when the steward reached for it. "I'm sorry, I don't care for Laphroaig. Might I have white wine instead?"

"Certainly," said Sarah. "Bong, some chardonnay for Mrs. Gray, please. There's a bottle in the refrigerator."

The steward complied, his face inscrutable.

Captain Sloane raised his glass. "A toast," he declaimed. "To truth!"

Dutifully, we all raised our glasses too and repeated, "To truth!"

Mum said, "*In vino veritas.*"

We all drank. The Laphroaig went down a little more easily the second time.

Captain Sloane put his glass down with a bang and cleared his throat. "This cruise is almost over. We've only one more day. These murders must be solved by then. Sarah and I decided that we must do everything we can to facilitate that, and to that end, we've decided to reveal the truth about everything as we know it."

Everything? Really? I was skeptical, but that's just my nature.

"I'll start," Captain Sloane continued. "When I had just graduated from maritime college, I was assigned as third officer to a ship of the line, the *Seven Sisters*. That was in 1983. I had an affair with one of the entertainers. I was not married at the time. I hadn't even met Sarah yet."

"Evie Hodges," I said.

"Quite. Five years later, I was assigned as first officer to another ship of the line, the *Southern Cross*. By that time I'd met Sarah, and we were engaged to be married. To my surprise, the cruise director on that ship was none other than Miss Hodges. She took me aside one day and informed me that we had a daughter, Maggie. I offered her monetary support, which she refused. She told me that her parents were taking care of the child and that I needn't worry; she had not told—and would not tell—anyone the identity of the father."

"Jessica told me she never did," I put in.

"I would have expected no less. Tragically, however, Miss Hodges was found dead the day we were to arrive at Southampton. Scotland Yard was called in. Nigel? Can you take it from here?"

"Everyone here knows what I'm about to say," Nigel said, "but I suppose it won't hurt to repeat it. Miss Hodges was found to have been murdered. She'd been strangled and beaten to simulate a fall down the stairs. Of course, since the ship had already sailed, it wasn't possible to investigate the murder because the evidence was gone."

"All these years, I never told Sarah about Miss Hodges," Captain Sloane said, "or Maggie. Today I told her."

Sarah put her hand over his. "He did," she confirmed, and her eyes filled with tears. "I know just how hard that was, because I had something to tell him as well." Her voice broke. "I had to tell him that our son, Keith, isn't his biological son."

"It's all right, Sarah," the captain said. "We've both shed enough tears today to float this vessel. I'm sure we'll shed more before this affair is resolved."

"I'm so ashamed," she said, sniffing. I handed her a Kleenex. "Thank you. I was already engaged to be married, and I should never have allowed myself to get into such a situation."

I opened my mouth to ask what situation, but a look from Hal stopped me.

Sarah went on. "Colin was away on a cruise ship, and some of my girlfriends wanted to go to a party." She wiped her eyes. "Nearly everyone there worked for the Constellation cruise line. My family owns it, you know. There was dancing and lots of drinking. I had too much to drink and passed out. When I woke up, I found myself in bed with Joseph Gerard."

"Oh my God," I blurted, ignoring Hal. "What did you do?"

Sarah blew her nose. "Well, first I threw up. Then I got dressed and went home. Two weeks later, I found out I was pregnant."

"Did you tell him?" my mother asked.

"I was so mortified, I didn't tell anybody. I was to be married in a month's time, and I thought I could just pretend it was Colin's." She gave a self-conscious little giggle. "It wasn't easy. Luckily Keith inherited my looks and not Joe's. I would have been hard-pressed to explain a redheaded baby."

That sounded familiar. I remembered my best friend, Jodi, telling me about something similar that had happened to her.

"Keith works in maintenance," Nigel said. "Does Gerard know he's Keith's father?"

Sarah shook her head. "Nobody outside this room knows."

"More to the point," I said, "did Keith know he had a sister?"

Captain Sloane poured more Laphroaig into his glass. He held the bottle aloft and waved it around. "Anybody need a refill?"

Nobody did. As a subject-changer, it failed miserably. Nobody was fooled.

He sighed. "He does now, more's the pity. It was a mistake to tell him. She might still be alive if I hadn't."

Both Officer Grant and Nigel snapped to attention. Officer Grant spoke first. "Captain, are you telling us that your son killed your daughter?"

"No, not intentionally," the captain said. "It was an accident, just as Dr. Day said. Miss Montague had told me several cruises ago that she was searching for her father, and we had talked about it on several occasions, but it wasn't until she told me that her real name was Maggie Hodges that I knew for sure that she was my daughter."

"Maggie Hodges isn't such an unusual name," Mum said. "Surely she told you more than that."

"Certainly. She told me that her mother had been an entertainer on one of the other ships of the line and had had an affair with an officer, and that when she, Maggie, was four years old, her mother had gone back to work as cruise director and was murdered. With that background, she had to be my daughter."

"So you told her then," Nigel said.

"No, not right away. I had to think about the ramifications, you know—like what it would do to Sarah if she knew, to say nothing of Keith."

"So when did you tell her?" I asked. "No, wait, let me guess. The night before we got to Barbados."

"Correct. Sarah was due to come aboard in Bridgetown the next day, and I envisioned some kind of happy family scenario with all four of us getting to know one another. I should have known better."

"Why?" asked Officer Grant.

"You know my son, Officer Grant. Apparently he inherited Gerard's temper. Keith always managed to spoil any family get-together he was ever involved in. I was hoping he'd get past that when he went to maritime college, but he's flunked out of six of the fifteen maritime colleges in the UK, which is why he's had to work his way up from the bottom. Now it's even worse, because he feels entitled and lets everyone he works with know it. I should have known that this would be no exception."

"So what happened?" I asked impatiently.

Hal gave me that look again. "Toni. Let the man talk."

Colin Sloane waved a hand tiredly. "It's all right, Dr. Shapiro. Leonie—Maggie—was here in my cabin after the show. I told her that she was my daughter. We hugged, she cried, I had Bong bring some champagne, and I called Gerard and had him send Keith up here. When he got here, I introduced him to his sister."

"How'd he take the news?" Grant asked.

"Not very well," the captain said. "He called her a gold digger and a slut. She slapped his face. He slapped hers, and the fight was on. She scratched his cheek and drew blood. He knocked her down and she hit her head on the coffee table and cut it open and knocked herself out."

"Oh dear," Mum murmured inadequately.

"You may well say so. Pandemonium ensued. Keith panicked, and I told him to get back to his quarters posthaste and try not to let anyone see him. I called First Officer Lynch and the doctor, who took her to the infirmary, and then Bong tried to clean the blood out of the carpet and off the coffee table. You know the rest."

"So nobody knows Keith was here except us," I said.

"Correct."

"When did the doctor call you to say that she had died?"

Captain Sloane looked perplexed. "He didn't."

"You mean you didn't know she was dead until her body was found the next morning?"

"No, actually I didn't know it was her until you and the Chief Superintendent told me the next evening."

"Really?" my mother asked. "You didn't recognize the dress she was wearing?"

"Uh, Mum? There really wasn't much left of it, and it was soaked with blood and embedded into her flesh."

Mum blanched. "Really, kitten. Was that strictly necessary?"

The captain gave a thin smile. "Sarah will tell you about my very limited fashion sense."

"It's only to be expected from someone who's worn uniforms all his life," Sarah agreed.

"So where do we go from here?" asked Officer Grant.

"To the infirmary," I said.

"Whatever for?"

"Because Rob told me that he did call the captain to tell him Leonie died," I said. "The captain says he didn't."

"Looks like our medical officer still has some explaining to do," Hal said. "Does anyone else here have a feeling of déjà vu?"

You are not permitted to kill a woman who has wronged you,

but nothing forbids you to reflect that she is growing older every minute.

You are avenged 1440 times a day.

—Ambrose Bierce

"That would explain your reaction when we told you who she was," Nigel said to Captain Sloane. "The last time you saw her alive, she was unconscious on your cabin floor and essentially uncrushed."

"That means we only have the doctor's word for it that she died when she did," I said.

"His and the first officer's," the captain said. "I called Officer Lynch right after I called the doctor. They both took her to the infirmary."

"That's not much better," I remarked. "Officer Lynch isn't medical. If Rob told him she was dead, he'd believe it even if she wasn't. If Rob asked him to help put her in the cooler, he'd do it without a second thought."

"Unless she started to regain consciousness," Hal said. "Then they wouldn't have put her in the cooler at all. They would have tried to medevac her to the mainland."

"Not the mainland," Captain Sloane said. "It's too far. Barbados is the easternmost island in the Caribbean. The eastern shore of Barbados is the Atlantic. But Bridgetown has a hospital. We could have medevaced her there."

"Like Joe Gerard," I said. "He didn't make it, and judging from the extent of Leonie's brain injury, she wouldn't have either. In fact, I can't believe she'd have regained consciousness in the first place."

"Don't people with severe brain injuries sometimes regain consciousness?" Hal asked. "I mean, you hear about a body being found in a different place from where they were attacked because they woke up and walked around? Didn't you tell me about somebody who did that in your emergency room back when you were an intern?"

"Oh God, yes," I exclaimed. "He got up off the gurney when we were all out of the room, and we looked all over and finally found his dead body in the stairwell."

"Now that's creepy," Grant declared. "Are you suggesting that they put her into the cooler while she was still alive?"

"Maybe they did," I mused. "I mean, maybe Rob thought she was dead, only she wasn't, and regained consciousness in the cooler."

My mother gasped and put her fingers to her lips. "What an absolutely horrible thought! Kitten, you can't be serious."

"As a heart attack," I said. "Imagine it. You're inside some small dark cold metal space with a locked door. What would you do?"

"Panic, of course," Hal said. "Try to get out. Bang on the door. Call for help."

"Dear God in heaven," Mum said. "I'm surely going to have nightmares tonight."

"Would that make enough noise that someone *outside* the infirmary would hear it?" Grant asked. "Because didn't the doctor tell us that he and Lynch put the body in the cooler and left?"

"I think one would have to be inside the infirmary to hear anybody banging around in the cooler," I said. "It's way down at the end of a long hallway behind a closed door."

"So if she regained consciousness before they had a chance to get out of the infirmary, they probably would have heard her?" Grant asked.

"It's possible."

"If they had, wouldn't they have gone to the rescue?"

"Depends," I said. "They would if they were innocent of any part of this mess. But we don't know that, do we?"

Captain Sloane picked up his glass, now empty, got up and went over to the bar. He put more ice in his glass, came back and filled it up with Laphroaig. At this rate, he was going to finish the bottle all by himself. "Dr. Day, are you trying to confuse us all? Isn't there anyone you *don't* suspect?"

"She suspects everybody," Hal said. "I wouldn't be surprised if she suspects all of us." His smile at me took the sting out of the words.

I smiled back. "I said it before, and I'll say it again. The only people I *know* are innocent are you, me, Mum and Nigel."

"You did say that," he acknowledged. "And we really don't know any more than we did then."

"On the contrary," Nigel said. "Now we have more suspects than we did then."

"So it's worse, not better," the captain said. "We actually know less."

Sarah yawned. "Excuse me."

Captain Sloane was instantly solicitous. "My dear, you're tired. Perhaps you should turn in."

"Maybe I should," Sarah said. "You should too, Colin. You should definitely *not* finish that drink."

The captain looked at her, and I could just hear what he was thinking. Woman, don't tell me what to do; I'm the captain here, not you. But before he could say a word, Nigel stood up. "We should all call it a night. We can resume this discussion tomorrow if we know anything more. Thank you for your hospitality, Captain, Sarah."

"You're quite welcome," Sarah said. "Fiona, will you breakfast with me tomorrow? It's our last chance."

"I'd be delighted," Mum said graciously. "But perhaps we should just have *one* Irish coffee this time."

"I couldn't agree more," Sarah said. "I've really been quite groggy all day, but the caffeine just wouldn't let me sleep."

I knew just how she felt.

Something was niggling at me, something to do with the cooler, but I couldn't quite put my finger on it. Maybe future discussions would refresh my memory. The problem was that we didn't have much future left.

"I don't know about you," Nigel said when we reached our cabins, "but I'm wide awake, and Grant is right about our running out of time, and there's a lot we need to discuss, now that we're not with the captain and Sarah."

"Okay by me," I said. "Hal?"

"Sure."

"Not me," said my mother with a yawn. "I'm going to turn in. Goodnight, loveys." She unlocked her cabin door and disappeared. I envied her. Why hadn't the caffeine affected her like it had Sarah and me? She'd actually been able to nap this afternoon and was still able to sleep now, where the rest of us who hadn't had naps were still wide awake.

"So do you want to discuss it here or go back down to the Ocean Lounge?" Hal asked.

"Let's go down," I said. "If I stay up here, I need to be sitting down or I'll get seasick."

"Take another pill," Hal suggested.

I looked at my watch. It was nearly midnight. Close enough. I went into our cabin and did just that.

If I'd had any worries about the Ocean Lounge being too busy for us to discuss anything there, they were dispelled as soon as we got there. There were only two other couples, and they were both on the other side of the room. The dance band had either taken a break or quit altogether.

We sat down, and the waiter, who was unfamiliar to me, came over to take our order.

"I for one," Hal said, "would like some decent Scotch. I didn't much care for that stuff the captain served."

Nigel and I both agreed. The waiter took our orders and went back to the bar.

Nigel pulled a notebook out of his jacket pocket. "Let's write down all our suspects and talk about each one. Maybe we can make some sense out of it that way."

"Okay," I said. "Let's start with the captain."

"I think we can eliminate the captain," Nigel said. "Now that Sarah knows about Leonie, he doesn't have any reason to have killed Leonie or Mrs. Levine."

"Not so fast," Hal said. "When Leonie and Mrs. Levine died, he still hadn't told Sarah."

"He's got a point," I said. "He doesn't have a motive now, but he did then. He had no idea how Sarah was going to take the news."

"That's true," Nigel said. "He didn't know she had a secret of her own."

"People were going around spreading rumors about Leonie spending so much time in the captain's cabin," I said, "including Mrs. Levine. Everybody thought they were having an affair. It wasn't much of a stretch to suspect the captain when Leonie's death became common knowledge."

"Do you think he killed Mrs. Levine too?" Nigel asked me.

"We can't rule it out," I said.

"Right, then," Nigel said, making a note. "The captain stays on the list. Who's next?"

"Let's keep it in the family," I suggested. "How about Keith?"

"He's the stereotypical angry young man," Nigel said. "Young, angry, and entitled. He was expected to follow in his father's footsteps as a ship captain, and he has now flunked out of six of the fifteen maritime colleges in England and Scotland. So Captain Sloane forced him to take a job on the maintenance staff, starting from the bottom."

"Which he hates," Hal said.

"So he chafes under the discipline required for his job and resents the chief engineer and everybody else he works with," Nigel continued. "According to Officer Grant, he frequently gets into fights with other personnel and openly flouts the rules. He's a constant disciplinary problem. There's not much Gerard can do about it either, and that makes him grumpy."

"Then he finds out that he has a half sister," I said. "That's got to be the last straw. He sees her as an interloper, someone with whom he has to share his parents' love and attention—and possibly his inheritance."

"He obviously wasn't thinking clearly," Hal said, "or he wouldn't be worried about his inheritance."

"The captain has confirmed that Keith attacked Leonie and knocked her down, causing her to hit her head and suffer a fatal brain injury," Nigel said.

"Unless he was lying about that," Hal said.

"I doubt that," I said. "We have forensic evidence. The handprint on her cheek matched Keith's fingerprints, and the tissue under her fingernails matched his DNA."

"That only proves that Leonie scratched his cheek and he slapped her cheek," Hal said. "It doesn't prove that it happened in the captain's cabin, or that it happened that night."

"Has anyone interviewed Bong?" I asked. "He was there the whole time we were in the captain's cabin tonight. He was probably there the whole time that night too. He probably saw the whole thing."

"Grant didn't mention it," Nigel said, "but I can't imagine that he overlooked something so obvious. I'll ask him tomorrow."

"Up until tonight, the captain's been covering for his son," Hal said. "He didn't want anyone to know that Keith was ever in his cabin. Anybody else would have been either summarily fired or put in the brig. Is there a brig on cruise ships?"

Nigel and I looked at each other and shrugged. We didn't know.

"There's got to be some place to put people when they get violent," pursued Hal. "He should put Chief Gerard there, don't you think?"

"Oh my God," I said. "If Keith reacts like that to finding out he has a sister, how's he going to react when he finds out that Captain Sloane isn't really his father?"

"Or that his boss, Chief Gerard, is," Hal said.

"Better yet," I said, "how's Gerard going to react when he finds out that his biggest problem in the maintenance department is his biological son?"

"I daresay we'll find that out tomorrow," Nigel said. "Keith has to be charged with second-degree murder at the most, manslaughter at the least."

"That's only true if the brain injury was the cause of death," I said.

"What do you mean by that?" Hal demanded. "Of course her brain injury killed her. You said so yourself."

"I know," I said. "I said her brain injury was severe enough to be the cause of death. But what if she wasn't dead when she was put into the cooler? Suppose she was still alive when she was taken out of the cooler and strangled to finish her off?"

"You didn't find any evidence of that," Hal argued.

"No, we didn't. Know why? Because her neck was crushed in the roof."

Hal stared at me, mouth open.

"I say," Nigel said. "You just might have something there, old girl. We've been struggling to figure out why the body was crushed like that. What better reason than to destroy evidence?"

"So who took her out of the cooler?" Hal asked.

"That's what's been bothering me," I exclaimed. "The cooler! There was no blood in the cooler. It had obviously been recently cleaned. It absolutely reeked of disinfectant. Rob said it got thoroughly cleaned between cruises and that there hadn't been a body in it during this cruise until Mrs. Levine."

"Why should there be blood in the cooler?" Hal asked. "Didn't Rob say she'd stopped bleeding?"

"Yes, he did, but if she regained consciousness and began yelling and struggling to get out of the cooler, don't you think it would raise her blood pressure and start her bleeding again?"

"Toni, old dear," Nigel said, "what does that do to the theory that whoever killed Leonie and whoever crushed her in the roof were two different people?"

"We've been struggling with that," I said. "We know that whoever took Leonie out of the cooler and put her in the roof had less than ten minutes to do it, but we don't know how they could be there so soon after Rob and Officer Lynch left the infirmary."

"We were going by what Rob said the time of death was," Nigel said.

"Exactly. We've been going by a lot of things Rob said. But we've already caught him in two lies. He lied about calling the captain to tell him Leonie died, and he lied about there not being a body in the cooler before Mrs. Levine. What else has he lied about?"

"Toni, you can't possibly suspect the doctor," Hal protested. "You two have been best buds through this whole thing. Why, he even loaned Nigel his cell phone to call Scotland Yard with."

"Right, then, let's discuss the doctor," Nigel said, making another note. "What do we know about the doctor?"

"He was engaged to Maggie Hodges in college," I said. "She broke up with him just before graduation. He followed her career. He kept calling her. So she takes a cruise job to get away from him. But when he gets out of medical school, he takes a cruise job to try to find her and finds out she's having an affair with the captain—or at least that's what he thinks. That's what everybody was saying."

"He stalked her, you mean," Hal said brutally. "He's a stalker, just like Robbie. If he can't have her, nobody can."

"But he's not the one who's responsible for her head injury," Nigel said.

"No, he's not. But picture this: he gets summoned to the captain's cabin in the wee hours of the morning when there's nobody around, and what does he find? The girl he loved and swore that nobody could have but himself, lying unconscious and bleeding on the floor. What a golden opportunity! Once he gets her out of the captain's cabin and into the infirmary, he can do whatever he wants to her."

"But he's not alone," Hal pointed out. "Lynch is there too."

"Right. When they get to the infirmary, he starts setting up to suture her head wound and discovers that she's stopped bleeding. He does a cursory examination, tells Lynch that she's dead, and Lynch helps him put her in the cooler. Then they leave together. That's what Rob said. But suppose they didn't? Maybe Lynch left and Rob stayed to clean up—and what should he hear but a lot of banging and yelling coming from the cooler." I waxed eloquent, gesticulating with my hands. "What to do, what to do? Should he pretend he doesn't hear anything and just leave her there? How long will it take her to die? What if she's still alive when *patients* start showing up? He can't take the chance. He opens the cooler and strangles her. Then he realizes that he's left marks on her. So now he's got to do something about *that*."

Hal applauded. "Quite a performance, sweetie. The theater's loss is our gain."

I made a mock bow. "Thank you. Thank you very much. And here's another thing. If he did all that, it would explain how he could be so blasé during the discovery of the body and the autopsy. He'd be expecting it."

"That's all very well," Nigel pointed out, "but you're forgetting something. He couldn't get her up to the observation deck and into the roof without help. Who helped him?"

"Maybe Lynch didn't leave," Hal suggested. "Maybe he helped."

"All right, let's talk about Lynch," Nigel said. "What do we know about him?"

"The only thing I thought was weird was that he showed up in the middle of the night and I wondered if he'd been sent to steal my cell phone," I said. "But Rob told me that Lynch started dating Maggie after college. She could have followed him to become a shipboard entertainer. Maybe they continued their relationship on board ship and he thought she was throwing him over for the captain because she spent so much time in the captain's cabin. And ..." I paused for effect. "He can open and close the roof."

"I seem to recall that the two of you had a rather lively discussion when he showed us to the captain's cabin after we looked at the videotapes," Nigel said. "What was that all about?"

"I took the opportunity to ask him about his relationship with Leonie," I said, "and I suggested that he must have been quite upset that she was spending so much time in the captain's cabin."

Hal put a hand over his eyes. "Toni," he said sotto voce, "tell me you didn't."

"But I did," I asserted. "He told me it was none of my business."

"Good for him," Hal muttered.

"Has anyone interviewed Lynch?" Nigel asked. "Because I haven't."

"Maybe Officer Grant did," I suggested. "You could ask him tomorrow."

"What about the ropes?" Nigel asked. "Whoever helped him had to be handy with ropes. We know it was all done with ropes because we saw it on videotape."

"Meacham?" Hal speculated.

"Maybe there isn't any Meacham," I suggested. "Maybe he's a figment of somebody's very active imagination."

"Oh, come on," Hal scoffed. "Officer Grant told Joe to have Meacham come to security to relieve him. Would he do that if Meacham was a figment?"

"He was supposed to relieve Joe so that Joe could concentrate on the security tapes from that night and morning. Joe was supposed to e-mail whatever he found to Scotland Yard, and he did that."

"What's your point, old girl?" asked Nigel.

"If Meacham came to security and realized what Joe was doing, wouldn't he have conked him on the head before he had a chance to e-mail anything?"

"Yes," said my stepfather, "that was rather the point, don't you know."

"But we know he did e-mail because your friend Hardwick said so."

"That's true, but …"

"What would be the point of knocking Joe out *after* he'd sent the tapes?"

Hal said, "Huh."

Nigel scratched his head. "You're right. That doesn't make sense."

"Suppose Joe found what he was looking for right away and e-mailed everything, and then went back to his duties without ever calling Meacham?"

"Well, then, who *did* hit Joe over the head?" Hal asked.

"Who else was present in security during Joe's shift?"

"Nobody," Nigel said, "except for the doctor."

"Bingo."

"Seriously?" Hal asked. "You expect us to believe that the *doctor* killed Joe? What for?"

"For the same reason we thought Meacham did," I said. "He was afraid someone would recognize him in the videotapes."

"But why would he attack Joe after he e-mailed the tapes?" Nigel asked. "You now have the same problem as you did with Meacham."

"Because he didn't *know* Joe had already e-mailed everything," I said. "He could have gone to security right after he finished sewing me up and done it."

"How did he know about the videotapes in the first place?" asked Hal.

"From me," I said. "While he was stitching me up, we talked about it, and that's when he told me the story of Bert Meacham. That's why we were on that Meacham wild-goose chase in the first place."

"Wild-goose chase?" Nigel echoed.

"I found the *Legend of Bert Meacham* on the Internet," I said. "It was practically word-for-word what Rob told me. He could have read it there and told it to me to cast suspicion away from himself. Don't you see? Meacham needn't be involved at all. It could be *anybody* who's handy with ropes."

"Like who?" Nigel threw up his hands in frustration. "And why has nobody seen Meacham since then?"

I shrugged. "Maybe he's shacked up with his girlfriend in her cabin. And there must be countless crew members who are handy with ropes."

Nigel clutched his head in both hands. "So you think that the doctor killed *both* Leonie and Joe."

"Think about it," I urged. "Whoever killed Joe ran away and left him there, lying on the floor. So who called the doctor?"

"Whoever showed up to relieve Joe in the morning," Hal suggested.

"But nobody else was there when we showed up. Right? I didn't see anybody else, did you, Nigel?"

Nigel shook his head.

"Joe certainly couldn't have done it. So how did Rob find out about it?"

Nigel sighed. "I see your point. He knew about it because he'd done it himself."

"It explains so many things if Rob did it," I said. "Who disposed of the evidence? Who hit me over the head in the infirmary and stole my cell phone? Who stole my laptop? We've been frustrated because the murderer seemed to always be one step ahead of us. If it's Rob, he knows everything we know."

"What about Mrs. Levine?" asked Hal. "Where does she fit into all this?"

I shrugged again. "She could have been a patient. She could have talked about the murder and the rumors and who knows what else, and Rob could have decided she knew too much and killed her and put her in the cooler."

"He would have needed help," Hal said. "She wasn't a small lady."

"He could have had any number of infirmary personnel help him," I said. "He could have told them she'd keeled over in the exam room. He could even have had them help him do CPR on her first just to make it more believable."

Nigel drained his scotch and put the glass down decisively. "It hangs together nicely, I have to admit."

"Doesn't it, though."

"There's only one problem."

"What?"

"We haven't a particle of proof for any of it."

Thursday | STILL AT SEA

But screw your courage to the sticking-place,

And we'll not fail.

—Shakespeare, *Macbeth*

When we woke up the next morning, the first thing we noticed was that the storm was still going on and hadn't diminished in force at all. Rain still battered our veranda door, and getting to the bathroom in one piece was an adventure in itself.

Packing, I reflected, was going to be problematic while being hurled from one side of the room to the other. So even though I'd already taken a seasick pill at midnight, I took another one, and I stashed yet another in my pocket for good measure.

Sarah had invited Mum to have breakfast with her in the captain's cabin, so Nigel, Hal, and I headed for the Lido restaurant. One quick foray into the pool area convinced us to eat inside the restaurant instead of out by the pool. If anything, it was darker, wetter and chillier than it had been the previous day.

There were also more people in the restaurant than there had been the previous day, so we opted not to talk about the case for fear of being overheard. Instead we talked about our preparations for going ashore the next day. We were supposed to be off the ship by seven o'clock, and we had to have our suitcases packed and outside our cabin doors before we went to bed. We had to have our purchases and receipts ready for customs. Luckily, most of our purchases came well within the $800 limit, but I was pretty sure we'd have to pay duty on my topaz earrings. The blue diamond ring I'd bought in St. Thomas was exempt, because St. Thomas was an American territory.

From the ship we'd be heading straight for the airport to fly back to Twin Falls, which required three flights—from Fort Lauderdale to Atlanta, Atlanta to Salt Lake City, and Salt Lake City to Twin Falls—and would take all day even if we managed to make all our connections. In January, the biggest obstacle was weather. Planes can take off and fly in rain or snow, but if they can't see the ground, they can't land. Both Salt Lake City and Twin Falls were prone to dense fog at this time of year.

To our surprise, when Mum joined us after breakfast, Sarah came with her. As Nigel and Hal pulled out chairs for them, both women were giggling as if they shared some joke they didn't want us to know about.

"What's so funny?" Hal asked.

They looked at each other and burst out laughing. "We're a trifle tiddly," Sarah explained.

"Mimosas," Mum added. "You know, orange juice and champagne."

"Then you should switch to coffee," Nigel said sternly, signaling to a waiter. "*Not* Irish, mind."

"So what did you three great detectives come up with last night while I was sleeping?" Mum asked.

Hal and Nigel took turns filling them in. "Toni's decided that the doctor did it," Hal said, "but my money's on Joseph Gerard."

"Keep your voice down!" I hissed, taking a quick look around. Fortunately, nearly everyone had left, and none of the stragglers were sitting anywhere near us.

"We didn't even talk about Gerard last night," Nigel reminded him. "Why didn't you say something?"

"Young Dr. Welch?" Sarah inquired in surprise. "But he's a sweetie. A right darling. He wouldn't hurt a fly."

"Gerard, on the other hand," said Hal, "threatened my wife."

"That awful man," Mum said angrily. "Nothing he did would surprise me."

"He's angry at me because I wanted to look at videotapes, and as a result his son was killed."

"Oh dear," Sarah said. "I heard about that. Colin was quite upset, and apparently Joseph didn't take the news well."

Joseph? Then I remembered that Sarah knew Gerard—in the biblical sense at least. "That's what Officer Grant said," I agreed.

"I'm afraid Joseph has always had a foul temper," Sarah said, "even as a young man. Colin has known him for decades, of course, ever since his first assignment on the *Seven Sisters*. They've always been at odds, because the young entertainer Evie Hodges was dating both Joseph and Colin. She preferred Colin, of course, and Joseph didn't like it."

"The captain told you that?" I asked. "I'm surprised he mentioned her, seeing as he kept their daughter a secret from you."

"Obviously, he didn't tell me *everything*," Sarah said, "but he did tell me about Joseph. Then when they were together on the *Southern Cross*, Joseph found out somehow that Evie had a daughter by Colin, and that really set him off. I believe he and Colin actually came to blows over it."

"Dear me," said Mum.

"Colin told me last night that Joseph threatened to tell me about Maggie, and Colin said he'd make sure Joseph would never work a cruise ship of the line ever again if he did that."

"Blimey," Nigel commented. "I'd say 'being at odds' is a bit of an understatement."

"Oh, they hate each other," Sarah said cheerfully. "It doesn't help that they now hold equivalent ranks."

I nudged Hal. "See?"

"Hmph," he replied.

"Colin says that it's very difficult to run a ship when one's worst enemy holds equivalent rank and can sabotage everything one does," Sarah continued. "Joseph probably thinks that Colin assigned Keith to maintenance just to get back at him."

"Damn," I remarked, "that sounds like Meacham."

"Bert Meacham?" Sarah inquired. "The 'gruesome twosome.' Just Colin's luck to get his two worst enemies together on the same cruise. One can only hope that it won't happen again."

"I thought Bert Meacham always showed up on every ship he captained," I said.

"That's pretty much true," Sarah said. "Meacham is the lesser of the two evils, I'd say."

"Have you told him yet that he's Keith's father?" I asked. "Gerard, I mean."

Sarah didn't answer right away, so I pressed on, disregarding the repressive looks coming my way from both Mum and Hal. "Or have you told Keith?"

"No to both," Sarah said. "I try to stay away from Joseph, and I'm afraid of Keith's reaction, so no."

"I was under the impression that Keith hates his father," I said. "Maybe if he knew, he'd be happier."

Sarah frowned. "Wherever did you get that idea?"

"When I saw him down in the food disposal, trying to get Leonie's skull cap out of the food grinder."

Mum made a face. "Antoinette, really."

I ignored her. "The way Keith looked at his father. Pure hatred."

"Keith is conflicted," Sarah explained. "All the psychiatrists I took him to agreed on that. You see, Keith craves his father's attention, but he didn't get it as a child because Colin was always off on a cruise ship. I'm afraid I spoiled him somewhat, trying to make up for it. He was given everything he ever wanted, sent to the best schools, given every possible privilege. But none of it made up for his father's love. He flunked out of countless schools. It's a wonder he ever made it to maritime college, and he flunked out of six of those. Colin finally put his foot down. No more partying, drinking, gambling, and drugs. He was put to work in the bowels of the ship in the maintenance department, and he hates that too. All the trouble he caused was the result of acting out, trying to get his father's attention. And he's still at it."

"I see," I said. "Then he finds out he has a sister, whom he thinks has taken away his father's affection, and he acts out by attacking her."

"Yes," Sarah said sadly, "and this is the end of the line, I'm afraid. Keith committed assault and battery on his sister, and she died as a result. It'll be manslaughter at the very least, and Colin put him in the brig that very night, pending trial when we get back to England."

"So there is a brig," Hal said.

"Of course there's a brig," Sarah said. "All ships have a brig. It's maritime law."

"So Keith couldn't have killed Joe Gerard or Mrs. Levine," I mused. "Speaking of Mrs. Levine, whatever happened to her body?"

"Colin arranged for her sister to take her ashore in San Juan," Sarah said. "They were going to fly her home to Miami to be buried there."

"I suppose there wasn't an autopsy," I commented, earning another glare from my mother.

"No," Sarah said. "Colin didn't mention one. Why? Should there have been one?"

"She was strangled," I said. "I found petechiae in her conjunctivae and a ligature mark around her neck."

"Colin must not have known," Sarah said. "Didn't you tell him?"

"She did," Hal said. "He was there when she found it. She showed him. She took pictures with her cell phone."

"Which was then stolen," I said. "It still hasn't turned up. Neither has my laptop."

"Dear me," said Sarah, sounding exactly like Mum. "Might I change the subject? Chief Superintendent ..."

"Nigel, please."

"Nigel, you said that you still suspect Colin in this dreadful affair. Might I ask why? Naturally I think you're dead wrong."

"Nothing would make me happier," Nigel said, "and I must say that the evidence implicates Keith much more than it does the captain. However, there are no witnesses other than your husband and your son. We have only their word to depend upon."

"Bong was there," Sarah said. "He saw the whole thing. He told me so."

"Bong is obviously a very loyal employee," Nigel murmured.

"Yes. He's been with Colin for twenty-five years, ever since the *Southern Cross*."

"You'll forgive me," Nigel said gently, "if I point out that Bong's testimony is somewhat suspect, rather like a wife testifying for her husband."

Sarah was unperturbed. "Yes, yes, I quite see that, but all the same ..."

"None of us really believe your husband is a viable suspect," Nigel assured her, "but there it is, don't you know."

We broke up shortly after that, with the excuse that we needed to return to our respective cabins and start packing and getting everything ready for disembarking. As Hal and I bounced between the walls and the bed with the pitching of the ship, laying out suitcases on the bed, emptying drawers, and retrieving toiletry articles from the bathroom, we continued to discuss the case.

"We're almost out of time," Hal said, "and there's not enough evidence to prove who did what to whom. So I guess somebody's gonna get away with murder."

"Murders," I corrected him, "and you may be right. But now that Scotland Yard is involved, surely they'll continue to investigate."

"There probably isn't anything we can do about it now anyway," Hal went on.

"Maybe there is," I said.

Hal stopped folding shirts and gave me that look he always gives me when he thinks I'm about to get myself into a dangerous situation. "Toni. I don't like the sound of that."

I ignored him. "We could set a trap. Force his hand. Or hands."

"No."

"Why not? It worked with Tyler Cabot."

"We're not dealing with Tyler Cabot. We're not in Twin Falls. We're dealing with maybe three murderers on board a cruise ship in the middle of the Caribbean in a storm."

"I bet I could get Nigel to agree."

"Not if your mother has anything to say about it."

The play's the thing
Wherein I'll catch the conscience of the King.
—Shakespeare, *Hamlet*, act 2, scene 2

"It could work," Nigel conceded.

Mum was not so agreeable. "Antoinette, I simply won't have it," she declared, hands on hips. "It's far too dangerous."

"Not if we get the captain and Officer Grant to help."

"In my humble opinion, which nobody ever listens to," Hal said with a withering glance at me, "if we don't have support from the crew, it will never work. Besides, who would you set a trap *for*? We've got, what, six suspects?"

"The captain, Keith, Rob, Gerard, Lynch, and Meacham," I recited, counting on my fingers. "We've all but eliminated the captain, and Keith has been in the brig since Bridgetown, so we've narrowed it down to four suspects."

"Oh, well, when you put it that way," Hal said, sarcasm fairly dripping from his lips, "it's as easy as pie. A child could do it."

"He's got a point, old girl," Nigel said. "It's one thing to try to catch one suspect, but four? How do you propose to accomplish that?"

"I think Hal's right," I said. "We do need to involve Officer Grant, and he can involve the captain, but I think if we have a lot of security guards around, it should be fairly safe."

"Fairly safe," my mother snarled. She slammed the lid of her suitcase shut. "*Fairly* safe? Have you all gone bonkers?"

"For this to work," Nigel said, "all the suspects have to think that each of us knows something incriminating about them but still hasn't told anybody. That way the guilty party will want to eliminate one of us to prevent our telling anybody."

Mum sat down on the bed and folded her arms across her ample bosom. "Oh, right. That sounds really safe," she said with a sniff. "Are you proposing to dangle yourself or Antoinette out there as bait? I'm telling you right now, if anything happens to either of you I'll never forgive you."

"Fiona, calm yourself," Nigel said. "The fact is that there are four suspects and four of us. Each of us will have a mission—even you. It's got to look completely innocent."

"Bollocks," said Mum. "Completely innocent, my arse."

My mother almost never swore. This was an opportunity too good to miss. "Mum, really," I said to her. "Your language!"

Nigel and Hal both burst out laughing, and even Mum produced a smile, although she strove mightily to conceal it. The tension was broken.

Officer Grant was more than happy to help us carry out our scheme. He assured us that members of his security staff could be concealed in whatever area of the ship we needed them. "But what do you each propose to do?" he asked.

"We're each going to confront one of our four suspects with the evidence we have that implicates that person, ask them to account for their whereabouts for each of the incidents, and see what happens," Nigel explained.

"Well, that's going to be a bit difficult with regard to Meacham," Grant objected. "We still haven't found him."

"Do you suppose he got off in San Juan?" I asked.

"Don't you think we would check something so obvious?" Grant responded. "He would have had to swipe his crew ID. There'd be a record."

"What if he didn't swipe his ID?" I persisted. "Could he sneak off without anybody seeing him?"

"I don't see how. There are always two people on duty at the gangway." Grant appeared to have had just about enough of this subject. "Can we please get on with something useful?"

His casual dismissal of what I thought was a perfectly legitimate question rankled, but I decided not to press it. I shrugged. "Carry on."

"We still have Gerard, Welch, and Lynch," Nigel said.

"I'll take Rob," I volunteered.

"I'll take Lynch," Nigel said. "Hal, do you think you can handle Gerard?"

"I think I can take him two falls out of three," Hal said. "It's that third fall that bothers me."

"Well, by that time," Grant said, "my men should come to your rescue."

"So where will we find them?" I asked. "I mean, we aren't allowed in crew quarters or anywhere below decks without a crew member."

"You can find Dr. Welch in the infirmary," Grant said. "That's not off limits."

Duh. I knew that. Grant didn't have to tell me that. But again I decided not to make an issue of it. "Oh, I know that," I said. "But what about the others?"

Grant thought a moment. "I can arrange to have all of them at the captain's table for dinner. It's probably best to wait until after dinner anyway, as they'll all be off duty by then. Dr. Welch will be done with evening office hours. You'll have the infirmary to yourselves after that."

"Except for the security guards that you'll conceal about the place," I reminded him.

We went our separate ways after that. Hal and Nigel went back to their respective cabins to finish packing, as the evening looked fairly busy. I went to the library and logged on to a computer to use my remaining Internet minutes. There was one more person I wanted to Google.

Everyone had finished packing by the time I got back to our cabin. Nigel proposed a visit to the Ocean Lounge, so he and Mum and Hal departed, leaving me free rein in our cabin to pack without anyone getting in my way. I asked him to let me have a look at the three ships' crew manifests, so he left them with me.

Since it was nearly five o'clock, I popped another seasick pill, as the pitching of the ship had not diminished. This must be a huge storm for us to still be in the middle of it after forty-eight hours. I finished packing, leaving out an outfit to travel in the next day. After I got the suitcases off the bed and out into the corridor, I changed into my black pants and a black sequined tunic with which I wore silver earrings and a wide silver choker. Then I curled up on the bed to peruse the crew manifests one last time.

The name I was looking for appeared on all three. How'd we miss that? Maybe we just hadn't had a reason to be looking for it—until now.

I stuffed the papers into my boat bag and went down to the Ocean Lounge.

After Boozey had taken my order, I hauled out the crew manifests and showed Nigel what I'd found.

"What are you trying to tell us?" he inquired.

"It's the same thing I've been telling you all along. The only people I don't suspect are the four of us."

"Did you Google him too?"

"Of course I did. I didn't find anything."

"Well, there you are."

"What's this all about, kitten?" my mother asked.

"Oh, nothing," I told her. "I just found somebody else that was on all three ships."

"What does it mean?" she persisted.

"I don't know."

"Kitten, I don't like it when you keep things from me."

"I don't like it either," Hal said.

Nigel intervened. "What Toni is trying to convey in her usual convoluted way is that we shouldn't trust anyone but ourselves, no matter how helpful they've been."

The captain's table was full.

Officer Grant had succeeded in his mission. Besides Captain Sloane and his wife, I recognized First Officer Lynch, Third Officer Alexander, Chief Engineer Gerard, Officer Grant himself, Rob, and a slightly built man with thinning blond hair who was unfamiliar to me.

Mum nudged me. "Kitten, who's that man sitting next to the doctor?"

"I don't know," I said. "I've never seen him before."

"That's Second Officer Bellingham," said the man across the table, "the navigation officer. He's the one who's been making all those announcements about the storm."

"Is he on all three crew manifests too?" Hal asked me teasingly.

I hauled them out of my boat bag and brandished them at him. "Why don't you look and see for yourself?"

"Children, kindly control yourselves," Nigel said reprovingly. "Toni, put those away. We don't need to be waving those about in here."

"What are those?" asked the wife of the man across the table.

"Some documents from Scotland Yard," Nigel said.

"Then why does *she* have them?" the man asked.

Nigel shrugged. "Because she has a purse and I don't."

The couple was prevented from asking any more uncomfortable questions by the arrival of the captain and Chief Gerard. Captain Sloane was all smiles, but Gerard looked like he'd bitten into an unripe persimmon.

Nigel jumped to his feet and performed introductions all around.

"Now then," said the captain, "Dr. Shapiro, Chief Gerard has finally found time for that tour of the engine room you requested. Isn't that nice?"

Hal looked bewildered. I nudged him. "Don't you remember? You asked about that at the beginning of the cruise."

Hal made a creditable recovery, although I didn't think there was any danger of him winning an Oscar anytime soon. "Oh, right. I'd forgotten all about that. Do you want to do that right now?"

Gerard shook his head. "Finish yer dinner. I'll meet ye at the main desk and we'll go from there."

"Great," Hal said. "I'll be there. Thank you."

Gerard left. Captain Sloane nodded to us and went back to his table.

As our waiter was clearing the dinner dishes preparatory to serving dessert, Officer Lynch came over to our table. "Chief Superintendent? The captain tells me you need to talk to me about an important matter. Would you accompany me to the bridge? We can talk in my cabin."

"Certainly," said Nigel. "Fiona, go ahead and have dessert. I'll see you back at the cabin."

"Very well, dear," said Mum.

"Shall we, Officer Lynch?"

And they left.

That meant it was now my turn.

I didn't have to wait long. Rob came over to our table and sat down in the chair Nigel had vacated. "Would you folks like to join me for cordials? I'm off duty."

Hal shook his head. "I've got a date with the chief engineer. I'm finally going to see the engine room."

"Terrific," Rob said. "I hear it's pretty impressive."

"You've never seen it?" I asked.

"Only through a window. Fiona? Cordials?"

"Thank you, Doctor, but I'm fair knackered. I think I'll turn in early. We have to be off the ship by seven tomorrow, you know."

"I guess that just leaves you and me," he said to me. "Shall we? I need to talk to you about something anyway."

"Okay," I said, "but let's go to the infirmary first. There's something I have to check."

"Let's go, then."

I stood up. "Hal, Mum, I'll see you later. This won't take long."

"Okay, kitten."

"Be careful, sweetie."

I waved to both of them. Officer Grant intercepted Rob and me as we moved toward the door. "You'll get there faster if you take the forward elevator." He led the way into the kitchen and pointed in the direction of the elevator.

We thanked him. It wasn't as if I'd never been on that elevator before, but Officer Grant didn't know that unless the captain had told him, and surely Rob used that elevator all the time.

Rob unlocked the door to the infirmary and let us in. "What is it you have to check?"

"I need to swab the cooler for blood," I told him. "Got a swab I can use?"

"Blood?" He frowned at me. "There's no blood in the cooler. That cooler is pristine. I cleaned it myself."

Aha, I thought. Have I caught you in another lie? "*You* cleaned it? I thought you said it was cleaned between cruises. You mean to tell me *you* did that? I thought somebody from housekeeping did that."

Rob recovered well, but I saw a blush creeping up his neck. "Oh, right, they do. I meant that I cleaned it again after Mrs. Levine was in there."

"Why? Mrs. Levine wasn't bleeding."

The blush crept higher. "It's just policy to clean it after a body's been in it, bleeding or not."

"Okay, that makes sense," I said. "We have policies like that at the hospital too. So when you cleaned it, did you get down around the edges and in the corners with a swab?"

"Well, no, I didn't go that far."

"Well, that's what I want to do," I told him. "I need a swab. Got one I can use?"

"I've got swabs, but look here," he objected. "Just whose blood is it that you're looking for?"

"Leonie's."

The blush was almost all the way up to his chin. Rob was getting angry. "Leonie wasn't bleeding either. She was dead."

"Ah, but was she?"

"What the bloody hell are you getting at, Toni?"

"Rob. Calm down. I'm not accusing you."

"The hell you're not!"

"Can we sit down and discuss this?"

Rob folded his arms across his chest defiantly. "I stay mad better standing."

I laughed. "Now you sound like me when I fight with Hal."

Rob expelled a breath and dropped his arms. "Come on, Toni. You and Hal don't fight. Do you?"

"Certainly. Because afterwards we can have make-up sex."

Rob laughed. "Let's go into my office. We can sit down there."

I hadn't known Rob had an office, although it made sense. Doctors do have offices. Rob led me around a corner into a tiny room containing only a desk, a bookcase, and an extra chair. He sat at his desk and I sat in the extra chair, which wasn't especially comfortable. He leaned back in his chair and put his feet on his desk. "Okay, Toni, say what you came to say. I'll try not to get mad."

"Good," I said, "because I wouldn't blame you if you did."

"That sounds ominous. Are you sure you're not going to accuse me?"

"Not necessarily, but it may sound that way. I'm going to propose some scenarios, and you're going to explain to me why it couldn't have happened that way."

"Okay, fire away. I promise I won't get mad."

"Let's start by supposing that Leonie wasn't really dead when you put her in the cooler."

He put his feet down and sat up straight. "Oh, come on. We've been through this before. What are you getting at?"

"Suppose she was still alive when she was taken out of the cooler and was strangled to finish her off?"

"We didn't see any evidence of that," Rob protested.

"No, we didn't. That's because her neck was crushed in the roof."

"Are you suggesting that I took her out of the cooler and strangled her? Because I didn't. How could I? Dave Lynch was here too. We left together. Just ask him."

"Nigel is doing that as we speak. One thing that's been bothering me is how anyone could have known exactly when you and Officer Lynch left the infirmary so he could go in and get the body and crush it in the roof. Well, what if it was you and Officer Lynch who took the body out of the cooler?"

"Toni, this is preposterous. Do you really think so little of me?"

"Rob, calm down. You promised you wouldn't get mad. This is all hypothetical."

"Are you sure about that? It sounds pretty accusatory to me."

"Hal and I were talking about a patient I had once in the emergency room when I was an intern. This man came in with a serious head injury. After we'd evaluated him, we called for radiology to do skull X-rays. While we were all out of the room, he regained consciousness and got up off the gurney and went wandering off. We found his dead body in the stairwell."

"So what does that have to do—"

"What if Leonie regained consciousness in the cooler?"

"She couldn't have. I'm telling you, she was dead. Ask Lynch."

"Lynch isn't medical," I said. "If you told him she was dead, why wouldn't he believe you?"

Rob put his face in his hands. "I can't fucking believe this."

"Picture it," I went on. "She wakes up in the cooler. She's imprisoned in this small, cramped, cold, metal space in the dark. She panics. She starts yelling for help and pounding on the door."

"Nobody would hear her outside of the infirmary," Rob pointed out.

"Are you sure?"

"I didn't hear anything. Neither did Lynch. Ask him. He'll tell you."

"Okay. What if you and Lynch were still in the infirmary? Or what if Lynch left and you didn't?"

"Why wouldn't I leave when Lynch did?"

"This was the girl you once wanted to marry. The girl you were engaged to who broke up with you. The girl who left you for Lynch. The girl you stalked until you ended up on the same cruise ship together. The girl who—"

"Stop!" Rob cried. "Why are you tormenting me like this?"

"Just bear with me for a little while longer. Remember, this is all hypothetical. Your job is to show me why it couldn't have happened this way."

Rob threw his hands up in the air. "I keep telling you. Just ask Lynch!"

"Don't worry. Nigel is asking him as we speak. It will be interesting to compare your answers with his."

Rob groaned.

"Here's the way I see it," I pursued. "You get called to the captain's cabin in the wee hours of the morning. You go there only to see the only girl you ever loved lying unconscious and bleeding on the floor. The girl who left you for another man. The girl who—"

Rob slapped his desk with the flat of his hand. In the cramped space of his office it sounded like a thunderclap. "You're doing it again. Cut it out, can't you?"

"Sorry," I said, although I really wasn't. I was on a roll. "As I was saying; here's the girl you loved and swore that if you couldn't have her, nobody else would either."

"I never said—"

"We're still hypothetical here, so shut up and listen. You've got a golden opportunity here. Once you take her down to the infirmary, you can do whatever you want with her, and no one's the wiser."

"Except Lynch," Rob pointed out.

"Except Lynch," I agreed. "But you could have fooled him. You could have pretended she was dead and he wouldn't have had a clue."

"Sure," Rob said, "but what for?"

"I think you really did think she was dead. You were probably glad that someone else had saved you the trouble of killing her yourself."

"Why would I want to kill her?" Rob demanded. "I loved her."

"But she didn't love you, and you didn't want anyone else to have her if you couldn't."

"You're making me sound like a stalker, and I'm not."

"Well, yes you are," I told him. "I've been there, and I know what I'm talking about. You kept track, you said. You probably kept calling her to ask her why. She took a cruise job to get away from you. So you took a cruise job too."

Rob got up and began pacing. "Toni, this is preposterous. I did no such thing! You—"

"I think you're protesting too much, but no matter. We're still hypothetical, remember. So you got here and found her hooked up with your childhood friend, Officer Lynch. Then she started spending time with the captain. So instead of holding a grudge against Lynch, you both held one against the captain."

Rob sat back down and put his face in his hands.

"See, by the time the captain called you, there was nobody else in his cabin but him and Leonie. You and Lynch both assumed the captain had assaulted her, which resulted in her severe head injury."

"Wait," Rob interrupted me. "Are you saying somebody else was in the captain's cabin when Leonie was attacked? Who?"

Of course. We hadn't talked to Rob since the captain and Sarah had made their big confession. "That's right, you don't know. It was Keith, the captain's son. He didn't take the news well that he had a sister, and they got into a fight and Keith knocked her down. The captain kicked Keith out before he called you and Lynch."

"Wow," said Rob. "I'm sure glad to hear that you don't think I did that too. So now what?"

"You were supposed to treat her—stitch her up, start an IV, get her medevaced to the closest hospital," I said. "But instead you told Lynch she was dead, and after he helped you put her in the cooler, he left."

"We both left," Rob said. "I told you."

"Quit interrupting me. You were just cleaning things up when you heard her yelling and banging around in the cooler. You went back to investigate, found her alive, and strangled her to finish her off. And then you realized you'd left a ligature mark on her neck. No way you could hide that, so you had to disfigure the body."

"Okay, suppose you're right. How the hell did I get the body up on the roof and crush it by myself?"

"You've got a point there," I admitted. "So maybe Lynch didn't leave after all. Maybe he helped you. After all, he had a grudge against the captain too. That way he couldn't have reported back to the captain that Leonie had died. See, that was one reason why I ever suspected you in the first place. You said you called the captain and told him she died, but the captain said you didn't. And apparently Lynch didn't either."

"So you'd take the captain's word but not mine."

"Not necessarily. But it's a discrepancy that hasn't been resolved. It's little things like that that can make or break a case. You also lied about not having had a body in the cooler until Mrs. Levine, but it absolutely reeked of disinfectant. It wouldn't smell like that if it hadn't been cleaned since the last cruise."

"Did it ever occur to you that it may have been cleaned after Mrs. Levine was in it?"

"No, because you didn't even know she was there until I told you, and when we went to look she was gone. Unless you were lying about that too."

"Why would I do that, pray tell?"

"Well, you could have killed her too. You know how she was, always talking and spreading rumors. Maybe she said something that you thought was incriminating for you so you killed her."

"When would I have had the opportunity?"

"She could have come in here as a patient. Maybe she had a sinus infection or something and needed antibiotics. You could have strangled her, and then you could have called a code blue, or whatever you Brits call it, and then gotten a nurse to help you put her in the cooler."

"That's ridiculous."

"I think you cleaned the cooler to get rid of Leonie's blood."

"But she wasn't bleeding. She was dead."

"You know, it bothered me that you said she died at five thirty-five, because she was still warm and dripping blood when the roof opened at seven. That's an hour and a half. She had to be alive when she was crushed in the roof. I think that when she regained consciousness in the cooler and started flailing around in there it raised her blood pressure enough for her to start bleeding again. That's why you had to clean the cooler, and that's why I want to take a swab."

"In case I missed something."

"Exactly."

"I suppose now you're going to accuse me of killing Joe Gerard too."

"It's not outside the realm of possibility that you did," I said. "Look at it from our point of view. You call Officer Grant to report a murder. We run down to security and find Joe on the floor with you bending over him. Nobody else."

Rob looked puzzled. "I didn't call Grant."

"Then how did he know about it?"

"I have no idea."

"Grant woke us up and told us there'd been another murder. He said you'd called him."

Rob shrugged and turned his palms up. "I didn't."

I looked at him narrowly. He seemed sincere, but I knew he'd lied before, so I remained suspicious. "Whatever. Joe was supposed to get Meacham to relieve him. But guess what? No Meacham. Meacham has still not been found. So if Joe didn't call Meacham, who called you?"

"Meacham called me," Rob said. "That is, I assumed it was Meacham. Then he left."

"And went where?"

"How should I know?"

"Well, since we can't find Meacham, he can't corroborate that. You could be lying about that too."

"To what purpose?"

"I told you all about watching the security tapes. I told you Joe was supposed to get Meacham to relieve him so he could e-mail the incriminating video to Scotland Yard. That's why you assumed it was Meacham who called you, because you knew he was supposed to be there. You told me the story of Bert Meacham. I found that story on the Internet, just the way you told it. You could have done that just to get us suspecting somebody who probably doesn't even exist."

"He does exist," Rob said. "I've met him."

"Oh, you've met him? On this cruise? When?"

"I did his physical, along with everybody else's in the crew."

"Okay," I conceded. "You've met him. But since we're being hypothetical here, this is the scenario I propose. You went to security right after I left you. You conked Joe over the head to disable him, and you killed Meacham. You've hidden his body somewhere, and that's why nobody's seen him. Then you notified Officer Grant when Joe's shift was over so that nobody else would find him first."

"And I did this why?"

"To prevent Joe from e-mailing incriminating video of you and Lynch crushing Leonie in the roof to Scotland Yard."

"Oh, for God's sake."

"It didn't work, you know. Scotland Yard told Nigel that they have the video that Joe sent them."

"Good for them. Are you quite finished?"

"Not quite. You see, it would explain so many things if you were the murderer. You were the one who put the evidence away. You could easily have disposed of it. You could have been hiding in the infirmary all the time we were in there looking for the evidence—and hit me on the head and stole my cell phone. You could have stolen my laptop too. You knew everything we did. You were in on the entire investigation. Remember when you said that the murderer has been one step ahead of us from the get-go?"

"I do. He has."

"Can you prove that you couldn't have done all those things?"

Rob leaned back in his chair. "Of course I can. Dave Lynch called me to the captain's cabin and was with me right up until we put Leonie in the cooler and left the infirmary. I went to my cabin and he went back to the bridge. Oh, and we both ran into Officer Grant outside the infirmary. He wanted to see the body, so I let him in and gave him the key to the cooler and then Lynch and I left."

"Oh, for heaven's sake," I exclaimed. "You couldn't have told us this before?"

Rob shrugged. "You didn't ask."

"So Officer Grant could have told us too, and he didn't."

Rob smiled. "You probably didn't ask."

"What about the night we wanted to get into the infirmary to get the evidence? You weren't there. Where were you?"

"I told you. I got a call from maintenance."

"Oh, right. But nobody knew what you were talking about when you got there."

"Correct."

"Can anybody corroborate that?"

"The captain. I called him to report it."

"Can anybody corroborate where you were? You could have called the captain from anywhere."

"How about all the people I asked about who was injured who told me they knew nothing about it?"

"Can anybody corroborate that you went to your cabin after you stitched me up and not to security?"

"Certainly. Officer Grant's cabin is right next to mine. His door was open. I said good-night to him."

"So you don't have my phone or my laptop?"

"No, I don't have your phone or your laptop," he mimicked. "How would I? I don't have keys to passenger cabins."

"What if somebody gets sick?"

"I have to get someone from housekeeping to let me in."

"But you didn't ask anyone from housekeeping to let you into my cabin?" I pursued.

"No, Toni, Goddamn it, I didn't! Now can we please stop this nonsense?"

Rob had raised his voice, and apparently it had alerted security, because the next sound I heard was a key turning in a lock and the door to the infirmary opening. "Everything okay in here?" a voice called. A burly security guard came around the corner, hand on his utility belt. I wondered if his hand concealed a gun. When he saw Rob and me sitting quietly in our chairs, not killing each other, he removed his hand. No gun. "Sorry. I thought I heard somebody yelling."

"No worries," Rob said calmly. "We were just having a discussion. It got a little lively."

"You heard us yelling from outside the infirmary?" I asked the guard.

"Yes, madam, I did."

"Would you mind assisting us in a little experiment?"

Rob looked quizzical. "Toni, what are you doing?"

"I want to know if you can hear someone yelling from inside the cooler."

The guard looked from Rob to me and back again. "Are you two having me on?"

"No," I told him. "We're dead serious. No pun intended."

"What do you want me to do?" he asked.

"You go back outside and close the door. Dr. Welch will put me in the cooler and close the door. I will yell and bang on the door. Give us thirty seconds, and then come back in."

"Okay, if you insist." The guard turned and started to walk away.

"Are you serious?" Rob demanded. "You want me to lock you in the cooler?"

"Yes. Let me yell and pound for thirty seconds, and then let me out."

"Okay, if you insist," Rob said. We went back into the morgue, and Rob and I horsed the cooler door open.

So much for our experiment.

The cooler was already occupied.

Again.

What I like about Clive

Is that he is no longer alive.

There is a great deal to be said

For being dead.

—Edmund Bentley

"WHO THE HELL is that?" I demanded.

"That," Rob said, "is Meacham."

"*That's* Meacham?" I asked in amazement. What with all the talk about the legendary Bert Meacham, I had envisioned someone like Ichabod Crane, tall and thin like a scarecrow with a sunken chest, wild black hair and deep-set eyes. The individual in the cooler was male, but there the resemblance ended. Will Meacham was no more than five foot eight and stocky, with curly sandy hair and freckles. He looked more like Andy Hardy than Ichabod Crane. Andy Hardy with a blue tongue tip protruding between puffy lips. Furthermore, he was much too young to have been on all three ships.

"What the hell's he doing here?" I demanded.

Rob turned up his palms. "Your guess is as good as mine. I'm just as surprised as you are to see him here. What? Now you think I killed him too?"

I sighed in frustration. "Damn it, Rob, how would I know?"

The burly guard came in. "Your thirty seconds are up. I didn't hear anything. Who's that?" Then he got a good look at the body. "Blimey, it's Will."

"The mysterious Meacham," I told him.

"Does Officer Grant know about this?"

"He does now," said a new voice, and Officer Grant loomed up behind the security guard. "What's Meacham doing here?"

"I don't think he's doing much of anything," Rob said, casting a disparaging glance upon the body. "I wonder what killed him."

"That's easy to figure out," I said. "What's hard is figuring out *who* killed him." As I said this, I loosened Meacham's collar and spread it wide. "Look. Ligature mark."

"He was strangled," Officer Grant said.

I pried up an eyelid. "Petechiae," I observed. I pulled down the lower lip. "More petechiae. And look at this ligature mark. What do you suppose made it?"

Grant peered at it. "A rope?" he guessed.

"Look at this pattern," I pursued. "It looks like something woven. You know, Mrs. Levine's ligature mark looked like this too."

"So you think the same person killed both of them?" Grant asked.

"Maybe," I said, "but not necessarily. All this shows is that it's a similar ligature."

"You think she was strangled with something woven?" Rob asked. "Like a piece of cloth?"

"Got a flashlight?" I inquired of Officer Grant. He shook his head, but the security guard handed me one off his utility belt. I aimed it at the ligature mark and saw something glint. "What have we here?" I mused. "Rob? Got some forceps?"

Rob opened a drawer. "These do you?"

"Perfect." I used the forceps to extract the glinting object from the folds of Meacham's neck. "This looks like metal. Something gold."

"What does that mean?" Grant demanded. "He was killed with jewelry? You think a *woman* killed him?"

"It's possible that whoever killed Mrs. Levine used her necklace to strangle her, and then again to strangle him," I said. "Because Mrs. Levine didn't have a necklace when we found her body."

"How long do you think he's been dead?" Rob asked.

I manipulated an arm. "Rigor is fully established. That takes about four hours. Maybe longer in the cooler."

"How much longer?" asked Grant.

"Hard to say," I responded. "What's more important is that rigor can last from thirty-six to forty-eight hours, and even longer in the cooler. So he could have been dead since …" I counted on my fingers. "San Juan. Maybe even St. Maarten. But he couldn't have been here in the cooler that long, because Mrs. Levine was in here until they took her ashore in San Juan."

"You can't narrow it down any more than that?" Grant asked.

"No, sorry, I can't tell you when he was killed. Only the killer knows for sure."

"I suppose you can't tell where he was killed either," Grant said.

I sighed. "No, I can't."

"He'll have to be off-loaded tomorrow in Fort Lauderdale," Rob said.

"I know that," Grant said. "What are you getting at, Doctor?"

"Maybe there'll be an autopsy. Then we'll know all that."

Grant turned and started to walk away. "Possibly."

"Officer Grant!" I said.

Grant stopped and turned back.

"How are Hal and Nigel doing, do you know?"

"I haven't a clue. No news is good news, as they say." He turned and walked away, and I didn't try to stop him. Instead, I asked Rob for a urine cup to put the metal fragment in, and I put it in my boat bag. I wasn't having any more truck with trusting evidence to the infirmary, by cracky.

Then I asked him for a swab.

"You still want to look for blood in the cooler?" he asked, as if our conversation had cleared him of complicity.

It hadn't. "Of course. Why not? If you're innocent, it shouldn't bother you."

He folded his arms. "Well, it does. Why isn't my word good enough for you?"

"We can't take anybody's word in a murder investigation," I told him. "The swab, please? And something to put it in also."

"Oh, for God's sake," he complained. "You never give up, do you?"

"Nope."

He opened a drawer. "Here they are."

"Thank you." I took one, moistened it with a drop of water, and then reached around Meacham's body to get into the edges and corners. The swab came away stained dark brown. "Yup. This is blood. See?" I showed it to Rob, who snatched it out of my hand and threw it in the trash can.

"What the hell did you do that for?" I demanded.

"I'm not going to let you do this, Toni. I've no intention of letting you ruin my reputation."

"Why would I want to ruin your reputation?" I asked. "How is this going to ruin your reputation?"

"If you intend to use that swab to prove that I killed Leonie, don't you think that would ruin my reputation?"

"All it would prove is that she was alive when she was in the cooler. It wouldn't prove you killed her."

"That's how much you know. Don't you think that the mere suggestion that I might have killed a patient will have a deleterious effect upon my reputation? Do you have any idea how hard it was to get this job? What shipping line would hire me after this? Not to mention the effect on my license. Every time I try to get a job from now on, there would have to be an inquiry."

"Rob, I think you're blowing this all out of proportion."

"I don't think so," he argued. "If you can show that Leonie was alive in there, how does that make me look? I pronounced her dead. Lynch was here when I did that. It makes me look incompetent."

"Rob ..."

"Also, I shut her up inside that cooler. It's airtight. She would have run out of oxygen eventually. That would have been murder."

"She had a depressed skull fracture and an intracranial bleed that would have killed her too. It's a toss-up which would have gotten her first, you know that."

"I know that, and you know that. But we're physicians. What do you suppose someone like Mrs. Levine would have made out of it?"

"I shudder to think. But look, Rob, Nigel saw it too, remember? He was here when we did the autopsy on the head. Nobody is going to question you for pronouncing her dead."

"Not unless somebody talks."

There was a threatening quality in his tone that made the hair rise on the back of my neck. Surreptitiously, I began to sidle toward the door. But it was too late. He turned and saw me. "Oh no you don't." He reached out to grab my arm, but I was too fast for him. I raced out of the morgue and got as far as the infirmary waiting area.

Rob caught up with me just as I reached the door, with a most un-Richie-Cunningham-like look on his face. "Damn you, get back here. I wasn't kidding, Toni. I'm not done with you yet." He grabbed my arm and began to drag me back into the main patient area. I struggled and tried to pry his fingers off my arm, and he hit me.

He clouted me so hard on the jaw that I fell to the floor. Then he bent over me. "Toni, I'm so sorry. I didn't mean to do that. Are you all right?"

I looked up at him in disbelief. "No, Goddamn it, I'm not all right. What the hell do you think you're doing? I think you broke my jaw."

"I don't think so. You wouldn't be talking if I had. I'm so sorry, Toni. Here, let me help you up." He reached down to take my hand and haul me to my feet, but I wasn't having any truck with that. I doubled up and kicked him in the crotch with both feet.

He howled in pain and doubled over. "Goddamn you, you bitch."

I scrambled to my feet and ran as if the devil himself were after me. I yanked the door open and ran out into the corridor, yelling for Officer Grant as I went. Where the hell were all those security guards who were supposed to be concealed within the infirmary to protect me? I was going to have a few choice words for Officer Grant whenever I saw him next.

I ran down the corridor to the security department where a security guard had just come out into the corridor. He caught me by the shoulders. "Here, here, what's all this?"

"Help me," I gasped. Behind me I heard running footsteps, and I looked back to see Rob coming down the corridor after me. He was limping. "Please," I pleaded. "Don't let him hurt me."

The security guard let go of me. "Madam, you shouldn't be down here at this hour."

I recognized him as Hodges, one of the guards who had been outside the doors to the Lido pool area the day we discovered Leonie's body.

"You don't understand," I protested. "Dr. Welch shouldn't be trying to kill me either, but he is."

At this point Rob came up to us, panting. The guard held up a restraining hand. "Hold it right there, Doctor."

"It's all right, Hodges," Rob told him. "Dr. Day and I were just having a little disagreement, that's all."

Little disagreement, my ass. I opened my mouth to object, but Hodges beat me to it.

"No, Doctor. We saw the whole thing on the security cameras. You hit the lady. We've already reported it to the captain."

"I've already apologized for that," Rob protested. "She kicked me in the crotch. Did you see *that* on your security cameras?"

"We did, sir. And I can't say as I blame the lady."

Rob turned to me, looking like Richie Cunningham again. "Toni, please, forgive me. Please don't file a complaint. It'll ruin me. Come back to the infirmary with me and I'll give you an ice pack for that bruise."

I shook my head. "No, Rob. I'm sorry. I know now why Leonie left you. You're an abuser."

Rob reached out toward me, and I backed up. Hodges restrained him. "No, sir, leave the lady alone."

Rob dropped his arm. "Toni, you don't understand."

"I understand all too well, Rob. This isn't my first rodeo." Both Rob and Hodges looked mystified at that, and I hastened to explain. "My first boyfriend was an abuser. I nearly married him, too. I broke it off when he raped me and beat me up."

A second security guard came out the door and joined us. "The captain and Officer Grant will be here straightaway."

"Thank you, Tibbetts. Better get back to the screens now."

"Yes, sir." The guard disappeared.

"You'd all better come in here too," Hodges said. "We may as well sit while we wait."

Inside, Hodges provided us all with chairs. I thanked him, and the others all murmured assent.

"Now then," said Hodges, "just what the bloody hell is going on here?"

"We're trying to solve a murder," I said. "I was asking Dr. Welch about his whereabouts when Leonie Montague was killed and crushed in the roof, and when Mrs. Levine was killed, and when Joe Gerard was attacked right here in this room, and he attacked me."

"You're that lady doctor, aren't you?" he asked. "The one who asked if we'd seen anybody carrying a human head."

"Yes, that was me," I said. "Do you mind if I ask you a personal question?"

"That would depend on how personal it is."

"Are you any relation to Evelyn Hodges?"

"She was my sister."

Surprised, I said, "I'm talking about the cruise director who was murdered on the *Southern Cross* twenty-five years ago."

"So am I," Hodges replied. "She was my sister. She left a four-year-old daughter, my niece Maggie. My folks took care of her, and now they're gone too. Sometimes I wonder what Maggie is up to these days, but after so much time ..."

Oh my God. "Then you don't know."

"I don't know what?"

"That Maggie changed her name when she became a professional singer."

"No, I didn't. What did she change it to?"

I knew it was going to be a shock to the poor man, but there was really no way to make it any easier. "Leonie Montague."

Hodges sagged. "Bloody hell."

"I'm sorry for your loss," I said gently.

"No one left to mourn the poor girl but me," he said sadly. "So it was Maggie who was crushed in the roof."

"Yes."

"That's the murder you're trying to solve."

"Yes, among others."

"What others?"

"Well, Joe Gerard for one, and Mrs. Levine..."

"Who is Mrs. Levine?"

"A passenger who liked to hear herself talk."

"Who was killed to shut her up, I'll wager."

"Undoubtedly. And also Meacham."

Hodges looked up, startled. “Meacham?”

“Yes. We just found him in the cooler in the infirmary.”

“Blimey,” Hodges said. “We were all wondering where he’d gotten to. Haven’t seen him for days. Has he been in that cooler all this time?”

“No, because Mrs. Levine was in it up until San Juan. She was taken ashore there and flown home with her sister.”

“Has he been dead all that time?”

I shook my head. “Maybe. I couldn’t tell.”

Rob stirred irritably. “What’s taking so long?”

“What’s your hurry?” Hodges inquired. “Do you have an appointment or something?”

Rob subsided.

A series of beeps announced the arrival of Captain Sloane and Officer Grant. “Hodges? Dr. Day? Is everything all right?” the captain asked.

“The lady claims that the doctor attacked her,” Hodges said. “We saw it on the security cameras in the infirmary.”

“What happened, Dr. Day?” Officer Grant asked.

I told him. “And that reminds me; where were all those security guards you promised? Did you leave Hal and Nigel hanging out to dry too?”

Grant didn’t have a chance to answer that, because Captain Sloane suddenly noticed the bruise on my jaw. “Did Dr.Welch do that?”

“Yes, he did,” I told him. “Are you going to tell me I need to see a doctor, because that’s not even remotely funny.”

The captain hid a smile. “No, I wasn’t going to suggest that.”

“I offered to give her an ice pack,” Rob said, “but she refused.”

“That’s not what I refused,” I said. “I refused to go back to the infirmary with him.”

“Dr. Welch, please fetch Dr. Day an ice pack,” Captain Sloane said.

“You’re going to just let him go after what he did?” I asked in amazement.

“Certainly. He can’t go far. After all, there’s always the chance that someone will need a doctor before we reach Fort Lauderdale. Go, Dr. Welch.”

Rob went.

"Disciplinary action will be taken," Captain Sloane said. "It's unlikely he'll ever work for the Constellation cruise line again with that on his record."

"Do you think he's the killer?" Officer Grant asked.

"I don't think so," I said. "I started asking questions, like we discussed."

"And he got mad," Grant said. "That's significant."

"He got upset at first, and then he calmed down and answered all the questions. He said that he and Lynch ran into you when they left the infirmary that night after they put Leonie in the cooler, and that you went back into the infirmary to check. How come you didn't mention that?"

"Because—"

I held up a hand to stop him. "Don't you dare tell me it's because I didn't ask. I've heard quite enough of that from Rob."

Grant sighed. "And now you're trying to intimidate me."

"Rob also said that you can alibi him for the night after we watched the security tapes."

"That's true. And he can alibi me also."

I feigned surprise. "Do you need an alibi for that night?"

"Are you serious?"

"Maybe, maybe not. You tell me."

"Never mind," Grant said. "What happened after that?"

"Then I asked for a swab to check for blood in the cooler. That's when he got really mad."

"Why do you think that upset him so much?"

"He said I was going to ruin his reputation."

"How?"

"By getting him suspected of Leonie's murder," I said. "He said that he'd never be able to get another job with that hanging over his head."

"Was there blood in the cooler?"

"Yes, lots of it. All around the edges and down in the corners. It was when I showed Rob the swab that he tried to attack me."

"How did you manage to get away?"

I told him.

"He's taking rather a long time," Captain Sloane said. "It doesn't take this long to get to the infirmary and back."

Grant rose to his feet with a grunt. "Perhaps it's time to see what's going on. Shall we?"

We all stood up.

"Not you, Dr. Day," Grant said. "You stay here."

"Not on your life," I said.

Grant sighed. "Captain?"

Captain Sloane shook his head. "You're on your own with this one, Grant."

The four of us went back to the infirmary. Rob was nowhere in sight.

"That's that, then," Grant said. "Shall we check his cabin?"

"We'd better check the cooler first," I said. "As I recall, we left it open."

We went into the morgue. The cooler was just as we'd left it, wide open, but with one rather glaring difference.

Meacham was gone.

What's done cannot be undone.

—Shakespeare, *Macbeth*, act 5, scene 1

"BLIMEY," GRANT SAID. "What the bloody hell happened to him?"

I clutched my head with both hands. "Seriously? What is this, the *Attack of the Body Snatchers*? This is getting out of hand."

"Well, at least you're not imagining things, because I saw him here too," Grant said. "Do you suppose Dr. Welch took the body?"

I turned up my palms. "To what purpose? What would Rob want to move the body for? And where would he move it to?"

"Maybe he hid it in his cabin," Grant suggested. "Let's go look."

"Wait a minute," I said. "There's a bunch of exam rooms in here. The body could be in any one of them. Shouldn't we check them first?"

"The lady has a point," Captain Sloane said.

It didn't take long with four of us looking. Nobody reported seeing a body.

I took the opportunity to check the refrigerator to see if there was an ice pack in the freezer unit. There wasn't one. Too bad, because my jaw was really throbbing. The inside of my mouth was cut, too, and that also hurt.

We left the infirmary and took the forward elevator up to the main deck. Grant took us through a door that said "Crew Quarters—No Passengers Allowed Beyond This Point" and down a narrow corridor. Unlike the corridors in the passenger areas, the walls were an unrelieved institutional beige with no pictures, and instead of plush carpet we were walking on vinyl flooring the same beige as the walls. Every so often we had to step over raised thresholds which I knew were there in case of flooding.

Rob's cabin was about halfway down, and I noted signs on the doors denoting whose cabins they were. Officer Dalquist lived down here, and so did Chief Engineer Gerard. As Rob had said, Officer Grant's cabin was right next to his. We bypassed it and Grant unlocked Rob's door. Nobody was inside.

"You don't suppose he stuck it in your cabin, do you?" I asked. "Do you guys play practical jokes on each other?"

Grant gave me a skeptical look. "Really, Dr. Day, this isn't college. We're all grownups here."

"You'd better check," I said. "That body has to be off-loaded when we get to Fort Lauderdale."

"Don't be ridiculous," Grant said. "He doesn't have a key to my cabin."

"Who does?"

"I do," Hodges said.

"Open it up," Captain Sloane ordered.

"But Captain," Grant protested.

"Do you have something to hide, Officer Grant?" the captain asked.

"Well, no, but ..."

"Go ahead, Hodges," the captain said.

Hodges did so.

No body.

Grant didn't exactly heave a sigh of relief, but I thought I noticed an infinitesimal relaxation of his neck muscles. Perhaps he wasn't altogether sure that the body *wouldn't* be in his cabin. And I wondered why that should be.

Oh, but that was ridiculous.

Still ...

I made a mental note. Just in case it mattered.

"Now what?" Hodges asked.

"Wouldn't it be more likely," I asked, "that if the body were hidden in anybody's cabin, it would be his own?"

"What are you getting at, Doctor?"

"Where's Meacham's cabin?"

"He's on B deck," Hodges said. "He's next door to me."

"What are we waiting for?"

A door opened, and Chief Engineer Gerard came out into the corridor in his bathrobe, which was bright red and absolutely screamed at his hair. Under the bright overhead light, his face was in shadow. "What's going on here? People are tryin' tae sleep." Then he saw me and frowned. "Doctor, ye shouldna be here. Did ye no' see the sign on the door?"

"She's with me," Grant said.

"And me," said Captain Sloane.

"Ah," said Gerard. "Captain. I apologize. I didna see ye the noo. What are ye doin' doon here?"

"We're looking for a body," I said.

Gerard folded his arms across his chest. "Anither one? Who is it this time?"

"Meacham," I said.

"Meacham? Isna that yer department, Grant? Canna ye no' keep track o' yer own pairsonnel?"

"Meacham's dead," Grant said. "I saw his body in the cooler in the infirmary. But now it's gone."

"Well, if it's in his cabin yer lookin'," Gerard said, "he's on B deck."

"Chief Gerard," I said, "didn't you give my husband a tour of the engine room?"

"That I did," Gerard said. "We finished up over an hour ago."

"Well, then, Hal's going to be looking for me," I said. "Let's get going."

"Good luck tae ye," Gerard said. As he turned to go back into his cabin, the light struck his face in a way that allowed me to see the shiner around his left eye.

Hmm, I thought. He hadn't had *that* when we'd seen him at dinner. Could it be … was it possible … that *Hal* had done that to him?

And if so, what had Gerard done to Hal in return?

Suddenly I was very anxious to see my husband. “Come on,” I urged my companions. “There’s no time to lose.”

B deck was a replica of A deck. We found Meacham’s cabin without too much trouble, and Grant knocked on the door.

“What are you doing that for?” I asked, but Grant didn’t have a chance to answer before the door was opened by a man who was clearly not expecting to see a woman outside his door, let alone a passenger, as he was stark naked.

“Put some clothes on, man,” Captain Sloane snapped.

With a mumbled apology, the man shut the door in our faces.

“Meacham has a roommate,” I said. “I didn’t realize …”

“Everybody has a roommate down here,” Grant said. “Only the officers get single cabins.”

The door reopened. The man was now wearing pants, although he was still naked to the waist and barefooted. “Sorry, sir. Captain. What can I do for you?”

“We’re looking for Meacham,” Grant said.

“Not here, sir,” the man said. “I haven’t seen him in days.”

“Sorry to disturb you then,” Grant said.

“Quite all right, sir.” The man closed the door.

“That’s it?” I asked.

“Certainly,” Grant said. “You could hardly expect me to ask him if he had a dead body in his room, could you?”

“I guess not.”

“Come on,” Grant said. “Let’s go back to the infirmary. Perhaps the doctor has come back.”

Captain Sloane said, “I’d better get back to the bridge. I left Officer Lynch in charge by himself.”

“Oh,” I said, “then Nigel must be done talking to him. Maybe he and Hal are waiting for me at the infirmary.”

They weren't. The infirmary was locked up, just as we had left it, and the corridor was deserted.

Hodges said, "Captain, if you don't need me anymore ..."

"That's all right, Hodges," said Captain Sloane. "You're dismissed."

Hodges left.

"Grant, are we done here?" the captain asked.

"Yes sir."

The captain left, leaving me alone with Grant.

Grant unlocked the door to the infirmary. The place was utterly silent and dark. Rob must have turned off the lights after coming back here, because they had all been blazing when I ran out of here.

"Rob?" I called.

No answer.

I turned on the light, half expecting to see Rob's crumpled body on the floor. But he wasn't there. I headed for the office. Perhaps someone had stashed Meacham in Rob's chair. I turned on the light. No Meacham. No Rob either.

"He's not in here," I called out to Officer Grant. "Let's start checking exam rooms."

"What for?" Grant objected. "We've already looked in all of them."

"That was when we were looking for Meacham," I called over my shoulder as I ran down the hall to the first exam room.

"Don't go in there," Grant called back. I heard his rapid footsteps behind me.

I turned on the light.

Meacham's body lay on the examination table.

How the hell had we missed that when we'd looked in all the exam rooms not thirty minutes earlier?

Oh. Realization dawned.

There had been four of us looking before. One of which was Officer Grant.

He must have been the one who'd looked in this room and then told the rest of us that there was no body. Which meant that he had been the one to put it here.

"Officer Grant," I said, turning to face him, "why did you—"

He didn't let me finish. He grabbed me from behind, looped

something around my neck, and pulled it tight. I gasped. Obviously he hadn't yet pulled it tight enough. He pulled harder. I grabbed for it and tried to wedge my fingers underneath it. Luckily for me, my silver choker collar that I'd worn to dinner interfered with whatever he was choking me with, which allowed enough space for me to get two fingers under it.

"Bugger!" he grunted through gritted teeth. He jerked back on the ligature. Maybe he figured if he couldn't strangle me, he'd break my neck instead. I let all my limbs go limp—except the fingers under the ligature—and fell to the floor.

Apparently Grant wasn't expecting that. It jerked the ligature out of his hands and he dropped it. Under the bright lights it gleamed gold.

"That's Leonie's necklace," I exclaimed. "You killed her!"

Grant dived for me, and I rolled to evade him, but he was too fast for me. As he pounced on me, I bent my legs and shoved upward as hard as I could. I'd seen it done on TV, but I had no idea if I could actually do it.

It worked. He didn't actually sail over me and land on his head, but I got him in the stomach and knocked the wind out of him.

He rolled off me, gasping for air. I tried to get to my feet and run away, but he grabbed my ankle and brought me down. I tried to pull away, but his grip was too strong. I thought about trying to scrape his hand off my ankle with my other foot but then thought better of it as he could have simply grabbed the other ankle and then what would I do? I'd have to resort to punching him in the gonads with my fist.

So I kicked him there with my other foot. As Rob had done, he doubled up and howled in pain. He also let go of me. I scrambled to my feet, hoping to put some distance between us. But it was not to be.

"You sodding bitch!" he screamed. Apparently he'd regained his wind. I didn't pause to reflect upon the physical impossibility of that epithet, but even so he managed to grab my ankle and bring me down once more. As I fell, I hit my head on the corner of a free-standing cabinet. I saw stars but didn't lose consciousness.

It did, however, give Grant time to get to his feet. He picked me up off the floor as if I were a rag doll and carried me into the morgue where the cooler door yawned open. My heart sank. He was going to lock me in the cooler. That's why he'd moved Meacham.

Well, he wasn't going to get me into that cooler if I had anything to say about it. I wrapped my arms around his neck and sank my teeth into his ear. He screamed and let go of me. I hung from his neck and kept my teeth locked on his ear. If I let go of his neck now, my weight would rip his ear right off. My jaw was killing me, but I didn't loosen my bite. I did, however, loosen my arms from around his neck.

He'd been so torn between holding me captive and pushing me away, neither of which had turned out well, that he was unprepared for the sudden shift in weight. He grabbed for me, but it was too late. His ear tore, blood spurted, and he clutched it and screamed. "You fucking bitch, what have you *done*?"

I turned and ran, spitting blood and flesh as I went. But Grant, maddened by pain, caught me, socked me in the jaw precisely where Rob had hit me, dragged me back into the morgue, and heaved me into the cooler like a side of beef. The last thing I saw before the door slammed shut was a face distorted beyond recognition with rage, blood pouring down one side of it, and a pair of bloody hands.

"By the time anybody opens this again, you'll be dead, you interfering busybody bitch!"

Well. Since I could hear that, it must be possible for others to hear me from inside. That cheered me slightly, but not enough to mitigate the cold, the darkness, the pain from my jaw, and the knowledge that I'd soon run out of oxygen because the cooler, according to Rob, was airtight.

Or was it?

I thought I saw a flash of light. I shifted experimentally, reaching to touch the roof and the walls. There was enough room for me to stretch out full length, which I already knew because both Meacham and Mrs. Levine had been stretched out straight and they were both bigger than I was. There was also enough room for me to curl up into a ball to conserve warmth.

One unexpected benefit was that the cold metal felt really good on my battered jaw. I moved it experimentally and came to the conclusion that despite the best efforts of both Rob and Grant, it still wasn't broken.

Moreover, there definitely was a sliver of light coming in under the door, so the cooler wasn't airtight after all, and I wouldn't be running out of air. It occurred to me that I'd better not say anything about it, though, or Grant would plug it up.

"Don't you have anything to say, bitch?" Grant taunted me.

He was really going to have to come up with some new insults, I thought, but I didn't say so, because it occurred to me that as long as he was out there, I had best keep quiet, or else he'd open up the cooler and finish me off as he had Leonie.

On the other hand, if I kept quiet, he might get impatient and open up the cooler just to make sure I was dead, and then I could take him by surprise.

But mostly I kept quiet because I was really, really tired.

I even thought I might fall asleep at one point, except that the hard metal was really not all that comfortable, even though its coldness felt really good on the various bruises I could feel developing.

Grant pounded on the cooler door, startling me. "Hey, bitch. You asleep in there?"

I kept silent.

He pounded again. "Hey!"

Eventually, I thought, he'll get bored and leave. Then what?

As if he'd read my mind, Grant said, "Oh, to hell with you. Goodbye, bitch." With that, the light went off and I heard the door shut.

Now what?

Outside the door, I thought I heard water running. Perhaps Grant was washing up before venturing out amongst people who would be shocked by his bloody appearance. I couldn't imagine that it would do him much good, though. He'd have to change his clothes, and how was he going to disguise his torn ear?

Maybe he'd find Rob and get him to sew it up or debride it or something. If he did, then I could make noise. I knew they'd hear it, because I could hear them. Then Rob could rescue me.

Unless they were in cahoots.

I hadn't considered that before, and I was sorry I'd thought of it. It was a depressing thought.

Now I understood why the security guards Grant had promised us had never materialized. If he'd killed Leonie with her own necklace, then he'd also used it to strangle both Mrs. Levine and Meacham, because the ligature marks matched the woven gold rope Leonie had worn the night she was killed. The reason we hadn't found it with Leonie's body was because Grant had taken it with him.

But he had to have an accomplice. Somebody had had to help him string up the body on the roof of the Lido deck. Had it been Meacham? Was that why Grant had killed him, so he couldn't talk?

Or had Joe Gerard called Meacham to relieve him, and Grant had had to kill Meacham so he could kill Joe?

So if Grant had killed both Meacham and Joe that night, why hadn't he strangled both of them?

I tried to visualize it. If Grant had tried to strangle one of them, the other would've tried to stop him. Grant would have had to disable one so he could strangle the other.

Yes, that would make more sense. Grant had had to kill Meacham. That's why he'd told Joe to call Meacham rather than some other security guard. Then he'd knocked Joe out, lay in wait for Meacham, strangled him, and put the body in the cooler. Then he'd gone back to security, expecting that Joe would regain consciousness and not remember anything, including the fact that he'd ever called Meacham in the first place. But Joe never did regain consciousness, which meant that Grant had to cover his shift and call the doctor—and then hurry up to the Nav deck to wake up Nigel before the doctor came so that nobody would know he'd ever been there.

He'd had no idea that Joe would find the footage he needed so fast and get it sent off to Scotland Yard before Grant could get back down to security after speaking with the captain. He must have been frantic, having to sit there being polite while Sarah played cocktail party hostess. And then I'd had the effrontery to fall and hit my head and require medical attention, which had delayed Grant even more.

No wonder he wanted to kill me.

But why had he wanted to kill Leonie?

Wait a minute.

Grant had been on all three ships. Had he known Evie Hodges?

More to the point, had he *killed* Evie Hodges?

Why?

Maybe it had nothing to do with Evie. Maybe Grant was having an affair with Leonie too. Maybe she'd rejected him. Maybe he'd raped her and killed her to keep her from telling anybody.

No, that didn't work. Leonie's head wound had been an accident. Perhaps the captain had reported it to Grant, and Grant had gone to the infirmary to evaluate the situation and had found both Rob and Lynch leaving the infirmary after having put Leonie in the cooler, believing she was dead.

So he'd gone and opened up the cooler and found Leonie alive. And he'd finished her off by strangling her with her necklace.

But that didn't make sense either, because if he'd raped her and didn't want her to talk, why wait? Why not just strangle her at the time?

No. It had to be some other reason. Actually, it had to be something that occurred to him when he opened the cooler, because otherwise why would he wait until then to kill her?

Suppose he had killed Evie Hodges. Did he know that Leonie was her daughter? How would he know that? On the *Southern Cross* she might have told him that she had a daughter, but her name was Maggie, not Leonie, and she was only four years old. Did Grant know that Leonie had changed her name?

He knew now because we'd all been talking about it, but had he known it beforehand?

Outside, I heard a door slam. Grant must have left. What had he been doing all this time?

But no, I heard voices. Somebody had come in. Rob? I thought about making noise and attracting attention, but what if Rob was in on it with Grant?

How would Grant get Rob to be in on it? Maybe Rob had been lying to me when he'd said that he and Lynch had both left when Grant arrived to check on the body. Maybe Rob was in on it because of his past history with Leonie. Or maybe …

"Grant? What the hell happened to you?"

It *was* Rob.

"It's this damn storm. I lost my balance and fell against the wall and my ear caught on something and tore."

"Caught on what?" I heard Rob say. "This looks like somebody bit it off. It looks just like what Mike Tyson did to Evander Holyfield."

"Come on, Doc. Who would do a thing like that?"

"You tell me. In any case, we've got to fix you up. Do you have the missing piece? I could try to sew it back on ..."

"No," Grant said. "I don't have it."

"Oh well," Rob said. "Maybe a plastic surgeon can reconstruct it. All I can do is stop the bleeding. You'll need a tetanus shot too."

"Whatever. Can you get on with it?"

"Come on. Let's go into this first exam room. I'll just turn on the light and— What the hell is Meacham doing in here?"

"How should I know?" Grant replied irritably.

Rob wasn't buying it, apparently. "He was in the cooler. Now he's here. What happened?"

"I told you, I don't know. Can't we use another room?"

"No!" Rob insisted. "Who's in the cooler?"

"Nobody."

"Let's just go look, shall we?"

"No. How about you just sew up my ear and quit going on and on about the fucking cooler," Grant suggested.

"Wait a minute," Rob said. "What's this on the floor? It looks like a piece of meat."

"Don't bother with that," Grant said. "Let's get my ear taken care of. Don't pick that up. You don't know where it's been."

"Well, what do you know? It seems to be the missing piece of your ear. Is this the wall you fell against, because there's nothing here that would tear off an ear. Are you quite sure somebody didn't bite it off?"

"I told you, Doc, I tore it. Nobody bit me."

"That would be good if it were true," Rob said, "because human bites are really bad. They almost always get infected. You're going to need prophylactic antibiotics too."

"Goddamn it, would you fix my sodding ear and quit talking?" Grant's voice was getting louder and louder and at least an octave higher. He was practically screaming.

"No, I don't think I will," Rob said. "At least not right now. I'm going to see who's in the cooler."

"The bleedin' hell you are," Grant snarled, and the scuffling began. Something crashed into the morgue door, something big, like a human body. I winced as I heard the meaty thunk of a fist hitting a jaw, or perhaps a cheekbone. I hoped it was Rob's fist versus Grant's face and not the reverse.

Someone wrenched the morgue door open, and the scuffle continued on into the morgue, where I could clearly hear the two men grunting and puffing as each strove to knock the other into the middle of next week. This is dinner theater, I thought. Where's the popcorn?

I heard another meaty thunk, and someone crashed into the cooler door. As the body slithered to the floor, Rob's voice said, "Take that, you son of a bitch."

From that I deduced that Rob had punched Grant and that it was now a propitious time to make my appearance. I doubled myself up and slammed my feet into the cooler door.

To my intense astonishment, it popped open. It must not have been locked properly.

But that was nothing compared to the effect it had on Rob and Grant. The door caught Grant on the side of the head and knocked him sideways into Rob, who sidestepped him. He crashed into the cupboard under the sink head-first. I rolled myself out of the cooler and landed on him. He didn't move.

Rob looked like he'd just seen a ghost. "Toni! What were you doing in there?"

"It wasn't my idea," I said, climbing off Grant and getting to my feet. "*He* put me in there, and I was just waiting to see who was going to win this fight before I made my presence known. I didn't want to end up like Leonie."

He threw his arms around me and hugged me tight. "My God, you're a sight for sore eyes! How long were you in there?"

"Too long," I said.

Grant stirred. Rob said, "Let's get out of here." We went out into the corridor and Rob shut and locked the morgue door. We heard Grant yelling "Let me out of here" and banging on the door.

"Let's get out of here before he remembers he has keys," Rob suggested. We made our way out to the reception area, with me moving slowly. Every muscle ached, and I was probably hypothermic to boot.

But we made it just in time to see Captain Sloane and Chief Gerard come bursting through the outer door.

"Where is he?" Gerard demanded.

I pointed.

Both men ran into the morgue and hauled Grant out. Gerard landed a haymaker on him that laid him out cold.

"That's for killing my son, you bastard. May you rot in hell."

Captain Sloane scratched his upper lip. "With Keith in the brig, I don't know what we're to do with him. There's not enough room."

"Put him in the cooler," I suggested. "That's what he did with me."

O villain, villain, smiling, damned villain!

My tables; meet it is I set it down,

That one may smile, and smile, and be a villain.

—Shakespeare, *Hamlet*

It would have served Grant right to be jammed into the brig with Keith Sloane, but I didn't really care what happened to him, because the next two people who came through the infirmary door were Hal and Nigel. Hal had a shiner that nearly rivaled my purple jaw.

"Toni! Oh God, Toni!" He swept me up in his arms. "Thank God you're all right. But are you?" He held me away from him and examined my face. "The whole side of your face is purple! And you look like a vampire. What did those bastards do to you?"

Nigel hugged me too and planted a mustachioed kiss on the undamaged side of my face. "It's good to see you, old girl. I do hope all that blood isn't yours."

I looked down at myself. My front was drenched in Grant's blood. "It's not," I told him.

"Thank God," Nigel said, "because we appear to be short one doctor."

"It's nothing an ice pack won't fix," I assured him. "And what about you? You look like you need one too."

"Well, we've come to the right place," Hal commented, looking around. "Surely we can find an ice pack around here somewhere."

"You'd think so, wouldn't you?"

"Come on, where's that refrigerator?"

"I'm telling you, I looked there. No ice packs."

"You need to look in the freezer."

I put my hands on my hips. "What do you take me for? Don't you think I did that?"

"Sorry, sweetie. Where did all that blood come from?" Hal asked.

"I bit Grant's ear off," I told him.

He stepped over to Grant's supine form, bent over and looked. "My God. You really did. Where's the rest of it?"

"I don't know. Around here on the floor someplace."

"Is this it?" asked Gerard, holding up a chunk of bloody tissue.

Captain Sloane averted his gaze.

"I think so," I said.

"Could the doctor sew it back on?"

"That's what he was trying to do when the fight broke out," I said.

"If ye want my opinion," Gerard growled, "he's not worth the trouble."

"So your mouth isn't bleeding," Hal said with distaste. "That's Grant's blood on your teeth."

"Some of it's mine," I said. "My mouth is cut on the inside. When we get upstairs I plan to brush my teeth with bleach. For an hour. And gargle." I hadn't even thought about blood-borne pathogens until now. I hoped Grant didn't have any. In a hospital setting we both would have had our blood tested for HIV and hepatitis B and C, but this was no hospital.

"What happens now?" I asked.

"We fly him back to England and let Scotland Yard deal with him," Captain Sloane said. "My son too."

"No, I meant what do *we* do now," I explained.

"I think you need a shower, an ice pack, and a good night's sleep," Hal said. "In that order. And get rid of those bloody clothes. Oh, and speaking of clothes, we still need to put our luggage out for pickup." He turned to the captain. "Is it too late?"

Captain Sloane shook his head.

"No worries," I said, remembering. "I put it out before I came down here."

"I hope Fiona put ours out," Nigel said.

"Under the circumstances," the captain said, "I will make sure that somebody picks it up before you go ashore."

"So we just disembark as if nothing happened?" Hal asked.

"I will let you know in the morning."

"Hell, it already *is* morning," Hal grumbled as we rode the forward elevator up to the Nav deck. "We'll have to get up in four hours."

"You go ahead," I told him. "I have to clean up first. And take some ibuprofen."

Hal went down the hall to the ice machine to get ice to make ice packs for both of us while I showered. I didn't brush my teeth with bleach or for an hour, but I did brush them for a really long time, and used up all my mouthwash trying to get the taste of blood out of my mouth, but it was no use. I think the scent had become embedded in my nasal passages.

By the time I'd gotten myself cleaned up and my hair dry, Nigel and Mum were knocking on the door.

"Sorry to disturb you," Nigel said, "but Fiona woke up and I had to tell her what happened, and she insisted on coming over here to see for herself that you were all right."

"Kitten!" Mum rushed in with every intention of clutching me to her bosom, but when she saw my face, she stopped. "My stars and garters! Your face looks like an eggplant. Are you sure your jaw isn't broken?"

I assured her that it wasn't.

"You must tell me everything. And I do mean *everything*," my mother insisted. "Leave nothing out."

So I curled up on the bed while Mum sat beside me, and I told her everything and left nothing out. I watched as my mother's expression went from alarm to horror to incredulity and back again. To her credit, she didn't interrupt me, although it was an obvious struggle for her not to.

"My goodness," she said when I'd finished, "Officer Grant seemed so nice and helpful. And that awful man Gerard wasn't so awful after all. Who'd have thought?"

"I guess you never really know another person until you get them mad," I said.

"And nobody does that better than Toni," Hal said with a wink at me.

"And what about you, Hal dear?" said Mum. "Where did you get that mouse on your eye?"

"Gerard," Hal said succinctly. Mum bristled, but before she could say anything, he raised a hand to stop her. "No, just listen to me. The captain asked him to give me a personal tour of the engine room."

"Yes, dear, I know that."

"First he showed me the engine control room. It's huge. There are what they call 'mimic boards' for all the equipment with screens and gauges showing what's going on and alerting people if anything goes wrong. There are always two engineers on duty there, while more engineers are actually in the engine room dealing with those things. The captain, or whoever's on duty on the bridge, notifies the engine control room if he needs more speed or more power, and the engine control room engineers notify the engineers in the engine room."

"That makes sense," Nigel said.

"Then we went down to the engine room, which is actually several rooms connected to each other. He showed me these huge diesel generators that make the electricity. There are six of them. There's also an emergency generator in case the others fail. Then there are the azipods."

"The what, dear?" Mum asked.

"Azipods. It's a new thing. Instead of propellers and thrusters, they have these podlike things that rotate 360 degrees to move the ship in any direction. They operate those from the bridge. They have hydraulic motors that rotate them, and internal propellers so they don't get fouled by anything floating around in the ocean."

"Get to the black eye," I suggested, tiring of all the technical talk.

"Well, it was all very interesting, but Gerard wasn't the most gracious host. I called him on it. He told me it wasn't his job to give tours to passengers and that he had better things to do, particularly when the passenger in question was the husband of the nosy bitch who got his son killed."

I gasped in outrage, but before I could object, Hal resumed. "So I socked him, and the fight was on. We exchanged a few punches, and then we both realized how ridiculous it was and started laughing. He apologized for calling Toni a bitch, and I apologized for punching him first, and for the last hour we've been down in the bar drinking beers and bonding."

"Aww, isn't that sweet," I said.

"All's well that ends well," quoted Nigel. "My adventure was pretty dull compared to yours. By the way, does Gerard know that Keith Sloane is really his son?"

"He does now," Hal said. "He doesn't care. He doesn't like him any more than he did before he knew. All he said on the matter was that if he'd raised Keith himself, he'd be a much better person. We had quite a discussion on environment versus heredity."

"You didn't come to blows over it, did you?" I asked.

"No, I think we both needed to blow off steam, and we'd already done that."

"To go on with my story," Nigel said, "I asked Officer Lynch all the questions we'd discussed. He was on duty on the bridge when Leonie had her accident, and he was still on duty when she was crushed in the roof. Officer Bellingham will tell you that nobody on the bridge opened or closed the roof until seven, which was when it was supposed to be opened. He was also on duty the night that Joe Gerard was attacked and Meacham was killed."

"What about Mrs. Levine?" I asked.

"That's a bit of a problem," Nigel said. "We don't know exactly when Mrs. Levine was killed."

"Well, she was alive and well when we were in Philipsburg, because she was on the yacht with me, and we found her body that night, and it was still warm. It had to have been during dinner, and Officer Grant wasn't at dinner that night."

"I didn't ask Lynch about that, but I doubt he had anything to do with it. Since he couldn't have killed Leonie, he had no reason to kill Mrs. Levine."

"Okay. Did you ask him about his relationship with Leonie?"

"I did. He said he started dating her after she graduated from university. Remember, he and Leonie had grown up together, along with the doctor and the cruise director. They'd all known one another as kids. He helped his sister Jessica get her position here, and they both helped Leonie. But he said that he and Leonie only dated a short time, and as far as the captain was concerned, Leonie had told Dave why she was spending so much time with the captain. So he had no motive to kill her for that."

"Did you ask him about running into Officer Grant outside the infirmary?"

"Yes. He confirmed that he and Rob ran into Grant, but they didn't go back into the infirmary with him. He said he went back to the bridge, and the other officer on duty can confirm that."

"Okay, scratch Officer Lynch," I said. "Does Gerard have alibis for those times?"

"He said he was either in the engine control room or in the engine room," Hal said, "and there are multiple engineers and other crew members who can vouch for him, and therefore he also had no reason to kill Mrs. Levine."

"So it was Officer Grant all along," I said. "He had Leonie's necklace, you know. He tried to strangle me with it. Maybe we were right about her regaining consciousness in the cooler. He must have strangled her with it. Otherwise, why would he have it?"

"I can't even begin to imagine," Hal said.

"Maybe he took it as a trophy," Mum suggested.

"Serial killers do that sometimes," Nigel said, "as a souvenir of their victims. But as far as I can see, Grant killed Leonie and the other murders were to cover that up."

"Maybe he killed Leonie to cover up an even earlier murder," I suggested.

"But we didn't have a previous murder," Mum said. "Did we?"

"According to the crew manifests," I said, "Officer Grant was on all three ships. What murder took place on one of the other two ships that we do know about?"

"Evelyn Hodges," Nigel said, "of course. But what reason would he have had to kill her?"

"It could have been anything," I said. "Unrequited love, jealousy, or maybe she had something on him and was blackmailing him. We'll probably never know unless he tells us himself."

"Maybe she knew he killed someone on the *Seven Sisters* and he killed her to shut her up," Hal said.

"This is getting positively Gothic," my mother said. "He might have killed someone before he even started working on cruise ships, and someone on the *Seven Sisters* knew about it."

"It's like one of those things where you see your reflection in a mirror reflected in a second mirror and the images go on and on and never end," I said.

"Well, Officer Grant is maybe fifty years old," Nigel said practically, "so it has to end somewhere."

"In 1983," Hal said, "Officer Grant would have been maybe twenty years old. Date rape? Statutory rape?"

"Maybe he got the poor girl pregnant and she killed herself," I said, getting into the spirit of the thing. "Although the pill had been around for about fifteen years by then, not all girls are prepared for being raped."

"And maybe Evie Hodges knew," Hal said, "and threatened to tell her buddy Colin Sloane about it."

"And we all know that Colin Sloane wouldn't hesitate to report it," Nigel said.

"Just like he did his classmate Bert Meacham," I said.

"It's a very pretty story," Nigel said, "but there's no evidence to support it, and it's all in the past in any case. All we know from the evidence we have is that Grant strangled Leonie, Mrs. Levine, and Meacham with Leonie's necklace."

"And tried to strangle me, don't forget," I said.

"I'm not likely to," Hal said with feeling.

"Children," said my mother, "and my darling husband, we have to be up and dressed and ready to disembark this death ship by seven in the morning, which is ..." she looked at her watch. "Three hours from now. I suggest we get some sleep."

Friday

FORT LAUDERDALE, FLORIDA

Love is strong as death; jealousy is as cruel as the grave.

—Song of Solomon 8:6

DISEMBARKATION DID NOT proceed exactly as expected.

The customs agent merely glanced at our customs declarations and tossed them into a box, so no duty was required. Two security guards then intercepted us and guided us into a room where my laptop and cell phone were returned to me. They were not at liberty to tell me where they'd found them. Then they put us in a taxi, which whisked us to the British embassy where we were interviewed at length about our contribution to the investigation.

As a result, our flights home were rescheduled, so we were required to stay overnight in Salt Lake City. Consequently, we did not get home until the following day, which gave us part of Saturday and all of Sunday to recover and be ready for work on Monday.

Mum and Nigel flew on to Long Beach from Salt Lake City. Nigel promised to update us whenever he heard from his buddy Alastair Hardwick.

Bambi and Pete met us at the Twin Falls airport with a hyperactive Little Toni who wrapped both arms around my leg and insisted that I pick her up—which I did, every muscle screaming in protest. No sooner did I get her settled in my arms than she reached out for Hal and insisted that *he* hold her. She paid no attention whatever to my purple jaw or Hal's purple eye, which was more than I could say for Bambi and Pete and every other person in the airport who stopped us and wanted to know what had happened to us.

"Most people come back from the Caribbean with tans," Pete said, "not shiners. This is going to put people off cruising."

"Then get us out of here," Hal said.

Miraculously, our luggage arrived when we did, in spite of the delay and rescheduling of flights. Within fifteen minutes we were on our way home. Killer and Geraldine greeted us with yips and whines and wagging tails. Spook, on the other hand, didn't make an appearance until I went to hang up our coats in the coat closet and he leaped out at me, yowling. He then jumped to the back of the couch, where he proceeded to groom himself and ignore us completely.

Mum called us as soon as they got home, but we didn't hear from Nigel about the case for a week and a half.

"Put him on speakerphone," Hal directed me when I answered the call.

"I heard from Detective Chief Superintendent Hardwick," Nigel said. "It seems that former Security Officer Desmond Grant made a full confession, and your speculations were spot on."

"Do tell," I urged. "Don't keep us in suspense."

"Grant said he went back into the infirmary to look at the body in the cooler, and when he opened the door, the 'corpse' was staring right back at him. He said it was the creepiest thing he ever saw. Then she lunged at him and screamed 'You killed my mother!'"

"Holy shit," I exclaimed. "That's spooky."

"He slammed the door shut on her, but she kept screaming and banging around in there. He panicked. He was afraid someone outside the infirmary would hear her and come to investigate. So he opened the door and when she lunged at him again, he grabbed her necklace and strangled her to shut her up."

"So are you telling us that Grant also killed Evie Hodges?" Hal asked.

"Al was able to get records from both the *Southern Cross* and *Seven Sisters*," Nigel said. "A girl was raped on *Seven Sisters*, a showgirl who was a friend of Evie Hodges. She told Evie who it was just before she killed herself. Evie recognized him on the *Southern Cross*, told him she knew, and blackmailed him. He killed her to keep her from talking."

"How did Leonie know about that?" I asked. "Her mother never came back from that cruise."

"She wrote to her parents," Nigel said. "They kept the letter."

"How come they didn't take it to Scotland Yard in the first place?" I asked. "Maybe Leonie wouldn't have had to die if they'd known about Grant at the time."

"There was nothing about murder in the letter, only blackmail," Nigel said. "Evie didn't mention any names, only that it was one of the security guards."

"If she didn't mention Grant by name, how did Leonie recognize him?" Hal asked.

"I don't think she did," I said. "With her damaged brain, she couldn't have been thinking clearly, or at all. She probably saw a security guard's uniform and what was left of her brain made the connection, and she just blurted it out. But Grant couldn't risk having anybody hear her, so he killed her."

"He probably figured that since Rob had already pronounced her dead, it wouldn't make any difference," Hal said.

"Unless somebody saw the ligature mark," I said. "Is that why he crushed her in the roof?"

"Precisely," Nigel said. "He blackmailed Meacham into helping him. It seems Meacham wasn't exactly the brightest bulb on the tree, and Grant threatened to give him a bad report and get him fired if he didn't help. Then, of course, he had to kill Meacham."

"But first he had to knock Joe out so he wouldn't remember anything," I said. "He must have hit him too hard. He didn't intend to kill Joe, but he couldn't have him conscious to watch him strangle Meacham and delete all the video files. Oh, and speaking of Meacham, how the devil did he manage to throw the weighted rope all the way across the Lido roof? He didn't look the like the athletic type to me."

"He used a gun," Nigel said. "Not the kind you're thinking of. These are guns that fire missiles that ropes can be attached to. That's how they can tie up the ship so fast. Instead of running around with ropes, they shoot them to whomever or wherever they need them to go."

"How would Meacham know about that?" Hal asked.

"Probably from his father," Nigel said, "who was an able seaman on the *Southern Cross*."

"What about Mrs. Levine?" Hal asked.

"That requires a bit of speculation," Nigel said. "But it wouldn't be too much of a stretch to say that he overheard her making accusations about who could have killed that girl, and maybe he wanted to shut her up before she got around to him. Who knows?"

"Then it must have been Grant who called Rob and said someone in maintenance had been badly injured," I said, "just to get him out of the infirmary so he could put the body in the cooler. She had to have been killed during dinner on Monday night because she was still warm when we found her."

"I'll bet he was still in the infirmary when we got there," Hal said, "just waiting for us to leave so he could leave. But Toni got too close, so he conked her."

"And stole my cell phone," I said. "He must have heard me say she'd been strangled. And then all of you came to tend to me, and then you had to find a gurney, which took forever. He must have been frantic."

"So who stole the head from the swimming pool?" Hal asked.

"Grant did," Nigel said. "He didn't want anybody to identify her. That's why he kept the necklace. They found it when they searched his cabin. They found your phone and laptop in there too, by the way."

"Maybe he also didn't want anybody to know she'd been strangled beforehand," I said. "I was the only one who saw the head before it was stolen. The next time anybody saw it, the flesh was falling off the bone."

"But, sweetie," Hal said, "didn't Grant know you'd gone into the pool to look at it?"

"Oh jeez," I said, "if that was the case, why didn't he try to kill me right away?"

"In his own words," Nigel said, "'the bitch was never alone.'"

"That's true," Hal said. "You were always with one of us or with Rob.

The first time Grant ever got you alone was in the infirmary when he put you in the cooler."

"And then," Nigel said, "the doctor screwed up his escape by insisting on sewing up his ear. Grant knew he hadn't killed you, and he couldn't figure out why it took you so long to make your presence known to the doctor."

"I still wasn't sure that Rob wasn't in on it," I said. "It wasn't until he and Grant started fighting that I knew he wasn't."

"You could hear all that inside the cooler?" Nigel asked.

"Yes, quite clearly."

"Then Grant was right about needing to silence Leonie," Nigel said. "He's lucky that she didn't start making noise while Rob and Lynch were still there."

"Too bad she didn't," Hal said. "Three people would still be alive if she had."

"It's a good job that Toni didn't," Nigel said, "or there would have been a fourth body."

"See there?" I said to my husband. "Don't ever tell me I don't know when to keep my mouth shut."

Hal put his arms around me and held me close, looking down into my eyes. "Now would be a good time," he suggested and kissed me.

The End

Praise for *Murder under the Microscope*

"*Murder under the Microscope* is an exemplary first novel."
—*The US Review of Books*

"As a winner of an IP Book Award for Excellence, I wasn't the least surprised that this book was selected."
—*GABixler Reviews*

Praise for *Too Much Blood*

"Munro's writing is entertaining, believable, and fast-paced. She takes you into the autopsy room, shows the fragility of the characters, and makes the readers feel they are inside the story. Readers will definitely be looking forward to solving more cases with this character."
—*The US Review of Books*

"Exceptional realism that only comes from personal, hands-on experience. Munro writes with captivating flair, and her story line is believable and realistic."
—Charline Ratcliff *for Rebecca's Reads*

Praise for *Grievous Bodily Harm*

"Sassy pathologist Toni Day shines in this modern-day mystery of corporate shenanigans and hospital politics ... A smart, enjoyable summer read."
—*Kirkus Reviews*

"Munro's story is a roller-coaster ride of suspense and intrigue, with twists and turns that will entertain a lover of mysteries and forensic crime novels for hours."
—*The US Review of Books*

"The author brilliantly shares her expertise in forensic pathology, allowing readers inside the room during the autopsy, and sharing her expertise and knowledge."

—Fran Lewis, *BookPleasures.com*

Praise for *Death by Autopsy*

"A solid mystery, far from *DOA*."

—*Kirkus Reviews*

"If this is your first Toni Day novel, you'll want to go back and start the series from the beginning."

—*BlueInk Reviews*

"Fans of medical drama and mysteries will be sure to love this fast-paced and fact-laced romp through the world of pathology."

—*US Review of Books*

"This book is a fantastic crime thriller. You won't be able to put it down until you finish reading it. I loved it. I gave it 5 stars but it deserved many, many more. I highly recommend this book to everyone especially if you enjoy crime and thriller books. You will love this one. I look for more from Jane Bennett Munro."

—Marjorie Boyd-Springer *for Goodreads*

"I suggest you do check this twisting, turning mystery out and have fun along with Toni as she gets close enough that now her life is being threatened!"

—*GABixler Reviews*

"I found myself thinking of Miss Marple in the Agatha Christie novels or Hercule Poirot since it reads very much like a classic whodunit. Told very effectively in the first person, the story moves along at a good pace as Toni slowly peels back the murder mystery like the layers of an onion and I look forward to the next Toni Day Mystery. Five stars for Jane Bennett Munro and *Death by Autopsy.*"

—Terry Rollins, *Amazon Top Reviewer*

Printed in the United States
By Bookmasters